DREADING THE DARK

Alison Saunders

Copyright © 2025. Alison Saunders

All rights reserved

The characters and events portrayed in this book are fictitious. Any similarity to real persons, living or dead, is coincidental and not intended by the author.

No part of this book may be reproduced, or stored in a retrieval system, or transmitted in any form or by any means, electronic, mechanical, photocopying, recording, or otherwise, without express written permission of the publisher.

ISBN-13: 9798285164708

Cover design by: Art Painter
Library of Congress Control Number: 2018675309
Printed in the United States of America

For Marion, my dear mum.

CHAPTER 1.

The barrack room clock struck 9.00pm. Lance corporal Harry Stevens knew it was now or never to grasp this sliver of peace and solitude for quiet thought, for reflection and something else. What was it? Remorse? Regret? Fear? Alone with his thoughts, sitting on a rickety chair, he took out the folded piece of writing paper from his breast pocket and laid it flat against his small bedside locker. He licked the short pencil stub, the same one that he had used to draw her portrait that evening in May before he left. And in that cramped, chilly room, Harry began to open his heart.

30th September, 1940.

My darling Lilly, I hope this letter finds you and little Marilyn both hale and hearty? Tell me please, how are Marilyn's nightmares? Is she still waking in the night? The blackouts must be fearful for her, being so young. It worries me so. How can you help her to understand all this? I miss you both and think of you constantly.

The raids over London remind me of that moving poem by Wilfred Owen that we loved so much, you know the one I used to read to you many years ago:

"Tonight, if thou shoulds't lie in that same room,
Dreading the dark thou knowest not how to illume
Listen, my songs may haply give thee ease…"

I hear such terrible news of the devastation which Jerry brings night after night. You must take Marilyn away from all that. Perhaps to Blackpool. That's a long way from harm, I think. We have had such wonderful holidays up there over the years, haven't we? Staying at the Cockington's, Sarah and Joe. Would you go there please? And soon. I have had an awful premonition about the bombing of the East End and I don't sleep well for fear of what might happen to you both. Please arrange to leave London as soon as you can manage it. You and sweet little Marilyn mean the world to me. You are everything I hold dear. Please write soon with your decision.

Your adoring husband, Harry.

The dancing shadows from Marilyn's candle night-light licking across the ceiling were not the only uninvited guests that night. Inside Lilly's overcrowded mind were hundreds of leering, mocking strangers laughing at her as she wept. They poked at her and she desperately covered her face. She screamed but they could not hear her. No-one could hear her. She screamed in silence while the little girl in the bed beside her slept on. Suddenly, Lilly was awake, bolt upright. Her drenched pillow offered her no comfort. She moved to the window, half awake and half in dream. The late summer breeze was only slight, but she was grateful for what little relief it offered through the heavy blackout curtain.

On the dressing table, Harry's letter was waiting for her reply. How should she respond to his request? Surely it was madness to leave everything behind and take Marilyn all the way to the other end of the country. What could they take with them? Hardly anything at all. A couple of suitcases. Not that they had very much. But the thought of going away made her feel sick to her stomach.

They had rented out her beloved house in Edmonton, North London for the duration of the war. It was their first marital home, their haven. Who knew what state they would find it in when they claimed it back.

It was tough coping in that cramped bedsit in Forest Gate where she and Marilyn had moved to be closer to her sister Laura and her ailing mother after Harry had been called up. Now she was torn between leaving them behind and seeking safety for herself and her daughter so far away up North. Life had become enough of a challenge without turning her back on what little familiarity she had left.

Lilly had always been a realist, but was she robust enough to take on such a new start? She could imagine herself in a boarding house full of strangers. Who might they be?

Thieves, pickpockets, vagabonds? And how would she pay her way? She had been a seamstress before she married Harry but that was five years ago. Who would take her on now? How would she present herself to a new employer?

What might become of Marilyn in Blackpool? She was still so little. Too young to be put on a train by herself surely. What could happen to them if they stayed in London? Harry was right of course. It was becoming more and more perilous in the East End with the raids coming each night now. The thrum of the aeroplanes shuddered through her whole body and her nerves were strained. Oh Harry, now I can understand why you have fretted so much! Lilly picked up his letter in her moist, unsteady hands and read it again in the dawn's tentative early light.

CHAPTER 2.

The heavy November clouds bearing down on Lilly and Marilyn held more in their threatening dark grey swirls than just rain. They evoked in Lilly's mind that cold foggy November morning three years earlier when she and Harry had brought their precious baby Marilyn home from hospital.

Now the unforgiving wind and rain had quickly drenched them through as they doggedly scoured the front doors for the right house. The deep brown puddles spilled into their shoes chilling their feet as they made their laborious way along the street. The drab terraced houses were dimly lit and the streets seemed to stretch for miles as they extended from the Marine Parade like the tines of a gigantic fork. Then suddenly through the gloom Lilly saw it. The dark green door, the welcoming wooden bench under the front bay window with its peeling light-green paintwork and the rusty nail sticking out of the left-hand arm. Just as it had been the last time when she was there with Harry back in 1936, when the sun was shining all summer long. How different everything was today. Marilyn's soft little hand in hers gave Lilly courage to go forward, for the first time without Harry's warm reassurance to guide her. How keenly she missed him and yet it was at his bidding that she had made this journey all those long miles from London. She knocked on the door as hard as her heart knocked inside her chest. They stood back to prepare for the door to open and to face an uncertain reception. Was this really going to be their safe haven, or would it turn out to be the most terrible mistake? Lilly noticed the chipped sign above the door. "Sunny View Guest House". It seemed to mock her with a cheerless irony.

Sarah Cockington bustled noisily from the kitchen to the front door. Thinking that Joe was upstairs, she called to him. Her husband was always in the wrong place when she needed him.

'Joe! Joe, they're here!' Then she noticed him sitting in the armchair with his newspaper and she tutted loudly. Opening the door, Sarah gasped at the two wretched figures standing there.

'Lilly, luv! Welcome! Welcome back to Blackpool. Ooh what a day you've picked...Not rained like this since...well since at least this time last week, I reckon!' Sarah laughed uneasily. 'But that's Lancashire for you, eh...And this must be little Marilyn. My! What a beauty you are. Come in, come in out of the wet. You've had a long journey. Oh, how was the journey? Long, very long I'm sure!'

Lilly led the reluctant little Marilyn over the threshold into the drab narrow passageway which was lit by a single lightbulb. Marilyn would remember that smell for many years to come. It was the smell of stale cooking where no fresh air ever had the chance to circulate and refresh the cramped space.

Sarah fussed over them until they had taken off their wet coats. Lilly was feeling tired and embarrassed. Their journey had taken almost twelve hours and the overcrowded train had made them both hungry and dishevelled.

'Yes, it was long,' she muttered finally. 'We had to stand for a couple of hours from Euston, not one of those young soldiers would give up their seat. And the train ran so painfully slowly. But never mind, we've made it and here we are!' She brushed Marilyn's head with her mittened hand to cover her awkwardness.

'Well, let's not stand on ceremony' Sarah said. 'Let me take your coats through, both of you.' But she was too flustered to take their coats. 'Joe! Lilly's here! Here at last, eh!'

Lilly stepped forward tentatively.

'Thank you, Mrs Cockington. Thank you for being so kind as to take us in at such short notice. It was Harry's idea, you know. He's worried sick about us, what with all these bombing raids you see...'

Sarah was starting to calm down and warmed towards her new guests. She had been a landlady in that house from the time when Joe had lost his job from the Railway where he had worked as a transport engineer since the end of the

Great War. He had been given little choice but to take his meagre war pension in the face of growing unemployment, worker unrest and strikes which had become rife across the county as the economy declined in the latter half of the 1920s and the tide had turned away from the early optimism of the first half of the decade. Taking in lodgers had begun as a short-term means of making ends meet, but then Sarah found that she enjoyed the varied company and it suited her to play the role of surrogate mother to a stream of mostly young boarders freshly snipped from their mothers' apron strings who were only just finding their way in the world. She was strict of course and didn't stand for any slacking with the rent or with standards of cleanliness. Her brusqueness was her stock in trade, the only way she knew how to make her business pay and to keep the house in order.

Sarah's hair had turned white literally overnight after they had lost their only child, a girl called May who had died of diphtheria at the age of nine. It had been the shock and devastation of this loss that had made her look prematurely aged. Now it was a subject rarely touched upon. Her fierce expression, exaggerated by her pencilled eyebrows which gave her a permanent look of surprise, frightened Marilyn into speechlessness at that first meeting. Marilyn wondered whether Sarah had in fact sat on a particularly sharp pin. Sarah carried a heady smell around with her, a mix of cigarette smoke and sickly perfume which Marilyn had never smelled anywhere else before.

'Please do call me Sarah. Aye, I just can't begin to imagine what it's been like for you down there in London. We hear such awful stories on the wireless about whole streets being destroyed in them air raids! And Joe says the papers are full of it -' Sarah stopped as she remembered little Marilyn standing there. 'Well anyway...'

Joe was at the door of the sitting room and ushered them all into the room. He was a gentle giant of a man who held in his aging eyes the spark of energy and dignity as though he were not yet ready to give up his youthful vigour to middle-aged weariness. His silver hair flopped carelessly over his eyes and he had a habit of brushing it back into place with never a thought to trim it into tidy obedience.

'Well now hello, you two!' He said, 'Here's a new addition to the family! How do you do, young lady?'

Lilly could see that Marilyn was too shy and over-awed to say anything at that moment. She had only just turned three and had been such a good girl. Good as gold all the way there. Joe smiled and was not put off by the silent response as Marilyn twisted herself around her mother's legs in an effort to hide from these overbearing strangers towering over her. Joe had always been struck by Lilly's diminutive stature and delicate build and her daughter was her tin type replica. Lilly was just twenty-seven years old and with her raven hair she was considered by anyone who met her to be an unquestionable natural beauty. This fact never seemed to affect her own self-regard and she was modest to the point of being blithely unaware of the frequent turning heads and appreciative smiles of the many servicemen and civil servants whom she would pass on her weekend strolls along the promenade in the years to follow.

'Well, it's a good thing that you've done, coming away up here. I hear they're taking so long to sort out the evacuations.'

Sarah chimed in, now regaining her stride in her role of the indubitable Landlady.

'Course, we had our fair share of bombs back last year didn't we, Joe! Remember? Not the Germans, it were the IRA that time. My God! Don't s'pose you remember that being reported down in London do you, Lilly, what with it all being overshadowed by the war. But I think it was just a kid what done it. A young Irishman wasn't it Joe, or sommat like that.'

'Brendan Behan, was his name...he were no more than a lad of 16. They said he was on his way to Liverpool to join his operational unit.'

Before becoming the renowned playwright, Brendan Behan had been the IRA's most famous contributor and he was to write about his experiences in his work "Borstal Boy" about how, on August 27th 1939, a bomb exploded near the door of Blackpool Town Hall. It was part of an IRA campaign which involved several English cities and most especially Liverpool.

Joe had followed his story. He was always up to date with the news and he took a keen interest in the world around him, even if sometimes he felt only a part of its periphery. Sarah began admonishing him.

'Lilly's not come all this way to stand here discussing the IRA, now have you luv? Why don't you do sommat useful for a change Joe and show them to their room upstairs?' Sarah laughed. 'Of course, you know the way. It were only in't summer of '36 that you were last here!'

Lilly's heart sank as she took in her surroundings. It had not seemed such a dreary house when she had stayed here in the past. But that had been in another time – a whole world away when war had never entered her happy world and she had Harry by her side. She had never noticed in those days how tired and forlorn the whole place appeared: the peeling paper on the walls, the yellow-brown stain on the ceiling above where Joe had presumably been sitting smoking his pipe throughout the long years, the damp around the windows, the grime-stained net curtains, the drooping plants in cracked plant pots. The combined front room and dining room had a door off to a small bare kitchen beyond. An immense sideboard, decades old, stood to attention watching protectively over the room. Its two drawers could barely close, so crammed were they with the myriad paraphernalia of everyday life. An old settee and two oddly matched armchairs, one of which had lost its shape and the other its colour, both stood in front of a small drab hearth. In spite of the paucity of luxuries around the room, Lilly noticed the wireless and a telephone. She hoped that these small comforts would be enough to relieve the long, lonely nights ahead.

As she and Marilyn stepped into the room, they noticed two young girls sitting at the table darning socks and giggling together. Sarah was eager to introduce them all to each other.

'Now then, these are our other two boarders, June and Ethel.' They smiled and nodded brightly to Lilly.

'How d'you do. Pleased to meet you.' Lilly noticed that

these two girls were dressed in rather a garish style and wore too much lip rouge for their age. Then a more pressing thought occurred to her and she turned swiftly to Sarah.

'Mrs Cockington, er sorry, Sarah, I would just like to clarify one thing up front, if I may please. We're paying guests. Just like in the past. No special treatment, well you know what I mean.' Then, for Marilyn's benefit she added: 'After all, we're only here on our holidays aren't we Marilyn?'

'Holidays...' softly echoed her daughter and they all smiled at that first sound of her voice.

Sarah dismissed any awkwardness with an abrupt wave of her hand.

'Well, there's plenty of time to sort all that out. We've had all kinds under this roof over the past few years. From all walks of life, haven't we, Joe, eh?'

'Oh yes,' Joe replied, 'I suppose so. It's funny how this war's thrown so many different types of people together. I mean to say, who knows how it'll all turn out in the long run...'

Sarah's patience was always thinly stretched at the best of times where her husband was concerned. He irritated her, sometimes without him even being in the same room.

'Yes, well don't you mind him, Lilly luv. He sits around the house with too much time on his hands, he does honestly. Anyroad, you'll both be needing some rest now, I shouldn't wonder...before you go out painting the town red tonight, eh!' Her earthy laugh was interrupted as suddenly the kettle began to whistle on the hob. Joe's response was always the same, a reflex action, their ritual.

'Baby's crying, mother!'

'Right you are,' replied his wife as she hurried off to see to it.

They watched the newsreels in mute disbelief as enemy armies marched across Europe in faraway places. As the air attacks on London intensified, the bombs fell over the East End and lit up the wide night sky. The Nazis claimed that they were aiming their attacks at targets of military importance, but to Lilly, the buses and trams that were blown sideways when the bombs burst across the road looked more like hapless children's toys than any military target. This was the Nazi's revenge for the heavy losses which they had suffered at the hands of the Royal Air Force, but it was the poor civilians who were taking the brunt of it. Why does the coward always attack the weak? She wondered out loud from her cinema seat.

When Lilly arrived in Blackpool in that Autumn of 1940, clutching her battered suitcase in one hand and her little daughter in the other, she found the town was booming. The contrast with London was staggering. With open-mouthed curiosity she spent her first few weeks moseying around the new buildings which had appeared since her last visit four years previously: the Derby Baths, the Odeon Cinema, the Casino, the New Opera House, the Solarium, Woolworths, St Johns Market. Blackpool was now a major war centre, one of the largest military training centres in the world during World War II. It was bursting at the seams with almost eight hundred thousand RAF recruits passing through their initial training in the town with forty-five thousand airmen billeted there. This huge growth in service personnel, together with the influx of some four thousand relocated civil servants was in addition to the many thousands of evacuees from the less fortunate bomb-battered towns and cities across Britain. Very soon, half the homes in Blackpool were said to be used as billets.

Marilyn was soon caught up in this massive inflation in the town's population. Evacuation of children from northern cities meant that her school, like so many others in Blackpool needed to operate a shift system. Not that they could see it at that time, but she and Lilly were the lucky ones, no doubt about it. There was much ill feeling among Blackpool residents who were forced to take in evacuees because the allowances paid to them were so modest. They complained that their young 'guests' were difficult and some wet the bed. Many of the children were from poorer homes and when they were billeted with middle class families, the culture shock was mutual. Unsurprisingly, a number of Marilyn's classmates had drifted back to their city homes.

Not long after Lilly and Marilyn had moved there, Blackpool suffered one lethal enemy bombing. A German aircraft dropped bombs which landed near North Station, only a few streets away from them. The aircraft was returning after a raid on Manchester. Eight people died and several houses were destroyed. However, to Lilly's amazement, this did not deter the holidaymakers who flocked to the resort as a much-needed morale booster and entertainment was much in demand. They saw this vibrant town as a safe place away from attack and it had a ready-made supply of accommodation. The bright lights of the London stages came to Blackpool in the wake of the bombing. Most West End theatres were closed and many plays premiered at Blackpool's very own Grand Theatre. Whilst its ticket prices were beyond Lilly's reach, she would sometimes take Marilyn to the foyer of this imposing building just so that they could both look around in wide-eyed awe of its beauty and splendour, evocative of pre-war London. Lilly allowed herself to pretend that she was about to take her seat in the Grand Circle.

Here was a climate of opportunity and soon Lilly began to feel certain that in this town lay her purpose and her destiny – at least for the duration of the war.

CHAPTER 3.

Lilly sat watching the skittish flames jiving across the grate. She held in her hands the tiny photograph of Harry and herself as they stepped out that sunny afternoon in 1937 dressed in their finery for some factory outing. She would have been just twenty-four and Harry twenty-five. It was Coronation year and in this 'walking picture' as they were called, the two of them were striding out confidently, full of hope and purpose. Dark-haired urbane Harry with his neat side parting and his fashionable moustache had his coat folded smartly over his left arm and his elegant young wife on the other. Her sober two-piece suit and striking red and blue silk scarf around her neck were complemented by white leather shoes and a matching ribbon in her hair. Lilly recalled that day tenderly and adored this photograph, although it was starting to look a little dog-eared in her purse. She put it to one side and set herself to the task at hand.

'Sunny View', Keswick Road, Blackpool, Lancs.
30th November 1940.

My dearest Harry
How are you keeping, my precious darling?
You will be pleased to hear that Marilyn and I are now quite nicely settled here in Keswick Road with the Cockingtons. The house is little changed from when we were both here in '36, except that it is rather more grimy than I remember it. Certainly there's a lot of coming and going all day with neighbours calling in and deliveries of this and that. Everyone comes round by the back door. The front door is reserved for formal visits, it seems and causes much consternation when used! Sarah keeps her front step spick and span. It's something of an obsession with her and she says, "That step were not put there for folk to stand on." You'd dare not argue with her.

We have some charming fellow boarders: a couple of young ladies called June and Ethel who have moved to Blackpool to try and make their living as best they can. I'm not sure exactly what they do to earn their keep and get by, but I think they must work long hours because they seem to come in at all times of day and night.

And of course, you remember how Mrs C (she insists on me calling her Sarah) was always a strong character. Well, I haven't yet made up my mind quite how to take her. She has made us feel so very welcome, but I sense a lack of much patience in her. She rarely sits still – I suppose she and I have that much in common, I hear you say. But there is also a kind of restless energy about her. She has something of a short fuse. She speaks to her husband as though he were a naughty child, which I find quite uncomfortable. The other day I was sitting in the living room when Mr C had evidently given the cat the wrong piece of fish or something. The poor man thought he'd done the right thing, but he had made an error somewhere along the line. I heard her shout at him "just get out of my sight, will you!" I was shocked. I could never imagine speaking to you like that, but then of course, you would never stand for it would you? She is rather a tyrant and Joe Cockington is a pushover, I'm afraid to say. I wish he would push back, but he never seems to. So, the house is run along her lines and to her orders. I cannot tell whether Joe is content to be so hen-pecked or whether he might one day rebel!

Anyway, Marilyn is doing well. She has her usual cough and stuffy nose that always plague her at this time of the year. She doesn't seem to mind being here at all, though I watch her closely for any signs of homesickness. She amazes me every day with her resilience and fortitude. Such a little thing and yet she teaches me how to soldier on!

Well, I'll close here for now. Please write to me again soon. We miss you so very much.

Your devoted wife, Lilly.

At the start of the war, the Cockingtons, like everyone around them, were getting increasingly irritated by the patronising red poster campaign which they encountered on every street corner. Ubiquitous notices claiming that "Your courage, Your cheerfulness, Your resolution will bring us victory!" Then these mysteriously disappeared as suddenly as they had appeared.

Blackpool's cinemas had closed by order of the government who feared mass casualties should any bomb happen to land on them. Joe was mightily relieved when, after only twelve days their cinemas all opened up again for business as usual. They were a far more effective means of getting information across to the population eager for guidance, quite apart from the essential morale boost that the cinema provided like nothing else could. He remembered well how hard it had been to get any progress updates during the last war. The newspapers were very one-sided and of course they didn't have these modern means of getting timely up to date information like the wireless and film reels at the cinema. It was going to be so very different this time. He felt sure that this war would be brought home to him in far greater detail and speed. And that would be essential if they were going to find themselves under a gas attack or in German hands at any time.

It was Sarah and Joe's habit to treat themselves to the matinee showing every Wednesday, even when this meant stretching their resources. They took themselves off to the local King Edward picture house one rainy afternoon soon after the outbreak of war in early September 1939, when they had a particularly empty boarding house and an uncertain future ahead of them. There in the smoky darkness, as they were watching the new Food Flashes on how to keep milk from turning sour during a storm and how to make the best use of powdered eggs, they suddenly both realised that they had a golden opportunity laying there before them.

They watched patiently and paid particular attention to Potato Pete and Dr Carrot encouraging mothers to give these important vegetables to their children. They turned to each other with an excited nod and could hardly wait to get home before they could get started on digging up their well-manicured lawn and pulling out their prized flower beds. Theirs was the prettiest garden in Keswick Road. Everyone had told them so. Now, like a pair of assiduous boy scouts, the Cockingtons put their middle-aged backs into their own vegetable production. Sarah would inform the inquisitive neighbours who craned their necks to peek over the fence,

'Our carrots and onions are just as good as any you'll find in't local stores tha' knows!'

They found that this was something they could do together, it brought them closer and gave them a mutual purpose. They listened with a shared sense of pride and satisfaction to the wireless broadcasts from John Raeburn, Minister of Agriculture when he spoke of the need to alleviate Britain's reliance on imported grain and vegetables from overseas and to turn to ship-saving foods like potatoes.

We want not only the big man with the plough, but the little man with the spade to get busy this autumn. Let's get going. Let "Dig for Victory" be the motto of everyone with a garden.

And so they did.

Inspired by this patriotic appeal, Joe went further by filling in his coupon ready to send off to the council so that he could secure an extra ten rod allotment, considering himself to be a suitable applicant. He looked forward to taking advantage of all the expert advice on offer to him from professional nurserymen care of the Ministry. Joe knew that there was good money to be saved from this effort too. He and his fellow plot holders, once they had organised themselves into a credible Allotment Society, could buy co-operatively all manner of implements, as well as collecting seeds, plants and manure. The sense of community, of co-operation and creation, filled Joe with a boundless excitement and purpose that he had not known since his youth. He was now a digger, a tiller of the land. He was ready to cultivate and to sow and plant. Just as the government had bid him do.

The Cockingtons were less in unison on the subject of the Anderson shelter. Sarah did not want the space taken up in the garden but was appeased when she realised that they would qualify for a free shelter as they fell below the requisite £250 per annum income threshold. Joe enlisted the help of the garrulous local baker Donald Bunn (who had never lived down his unfortunate surname) and they set about constructing the shelter down at the very bottom of the garden. They bolted the two steel plates together at the top to form a perfect arch, reinforced with a heap of heavy soil which offered extra protection over the four-foot ditch that took most of the day to dig. Inside, they decided to assemble two benches on each side of the six foot-long shelter. Joe had read up on this subject in detail and remembered the value of incorporating a curved entrance to stop any potential bomb blast. They painted the shelter an encouraging, if somewhat sickly shade of pale green from an old paint tin which had been languishing at the back of the shed since long before the war. He had even rigged up a small stove in there.

'Our little home from home,' Joe had said and he commandeered as many tin washbowls as he could lay his hands on having read about how useful they were as potential helmets in case of an air raid.

Sarah thought it was awful and she wasn't at all looking forward to being squashed in there like a sardine. She remained resolutely unconvinced and deemed the whole enterprise to be a complete waste of time and struggled not to say as much out loud. She simply pursed her lips and hoped that she would never have to be proven right.

Lilly came in from the kitchen where she had been discussing her rent with Sarah over the washing up. She joined Marilyn as she was sipping her tea in the dining room. It was still early on Saturday morning and as the weak February sunshine reluctantly trickled into the room, Joe was trying valiantly to stuff some papers into a drawer in the sideboard. The drawer was clearly over-packed already and he was struggling to close it as Sarah entered briskly from the kitchen carrying a vase of early home-grown daffodils from the front garden. Their light and brilliance immediately filled Lilly with a warm feeling of optimism and delight.

'How many times have I told you to stop cramming that drawer full with all your junk, Joe Cockington!' cried Sarah.

'There's no more room to be had in there until you chuck sommat out!'

Joe ignored her.

'It's no bother. Don't start in with your fretting. I've done it now.' With one final determined push, Joe shut the drawer. A smug little grin spread momentarily across his face and he sat down in the armchair, taking up his newspaper. Sarah sighed, exasperated.

'So you see, Lilly, now that you've been here with us more than three months, it puts us in rather a difficult position, what with us giving over that room to you that we'd otherwise use for tenants or evacuees…I hope you do understand, luv.'

Lilly had been expecting this. She had her response carefully rehearsed and ready.

'Oh yes, Sarah. Yes of course. Well, I have a job now in any case, so I can afford the increase.'

The room came to a sudden halt.

'Oh, a job. Is that so?' asked Joe who had never got used to so many young women under his roof going out to work. This war was turning the world upside down. He thought of the two girls, June and Ethel. What had this war made them turn to for a profession? He could hardly countenance it…

His wife's razor-sharp voice sliced his thoughts into fragments.

'Don't interrupt us Joe, you just go back to what you do best, lounging about with your newspaper,' Sarah chided him. 'We were just discussing the rent, Lilly and I. Now then, what kind of job did you say, Lilly luv?'

Lilly was unabashed.

'Well, it's not much,' she said. 'I'm sewing buttonholes for Mrs Bennett the dressmaker in her shop in the high street. Mornings only, but it's not so bad. Do you know, George Formby - and Beryl, his wife - have been known to frequent Mrs Bennett's shop. I haven't seen them in there yet, but you never know!'

Joe lowered his paper.

'Oh, she's a funny one, she is…'

'Who, Mrs Bennett?' said Lilly. 'Oh, she's alright, a bit

strict, but she's – '

'No, no', chuckled Joe, 'I mean Mrs Formby. Wears the trousers, she does! And she goes everywhere he goes-'

'She don't trust him, obviously!' Sarah said with a dismissive sniff.

Joe was in full flow.

'I read in the paper that Formby did volunteer for the army, but he were turned down by the military 'cos of his flat feet! He's done a stint in the Home Guard as a dispatch rider, he has, did you know that?'

Lilly had heard from Harry about George Formby's troop concerts. Since the early days of the war, Formby had been working extensively for the Entertainments National Service Association, entertaining civilians and troops. He would go on to perform in front of some three million service personnel, many of them wounded British soldiers and often in improvised theatres all over the world. The famous comedian was almost always accompanied by his wife, Beryl.

His tour of North Africa had only lasted for a couple of months, but Harry had reported in his letters to Lilly that in some places Formby was giving as many as four shows a day.

'He's doing his bit by keeping up the morale of the boys overseas, like my Harry...'

'Oh, the boys love him!' chimed Sarah. 'And he's cheering us civilians up at home too! What's that song of his, Joe? Hitler can't kid us a lot, his secret weapon's tommyrot' Joe was clearly embarrassed in front of Lilly.

'Er...yes well not now, Mother, eh?'

Lilly's attention was still overseas with Harry. She pulled herself back to the matter in hand.

'Anyway, as I was saying, I'll be able to get you the extra money in a week or so. How does that suit you?'

That was fine with Sarah. She was slightly ashamed to ask and hoped that Lilly understood, because she did have her business to run and after all, there was a war on....

Sarah's thoughts were suddenly interrupted by the shrill ringing of the telephone.

'Oh, excuse me, luv.' With her posh telephone voice, she purred into the telephone.

'Hello, Sunny View guest house, Mrs Cockington speaking...oh, well yes she's just here as a matter of fact. I'll call her to the telephone, if you'll just hold the line...er Lilly, there's a gentleman who wants to speak to you, from London so he says.'

Joe saw that Lilly's hands were shaking as she grabbed the receiver. She spoke into the phone with an over-powering sense of foreboding.

'This is Lilly Stevens speaking...Yes, yes that's right. Er, Number 19, Brindle Road, Forest Gate, London E7.' She was getting agitated. Her mouth dry as cardboard. 'What? Oh my god. No! When? Are there many hurt? Are there any... killed? What do I do? What do I do? Er, yes, yes my husband is away in the Army...in Africa somewhere. Oh dear, I'm not supposed to...am I supposed to...? I'm sorry....Yes, I will. I will do. Yes of course, thank you for calling me up to let me know...Thank you...Goodbye.'

She stood there winded, rooted to the spot in disbelief. Sarah rushed to her side.

'What on earth is it, my dear girl? What's happened?'

Lilly felt as if the full force of a shockwave had hit her hard in the face and was sucking out the air from her lungs. She could hardly breathe.

'Our home has been bombed in Forest Gate. Direct hit. It's gone. The whole street has...it's gone.'

'God preserve us,' said Joe. 'When?'

'Last night. I have to go and see to Marilyn. We have to get back there. We just have to!'

Nearly every street had been destroyed across the East End of London during those intense months of German bombing in 1940. Lilly's sister Laura had spared no detail in her hastily-written letters, describing how many people she had seen as she ran for cover in doorways, caught out by the abruptness and rapidity of the raids. The dead and dying, ordinary people, men and women alike and even toddlers, rushing forwards and backwards through the wreckage, desperately trying to flee to the shelters but they were impotent, too late to save themselves. Shouting for their loved ones. Searching, sobbing for their children, screaming where can we go? Everywhere seemed to be in flames, smoke and fire billowing from the docks right across town to the back streets and alleyways. Above this anguish, the appalling red-yellow sky.

Yet that was just the beginning. The incendiary bombs were effective in starting lethal fires and the robust flames which leapt from those first surprise raids over the river were intended by the Nazi war machine to provide guaranteed beacons to guide their later raids on those same nights, leading the bombers into the city so that they could easily take out whole streets, raining down their explosives and reducing London to columns of dust and debris. No more phoney war now, no more vicarious conflicts happening to others across the Channel related from a safe distance by the Press and the BBC. This was real war on the streets of London.

In Stepney, where Lilly and Laura were born, where two hundred thousand people dwelt around the dockyards, war had come earlier than to other parts of town, as soon as war had been declared, in fact. Their mother had been sent home early from hospital to make room for anticipated casualties. Lilly had wandered from shop to shop trying to get supplies of sugar, candles, night lights for Marilyn and black paper. All these had run out almost within the first forty-eight hours. These were once familiar districts where now chaos raged in sheets of flame as every night houses were demolished and roads torn up. Every night the same heartbreak, loss, bewilderment.

Hopelessness pervaded the East End. In the first light of dawn, dust-ingrained inhabitants were forced to inspect the wretched vestiges of their lives, often where nothing remained, not even the smallest item. Children left without clothes or toys, adults left with nothing but memories of the lives they had lived up until the night before. Most of them thankful to be alive but many were angry and bitter, pushed aside by the horror and suffering.

The King and Queen had stepped gamely through the destroyed city streets to sympathise and offer the people of the East End comfort in their suffering. A few scant but heartfelt words of encouragement provided a remarkable tonic, a touch of humanity among the debris of their shattered lives. These ordinary people were meant to be the indestructible wall of British tenacity and courage. They were to keep going, determined never to bend their knee to force, whatever may befall them.

Joe gently blocked Lilly's path to the stairs.

'Well no Lilly luv, I think perhaps it's best if you don't go. Don't do that, please, luv. You need to take your time. Gather your thoughts, like. You can't do owt until you know more about what happened there.'

'But my mum, my sister...they're not on the 'phone you see. I need to know if they're alright. Where they are... Oh my God, Harry was right, he was right!'

And then Lilly swooned as the room began to swirl about her. She reached for Marilyn with her arms outstretched but as she groped, she suddenly felt a cold darkness close in around her and she fell forward.

'She's passed out!' Sarah tried to rouse her. 'Oh, get me smelling salts, Joe. Quick!'

CHAPTER 4.

'Right, Lilly luv, it's five shillings for Board plus two shillings for your laundry.' On returning home from collecting Marilyn from school, Sarah caught Lilly before they had even taken off their hats and coats. Lilly knew the routine. Since she had made the decision to stay put in Blackpool and there was a comfort in the regularity and normality of their lives now. Lilly concentrated on setting in place a routine for Marilyn and herself which could wrap its mundane predictability around them both and help them to carry on in these darkest of days.

She could not now contemplate going back to the East End Street where her lodgings had been obliterated. Neither did she want to summon Harry to rush back to her side on compassionate leave to help her recover from the shock of what had happened. So many of his unit had had to do this since the start of the bombing raids over the country. Much to Harry's surprise, Lilly was determined to carry on carving out a life in Blackpool. She had never been so truly tested in all her young life and she wanted now to develop a stoicism and resilience which she knew would be essential to her survival as well as being able to protect her little daughter. Harry simultaneously respected and worried about her restraint and about the fortitude that he had never expected to see in her. But he was unaware of the fury which was also building up inside Lilly. She would not share that in her letters to him. It was her own private rage. Not even something that she would want Marilyn to see. Not yet. It had been her home and her possessions which had been destroyed, although she had only been renting the place for a matter of months. But it was the narrow escape, the narrow luck of her timing and the precariousness of fate that had prompted her to heed Harry's plea and leave the East End when she did. Had she resisted, ignored him and remained there, that might have been the end of them. How dare the Germans reduce their lives and those of ordinary townspeople across the country to little more than a game of chance. A nightly gamble whose sickly stakes were based on whichever street or neighbourhood they happened to dwell in.

Eventually, her anger and bitterness gave way to an acceptance that life was now a perilous tight rope walk in which the unexpected could happen at any time. The more trivial details in Lilly's life were now less important to her and she noticed how the shock of the bombing had made her often confused and forgetful even of basic facts, all except those concerning Marilyn. She frequently felt muddle-headed and lacked focus or mental clarity. She had never been a good sleeper at the best of times, but now she was wakeful most nights and her appetite was non-existent, not aided by the paltry offerings emanating from Mrs Cockington's frenetic kitchen. Rather than worry about her own lack of nutrition, Lilly watched over her daughter with a greater intensity, almost to the level of obsession about what she was doing, how she was eating, sleeping, playing and speaking. She would hug the little girl tightly, reluctant to let her go, even when Marilyn squirmed to break loose, unaware of the effect this might be having on the child. And she was sick with worry about how her own mother and sister Laura would survive in the thick of it all. She knew that it was futile to try to get them to move away, both of them unable and unwilling to leave their East End home, destined to sit out the war like sitting ducks without decent protection. The thought was unbearable to Lilly.

Although she was not always able to keep up with her landlady's ambiguous financial thinking, she paid up without any quibble. She made a mental note however, to take back her own laundry from now on and save a few bob each month where she could.

'And little Marilyn, how's she going on?' asked Sarah. 'No more illness? Not sickening for nothing any more now, I take it, like she has been?'

Lilly was on her guard. Marilyn had always been a sickly child. She was often poorly, but since coming to Blackpool during that damp Autumn, her health, both physical and mental, had taken a definite downward turn. It was constantly tough-going for Lilly. The doctor's fees took a substantial chunk out of her modest income.

First it was Marilyn's tonsils and adenoids, then she had a bad bout of flu which had lingered as a persistent, chesty cough, keeping Lilly awake at night and scaring her witless. The last thing Lilly needed now was to have Sarah Cockington on her back nagging her about the rent – or worse still, pushing them both out the door if she thought that there was ever the slightest danger of her not paying her rent on time.

'No, thankfully.' Lilly said decisively. 'Not since those horrible nits last month. Mind you, the whole class got those. She's right as rain now. Aren't you sweetie?'

Marilyn looked up at her in mute bewilderment as Sarah swooped down on the poor unsuspecting little girl.

'What's the matter, cat got ya tongue?' Sarah laughed but Marilyn preferred to turn away from her irritating face which was too close to hers. Her breath reminded Marilyn of the rotting leaves in the park.

'No, she's still very shy. It's been rough on her, all this upheaval. New home, new school, new friends…It's no wonder she's still having trouble sleeping through the night. The dark, you know, it affects her terribly. At home, back in London, she was used to more light from the streetlamps at night-time. And she's still tending to wake up in a panic, forgetting where she is!'

Sarah was only half-listening.

'Of course, poor little mite…anyway, talking of cats, my own little puss will be along in a minute cos he knows it's his tea-time.' Marilyn listened eagerly for the familiar hungry meow of her best friend. It was what gave her the most joy since arriving in Blackpool and Sammy the cat was always happy to be petted by her.

'Ah, there he is. What did I tell ya? Regular as clockwork, he is. I'm coming Sammy my boy!' Sarah dashed out to the kitchen. Lilly followed Sarah and stood for a moment looking at the cat from the kitchen doorway as

Sarah crooned 'Mammy's gonna give you your din dins and then you'll get your tummy rubbed...Who's pleased to see mammy...?'

'Umm, he looks...doesn't he look...?'

Sarah straightened up. She had the remnants of the inane grin that she had proffered to the cat.

'Looks what, luv?'

Lilly hesitated, searching for the elusive words that she knew she must find.

'Well, I think he looks sort of...pregnant. Could he be a... she, possibly?'

Sarah's grin crashed to the floor. Marilyn thought it clattered like a saucepan lid.

'Don't be so daft! Of course he's not a she! I know my little Sammy and he wouldn't go all soft on me. He's a Tom, alright. The toughest Tom around 'ere! In fact, he's quite the little raver!'

The front door opened and Ethel and June walked in, giggling. They were always so thrilled to see little Marilyn.

'Hello, hello Mrs Stevens. Hello Marilyn.'

'Hello.' Marilyn's face lit up as she watched the girls bustle in and take off their hats and coats.

'Oh June, do please call me Lilly. After all, we've been living under the same roof for almost a year now!'

Sarah had their tea ready and knew they would be ravenous.

'Well, you young girls just sit yourselves down and I'll bring your tea through. Go on through, Lilly. Make yourselves comfy and I'll bring you sommat to eat. I'm off out myself tonight to the George Hotel while Joe's doing his night shift. So, it's catch-as-catch-can if you're alright with that'.

'Of course, we don't mind,' June spoke for them both. 'Come on Lilly, come and have a cuppa with Ethel and me.' She picked up Marilyn who started to giggle. 'And you, trouble, you can come and sit on my lap.'

Lilly felt a momentary pang of inexplicable resentment mixed with some relief.

'That's a first! You must be a miracle worker, June. Marilyn doesn't usually take to strangers, let alone sit on their laps...'

June smiled sweetly.

'But we're not strangers, are we? You just said so yourself.'

Sarah entered with some unappealing paper-thin shrivelled up sandwiches on a tray which she put down on the table by the teapot already placed there. She switched on some lively music on the wireless as she exited back into the kitchen with a wiggle of her hips in time to the rhythm. The three young women smiled to each other and June rolled her eyes. They had begun to form a warm bond. For Lilly, it was a welcome chance to relax and talk freely. Something she had not done for so many months.

Both June and Ethel noticed how Lilly's hands were shaking as she poured the tea. She cleared her throat and filled the pregnant silence with a question which she had been long wishing to clarify.

'So, tell me girls, did you both grow up here in Blackpool?'

Ethel loved to chat about how she'd made the break from the shackles of her homelife and come up to town.

'Oh ay, we come from Bispham just outside, don't we June?'

'That's right,' said June. 'Bispham born and bred. There's not much doing there, mind, oh except for the Dominion on a Saturday night! But tell us Lilly, what's it like in London? We've never been, have we Ethel? Well, not yet anyway.'

Lilly felt her face grow hot. It was hard these days to think back to her London life with Harry, with her baby and all the memories of a life on hold.

'Well, it's pretty dark and dreary there at the moment with all the blackouts and the raids and what have you. But before the war, it was so colourful and full of wonderful places to visit. Harry and I loved to go dancing. Every Friday night, we'd go. We used to finish work around six o'clock and then head straight for the Hammersmith Palais. That's a dance hall up West, I mean in West London, that is. Of course, I love the pictures too. The grand picture palaces up West, especially Leicester Square, they're so beautiful...I do hope we can go back there again someday before too long.'

And then she could feel her emotions soaring to the

surface and she wanted to change the subject.

'Anyway...you know, I swear that cat there has gone and got itself pregnant, but Mrs C, won't hear of it!'

June broke out into laughter again.

'Oh, Lilly, you really mustn't mind old Cockie. She's pretty bats most of the time!'

Ethel couldn't resist.

'Yeah and she's so bloody tight with it as well! Oh sorry Marilyn.'

It was time to get Marilyn off to bed. Lilly told her to say good night to Auntie June and Auntie Ethel.

'Nighty Night, Auntie Ethel and Auntie June. Sweet dreams.' Marilyn blew a clumsy kiss with her little hands and waved to them as she scampered away up the stairs. It always made them smile.

'Ah just look at her,' said Ethel. 'I bet butter wouldn't melt in her mouth...'

Lilly knew that this wasn't quite true, but she thought it better not to shatter their illusion. So she decided not to mention the fact that when she had sent Marilyn down to the chip shop in Bloomfield Road for six penny's worth of chips last Friday, the little scallywag had come back empty-handed because she'd eaten them all on the way home!

'Why did you do that, Marilyn, for Heaven's sake?' She had scolded Marilyn, grabbing her by both wrists.

'But the chips were hot and – and I was really really hungry.' replied the little girl, self-righteously. 'I didn't think that you'd mind all that much mummy. So I ate them all up. I'm sorry.'

Eaten the lot, she had. Lilly was still furious.

'Anyway goodnight girls, goodnight.' The girls both cooed as Lilly followed Marilyn out of the room. Ethel sighed.

'Poor luv, she looks exhausted. Must be hard on her, what with having the little'un in tow and her hubby so far away fighting and not having had any word from him for so long. I could cry for her, I could really.'

June had one eye on the clock.

'Well, Ethel, it's gone 8:30 so let's look lively, eh! Our first gent will be waiting for us at the Palatine.' She got up from the table and went to see to her hair.

Lilly fell straight to sleep as soon as her head nestled into her pillow. A deep and malevolent sleep which, rather than bring her rest and renewal, seemed to reflect all the dark unsettling events that had besieged her since the start of the war.

It was the sort of dream which persisted as she tossed and turned fitfully and which would hang on her still when she woke. She dreamt that she was on her way to find the Wizard of Oz and there she found herself face-to-face with the Wicked Witch of the West. She could see thick branches silhouetted against an ominous purple sky and strange sounds were twirling on the wind. Monkeys were screeching and birds were gloating. And that monstrous vile, green-faced witch was screaming some manic diatribe at her:

'It was such a surprise to see you, my dear,' said the witch. 'My party was just beginning. And then you had to go and throw that bucket of water over me and in that moment, you destroyed my world, my beautiful world. I was melting! Melting! Then there was nothing left of me but my black cloak and hat. I was driven to hatred by the goodness of that righteous Good Witch of the North. She is so sickly and contemptable. I needed to kill anyone whom she touched with that stupid sparkly wand of hers!'

'And oh, how I wanted those ruby slippers. You wouldn't give them to me. She had given them to you and I was consumed with jealousy and rage. Then I remembered that those slippers would never come off as long as you were alive.'

'My winged monkeys were only too happy to do my evil work for me. They flew everywhere, grasping at you and your stupid friends. There was no way you could catch them. And that pesky dog of yours, Toto. What a pathetic creature. The monkeys took him off without a struggle and I knew that would hurt you the most. Until even he ran away out of my clutches.'

'I never imagined that you would have such clever friends

to save you and destroy me. That silly Scarecrow without a brain. Who could have thought he would out-smart me! Even that Cowardly Lion! I thought he would be an easy conquest. But he found his voice alright – and his courage. She, that Good Witch was behind him, egging him on with her trickery and deceit and taking him out of my grasp. And as for that Tin Man. I was so sure I could ensnare him and break his chest with rust. It would be like cancer to his rivets and screws. But, no it was not to be.'

'It seems that you had the power all along – to escape from me by your own tenacity and guile. And so you found that dreaded bucket of water and threw it over me. Oh, you say it was not meant for me and that, had I not set fire to your scarecrow, it never would have happened! Well, that may be so, but how could you do that to me when you knew it was the one thing that would destroy me! My Achilles heel, my deadliest enemy.'

'You have your victory now and your escape. My face will appear in your dreams and turn them all to nightmares. Yes, technicolour nightmares, the green witch who took away your pink childhood innocence.

'But just three clicks of your sparkling ruby heels and there you were gone from my world. Home again and safe. There is no place like home - but your memory will never be rid of me.'

And then the Witch would not stop her demented laugh until Lilly woke up. It was nearly two years now since she had been with Harry to see the Wizard of Oz at the Odeon in Leicester Square. It seemed so odd that her favourite film, the one which she had loved so much that she had gone back to see it three nights in a row, had now given her the most alarming nightmare. She could not understand what had put it into her mind. Being so far away from my home, she supposed, yet knowing that her house had been destroyed, not by a violent storm, but by the enemy's bombs and she had not the first idea of how or when she would ever get back there.

'For the love of God Joe! Turn that bloody wireless down, will you, please.' Sarah was leaning against the kitchen door. Her face was a curious shade of green and she was clearly very hung-over. An excited reporter was describing every detail of the scene as an Allied convoy came under attack from the air. Joe had cranked up the volume and was now sitting rivetted. To Lilly it seemed that such a close eye-witness account was too vivid, too intense; it reminded her of the gory sporting contests which Harry used to follow back before the war.

"Germans are dive-bombing a convoy out into sea...there are one, two, three, four, five, six, seven German dive-bombers - Junkers 87s - there's one going down on its target now... bang...no, missed the ship, so he hasn't hit a single ship...there are about 10 ships in the convoy...but he hasn't hit a single one. There you can hear our anti-aircraft going at them now...there are one, two, three, four, five, six....there are about 10 German machines dive-bombing the British convoy...which is just out to sea in the Channel...I can't see anything...no...we thought a German one had been got then...but now the British fighters are coming up...there's one coming down in flames ...somebody's hit a German...and he's coming down...there's a long streak...he's coming down completely out of control...a long streak of smoke...oh ah, the man's bailed out by parachute, the pilot's bailed out by parachute...he's a Junkers 87 and he's going slap into the sea...and there he goes - SMASH! Only one man got out by parachute so presumably there was only a crew of one in it..."

Lilly could not resist. The devil was at her shoulder.

'Morning Sarah. How was your evening?' Sarah could feel her ear drums wobble painfully.

'Agghh. Morning to you too Lilly, luv.'

'Marilyn was hoping –'

'Who?'

'Marilyn – my Marilyn – she'd like to have a go at making us a cup of tea...'

'Oh yes, but please don't shout, luv! Me head! I feel like I'm stuck inside a drum and some bugger's banging on it right now…'

Lilly humoured her.

'I am sorry to hear that. Sounds like you made rather a night of it then.'

Sarah knew it was her own silly fault.

'Bit tipsy I were, last night at the George. But then what other pleasures do I 'ave, really?'

June and Ethel came through the door breezy as ever.

'Agghh! Oh hello June, Ethel….'

Ethel caught Lilly's eye and winked.

'Nice evening you had by the look of you this morning, Mrs C!'

Sarah snapped.

'You're always giggling and laughing, you two girls. It'll get you into a lot of trouble one of these days, you see if it won't.' Sarah sighed and turned to Lilly. 'Lilly, luv, you must join me one evening at the pub. It would do you the world of good, I'm sure! My treat. What d'ya say?' She was nursing her head.

Lilly wasn't really a pub kind of person. She rummaged in her mind for a gentle refusal.

'My Harry wouldn't really like me to…and of course I have Marilyn to think of.'

June chimed in casually.

'Oh, don't you worry about that. Ethel and me, we'd be happy to mind the little'un for you. Wouldn't we, Ethel? We might as well. When we're not er, you know, working, like.'

Lilly was humbled and grateful. It was kind of them both, but still…

Sarah was refreshed by a new thought.

'Ah, that reminds me, I'm expecting another evacuee arriving on Saturday. Just the one little lad. I said to them, just the one will do, thank you. What with me having a house full, as it is! They wanted me to take on more, but I said to 'em, I said "What about the cost? I'm not made of money, tha knows!" I said to 'em.'

Lilly was concerned.

'Will you have enough room? Where will you put him?' But Sarah didn't hesitate.

'Oh, he'll not need much room. I'll put him in the attic – that way, if he cries himself to sleep of a night, like the last one used to do, well, he shan't disturb the rest of the house, will he?'

No-one answered. They were suddenly aware of a sharp meow from the kitchen.

'Ah that'll be Sammy.' Sarah said. 'Eh, I'll tell you what, my Sammy's not been himself of late. He's right poorly looking, don't you think, eh?'

Lilly was defiant.

'No, I don't suppose he is himself, especially if he's a she… but let me take a look. I'm quite good with these things.' She went into the kitchen with Sarah hard on her heels.

'He's a he, if you don't mind. Like I said before.'

Lilly persevered

'You see, the thing is, Sammy does have those nipples, six of them in fact…'

'Well, don't Tom cats have those an' all?'

'Possibly,' Lilly pressed on. 'But then there's also the absence of a certain, um you know…down there…anyway, it's just my guess, but I reckon your Sammy might be expecting kittens.'

June and Ethel couldn't help their sniggering despite having been admonished by Sarah.

'What?' Sarah was beside herself. She remembered her head. 'Ouch! Oh, that can't be right. Don't be so soft. Sammy wouldn't do a thing like that. He wouldn't do that to me!'

Through her tears of laughter, Ethel could barely catch her breath.

'Well. We'll just have to wait and see then, won't we!'

CHAPTER 5.

'Well, dear me, whatever next?' Sarah said out loud. She was exasperated, although that was nothing new. 'Apparently, it's now patriotic to be shabby. Have you ever heard anything so…'

As often happened when the right word for the occasion eluded her, Sarah's voice trailed off as she handed Lilly a copy of the latest booklet on Make Do and Mend. It had cost Sarah an extravagant threepence, but she considered the outlay an investment if it would give her some significant money-saving hints. She had been in shock from the sudden rationing of clothes in June 1941 as the supply of cotton and wool dropped dramatically and the factories that had spun and woven them had been turned over to other priority war work to supply blackout material, parachutes, blankets and of course, uniforms. Little was left over for the rest of the population who had to put up with the "fair distribution of available supplies." Only hats did not require coupons and Lilly knew that these had all but disappeared from the shops.

Lilly eagerly foraged through the little pamphlet for encouraging hints and tips on how to help make her clothes last longer. There was plenty of information on better ways to mend collars, cuffs and gloves and most urgent of all, there were ideas on how best to store the precious few clothes that she and Marilyn had brought with them from London in haste. Lilly knew that these simply had to last longer than before and she tried in vain to halt the spread of holes and frays from showing as long as possible. Spurred on by the Board of Trade's confident recommendations to everyone about making simple, practical alterations to clothing, Lilly had even tried to persuade Mrs Bennett to host a new needlework class at the back of the shop which might help boost the confidence of local women in learning more skills in how to re-fashion or repair what they already had in their wardrobes. She was keen to show them how a pair of old trousers could be turned into a new skirt or how two old dresses could be unpicked and adapted into a smart new one. This was second nature to Lilly who had developed her needlework skills since childhood from her mother and grandmother.

Unfortunately, her enthusiasm went unshared and the needlework class idea came to nothing as no-one had shown enough interest, least of all Mrs Bennett. So much for community spirit. Lilly would have to motivate herself to turn every scrap of good material she could lay her hands on to advantage and resist the need to buy new, for which the cost and lack of supply proved prohibitive anyway. Marilyn was growing, but thankfully not as fast a rate as the many other children around her, for she was so often sickly and like both her parents, would never grow tall or broad. That was a blessing now and Lilly was not too proud to accept hand-me-downs and dress her daughter in other mothers' cast offs. She was happy to adapt larger dresses and made a game for Marilyn out of seeing what they could create anew from seemingly dog-eared and dilapidated garments. In addition, second-hand clothes were not to be limited by rationing which meant that Marilyn, like many of her school friends could be well served by jumble and bring-and-buy sales which sprang up almost every week.

Sarah's Make Do and Mend leaflet also explained how to best clean these precious garments, both old and new so that their life could be extended and how different washing methods should be applied depending on the type of fabric. This was useful to Ethel and June whose rayon stockings were among their most prized possessions. Lilly stopped them from ruining their precious last pairs one day when she caught them diligently washing them with much vigour.

'Dirt doesn't sink into the fibres apparently, it just sits on the surface of the stockings, you see, girls.

So, you really shouldn't need to rub them and wring them, or else they'll distort and break. All you need to do is to dip them into the water and then squeeze them, gently. Like this.'

They were both so grateful to her as she demonstrated

her point that they couldn't stop thanking her all evening.

Sarah for her part, was all for making her cleaning products stretch as far as possible. With such punitive rationing of soap, she was constantly striving to make what little soap she could lay her hands on go that little bit further. Not a sliver would she throw away.

'It's just ridiculous, that's what it is!' she exclaimed to Joe as she read out the ration card. 'How can we get on with four ounces of hard soap for the floors or six ounces of soft soap for the dishes and that or three ounces for washing ourselves. No wonder we're all starting to stink!'

Then Joe had an idea. He rummaged around in the drawers of the dresser in his usual noisy chaotic fashion, as he always did whenever he was in the grip of inspiration. Sarah didn't hold her breath and was about to walk out of the room when he suddenly waved a piece of paper in her face.

'Whatever are you doing now, Joe?' she was tetchy with impatience.

'Soapwort! I don't know why I didn't think of it sooner.'

'No, I wish you had. What are you on about?

'The lads on the allotment were telling me all about it a few weeks back and, well it went right out of me head. I clean forgot all about it, as you might say.' He chuckled to himself as Sarah waited, a stoney look of exasperation shaping her features. 'Well, you see, there's a corner of the allotment up there that's full of the stuff. The boys were in favour of digging it all up to make more room for the onions and carrots. Only then Jim Herbert who's always reading up on these things, he says we should keep the soapwort and give it to our wives to make a go of shampoo. Our own shampoo! What d'you reckon, Sarah?'

'What do I reckon? This is just one of your usual harebrained schemes, that's what I reckon.' Again Joe chuckled but only he appreciated the pun.

'No, you just have a listen to this, before you dismiss it out of hand. Jim Herbert says that, hang on, I wrote it all down as he were telling us. Ah yes, here we are, according to Jim, all parts of the soapwort plant contain what he called saponin or sommat, I can't read me own writing here.' Joe pushed his glasses further down his nose for a better focus.

'You have to wash the roots and then hang 'em up to dry for a few days. Then you have to pack 'em away in storage and then later on in the year, you can just get the saponin out by soaking the roots in water overnight, mashing them up and then straining out all the bits. It makes a sight for sore eyes by all accounts, but old Jim says his wife's hair has never felt so soft –'

'It's you that's soft!' cried Sarah. 'I'm not mucking about with nasty green slimy plants. No no, we'll stick to what they give us int' shops if you don't mind. Thank you all the same.'

Joe was used to his wife pouring scorn on any new idea and decided that this battle wasn't worth the choosing.

'Well in that case, why don't we just use me shaving soap for washing in? That's not rationed at all. Why don't we do that then, eh? The boys on the allotment are doing that an all –'

'Now that is a good idea! I do like that, I must say! You are a clever man, sometimes, Joe Cockington!'

Sarah put the last little slivers of all the different soaps into a jar with warm water so that it turned into a disgusting jelly of indeterminate colour and odour but which could be used for washing up or soaking dirty woollens. She also took to placing a small square flannel between the soap and soap dish so that she could collect enough residue to eke out another wash or two. It all became routine practice for her and she encouraged all her boarders to do the same. She could not bear to see anything go to waste. And then when all the soap had run out, she came up with other ways to keep the house clean without it. Vinegar, salt, borax, bicarbonate of soda, all the substances her own mother used to use. All it took was a little imagination and a very strong stomach to cope with the smell.

83 Lansdowne Drive, Hackney, E8.
12th October 1941.

My dear darling girl

I am writing this to you over the wail of air-raid sirens. Wouldn't you just know it! As soon as I sit down with pen in hand, Hitler starts his nonsense again.

My neighbour, Enid, (Mrs Morrison as you know her – we all seem to be on first name terms these days) was telling me over the fence this morning that her daughter Rose, the trainee midwife down in Plymouth, was on night duty last week helping to prepare for a difficult delivery, when a bomb struck the children's ward next door. She said that there was dead silence and then you could hear the poor children crying. By all accounts, another bomb came down right onto the maternity block itself and poor Rose had to deliver this baby all by herself by torchlight on account of there being no lights and all the debris falling about her. Can you imagine such a thing? Bringing a precious baby into the world amid such muck and filth? I wonder if the German women are being subjected to this same horror and chaos. Serves them jolly-well right I suppose…

Lilly stopped reading the letter. She couldn't bear it. She could well imagine what sort of hellish inferno that hospital in Plymouth had endured. She had read about it in Joe's newspaper. It had been reported, minus most of the details, with the usual focus on carefully managing the impact on morale. Yet it was enough for Lilly almost to smell the putrid odour of blood and burnt skin, rubble and dust all mixed up together. The horror of it made her want to weep, but she read on. Her mother's letters were rare these days, but always as frank and unsentimental as the woman was herself and this brought Lilly some comfort, as if her mother were sitting there beside her.

…They've tied notice boards to the Town Hall railings. Each morning after the raids they pin up lists to these boards of the dead and the missing. I have to walk past there every day to fetch our milk and bread. It's such an awful sight, Lilly. So many women desperately worried as they try to find out whether anyone they know has been killed….

Lilly was shocked by this stark account from her mother and guilt lay around her shoulders like a damp heavy blanket. She and Marilyn had turned their backs on that peril, hadn't they? She knew in her heart that there was no rancour nor resentment in her mother's letters. But the down-to-earth detachment in her descriptions of life around her in the East End was somehow far harder for Lilly to take than if each line had been under-scored with her mother's bitter recriminations. Lilly could feel the pain and the determination of these Londoners whom she had left behind her. But after all, wasn't she simply following the Government's advice dished out to the many thousands of people made homeless by the Blitz, to "make their own arrangements"?

It was the hatred that got to her the most. It seemed to be pouring out of every street, every bomb shelter.

Every letter she had received from her London friends and family conveyed it. Publicans, butchers, bakers, everywhere she turned she could hear it, see it, feel it. "An eye for an eye! If they can do this to us, we should do it back to them!" And worst of all "If they can kill our children, then we should kill theirs!" This way madness surely lay. Lilly could barely understand how people of her own age, her own background could utter such horrific sentiment. The world was changing swiftly, utterly, irretrievably. Her world. Marilyn's world. Lilly could not comprehend it. What kind of humanity could embrace such bitter intolerance of itself?

The wind had got up and was blowing a noisy gale. It threw the leaves into a rhythmic swirl across the pavements and on the lean-to behind Mrs Bennett's shop.

Lilly had moved to a lighter, less drafty corner and poured over her work with renewed alacrity. Only one more day this week and then she would have a couple of days off to spend with Marilyn exploring the beach, the lanes and the parks around the town. Walking was her favourite new past-time since her move to Blackpool. She had never been keen on it before the war and Harry was always driving her around in the smartest car he could afford.

But now, here she was without a car and everything was close to hand and convenient, doctors, shops, even the local picture house. She had surprised herself by how much she looked forward to walking just for pleasure, instead of it being a means to an end. It was good for little Marilyn too. They would chat together hand in hand, pointing out new details to each other and listening, really listening to the novel sounds dancing around them as they walked. Sounds which they never heard at home in London: the seagulls, the crashing waves, laughter on the beach and the rustling of leaves susurrating through the trees around them. Walking slowed her thoughts, gave her an inner peace and a brief respite from her daily anxieties replacing them with something approaching a feeling of contentment and sometimes almost elation. The excited mew call of seagulls swooping above her in the mornings added joy to Lilly's life and lit her face with a grateful smile.

Fred Ackroyd, the twenty-year-old local delivery boy had just crept in through the back door. To him, Lilly Stevens was the most beautiful creature in the world. His life was more colourful and entrancing from that very first moment when he met her just before Christmas. She was wearing a pale grey-blue dress today which flattered her slim figure and her hair was swept back giving her an unquestionable elegance and grace. In his eyes, Lilly was near perfect. She looked like a film star, a glamourous, exotic actress...

'Morning Fred. Oh, you made me jump, you did! What are you doing skulking around?' Lilly smiled at him.

Fred froze on the spot. His acne-scarred face flushed red hot. He had been caught in the act of admiring her from the safe distance of the backdoor step.

'Oh good morning, Mrs Stevens. I've brought the milk and tea for Mrs Bennett. I'll just pop them here on the side for you, shall I? Just 'ere, like?'

'Right you are, thanks Fred.' Lilly was engrossed in her buttonhole work and didn't look up. Fred stood there a moment longer than he should, willing her to look at him for just one more fleeting moment. The merest glance from Lilly could warm him through and sustain him for the rest of the day.

Fred thought to himself, *now then, how about throwing out*

a witty line here, eh? He wracked his brains. It was early morning, only just light. He had run his patter over and over in his head as he dragged his bicycle out of the coal shed, rolled his witty lines around his mouth as he cycled over the bumpy cobbled streets. But he was grateful when she prompted him.

'How's that bike of yours this morning, Fred? You were mending that rusty chain guard last week, weren't you?'

'There's talk of me getting me own van, tha knows, Mrs Stevens. This bike was all very well when they were wanting to take all vehicles off the road in case the enemy got hold of 'em. But now that looks unlikely, I might get given a proper delivery van.' He puffed out his chest for no good reason and waited for Lilly's astonished reaction.

'You always cheer me up in these dreary mornings, Fred. You did make me laugh yesterday with your daft story about that lady on the pier and her hat flying into the sea. I was chuckling all day about that.' Still she didn't look up at him.

'Shall I make us both a cuppa if you've got the time, Mrs Stevens?' Then she gazed on him at last. 'Oh yes please Fred, you are an angel.'

With an effort of will, Fred turned from her and filled the kettle. She had no idea what tumultuous feelings he was wrestling with. How could she possibly?

'I suppose Mrs Bennett will want to join us. I'll just go and fetch her.' Lilly swept out of the room with her usual flurry. Mrs Bennett had little time for Fred but indulged him this one small luxury of a quick cup of tea before he went on his way. Ten minutes tops she gave him, then she would shoo him out the door. He should know his place after all. Charlotte Bennett, an austere buxom lady of advancing years, had a very shrewd eye for liberty-takers and shirkers. In her book, that boy Fred Ackroyd was both of those. Give him an inch, he'd take a mile. Lilly Stevens must be so naïve; she should be more careful than to encourage the likes of that scrawny lad. Tut tut. Oh Lord, why did this battle-axe of a woman always feel the need to stamp all over his elation? The two ladies came back in and sat down.

'Here, I'll put the tea in the pot,' said Lilly. Some fleeting memory flashed through her mind, but it escaped her too quickly before she could grasp hold of it. What did that comment remind her of?

'I had a letter from my brother Alan yesterday.' Fred blurted with a forced composure.

'Did you? How lovely.'

'Oh aye. He's a right champion letter-writer is our Alan. Never neglects to write.'

But as they were sitting there sipping their tea, the conversation had got off to a false start. There was a lull, a hiatus, a chasm which his limited wit failed to bridge. He felt himself falling. Until Lilly picked him back up again.

'So, what did he say in his letter?'

'Oh well, he's finished his reconnaissance training and now they're getting ready to push off to France. That's all he can tell us at the moment, you know. Me ma's so proud of course.'

And as if to answer the unformed question in Lilly's mind, Fred began a coughing fit, a deep wild chesty cough which took all his strength to tame.

'Yes, well, we've had enough careless talk around here for one morning,' pronounced Mrs Bennett in a way that invited no retort or clever one-liner, witty or otherwise. 'You'd best be on your way now, me lad.'

'See you tomorrow, Fred.' Lilly said breezily without any inkling of the momentous impact of those words on Fred's delicate self-esteem. 'And do wrap up against the cold,' she added. 'You need to take care of that chest of yours!'

Fred nodded to her in dumb obedience and he stumbled backwards out of the door, nearly falling over his bicycle which was propped up against the wall.

All his awkwardness went mercifully unnoticed by Lilly, but Mrs Bennett saw it all. She tutted and dismissed his exit with a contemptuous sneer, just as she did every morning.

'I don't know why you let him bother you, Lilly I must say.'

'He means no harm, Mrs Bennett. I rather like him. He makes me laugh. And besides, you know, he and his mother are our very good neighbours in Keswick Road.'

Her employer saw nothing in that statement with which

to agree and she turned tail and swished contemptuously back into the shop just in time to hear the doorbell usher in her first customers of the day. And Mrs Bennett was restored once again to her proper, well-ordered world.

CHAPTER 6.

Some days she could put it out of her head completely, but not today. Lilly was wandering about the kitchen trying to find things to take her mind off the horror of it all. June came in to look for a bottle opener. She was always noisy in everything she did. It would often irritate Lilly but at this moment, she welcomed the interruption to her prowling thoughts.

'Hello there Lilly. I've just been chatting to a woman at the bottom of the road there and she were telling me that she'd heard about a young woman evacuated from London with her baby boy and she'd been made to sleep in a barn just because the little lad were handicapped. So evidently, she took one look at the place and turned tail and went straight back to London, bombs or no bombs! Have you ever heard anything so awful? In't it disgusting, eh? You wouldn't credit it, would you!' Then she noticed the strange look on Lilly's face as she turned to her.

'What you doing?' she asked casually. Lilly didn't answer. She was looking down at the leaflet in front of her on the little kitchen table.

'This has just been dropped through the letter box. It's quite unnerved me. I mean, why do they have to keep on and on? Giving out instructions, barking orders at us as if we're all mindless morons. I can't stand it-'

'Oh, I see,' said June as she creased up her face to try to make out the tiny type face on the leaflet. She couldn't read it too well and so decided it shouldn't worry her. But Lilly's anguish was something she couldn't ignore. She sat down by her side and picked up the leaflet closer to her face.

'What to do and how to do it…' she read turning it over in her grimy little hands. Her filthy fingernails turned Lilly's stomach.

'There's nothing in here that we don't already know. Oh June, I can't believe we'd ever really be invaded. Not here in

Blackpool.'

'Well, then what are you getting yourself so worried about?'

'No, it's just that I'm frightened for Marilyn. For all the children. What would happen to them? I can't imagine it.'

'Seems to me, Lilly that it'd be far better if we *don't* imagine. I mean, what good would all the advice in this silly pamphlet do us if we had to face the Germans with all their might, eh? What a lot of rot, I ask you. "You must remain where you are. The order is stay put...don't spread rumours, keep your heads, use your common sense...." Oh and I like this bit here, "Think before you act. But think always of your country before you think of yourself..." I'd be surprised if people do that, eh! Come on Lilly, it'll be alright. We can't do much about it and you know what they say, "why worry about what you can't do nowt about? Or sommat like that, anyway, you know what I mean.'

Lilly put on her tatty coat and picked up her bag and quietly left for work, too preoccupied to say anything more to June sitting there. June softly wished her a nice morning, knowing well enough that Lilly's day would be far from easy. Then she brushed away the tear drops which Lilly had left on the leaflet so that others might read it later on.

'Hey Sarah, luv, I'm done with scrubbing floors, tha' knows!' Sarah blinked hard in the unforgiving Autumn sunshine. She was not best pleased at the interruption as she had a busy morning ahead of her, but she could not escape quickly enough the advancing Betty Ackroyd who was particularly fleet of foot on this early morning.

'What's that you said?' sighed Sarah straining to hear her neighbour over two fences with a garden in between them.

'Well you see, me new linoleum is being delivered to me today. Hang the cost, I say! I'm having the downstairs all done out in it. It will really make a difference. All I'll have to do is wipe it down to keep it clean, you see. Wipe it down with a mop. Well, there's no bother in that, is there?'

'Sounds expensive!' Sarah dismissed it with a snort.

'No, no, it's not at all expensive, tha' knows! They're just gonna lay it down directly on top of me old stone flags, they are. Not a big job I don't reckon. You wanna think about it too, Sarah, luv. It'll make such a difference to you. You'll not have to get down on your hands and knees to scrub them floors no more, oh well, except for them corners and tricky places, like. But that's nowt, is it!'

Sarah was not convinced. This was extravagance beyond the pale. The unintended pun made her chuckle to herself and she cheerfully dismissed the idea of her own kitchen swathed in linoleum from her mind.

'No, it's out of the question, Betty luv. We don't have the money for all that sort of thing. Why, you remember all the bother and hullabaloo we had when they put in them boilers and indoor pumps back '37? Just so that we could have running water int' kitchen and upstairs? Well, I can't think as we could get any more modern than that, eh?'

'Oh well, please tha'self!' was all Betty had to say. Nothing could deflate her excitement. She tapped her hand on the top of the fence and danced off back indoors. Each lady felt that she'd scored a self-righteous victory over the other.

A knock at Sarah's front door recalibrated her stance.

'Oh, that'll be the Billeting Officer,' she cried out loud to herself. 'About time an' all. She's over two hours late.'

As soon as Sarah opened the front door, the local Billeting Officer wasted no time in nudging forward over the threshold a stout little boy with grubby cheeks of about eight years old. The boy looked down at his shoes. He seemed terrified.

'Good afternoon, Mrs Cockington. This is your new evacuee. His name is William Hackett. He's eight years old and comes from Stepney in the East End of London. In you go now, Billy. There's a good lad. Oh, he prefers to be called Billy. Here's all the paperwork to go with him. Anything you need, there's our telephone number on the bottom. But of course, you know how it all works, I dare say. Thank you so very much. Good day to you Mrs Cockington.'

Without waiting for Sarah to sign the chit as was the usual procedure, the Billeting Officer turned on her heels, clicked away down the path and was gone.

As she closed the door, Sarah took in the musty smell of fried food that clung to the sorry little mite. He was playing with his destination tag which by now had become dog-eared and tatty. Someone had misspelled Blackpool as Blackpill which had only added to the little boy's confusion. Sarah was shocked at his condition. He looked as though he hadn't had a good proper wash for months. His eyes were red and sunken and he was so pale and miserable-looking that she wondered whether he had in fact just been hauled out of a ditch.

'Well now, so here you are. You'd best come on through, Billy Hackett. Here's your new home. Hope you like it.' Billy stayed silent. Sarah continued with her drill, knowing full well that the wretched boy was trembling on the brink of tears.

'So, here's the rules. We don't stand for any crying and nonsense. You are the only man about the place, apart from me husband, I should say. So, you'll be expected to behave like a man. You understand me?'

Ethel had heard the front door and was skipping eagerly down the stairs wondering whether the caller was for her.

'Oh hello, you must be the new boy. I'm Ethel –'

Billy couldn't help himself any longer. He gave way to the flood of tears that had been welling up inside him like a hot fountain ever since he'd first stepped onto that huge train which his mother had promised would take him on his first big adventure away from the city smoke. If big brave cowboys weren't supposed to cry, then he didn't want to play that game anymore.

Billy and Marilyn had little in common other than their shared beginnings in the East End of London and the fact that neither of them understood why they had been moved to Blackpool and why their favourite grown-ups were always disappearing. They played together as nicely as they could, given their lack of interest in each other. For a time, Billy and Marilyn would walk to school together. At the weekends, Billy was happy for them to play quietly together in his malodourous messy little bedroom if in the early mornings the adults were particularly tardy in getting up. Marilyn believed that the boy was a bit too slow to keep up with her, despite her being so much younger than him and she tested this theory one day when they were playing with the cruet set before tea. Billy asked her what the pepper pot was for.

'Why don't you sniff it and find out what it smells of?' she innocently suggested and when Billy took a sniff, he couldn't stop sneezing for half an hour. None of the adults took much notice as the boy was always sniffly and wiping his nose on his sleeve.

On Sunday morning when Sarah had covered the dining table in an enormous dark red velour tablecloth, the two children hid themselves under the table as Marilyn thought it would be fun to see how long they could sit there undetected by anyone else in the house, until they both became scared of the dark confined space and of the thought that they might be forgotten there.

One morning when everyone was sitting around the breakfast table, Billy was becoming more and more agitated among the chinking of cups and scraping of butter knives against burnt toast. Sarah noticed with growing annoyance that the boy was upset and wouldn't stop his fidgeting. Joe meanwhile was engrossed in his newspaper.

'Eh, just listen to this! It's Churchill's latest speech yesterday. He's saying, here listen, he says:

"...Never give in, never give in, never, never, never, never - in nothing, great or small, large or petty, never give in except to convictions of honour and good sense. Never yield to force; never yield to the apparently overwhelming might of the enemy..."

Joe lowered his paper and cleared his throat, almost moved to tears.

'Well, well, what d'you all make of that then, eh?'
Sarah was oblivious to any historical or emotional significance in Churchill's latest bit of fine talking. Her attention was trained on Billy. She could take it no longer.

'What's the matter with you, Billy lad, eh? Sommat wrong with your breakfast?'

'I bet it's just that he's not hungry, Mrs C. That's all.' Ethel said.

Billy spoke for the first time that morning. He had a way of avoiding eye contact with any of them which Marilyn found particularly frustrating.

'I'm not hungry.' Billy groaned to no-one in particular.

'See, I told ya, that's all that's the matter with him.' Ethel understood the troubled child. Of course she did.

'Well, why aren't you hungry? Eh? Kids just like you are starving across the continent 'cos there's not enough for them to eat.'

Lilly was suddenly aware of something strange.

'What's that smell?'

Ethel noticed it too. What was it?

'Billy! Is that you? Have you pooped yourself, young man? Eh? Have you?' Sarah barked at the boy and was almost ready to drag him up from his seat by his grimy little pullover. Lilly came to his rescue.

'Have you had a little accident, Billy?' She asked him quietly.

Billy nodded and started to sob. He was mortified.

'Come on, come with me then.' Lilly took him gently by the hand.

'It's alright, I'll see to him, Sarah. Come on Billy, let's go upstairs.'

As she was taking Billy out of the room, Lilly suddenly stopped by the fireplace.

'I left my ExLax chocolate on the mantlepiece here. Has somebody moved it? It was just here – '

'Was that your chocolate, Lilly luv? I am sorry, I gave it to the lad here,' Sarah replied innocently.

'No! It wasn't just chocolate. It was my ExLAx. You know - for my tummy, for my *constipation*!'

June and Ethel both let out an involuntary snigger. Sarah went on self-righteously.

'Well, if you will leave your stuff just lying around –'

'But it says clearly on the box-'

'Well I didn't see nothing clearly on't box, did I? And besides, the lad wanted some chocolate.'

June turned to a bewildered Marilyn.

'Poor old Cockie, she doesn't see too well these days, does

she Marilyn?'

Lilly pursed her lips. Wasn't Harry's mum always advising "*Bite your tongue...*" whenever a row was bubbling up? This was the best thing to do right now. She took a deep breath and swept the unfortunate Billy out of the room. Joe rolled up his sleeves and cleared the table with the help of June and Ethel. As they carried the breakfast debris out into the kitchen, Sarah began searching for some music on the wireless. She took up some socks and started darning. Marilyn was only too pleased to get back to her spot on the floor at her feet and resume the absorbing task of cutting out pictures from a pile of magazines. Sarah stopped her sewing to watch Marilyn.

'Careful as you go there, Marilyn luv. Them scissors can be sharp. I'll have your mam to answer to if you snip your fingers off! What are you cutting out there, anyroad? Mm?'

'Pretty dresses, for my dolls,' Marilyn proudly held up the magazine she was working from for Sarah to see.

'Oh well, that's nice. Pretty dresses, good girl.'

There was a knock at the door. Her neighbour from next door but one, Betty Ackroyd popped her head round the door before bustling in. She was a short, plump fusspot of a woman with an air of restlessness about her. Betty had a habit of pulling her worn, shapeless cardigan around her substantial abdomen in a way which added to her air of drabness. Much the same age as Sarah, she was a good-natured but unworldly woman who had never travelled very far. She had once spent a weekend in Manchester with her late husband many years ago but didn't like the noise and the crowds. She had never seen London and had no curiosity to travel that far. Sarah admired how she channelled her nervous energy into a stoic fortitude to cope with the separation from her beloved son Alan who had left for the war nearly a year ago.

Betty had been a prolific cake-maker before wartime rationing had kerbed her zeal. Many a good cause had gratefully received her contributions at jumble sales, Mothers Union coffee mornings and country shows.

She had lived in Keswick Road a decade longer than

the Cockingtons. Sarah and Joe had never forgotten that afternoon they moved in when there was a knock on the door and with a kind and hopeful expression, there stood Betty on the doorstep holding out a date and walnut cake as she welcomed them to the street. Sarah had preferred to keep a respectable distance between them and assiduously fended off Betty's attempts to draw her into the sphere of the Mother's Union. Sarah believed that their modest fences and hedges were enough delineation between friendship and neighbourliness, but then the war had changed that. Now they were rarely out of each other's kitchens and shared many a knitting pattern or recipe.

'Only me, Sarah luv.'

'Oh, how do, Betty. Come in luv. How's things?'

Betty was already seating herself comfortably.

'Oh, now, we mustn't grumble, must we?'

'And how's that young Fred of yours going on?' Sarah asked.

'Oh he's alright, you know...' Betty sighed heavily as she straightened her head scarf. She barely disguised her disappointment in her Fred who had not made much of himself in life and compared less than favourably with his twin brother, Alan whom she thought had shown distinct initiative and signed up to the Air Force and very handsome in his uniform he looked too. She still had Fred at home and, whilst he was company for her, that sigh encompassed a multitude of secret, long-forgotten dreams that she had harboured for the lad.

'He gets up at half past four every morning to start his deliveries. He stops in for a quick cuppa at Mrs Bennett's, you know the dress maker in the high street, just before she opens and then he's home again by nine o'clock for his breakfast.'

Sarah leaned forward conspiratorially.

'He must know one of my boarders, Lilly Stevens. She works for old Mrs Bennett, she does. Her hubby's away in Italy.'

Sarah lowered her voice, conscious of Marilyn sitting there.

'Only she's not heard nothing from him in weeks. Not a dicky bird. She's in bits, the poor luv. Well, we all are of course.'

Betty sat forward, her dry florid cheeks wobbling in anticipation of imparting a juicy morsel of gossip.

'Oh aye, that lass from London? Oh, he goes on about her all the time, does my Fred! What she's said, what he said to make her laugh, how she's ever so gracious and polite…he's quite taken with her, tha' knows.'

Sarah smiled down at Marilyn.

'Yes, and this is Marilyn, Lilly's young daughter. I look after her some mornings while Lilly's in't shop. We get on a treat, don't we Marilyn, eh?' Marilyn was far too engrossed in her cutting out to be drawn into the conversation. Sarah whispered,

'They lost their home in the Blitz a while back, poor luvs. It were dreadful. Can you imagine it?'

Betty was not one for indulging small children, but in spite of this, she was struck by the little girl's beauty.

'Well, yes. How d'you do Marilyn. And what have you got there?'

'Bright as a button she is too.' beamed Sarah.

Betty noticed Marilyn's ringlets which cascaded around her shoulders. Lilly's pride and joy.

'You're a pretty little thing, aren't you. Happen you'll break a few men's hearts one day. Oh, well, Sarah luv, the reason I've called in is 'cos I'm all out of sugar again till me next lot of coupons. Could I borrow just a small cup from you luv? I'll bring it back to you next week. I wouldn't ask, only – '

Sarah was one step ahead of her neighbour. It was a weekly ritual that they played out between them.

'I'm afraid I've nearly used up my week's ration of sugar too. Let me go and see what I've got left.'

'Oh you are a good soul, Sarah Cockington.' Betty threw a wink at Marilyn.

Sarah busied herself in the pretence of rummaging through her kitchen cupboards.

'All that baking you're doing of late, feeding that young lad of yours –'

'Oh, it's not for Fred.' Betty sat up impatiently. 'No no, it's for me new evacuee. I've got a young lad of seven. He won't eat nothing but cake! I've tried him on everything I can find: powdered egg, me home-made black pudding, porridge, the lot. But he won't touch it. None of it. I'm at my wit's end!'

Sarah popped her head out of the kitchen.

'What about plain old bread and margarine, or bread and _'

'Now then, don't get me started on margarine!' cried Betty. 'You know what the little beggar went and did the other week? He'd only been with me a few days. I were sitting in't kitchen doing me knitting and I thought to meself, that lad's gone a bit quiet. What's he up to? You know a mother's instinct, like. Well, guess what I caught him doing. No, you'll not guess. Not in a million years! He'd only got hold of my whole week's margarine ration and he were smearing it down the door jam and around the door frame.' Marilyn looked up at this. It was a new one on Sarah too.

'Whatever for?' she asked.

Betty went on, relishing the chance to share her tribulations with someone who would understand.

'Well, when I asked him what on earth he were playing at, he told me, bold as brass mind you, that he thought that the door jam and the cracks around the door needed filling. I don't know, he went on muttering something about there being a draft coming through or sommat. I couldn't make him out. Anyroad, he wasn't happy about them cracks around the door evidently, so he were filling them in... with my margarine! Honestly, these London kids, they'll be the death of me yet!'

Betty stood up as if to emphasise her woes. Sarah let her guard down now as well.

'Well, it would be a blessing if mine got called back by his mother.'

'Oh, you mean young What's His Name, Billy?' Betty knew whom she meant.

'Aye, his mother's looking to move out to some country village in Essex by all accounts and she said she could give him a safe home away from any bombs and the like. It would be quite a relief, I don't mind saying... Well, the lad's not quite all there, if you ask me. You know, he's a bit...'

But Sarah never got to find the word she was looking for. Suddenly the front door flew open. Betty's son Fred Ackroyd rushed in holding a screwed-up telegram. He was a scrawny, sickly young man at the best of times, but Sarah believed he now looked as if he'd been crying.

'Mother? Mother, a telegram's just come! It says...oh god...it says our Alan's been shot down. Been shot down over France. He's dead Mother, he's dead!'

Betty felt winded. She sat down blindly, not caring where she landed.

'What? No! There must be some mistake. You've made a mistake, lad!' Fred handed her the telegram. Sarah was shocked too.

'Where's me smelling salts?' She cried. 'I've got 'em here somewhere.... Betty, you poor, poor luv. I'm so sorry for your loss.'

Betty stared blankly at the telegram. She couldn't understand. She couldn't take it in. How could this happen to her Alan?

'You'd best take your mam home with you, Fred.' said Sarah. 'I am so sorry for your loss, both of you.'

As they were leaving, Lilly came back into the room. They took only brief notice of her. She watched them open the door and leave like two ghosts chastised into silence.

'Hello, what's happened? Are they alright?' Lilly asked Sarah.

'Oh Lilly, Alan Ackroyd's been killed. Fred's twin. They've just found out by telegram.'

Lilly was distraught.

'Oh no, how awful. Poor Mrs Ackroyd. Poor Fred. They're both so proud of him. What happened, do you know?'

'By all accounts, he were shot down over France. That's all they said. Alan, he were a gunner in the RAF, you knew that, did you? Oh yes, she was so proud of him.' Sarah sighed and went off into the kitchen. 'Just goes to show you, eh...'

'Show you what?' Lilly felt tears rush to her eyes. 'The sheer pointlessness of it all? This awful war! When will it end? What a mess it's all become.'

She picked Marilyn up in her arms.

'How's my Marilyn? I do so wish you hadn't seen all that, my precious darling.' Lilly hugged her tightly, but Marilyn was only bemused by the whole thing and wanted to get back to her cutting out.

CHAPTER 7.

'Sunny View', Keswick Road, Blackpool, Lancs.
22nd March 1942.

My dear Laura

Thank you ever so for the book Sad Cypress that you sent me with your last letter. I did enjoy it very much. I do love a good Agatha Christie intrigue! Will you want it back or can I pass it on? I have a young friend at work who I think would enjoy it. I certainly have no shortage of opportunities to read these days. What with all the black outs and the long quiet Sundays that seem to stretch out for an eternity! Our little local library around the corner from the house is such a blessing and always stocks a number of classics from before the war. I am steadily working my way through their collection. Last Wednesday, I popped in on my way home from work and was intercepted by the gregarious young librarian who has bright red hair and huge spectacles perched half-way down her nose. She grabbed my arm and whispered in my face like some breathless conspirator,

'Oo Mrs Stevens, have you seen this new thriller from America? It's called "No Orchids for Miss Blandish." Ever so good it is too!' So I was compelled to take it and honestly, Laura, she was right, I could not put the book down! I read it from cover to cover in a single evening down in the Anderson shelter, in spite of the cold water swilling about my feet – and in spite too of Mrs C and her incessant chatter which I am now thankfully able to block out whenever I need to after much concerted effort. (I wonder that her dear husband has never managed to do the same.) I offered the book to her, but she politely declined saying that Miss Blandish would have to keep her exploits to herself and that she, Sarah, had quite enough of her own thrills and spills during each working day which kept her from peaceful slumbers and she had no need of any further excitement from no books! See what my life is like living here?

Anyway, my dear, keep yourself safely out of danger and give my kisses to Mother.

All our love,
Lilly and Marilyn.

It was beginning to look like a perfectly still Spring day and Sarah cheerfully threw the doors and windows fully open wide. Marilyn sat down on the bottom stair, tucking her dress neatly under her thighs. She could hear the birds singing in the yard outside. For want of anything else to do, she sat idly watching Sarah at work and silently wondered to herself what was going on. Gracie Fields was warbling softly on the wireless about a lovely lake in London, an unwitting accomplice to Sarah's grim work. Marilyn was aware of the sound of kittens meowing in a desperate panic, but she couldn't place where the sound was coming from. She was transfixed. Sarah, meanwhile was unaware of Marilyn sitting there and had her back to the child. She shoved the kittens into a large bucket of water.

'No, no you don't. You little beggars! In you go, into the bucket and stay in!' Sarah checked to see whether she had put in enough water to cover them all. She then grabbed a large plank of wood which she had fashioned as a lid to cover the bucket and promptly sat on the plank and folded her arms as if this would give her more strength to finish the job.

'Just you quieten yourselves down. Want to attract the neighbours' attention, do you? I've heard just about enough from you lot!' She adjusted her position on the plank and waited. Eventually, the kittens stopped struggling and were silent.

'Thank heavens that's done. That'll do them proper.'

Sarah was brisk and business-like in her work. 'Now I'll just fling these little beggars onto the fire and make a nice cup of tea. Oh!' She noticed Marilyn sitting there.

'Oh hello, Marilyn luv. What are you doing just sat there on't step for, eh? Where's your Mam gone to?'

At that moment, June was hurrying down the stairs in search of Marilyn.

'Lilly's working in't shop this morning, Mrs C. We're

looking after her, just until dinner time.'

'Yes June, well see that you do. She's under my feet. Kindly take her away from under my feet if you please.'

June was always in tune with the little girl's feelings. She took her hand.

'She seems very upset. Did she see what you were doing to them kittens, Mrs C?'

'I've no idea. Anyhow, them little beggars won't be bothering us no more with their mithering and peeing all over the place.' Sarah took a deep sigh. 'Oh Sammy, how could you do such a thing to me!'

If only June could have come downstairs five minutes sooner, she could have protected her charge from such a traumatic experience.

'That's not something a little'un should have to watch, Mrs C. Come on Marilyn, let's go back upstairs. That's it, come upstairs with your Auntie June.'

Sarah was unrepentant.

'Well, I don't recall inviting her to sit there and watch me, the little madam. I would have thought she'd have found sommat better to do with her time.'

If only Marilyn *could* have found something better. But too horrified to speak or even to blink, she sat there immobile with terror. This was a sight which would haunt her for the rest of her life. But at that moment, she was too young and wretched to comprehend that in those stark, pragmatic times, under the shadow of wartime austerity, it was the usual practice to drown unwanted kittens.

'But it's so cruel! She's cruel. How could she ever do that to kittens?' she sobbed as Lilly tried to comfort her on their bed later that evening.

Lilly had found her bawling into her pillow and she searched for the right words to explain to her daughter how, with the absence of wartime vets to neuter adult cats and a lack of any other more humane way to euthanize animals except by poison, violence or drowning, many people were unable to find homes for unwelcome litters. Drowning the poor hapless animals by the batch-load was one preferred option. It was quick, cheap and easy. Lilly could understand how people had become hardened to the reality of it. She had heard tell that right at the start of this war and then later at the onset of the Blitz, thousands of pet cats and dogs had been destroyed, their owners broken-hearted although convinced that it was kinder to have their pets destroyed efficiently than to subject them to the unimaginable horror of the bombing raids. Precious seconds could be lost, as the air raid sirens began to wail, searching for or rounding up wayward cats and the dogs would have hated the confines of a shelter already crammed to capacity with quaking humans. Three quarters of a million household pets had been put down, most often using a Bolt pistol which was accepted as the most efficient means available. Heartbreak and panic were barely contained under the pretence of pragmatism.

'After all, sweetheart, Mrs Cockington can hardly afford to feed all of us here in this household. You do see how it is, don't you? She really doesn't mean to be cruel. I promise you that.'

But the damage was done. Marilyn wept night after night following that awful spectacle. She could not reconcile herself to what she had watched Sarah doing to those kittens.

'But mummy, if only I could had saved them,' she wept. 'I should have tried. I could have run over to that bucket and pushed Mrs Cockington out of the way and pulled that big brown sack out of the water.'

Marilyn could imagine herself doing that, she would have grabbed the little mites, unconscious at first, held them upside down by their hindlegs to allow the icy water to come out of their little petrified mouths. She would have given them the kiss of life just like the man in the film showed them at school and she would have eased their pained cries and stopped their intense distress. But she hadn't done any of that. Instead, she had sat and watched the final horrific moments before death came to them.

'Here, put this on your face, luv.' They were sitting in the front room. June was administering a cold flannel to Ethel's face which was raw and badly bruised.

'Oh thanks.' Ethel flinched. 'Ouch... It's still sore but it's not stinging so bad now. Oh honestly! Just when I've got one of my favourite regulars booked in this evening an' all! My bad luck.'

June was philosophical.

'That's just the way it goes, in't it? Just the way the cookie crumbles, or the piss pot cracks, as they say. But it's rotten luck you getting knocked to the ground like that. I mean, a couple of seconds either way and you'd have missed that horrible toe-rag altogether!'

Sarah entered with Marilyn and began setting the table for tea. She was eager to share some momentous news with them but she stopped suddenly and was shocked to see Ethel's face.

'Whatever's happened to you Ethel, luv? You look like you've been hit by a bus! You've not been hit by a bus, have you? Eh?'

Ethel managed a painful half-smile. She and June had been strolling arm in arm along the high street that morning. Their thoughts were on where they would like to go out that evening now that the weather was picking up. They were so engrossed in their plans and excitement as they reached the door of Thomas' the Chemist that they did not see the young lad come rushing out of the shop at the speed of lightening. He knocked straight into them sending Ethel careering through the air. She landed clumsily on the edge of the pavement, narrowly avoiding smashing her head on the edge of the kerb. She was in a total daze. The lad did not stop, did not even notice her and he kept running, making his escape before any other passer-by could notice what had happened.

'She didn't know what had hit her, the poor lass!' June declared. 'He were shoplifting. Nicking sommat, looked like painkillers or sommat, but he were gone too fast to see. He scarpered, got clean away. No point in calling the Police.'

No-one went after him. The Chemist, old Mr Thomas, was behind the counter and he did not have the speed of response to anticipate or prevent this misfortune. His two ancient assistants out the back saw nothing and were mortified when they realised what had happened.

They fussed around the girls, trying to help the best they could, insisting that Ethel sit herself down while they made her a hot cup of sweet tea for the shock. June noted with some resentment that they didn't offer her a cup, even though it was just as much a shock for her.

Looting was rife. The war had brought with it a raft of new restrictions and regulations which many people chose to break or circumvent. Wider restrictions on various staples of life offered huge opportunities to fraudsters, forgers and thieves and created a vibrant black market.

A vast range of new and expanded criminal opportunities emerged and Blackpool had not been spared this scourge. There were many cases in which looters were not just criminals or petty thieves. Rumours began to circulate that firemen, wardens and other members of the defence forces often joined in too. Despite the severity of the courts, the government was so concerned about the looting getting out of control, that it had recently brought in the death penalty and life sentences as further deterrents. However, no-one was actually executed for looting and those perpetrators who were unfortunate enough to get caught were given heavy fines or shorter sentences. Much of this crime wave occurred under the cover of blackout and so it was almost impossible to contend with, adding more misery and fear to the lives of ordinary people, the like of which had been virtually unheard of before the war.

'I don't know what this world's coming to, honestly, I don't.' Sarah sighed. 'He should be away fighting for his King and country, instead of running about stealing from shops. This never would have happened in the last war, I can tell you that. Oh no, we all pulled together then. And the young men, they knew what they were about and what was expected of them.'

Just as June and Ethel were exchanging weary glances, Lilly entered the room. She was carrying a small piece of paper which she had picked up as she came through the front door which no-one else had noticed. It was issued by the Home Secretary and entitled THE NEW EXPLOSIVE

INCENDIARY, instructing the public on how to help the Fire Guard service by taking certain precautions to allow access and reducing risk when dealing with the incendiary bombs that were gathering pace in many parts of the country. Lilly was sick of this endless stream of official instructions, guidelines and advice. For a country working so hard to conserve paper, it seemed ludicrous to her that so many leaflets and pamphlets were being distributed almost every week. And so she glanced only briefly at this latest missive and barely took in its repetitious instructions about black-out curtains and extinguishing lights before she then stopped in her tracks as soon as she noticed Ethel.

'Hello. Oh Ethel, what on earth's happened to you? You look like you've been hit by a –'

'Oh, we've done all that!' Sarah chimed in. 'You'll never believe it Lilly, but Ethel here's been knocked down by a shoplifter in the high street!'

'A what? A shoplifter?'

'It's a long story,' explained Ethel. 'Anyway, I'm doing alright. With my nursemaid here to look after me. How's your day been? How's the old battle-axe Mrs Bennett?'

Lilly was tense.

'Oh, same as always, you know. She never changes.' She paused. 'By the way, was there any post for me today, d'you know?'

'No Lilly luv, nothing for you today, I'm sorry.' Sarah felt her frustration.

'Oh, I see. Oh well, that's that then.' Lilly was not about to break down in front of them. She sighed.

'Strange not to get anything from Harry. This isn't like him. I do hope it's nothing bad.'

Sarah was feeling like Mother Hen to them all, but even so, she was helpless.

'Oh now, don't you go fretting luv. He's probably just on the move somewhere. You'll hear sommat soon enough. You see if you don't.'

Lilly knew that Sarah was trying to ease her worries and was grateful, but it did nothing to calm her.

'But he's been writing at least once a month, without fail.

I've not heard anything from him in over three months now. It was three months yesterday in fact.'

Lilly felt her loneliness envelop her. It was a quiet desperation. Each day she would return to the house weary with strain and apprehension. The house was full of friendly faces and a distinct camaraderie, but this was not nearly enough for her. Living in a house full of people brought her the strangest feeling of aloneness. The long days without any word from her beloved Harry were torment for her. She could feel herself slowly succumbing to bitter resentment. Resentment that she was living the life of a single mother with nowhere to land between wife and widow. She missed him. She missed all those brief but comforting moments that they would share together, a silly joke, a shared understanding, a glance between them, the warmth of his hand wrapped around hers. They could never make up for those lost years, never grasp that time back again. And how many more lonely months would she have to endure? Would it be six, twenty-four, fifty, forever? How on earth did all the other wives, girlfriends, mothers, sisters manage to put one foot in front of another each day and carry on? Her stomach was constantly in a knot and her knees were weak with worry – how could she not fret about him? He was her rock, her whole world.

Harry and Lilly had met at the factory where they had both worked since leaving school. He was twenty-one and an assistant in the Managing Director's office and she was a machinist, just turned twenty. Lilly had been one of a close group of girls who went down to the canteen together every day, shared their bus ride home together and would go out at least once a week to the pictures. The girls all stood up for each other when they had to. The Management knew that they were a force to be reckoned with and gave them a fair deal and a decent working environment, more so than many other local employers at that time between the wars. When one of the girls got married, Lilly and Harry were both invited to the evening reception and were seated together at the table. It was a moment of serendipity for both of them. They danced together all evening. They talked and laughed right up until Harry saw her home to her door. Neither of them could bear to part and say goodnight and they both knew that from that moment on, that they were destined to share a future together. Their two-year courtship was easy and carefree, filled with lazy Sunday afternoon picnics at the coast and dancing in the West end, with pleasing the parents, saying the right things and enjoying smoky evening singsongs around the piano in his sister's front room. Harry was making very good money at the factory. He became the first person in his street to buy a motor car which stood in proud isolation outside his house. And only a couple of short years after they were married, he had earned just enough to buy their first little house in Edmonton, North London for the princely sum of £300. He believed whole-heartedly in the benefits of investing in bricks and mortar. They buffer you for life, he would always tell Lilly.

He had secret aspirations to buy the entire street one day. He married Lilly on a bright, crisp day in April 1936 in Stepney with their modest-sized families around them. They made a handsome couple, Lilly and Harry. Everyone thought they looked like a pair of film stars, he like Ronald Coleman and she like Vivienne Leigh. Her dress was made of luxurious cream silk with a veil of lace.

The lace covering her chest was rounded at the neck and the silk shoulders continued into long sleeves with three buttons at each wrist. The dress swirled around her, complimenting her tiny waist and made an extravagant circle of fabric about her feet. She carried a tiny bouquet of lily of the valley which had only just started to appear in late March. She would have liked to include the larger highly scented, white bell-shaped lilies, but they were not yet in bloom. That hardly mattered to her though. She was too full of pride and delight as she marveled at the fine-looking groom by her side. She believed his mourning suit gave him the air of an elegant Earl. In that wedding photograph, Harry thought that he looked every inch the cat that got the cream.

There was an intensity about Lilly, an energy, a force which attracted Harry to her. He had a simple, balanced range of emotions and he was more often baffled by her outbursts rather than repelled by them in the way that many other men might have been. Instead, they drew him closer to her, perhaps because of his wish to protect her, to soothe her and calm her fears. While he was not blind to her shortcomings, he simply adored her. It was his unshakeable belief that she was his soulmate and that he was one hell of a lucky fellow to have won her affections in the first place. He would move mountains to keep her safe by his side. Till death us do part. That was good enough for Harry.

One morning however, long before the war had driven them so far apart, when they had in fact only been married a few short exhilarating months, a row broke out between them. It was a silly, unnecessary row, the kind that would be forgotten soon after. It had stemmed from Lilly's fears about money being tight and what she saw as Harry's inveterate extravagance. They never would see eye to eye on money matters. Lilly was obsessed about saving for that inevitable rainy day, whilst Harry was keen to live for today, given the storm clouds brewing over Europe and the thought that tomorrow might be snatched away from them at any moment by forces way beyond their control. Lilly began to panic in the face of an imminent strife that was so foreign to her.

She could not abide the potential indignity of failing to meet the rent, the sight of the bills that remained unpaid piling up on the kitchen table and they never seemed to have anything left over at the end of the month. This was not how she wanted her married life to begin and she felt unable to take control or make him understand. For Harry's part, this endless nagging, his romantic ideas of candle-lit dinner dances and surprise gifts of perfume or a new frock thrown back in his face were not conducive to a harmonious partnership. He was getting sick and tired of her frosty resistance to his spontaneous gestures of affection. It was impossible to comprehend her. Wasn't this what all women wanted? After all, didn't a man work hard enough each week to share a few luxuries with his wife? Who else did he have to share his pay packet with anyway? She was just being ungrateful. A spoilt child, determined to create an atmosphere of tension and conflict where there didn't need to be one. He was frustrated and angry with her. And now there she was screaming at him through the closed bathroom door and calling him reckless and profligate. It was the reckless part that so offended Harry. Where had that come from? It was just like Lilly to add another arbitrary dimension to her argument, rather than stick to the point. No, there was no point! She was just making his life a misery, reducing their relationship to an unreasonable, penny-pinching, nit picking battle. It was all so unnecessary. This row was unnecessary too. Its cadence had grown more and more intense until Harry came out of the bathroom wearing only his under garments and a towel around his shoulders, looked at his young wife directly in the eyes, taking her roughly by her slim shoulders and yelled,

'Enough Lilly, alright? I say enough is enough!'

And with that, he stormed dramatically into the bedroom of their small Mile End flat and flung open his wardrobe groping for the first shirt that met his clumsy distracted grasp. He was shaking with fury. Watching his every move, Lilly froze. Her blood rushed to her feet and she felt a cold stab of ice-white panic clutch her heart.

'What are you doing, for Christ's sake, Harry?' she screamed.

'Putting my shirt on. What do you think I'm doing? It's too cold to be standing around here arguing in my vest.'

He had not the slightest inkling of what had passed through Lilly's mind in that moment. She had thought that Harry was leaving her, packing his clothes and going. It was an irrational fear stemming from deeper insecurities and a melodramatic tendency which had plagued Lilly from her earliest years. That split-second of dread brought her to her senses. It left her weak with relief. She turned away from him and wept quietly to herself. Why take him to the edge, you fool, she reproached herself.

'I'm sorry, Harry, dear. Please forgive me, I was panicking again. I don't know why I let everything get on top of me like that…'

Harry was starting to calm down and he turned to look

at her, not ready yet to take her in his arms but wanting so desperately to recover their familiar equilibrium.

'No more anger, Lilly love. Only joy from now on, eh? God knows, there's enough trouble in the world, without us two adding to it.'

And so they went forward, the two of them against the world, preparing to face whatever life held in store for them, together, united in a common purpose, a lifeline for each other, almost always harmonious and robust.

Now he was somewhere miles and miles away from her, unseen and incommunicado. She could not, would not contemplate a future without him. Neither had she ever expected to be struggling with all the upheaval of a long-distance marriage. She knew she must keep herself in check. This was petty nonsense. Of course he would be safely returned to her. It was only a matter of waiting.

She should just shut up and wait. That was her only option. But it was just that... no, she would be strong. Marilyn needed her to be strong and cheerful.

Lilly looked down at Marilyn sitting there patiently at the table, her arms at her sides.

'Oh Marilyn, give your Mummy a big cuddle. Have you been a good girl helping Mrs C with the tea things?'

'She's always a good girl, this'un.' Sarah chuckled. 'Proper little angel she is too.'

'Please don't worry Lilly, I bet you'll hear from Harry any day now.' said June. She could see that Lilly was grappling with a dreadful sense of foreboding. She felt it too. Dear God, she thought to herself I do hope nothing awful's happened to young Harry Stevens. But Sarah was more matter of fact, always the pragmatist.

'Now then Lilly, luv, let's not give in to our fears, eh? We can't go worrying about what we can't do nowt about, eh? Now can we! Just bide your time, luv, bide your time.'

Lilly knew she was right, of course. She needed some air. She left the room and went upstairs where it was always cool, to freshen up before tea.

It was an unusually cool evening for August. In the living room, Sarah sat down in front of a hastily improvised fire which spluttered and moaned and threated to fizzle out at any moment as soon as they took their eyes off it. Sarah pulled the old hearth rug towards them and smiled to herself as she recalled how she and Joe used to sit together in her parents' kitchen as a courting couple so long ago making this peg rug for their new home. Many hours they would spend cutting up old coats and rags into strips, weaving them into the old hessian sack backing.
The sturdy rug had no obvious beauty, but it had endured many years of foot wiping and had valiantly quashed countless stray embers from the fireplace.

Joe was engrossed in a newspaper article about Prince George, Duke of Kent who had just been reported killed in action in a plane crash.

Sarah was thinking about the huge pile of Joe's discarded newspapers on the floor in the corner of the dining room. She was so tired of seeing them there, of having to step around them. It would be a blessing when the Council finally came to collect them as they had been promising to for so long. In the meantime, she was grateful for that little girl guide from across the road, whatever-her-name-was, who would be knocking on their door again probably at the weekend with her mother's old pram stacked up to the gunnels with scrap paper. It was bigger than she was, that pram, but she was a determined little mite. Yes, it was all part of the war effort – and goodness knows how much recycled paper would be produced from Joe's avid newspaper reading, but even so, they did clutter the place up!

'What a terrible thing.' Joe muttered with his pipe clenched between his teeth. 'He were in some sort of flying boat, so it says here.'

Joe adjusted his reading glasses further down his nose to get a better focus on the newspaper column. 'Prince George and another fourteen others with 'im were on their way to Iceland and they've crashed on a hillside up in Scotland. He were not yet forty years old. Aye, the poor King. I mean to say, I bet he were fond of his brother.'

'Well, what do you know about it, eh?' Sarah turned towards him with her customary dismissive snort. 'They might have hated each other! There's a lot goes on behind them palace doors that we don't get to hear about, tha' knows.'

'Oh no, I can't imagine our King hating his own brother, well not that one anyhow.'

Sarah wasn't at all sure what had put it into her mind, perhaps it was the mention of Scotland, but she allowed her thoughts to wander back to that more distant time of Queen Victoria's funeral. The old Queen's haughty portrait had hung on the wall over their bed ever since they'd moved in. Although they had almost come to forget it was there, it had been her mother's much treasured possession and Sarah had solemnly promised her that she would not throw it away but would pass it on down the line to her own daughter. As that line had halted now with Sarah, she felt obliged to revere the portrait just as her mother had done.

'Of course,' she began, as images of Queen Victoria's white ponies and gun carriage flashed vividly before her eyes. 'Do you remember old Queen Victoria's funeral? Forty years since! I were only a lass, not much older than little Marilyn is now. Me dad used to call me his pretty little doll...' She went on, ignoring Joe's involuntary scoff.

'Me mam and dad took me to the Royal Pavilion in Rigby Road to see the Pathé film, but that were some years afterwards of course.'

'Oh yes,' Joe recalled with a spark in his eye. 'I remember the sight of them horses breaking free. Oh, the crowd did catch a fright when they saw the Queen's coffin resting on the gun carriage and then suddenly no horses to pull it! The poor Navy-Blue Jackets then had to get roped into dragging her along instead. What a palaver for them!' Joe shivered as though the Old Queen's ghost itself had just walked through the room. He got up to fetch his crumpled pullover from the back of the kitchen door. 'Fancy a bit of chocolate while I'm here?' He called to Sarah as he passed by the dresser.

He had been given a slab of the dark sweet stuff along with a neat little box of peppermint lumps by a grateful housewife who had accosted him last week on his way home from the drill hall. He had noticed a little kitten high up in a tree crying and too scared to jump down by itself. As he shone his torch into the branches, he could see that the little wretch refused to budge an inch. How it had got up there was a mystery, but Joe decided to pop into the pub at the end of the street to borrow a bar stool and he carried it all the way back to the tree.

He climbed up, almost tipping over which prompted the little fella to stop its meowing and jump down on the pavement of its own accord to be swiftly scooped up by the distraught housewife and smothered in her voluminous arms. Joe was left clinging on to a precarious branch with nothing to rescue him but his own pride which had rapidly given way to frustration and embarrassment. His good nature was soon restored however and the profuse apologies and hearty laughter from the kitten's owner soothed away any potential ill feeling. Then she prevailed upon him to stop there while she popped the little mischief-maker into the house and go and find something to recompense him for his trouble.

Joe was suddenly rocked by a preposterous thought which flooded his mind as he stood there at the lady's gate until she returned a couple of minutes later with the sweet treats and thrust them into his hands.

'It's the very least I can do, when you've been so very kind and obliging,' she insisted as she fluttered her moist eyelashes at him. Joe noticed the curtains twitch on either side of this lady's house. What must it have looked like? he contemplated with a reluctant smile.

'Ill-gotten gains, I call this!' Sarah claimed after Joe had relayed his little adventure to her on his return home that night.

But at this moment, she was stuffing the dark chocolate into her watering mouth. She disliked the powdery texture that chocolate had these days now that milk was in such short supply. But it was better than going without, so she persevered.

'This is my reward, is this! Anyroad, thanks for saving me some. Watch the crumbs you're making there on't rug there.' Joe moaned. 'You know, we really ought to save some for little Marilyn,' said Joe as he watched the rapidly disappearing chocolate.

'She's too shy to ask for herself and she gets precious few treats as it is.'

But before Sarah had a chance to finish her mouthful and reluctantly agree, Lilly burst into the room with an urgency, bordering on panic. She stopped in the doorway and stared at the Cockingtons for a moment. Joe could see more of the whites of her eyes than normal.

'I need to ask you both please,' Lilly began breathlessly. 'What did you do with the soap in the bathroom? It was my last piece.'

Sarah was used by now to seeing Lilly on the brink of tears, but she was startled and she knitted her brows.

'What a strange question. I've not taken it, luv.'

Lilly was not in a mood to be trifled with.

'Well, it's not there now and it's not walked off by itself, I assume.'

'I can't explain that, sorry luv.' Sarah persisted. 'But if you want to talk about strange mysteries, then perhaps you can explain to me, now that you're here, why the pulley on your bedroom blind looks like it's been chewed – and you,' she rounded on Joe, 'I noticed all the envelopes in that ruddy drawer of yours had all been shredded t'other day. Been meaning to bring that up. Thank you, Lilly for reminding me, luv.'

'What? Let me see,' As Joe crossed the room, he suddenly stopped short and noticed something small but distinctive on the rug which he narrowly escaped stepping on.

'Oh God! Is that what I think it is?' He stepped back. 'Ah, yes well that explains it all then, eh? These little parcels on the floor, they're mice droppings, I'm afraid –'

The ladies screamed in perfect unison.

'Mice! You sure?'

'House mice most probably. Coming in from the garden

'cos of this cold snap, I shouldn't wonder.' Joe was taking command of the situation now.

'Oh my God!' Lilly was uncertain about whether to faint or throw up.

'Now then, it's alright, no need to get all fluffed up and unnecessary. I'll pop into town first thing tomorrow and pick up a couple of mouse traps from the hardware shop on't corner. You load them each with a piece of this chocolate here and hey presto – then we'll simply let the sorry little also-rans go free outside. Aye, it's a bit of luck we didn't eat up all the chocolate ourselves, eh!'

Lilly stood there, incredulous.

'How can you be so calm about it, Joe? It's disgusting! Where are they? They could be anywhere!'

'Well, we can block up their entry points. At least now we know what those strange tapping and rustling noises are coming from that 'ave been keeping us awake in the night, eh Mother?'

'And I suppose that's what set that little lad off crying all night up in't attic...' Now at least, one little mystery had been cleared up for Sarah.

'Who knows how many of them there are!' Lilly was not satisfied. 'They could be staring at me when I'm getting dressed in the mornings. We might need harsher methods than your traps, Joe!'

'Oh now then, do get a grip, for goodness's sake! Why don't we put the kettle on – unless the mice have chewed through all our precious packet of tea...'

'Well, I shall have to have strong words with me precious Sammy about this! He's not doing his job properly, not earning his keep,' Sarah muttered. 'In't it his job to keep them mice at bay? Honestly, why have a cat and wag your own tail, eh?' Sarah stomped out into the kitchen for the dustpan and brush before Lilly could utter any response. Joe stepped forward to correct his wife but quickly thought better of it.

CHAPTER 8.

Joe could see clearly enough that Lilly was trying hard to control her temper and he could make an intelligent guess as to its cause. He had a couple of thoughts as to how best to douse the rapidly increasing flames of her ire, preferring instead to retreat behind his newspaper.

'They say here in't Gazette, Lilly luv, that "The Blackpool Savings Committee sends its congratulations and thanks to the citizens of Blackpool who have saved and worked to such effect that the sum of twelve million pounds has been invested in Government securities in Blackpool during the past four years. The standard of weekly savings now reached, if maintained, must have its effect on shortening the war..." Well, that's quite a show, in't it! What d'you suppose Government securities are, when they're at 'ome, eh?'

He glanced at Lilly, but she wasn't listening to him. She was shaking with rage.

'Why on earth have you never told me, Joe?' Her anger was white-hot. Hotter than the electric iron plugged into the light socket above her head. She was trying to steer it in a straight line across Marilyn's only school blouse but was blinded by the sting of shock. She was in confusion as to what to do next.

'I had no idea until I found out from Mrs Bennet this morning. Of course, she knew all about them.' Lilly felt so foolish. How could she have missed the signs? She wasn't that naïve, that prudish, surely. Then her anger washed over her. Her world had been turned up-side down yet again. Why did this keep happening? She had had enough.

Joe could see that this was not going to be an easy conversation to have. He could barely find the words to explain it all to her. He himself had tried hard to ignore the reality of the situation, but his own moral outrage had been supressed for so long now.

'But you see, Lilly luv, it doesn't alter the fact that June and Ethel are two of the kindest, most reliable girls you'll ever come across.'

Joe's voice petered out as he watched Lilly trying hard to compose herself. What did she, or any of them in that house really know about these two young girls? Only that they had come to Blackpool together in late 1939 as soon as they had both turned seventeen. Inseparable since they were six years old, the two girls had often dreamt together of someday living the high life as far away as possible from their sleepy village of Bispham. But for now, the bright lights and lazy days on offer in Blackpool were enough of a lure for them.

June Hetherstone, was a naive and cheerful lass, the oldest of four daughters. Her shape seemed to be uniform from her neck to her ankles. She carried an air of secrecy about her, and yet behind her thick glasses, her eyes sparkled with an inquisitive, optimistic quality worn down into the ordinariness and conformity of her class and dreary surroundings. Since the age of fourteen, she had willingly helped her widowed father, Arthur to run the home and care for her younger siblings. Arthur Hetherstone himself had led a varied and challenging life. Although suffering the loss of his young wife in childbirth, he had achieved an exemplary military record, having signed up as a Private but leaving as Sergeant. He doted on his girls and they provided him with all the colour and warmth that he wished for each day. June had suffered from meningitis as a child which left her partially paralysed. She walked with a pronounced limp and struggled to use her right hand effectively. Nevertheless, she didn't let this dampen her spirits and she dreamed out loud of the lively nightlife on offer in Blackpool. It was inevitable, her father privately conceded, that June would fly the nest in search of more stimulating and gratifying pursuits.

Ethel Scott was the only daughter of the village butcher. Her father was stern and often aggressive. He terrorised his wife and daughter with threats and foul language. It got to the point where just his glare or slight lift of his meat cleaver were enough to silence them into a sickening dread whenever they did or said something that displeased him, no matter how trivial it seemed to them. But for Ethel enough was enough.

She packed her favourite clothes into a battered old hand-me-down suitcase belonging to her mother and with trembling bravado, announced that she was going to live at her friend June's house. Expecting to be subjected to her father's wrath, she was stunned to find that he just laughed at her and turned his back growling that he was glad to be rid of her. One less rotten mouth to feed as far as he was concerned. Her mother silently wept in the corner of the room. Ethel was uncertain whether it was for her daughter or for herself, for she knew that she was leaving her mother to face her own fate without her being there to hold her hand and the guilt stayed with her for the rest of her life.

The sense of release when she closed the back door behind her smothered her like a giant gust of fresh air and she never returned. Not until the day of her mother's funeral years later when her father had long since hung up his butcher's apron and she was shocked to find him so lost and withered sitting by the depleted fire in the kitchen, a stranger to his daughter.

Lilly was still indignant.

'No, I'm sorry, but it just doesn't wash with me, Joe. I have entrusted my daughter to their care, those two girls! I never would have done that if I'd known. Heavens, we would never have stayed here under this roof as long as we have.'

Then Lilly rounded on Joe.

'You, of all people should have told me. I have every right to know who I am bringing my little girl to live with, who we're sharing a house with!'

'We didn't want to lose you from here, Lilly.' Joe said simply, almost whispering. He could only speak as his heart guided him. It was how he had always tried to live his life, listening to that quiet voice of his conscience deep inside him.

'We both wanted you to stay here with us in safety. We thought it was the best thing for you and little Marilyn to do. You know that we only had your best interests at heart, luv.'

That cut little ice with Lilly's hardened scepticism. She slammed down the iron.

'How, tell me please, can it possibly be in the best interest of a four-year-old child to be baby-sat by a pair of, of prostitutes? Please tell me that!'

Joe was taken off guard. His reasoning was all in a turmoil and he could hardly look her in the eyes, much less answer her as plainly as she was demanding of him. He and Sarah had both known, of course they had known. But as long as the girls conducted their business away from the house, strictly not on their premises, under someone else's roof, then what could they say? There was the Palatine Hotel situated on the Promenade and well-known locally for ladies of a certain profession to ply their trade discretely. That was how it had all begun. A simple introduction, a short chat and some easy cash. This was their world and it was far enough out of sight.

Ethel and June had not yet come of age and they weren't exactly the sharpest tools in the toolbox, now were they? So what other employment would they be able to find until they got themselves called up? Joe and Sarah had had their own battles with the morality of what their two boarders got down to when they went out of an evening. But until this government saw fit to summon the girls to a more urgent, dignified role...well, there but for the grace of God and all that.

'It's this damn war, in't it.' Joe sputtered at last. 'Ethel and June are just trying to survive, Lilly luv. You know you have to do lots of things in this world, unpleasant things, just to survive these days. I'm sure it's the same down in London or anywhere...I mean to say, you just can't see this thing in black and white, luv.'

He spoke with a passion bordering on resentment, but that was it. That was all he wanted to say on the matter. It was the first time that he had ever tried to put his own ambivalent thoughts into some kind of cohesive order. Lilly stared at his satisfied face for a moment. How could she refute his simple, succinct castigation of the world around them?

He had explained himself and he was right, she knew that. And after all, she had grown to like these two girls very much and Marilyn adored them of course, hanging on their every word. The fact was that Lilly had only just cottoned on, only just twigged as to where the girls went almost every evening and why they sometimes came home at odd times in the morning. More than anything, she knew that her anger stemmed from her own naivety about what everyone else knew but her.

She resolved to speak to them both at the earliest opportunity. She had her principles, after all. It rankled with her that June and Ethel, still too young to be called up for compulsory war work were at leisure to skulk around all day – and night - while the older women were doing hot and dangerous work to serve their country. Women like Lilly's sister Laura who had been drafted in to do men's jobs for less pay and in the face of resentful prejudice from the munitions factory floor.

And then what would Lilly say to Harry? He would expect her to tell him the truth and, surely he would insist that she take Marilyn away to find another boarding house somewhere else in town. Not that there was much choice now that the Americans had taken over the nearby airbase and had gobbled up much of the local accommodation. Move on? Really? Wasn't it a case of better the devil you know? But still...! Lilly ran her slender hand through her hair in a gesture of exasperation. Perhaps it was best if Harry didn't find out just yet. There would be plenty of time to tell him later on.

'I suppose I really ought to get this into some kind of perspective.' She said as she perched on the arm of the sofa. Joe felt a wave of relief sweep over him. He was tempted to retreat gloriously behind his newspaper, except that he wasn't sure whether the danger had passed completely.

'That was the conclusion that Sarah and I came to. I mean to say, they have to pay the rent at the end of the day, just like everyone else-'

'No Joe!' Lilly wasn't able to let the matter drop yet. 'No, please don't dismiss it out of hand, just like that, like it doesn't really count for anything much.' Then she softened again. 'Let me please find my own way to come to terms with it.' Lilly stood up and, thankful that Marilyn was still at school at that time of the afternoon, she put her ironing away and then grabbing her coat and hat, she made a hasty retreat for the front door, out into the tranquil autumn sunshine where she hoped to regain the soothing sense of stability which she had only recently started getting used to.

Lost in thought, mulling over the conversation and its conclusion, Lilly's stroll turned out to be anything but soothing. The warm autumn sunshine had caught many people out. Along the promenade, men were stripping themselves of their heavy overcoats. Ladies were discarding their warm mittens and stuffing them into bags. Others in uniform, allowed themselves an open top button, or a loosened belt. Lilly had only her thin dress on underneath her coat, so she was comfortable and thought nothing more about the temperature, nor of her surroundings. She did notice however, the elderly man staggering towards her. She felt an instant disgust.

Give him a wide berth, he's obviously one over the eight, most likely had too many at lunchtime. The fool. How do they let themselves go like that...

The man was haggard and was swooning as if he were about to lose consciousness, grabbing the railings for support. As the space between them narrowed and she drew closer, Lilly noticed that his face was a sickly yellow-grey. She felt that she ought to go over to him to check whether he was suffering. He did look very unwell.

She decided against it. Better to leave him to his own devices, don't get involved. And so she walked on past him, resuming her swift pace.

Something made her turn around to look at him again. As she turned, she saw the man, this stranger, suddenly collapse onto the pavement. She saw him groping for something, moaning and then he was clutching his chest.

Lilly rushed back to where he now lay prone on the

ground. He looked up at her through squinting eyes as if imploring her. Lilly looked about her for someone to come to her aid.

'Can anyone help us here, please!' She bent down to loosen his tie and his belt. She stood up again as a crowd rapidly gathered around them. She thought she heard a woman say that she recognised him. She could pick out snippets of conversations, comments peppering the small arena of worried bystanders forming around the stricken man. Epileptic...Apoplexy...His heart?...Not very dignified... Get his some water...Someone put a coat under his head...

A young airman offered to find a St John's ambulance and was gone in an instant. The intense afternoon heat played brutally on the man's ashen face. He seemed to be passing in and out of consciousness now and could barely move.

And so they waited. Lilly held his hand until help arrived, uttering reassuring words to him as she would to Marilyn when she was in distress, not knowing whether he could hear her or not. It seemed to take an age before the ambulance reached them. The two ambulance drivers, one ample, energetic woman and one more reticent insipid girl of about nineteen attempted to lift the man off the ground and lead him away from the eager eyes of the crowd. And that was the last Lilly saw of him. She wondered what would become of him. How ill was he? Would he survive? How could she ever find out? All she had known about him was what she had heard him utter breathlessly to the ambulance drivers. His name was Ken and he was staying in Abercorn Place. And she wished that she had entered his life just five minutes earlier.

CHAPTER 9.

Sometimes the low autumn sunshine streamed in so strongly through the front bay windows of 'Sunny View' that Lilly found it hot and blinding in its intensity. The identical houses opposite stared back at her as she gazed out. The back of the house, north facing, was cold and austere. Joe had chopped down a deceased plum tree some years ago to provide more sunlight into the house. Marilyn liked to sit on the stump and command the attention of her dolls whom she arranged in an obedient circle around her to take imaginary tea. This scene aroused a pang of sadness in Lilly's chest and she wished that Marilyn had more real friends to play with. Better still, a little brother or sister, someday... still, Lilly would often catch herself looking at her tiny daughter and wondering what she would make of her life. Would she become a professional in some field or other, or would she have a big family of her own and surround herself with children. Whichever path Marilyn would choose, Lilly hoped it would be full of light and joy and health. Of course she wanted this, although looking too far into the future made her feel giddy and it was a pointless exercise all the while this war was occupying her life and plans.

She shrugged off the very idea as she set up the clunky old mangle which was kept by the back door. Lilly wanted a tiring job to wear herself out and help her to sleep better at night. She lifted the wet, heavy clothes out of the dolly tub, tucking the buttons inside the folds of the garment to save them from being crushed and then fed them though into the rollers so that the mangle could grip them. This was a job she would try to do away from Marilyn's prying eyes so that she would not be tempted to try this herself. The mangle and all its potential menace was strictly out of bounds to small children. So lost in her thoughts was Lilly as she began to hang out the washing onto the line with her new set of dolly pegs, that Sarah had to call her three times for her cup of tea.

'I was just wondering whether Marilyn is missing Billy, you know.' Lilly had not expected her to but now she could detect little telltale signs. Signs of loneliness. She was sure Marilyn would remember the boy longer than she herself might.

'Well, I'll not miss that lad, you can be sure of that.' Then Sarah softened. 'The poor little beggar.'

Lilly had watched Marilyn during the long night before as the child whimpered softly in her sleep. She had smoothed her hair and stroked her cheek, thinking how lucky she was to have this little child in her life. Marilyn was her whole world. The rain punching the window, making an incessant tap-tap-tap on the stone sill, had seemed only to close in this world ever more tightly. As Lilly watched Marilyn breathing in and out, she found herself wondering whether Billy Hackett had ever felt the soft sweet tenderness of his own mother's hand or slept within the certainty of her devotion. Somehow, Lilly knew that this was not the case. Billy had the struggle ahead of him which only the lonely unwanted child would ever have to face. She felt certain that Marilyn in some unspoken way also understood that. Lilly let a solitary tear trickle onto her pillow. A tear as much for the absent Billy as for the little girl she had brought to Blackpool to keep safe by her side.

When Lilly felt maudlin like this, she would rouse herself and sit down to write a letter, most often to Harry but today she was missing her sister Laura and her thoughts turned to her. Laura's latest letter had run to eight pages filled with all the horrors of life at her local munitions factory.

Since last December, when Parliament had passed a second National Service Act, it had broadened the scope of conscription making all unmarried women between the ages of twenty and thirty liable to call-up to roles in nursing, munitions and transport. Laura had been called up to work there two weeks ago and her letters detailed how she was set to work filling empty shells with cordite powder and packing explosives around fuses on a never-ending assembly line. Laura said that all the workers looked a fright. No-one was allowed to come to work wearing hair pins or jewellery on account of the risk of a spark caused by the metal which could blow up the whole factory in an instant. The girls wore heavy overalls and boots with rubber soles to minimise the risk of sparks and static. The floor was covered ankle-deep in water in which Laura would stand for the entirety of her long shifts.

She described to Lilly how she and the other girls around her would sing songs all the time to keep their spirits up, although now and again they could not resist the temptation to allow a rude word or two to creep into their verses which would inevitably prompt their supervisor to bellow at them to shut up. Laura was disgusted to discover that her beautiful fair hair had taken on a sickly yellow hue and that her skin and nails had also absorbed the pigment of the explosive powders. She added in one of her letters that she knew of a girl in the factory whose baby was born yellow.

Lilly fretted about the insanity of siting a munitions factory in the East End of London where so many enemy bombs were dropping. She was also humbled by these accounts by Laura. They pulled her up sharp and reminded her of just how fortunate she had been to have avoided that fate so far, simply by dint of her motherhood. Only single girls were being called into the factories for the moment, so she believed. Maybe soon, if the war went on for many more years to come, they would be calling all women in to do their bit on the production line. How awful, she thought. She couldn't face putting pen to paper right now. It would have to wait.

Billy's little attic room had been empty for two weeks now. The musty odour he had left behind had reluctantly dissipated through the open fanlight which Sarah had refused to close, despite the cold inhospitable air creeping in.

Sarah was anxious to fill the vacant space with a new paying lodger as quickly as possible. She knew that she was obliged to get in contact with the Billeting Officer now that she was once again in possession of a spare room. But the whole Billy experience had sapped her of her willingness to start all over again with another evacuee. They were so messy, so unpredictable. They all seemed to her to come from scruffy, chaotic homes. She did not have the patience nor the appetite to go through all that again. Maybe, she hoped, just maybe, the war might be over before she would be forced to take into her house any more of these rotten little London urchins and the pathetic clothes they stood up in.

Sarah had begun the following day in a bright optimistic mood as she squinted in the fresh early morning brightness hanging out the bed linen, freshly boiled and bleached, one final act of purging Billy from her house. Joe had given her a wide berth this morning as his permanent aversion to bleach drove him as far away from the house as he could get.

'You know Lilly,' Sarah said as she gulped down her tea, 'I've got a good feeling about today. And I don't often say that, now do I?'

'What's given you that, then?' Lilly was happy to indulge this happy mood of hers. It made for a cheerier atmosphere for the whole household.

'Oh, I don't know luv. It's been just such a fine morning. And these palms of mine have been itching since yesterday. You know what that means.' Sarah tapped the side of her nose extravagantly – she could be grotesque at times. Lilly simply smiled. Although she had little idea of what Sarah was talking about, she noticed a twinkle in Sarah's eyes and a bristling energy, the source of which was an enigma to her.

The urgent rap on the front door brought just the opportunity that Sarah had been hoping for. It was serendipity, surely.

A young woman stood squarely on the bottom step smiling serenely up at Sarah as though they had already met and had arranged this moment in advance.

Sarah, whom Joe had always reckoned to be an excellent judge of character, took a moment to focus on the woman silhouetted there against the bright midday sunshine.

'You have a room to let, I believe.' A statement rather than an inquiry. The woman's smile fixed itself rigidly beneath a pair of little round glasses perched on her narrow nose.

'Oh yes, yes, that's right, luv.'

'My name's Trench. Miss Rosalind Trench. I'm here with the Civil Service.' There was an air of worldliness about her. She stood tall with her dazzling blond hair swept back in a severe bun at the nape of her neck. She wore smart leather shoes and her dark blue suit was of a good cut and made from robust material. Her clipped accent suggested fine breeding to Sarah and her pulse quickened.

'I saw your vacancy sign when I walked past the house last Sunday on my way down to the Promenade.'

'Why don't you come right in. Would you like to take a look at the room? It's just this way.' As she swept aside to let the younger woman in to the hallway, Sarah began to worry that she had not left the room as aired and tidy as perhaps she should have. But it was too late now. She led Miss Trench up the rickety stairs, cringing anew at each creak and squeak. As they approached the top landing, Sarah glanced at the young lady's inscrutable face.

'Mind your footing though, luv. We have an intruder step just there. These old houses all have 'em. Evidently, they're meant to keep the thieves and varmints at bay!' Rosalind was suddenly startled. Not understanding what Sarah meant, she tripped anyway. Despite this brief awkward moment, Sarah sensed that her potential new lodger was a sophisticated and obviously cultivated young lady. She will do nicely, she thought.

'You're up from London, I take it?'

'Yes, that's right. They've moved us all up here. It was quite without warning. Two weeks' notice they gave us to arrange everything. Can you imagine it!' Rosalind smiled sweetly as they climbed.

'Well, it must be an upheaval for you. Did you leave much family behind?' Sarah was always direct. No point in beating around the bush. But Rosalind didn't seem to hear her question.

'I notice how much sweeter the air is here. In London there is the constant smell of acrid smoke in the air all the time. It's quite choking.'

As they reached the second-floor attic room, Sarah was already charmed. She grinned as a purring cat when it's being tickled.

'Here we are luv. I do hope it's to your liking.'

They briefly discussed the rent in a perfunctory way, each of them having already made up her mind that the arrangement would suit them fine.

As Sarah skipped contentedly back down the stairs, she only briefly wondered how this Rosalind might fit in with the other boarders. She was so smartly dressed and posh spoken, more elegant even than Lilly was when she had first arrived. Oh well, at least those two ladies would hit it off. Sarah was sure of that, at least once Rosalind had got her bearings and settled herself into her new surroundings. How lovely it will be for Lilly to board alongside another lady from London, better educated and with a career of her own. Then she turned back up the stairs and tapped gently on the closed door.

'I expect you'll be wanting a nice cup of tea.' She asked her new boarder, not without a degree of obsequiousness.

'Yes please, Mrs Corrington. I like it good and strong with two sugars, if you have it.'

'It's Cockington, actually, luv.'

'I beg your pardon?'

'The name's *Cockington*. Just so as you know. It can trip folk up sometimes.'

'I see. Yes, well. Just a dash of milk.'

'Right then.'

Sarah was somehow too overawed by Rosalind's sophistication to take this slight too much to heart. She was surely the highest class of boarder that she had ever had under her roof. Joe would be equally impressed. He would enjoy cosy evenings discussing some news article or other over a mug of cocoa with Rosalind Trench, no doubt sharing his opinions on Churchill's latest announcement in Parliament or whatever else had caught his eye in the newspaper that day. Oh, but then, what did he know about owt? Sarah dismissed this thought of Joe with a shake of her head.

Of course, it was best if no-one mentioned the recent mice which she was sure had been banished from the house once and for all. She would definitely have to manage the situation with June and Ethel very delicately, most carefully. Rosalind might have certain sensibilities and would expect Sarah to keep a strict and decent house. Lilly and Marilyn would back her up if it came to that.

She grabbed Lilly's arm as soon as she came back into the kitchen. Her tea was stone cold, but she gulped it down anyway.

'Lilly luv, it's a new boarder we've got here! She's grand and ever so well-to-do. You'll meet her presently.'

Lilly finished wiping the cutlery and smiled gently as she shut the stiff drawer with her hip.

'That was a bit quick, wasn't it? Does she have her documents with her, identity papers, references and all that sort of thing? Oh well, you know about all that better than me, I dare say.'

Sarah dismissed this unnecessary detail, oblivious to her own sudden uncharacteristic recklessness.

'But she's with the Civil Service.'

'Oh, I see. Well then. You know best, I suppose Sarah.'

'Aye, that's it. It'll be fine.' Only the slightest moment of caution flitted across Sarah's mind and then it was gone as Rosalind appeared in the kitchen doorway.

'I'm about ready for that cup of tea now, if you don't mind.'

Sarah pursed her lips in that peculiar way of hers which Lilly had come to know so well. Rosalind eyed Lilly and the two of them shared a momentary hesitation before Lilly stuck out her hand and greeted Rosalind warmly.

'How d'you do. I'm Lilly Stevens. We've come up from Forest Gate. Do you know it? It's East London.

'I know of it,' replied Rosalind with an undisguised sneer framing her smile. 'I'm not like the King and Queen. I don't frequent that part of town.' Lilly smarted from the sting but she wasn't fazed.

'Well, you've probably missed the boat now, of course. Much of the area has been flattened by Jerry. My own street included!'

'Oh, I am frightfully sorry. How dreadful for you.'

'Yes it was.'

Lilly was embarrassed at having revealed so much information so readily. This was not her usual introverted "less is more" style into which she instinctively retreated whenever she met someone for the first time.

'Will you be staying here long?' Even that sounded too direct, even rude. But Lilly felt that there was something odd about this Rosalind Trench woman that seemed to be sucking the ease of conversation right out of the room.

Perhaps June and Ethel will help me out. They always manage to break the ice. She was eager to see the two girls come stomping through from the front door.

'My little girl Marilyn is just outside in the back garden. She's out there catching cabbage white butterflies and caterpillars. She loves helping in the battle against garden pests...' She hoped that this might lead them to some common ground.

'Children? In this house?'

'Just the one child and little Marilyn's no trouble at all. Quite a cherub, you'll see.'

Rosalind's stony silence unnerved both Sarah and Lilly as they watched her mutely move into the sitting room and sit herself down gingerly on one of the armchairs. She looked as if she feared that the chair might produce a sudden bolt of electricity beneath her buttocks at any minute.

'It won't bite you luv.' Sarah followed her into the room a moment later and sat down on the settee opposite her. 'Well, at least not until it's got to know you better.' But there was no reaction from the deadpan Miss Trench.

'So er, it were the Civil Service, you said you were from? That's interesting! And what sort of work is it that you do there?'

'Please don't ask me about my work, Mrs Corrington. It's rather confidential, you know. I don't suppose you would... not many people of your sort... well I mean, it's all very complicated actually.'

'Oh well, please yourself, luv. I don't mean to pry. And it's Cockington...but I think maybe you should call me Sarah. Everyone else does. Just plain old Sarah. Anyway, you're alright luv, we've all got our own lives to lead in this house and plenty to be going on with, in't that right, Lilly luv, eh?'

Lilly had sauntered warily into the room and sat down beside Sarah sensing she was needed as reinforcement.

The concept of 'harmony' had never occurred to Sarah Cockington before, nor to Joe or Lilly, come to that. But it was about to become of the utmost importance to them all. When something is threatened it becomes most precious.

Over the coming weeks, the residents of Sunny View noticed that Rosalind Trench was not someone who could easily relax. She emitted tension in her every movement. She eschewed any attempt made by Joe to find out her views on the current developments of the war. She overtly bristled when Ethel or June tried to bring her into the teatime chatter at the table and Marilyn failed to warm her heart as she had done with everyone else in that house. Lilly was keenly aware of this. She was saddened by the distinctly gloomy change in the atmosphere since Rosalind's arrival.

'I don't think she's very happy.' Lilly declared to Joe one afternoon when it was just the two of them clearing the table.

'The poor lass is so far from her friends and family. It's only to be expected.'

'I know how she's feeling on that score,' said Lilly. 'If she'd only let us, we could help her. I'll make her a nice cuppa when she gets in from work later.'

Unlike the rest of them, Rosalind tended not to pop her head in to say hello when she got home. She just went straight upstairs to her solitary attic room and shut the door, no doubt in fear of anyone catching her and asking her how her day had been.

Lilly left her for twenty minutes to settle before approaching with cup and saucer in hand and knocked gingerly on Rosalind's door. She was not prepared for the response she received.

'Who is it? What do you want?' Rosalind's voice was harsh, stinging.

'It's only me,' Lilly persisted. 'I thought you might like a nice strong cuppa before you come down. I made it just as you like it-'

'You can leave it there outside the door.'

Lilly wasn't put off by this rebuff, although looking back much later on, she sorely wished that she had taken the hint that evening, acknowledged Rosalind's offensiveness and turned tail back down the stairs. But for some reason, loneliness on her part she assumed, Lilly was intrigued by Rosalind. She was determined to melt this woman's frostiness and forge a friendship out of their dramatically contrasting characters.

'I bet you've had a tough day,' Lilly said as she breezed into the room and searched for the nearest surface on which to place the tea down. She found the little bedside table, but a lamp and a cracked porcelain dish, a souvenir from Bridlington, already took up most of the surface and Lilly wondered for a moment whether she had misjudged the wisdom of her decision to come in. She stopped short of making herself too much at home and stood awkwardly between the open door and Rosalind who was glaring at her and then at the cup.

'Go away. Get out now. Now, if you don't mind!'

It took a moment for this remark to register with Lilly, so unexpected as it was. She ran out speechless, leaving the door open and went straight down to her own room. Sitting on her bed trembling with indignation, she wanted to cry out loud, *'I hope the tea bloody well chokes you!'* But then as she caught sight of herself in the dressing table mirror, Lilly took a deep breath, brushed herself down and muttered *It takes all sorts to make this world.* That's what Harry would say. She determined to keep her views about Rosalind Trench to her letters to him and say nothing about this to anyone else in the house. She could pour her heart out to Harry and he never seemed to mind. In the meantime, to Rosalind, she would give a wide berth from now on.

It was some days later, completely out of the blue when

Lilly spotted a piece of paper folded up into four and popped through the door. It was addressed to her. So many letters nowadays were envelope-less due to the paper shortage. Shops often ran out and didn't bother to re-stock. The prices would be too high for their customers to bear in any case. Without knowing why, Lilly had a presentiment that this note would need to be read in private and she took the little piece of paper upstairs with her.

Sitting on her unmade bed where Marilyn had strewn her night attire before rushing downstairs and out to school, Lilly smelled a vague mustiness in the note. It was from Fred Ackroyd. She sighed. He had sent her another poem. It read simply:

To Lilly, please forgive my writing this poem for you, but I need to get these feelings out of my system before I go barmy. I hope you like what I have written down here. It's called 'Some Day I'll Say I Love You'.

> *Each day, as my hand reaches out to take,*
> *I have a heart that extends to give*
> *With the same desperation that I snatch,*
> *So my heart longs to touch you.*
> *Sometimes my hands quiver with indecision*
> *Always my heart flutters with fear*
> *The tied hand and the trapped heart are both imprisoned in a mind*
> *Tortured with the fear of rejection.*
> *But freedom comes when for the first time*
> *I can give with my hand and you can feel*
> *That which is in my heart*
> *I want to be part of your life.*
> *However small, for however long you want me.*
> *I will ask for no assurances,*
> *I will expect no returns,*
> *For that which I give is yours.*

Lilly was at once shocked and touched. How should she respond to Fred about this? He had made no other sign of his feelings towards her, as far as she could make out.

Had he dropped some hint somewhere, sometime that she had simply missed? Surely not. Well, with everything else going on around her, Lilly had not the time nor patience to indulge Fred's silly callow notions of love and affection for her. It would not do to raise his expectations in any way. But she could not think of what to say to him. She decided simply to ignore the poem for now. Pretend it never got to her. Perhaps one of the girls had picked it up by mistake. No, it would crush him to think that they might even now be giggling and belittling his genuine ardour. Best just to leave it alone. The poem wasn't half bad, mind you. But no, he should direct his poetical prosing elsewhere to far more appropriate objects.

She didn't have to wait very long before she picked up another of his missives. This time it was inside a book that he had left for her on her workbench early one drizzly morning before she had arrived in the shop. It was a short poem this time. Short and to the point, but thankfully not directed at her.

Where is it that men must kill and innocence die?
Where the scar remains and the bodies lie,
Where civilian and soldier are but one,
And all government is lead from gun?
Where is it that men must kill?
The where is war and the war is will.

'This is very good, Fred!' Lilly was relieved and impressed by his writing. 'You have a real talent here, you do really.'

Fred said nothing. He blushed his usual crimson as he turned away from her to busy himself with unloading his groceries onto Mrs Bennett's damp wooden draining board.

'Really you do, Fred. I wouldn't say so if I didn't truly mean it.'

'Oh, thank you, Mrs Stevens.'

'Lilly, please.'

'Lilly, yes.'

'Well, I hope you'll write more. I think it's a good idea if you have lots of feelings inside and you need to make sense of them somehow.'

'Yes, that's it! I knew you'd understand!' He spun around and sat clumsily on the stool opposite Lilly.

'I've written more, tha' knows. Lots more. I've been writing poems ever since I were a little nipper. I never could share them with me folks, of course. Well sometimes, just sometimes mind, I'd show 'em to our Alan. He never much cared for poetry, he didn't, but he was always kind about what I'd written. And then some of me teachers in school, they didn't think much of 'em and scolded me for bringing them in 'cos poetry was a girl's thing, they said. But I never stopped thinking them up, me poems, all the same. They just keep coming to me. Sometimes like, they just pop into me head as I'm cycling along the lane and I have to stop me bike and write down a phrase or a rhyme so as not to forget or lose it. P'raps I'm a bit soft, but anyhow, well, with our Alan gone, I need to get me thoughts out, just like you say. I knew you'd understand. I just knew!'

'Yes, Fred. I do understand. But please try to stick to any subject other than me. I'm way too ordinary to inspire poetry! Why don't you try and find more interesting subjects to write about!'

But Fred was deep in thought, already composing his next verse and it was all about her.

CHAPTER 10.

'Sunny View', Keswick Road, Blackpool, Lancs.
29th November 1942.

My own dearest Harry

I hope this finds you safe and sound.
We go on as usual here and I notice particularly how little is said about Christmas this year. Very little in the shops or on the wireless. You'd think they had cancelled it completely! Poor Marilyn and poor children everywhere. It really is extremely sad.

Air raid warnings have now become a regular event here in the town but, so far thankfully we suffer very little in the way of bombings, please rest assured on that front. Joe said he was standing on the cliffs last night where he could see the dark shapes of the German bombers crossing the sea between Liverpool and Barrow-in-Furness. He said he could see these places as distant orange glows. Please God, they don't come any closer to Blackpool.

As a safety measure, you know they have now removed all signposts to the town as well as the place names. It makes me so sad to see the word 'Blackpool' painted out on signs in the town centre in case (and it's surely a big 'in case'!) the Germans should come ashore. I can just imagine the enemy standing around underneath the Tower, scratching their Nazi heads and wondering where on earth they were!

I took Marilyn into town last Tuesday to show her the large metal braces that they have fitted to most of the shop windows. You'll never guess what we saw there, Harry darling! It was a Messerschmitt 109 fighter captured intact on display in the open market. (I wrote the details down on my shopping list so as to get my facts right for you.) Marilyn's eyes nearly dropped out of her head. I was worried in case it might add to her bad dreams. Why they have to put such an ugly monstrosity in the middle of the marketplace like that, the Lord alone knows. I don't think it's right and I said as much to the Cockingtons. They didn't know what to make of it either. What is this world coming to?

Anyway, I love and leave you now, darling and hope that you continue to keep yourself safe. Are you eating well? I kiss your picture every morning and night, the one of you in your great coat and cap, your cheeky grin and dimples. I still find it rather amusing how you are smiling right at me and I hope you have not lost any of that sparkle in your eyes when we meet again.

Ever your devoted wife,
Lilly.

"Send your saucepans flying!" They listened to the Food Facts on the wireless. It was one of the highlights of Sarah's evening. She tuned in at the same time, 8.15pm to hear the plentiful culinary advice being dished out by the Ministry. Tonight, they were imploring every housewife to give up her prized cooking utensils to provide invaluable metal for Spitfires and other aviation vital to the war effort, never mind the fact that, as it turned out, these utensils were the wrong grade of metal for that sort of production.

'Not blinking likely!' Sarah cried out loud. 'They can't have mine. They were a wedding present from me mam and dad and I'm not parting with 'em! Let that Beaverbrook fella hand over his own pots and pans first. He'll not notice 'em gone.'

Joe, Lilly and Marilyn were at the table finishing their early evening meal of baked potato pudding with raspberry jam. It was the usual dull tasteless fare that Sarah served up these days.

She thought that she had shown considerable ingenuity in feeding her household of boarders, her husband and herself on whatever food she was able to obtain on ration these days. And that inevitably meant few treats, if any. There were only so many ways to skin a potato after all.

Everyone else was out of the house. Lilly was run down and suffering from a streaming cold. Sarah was concerned that she hadn't eaten anything all day.

'Oh Lilly luv, you do look pale. Maybe you should have yourself an early night, don't you reckon Joe?'

'Oh I'm alright.' said Lilly. 'It's nothing. It's only a stupid head cold, that's all. Lots of it about at the moment. Some silly old lady sneezed all over me in the shop last Monday. Just what I didn't need!'

'No, I'll tell you just what you do need, lov,' said Sarah as she laid her damp fingers across Lilly's burning forehead, 'and that's raw onion juice and sugar. It'll soothe your throat and stop your sneezing. Come to think of it, I might have an onion out back...' Lilly screwed up her face in revulsion at the idea.

'Hot water, whiskey and sugar, that'll do you a treat,' suggested Joe who was packing his haversack with an unusual sense of urgency. But as he grabbed his black-out torch, his pipe and tin of Three Nuns tobacco, he stopped and rummaged about in his coat pocket for his scrunched-up bag of Victory V lozenges which he always had to hand throughout the long unpredictable Winter months. He swore by them and held them out for Lilly to take one.

'Coughs and sneezes spread diseases. That's what they're telling us, in't it? Obviously, some folk haven't quite got the message yet. Well anyway, ladies, I'll bid you a good evening. I'm due at the drill hall by 8.30 sharp. We've got a lecture tonight on the smells and effects of different types of gases. I just hope they know what they're talking about. Should be very useful indeed.' He tapped the side of his head, the way he often did when he felt as though he were party to some intriguing priority information. This always rankled with Sarah.

'Oh, you and your Home Guard nonsense! Playing at soldiers the lot of you, if you ask me. God help us if Jerry invades and all we've got is your mob to defend us!'

In spite of himself, Joe could not let her criticism go unanswered.

'Now then, don't start on me. It's not nonsense. We're all trying to do what we can to keep this town of ours safe from the Jerries....and I'm not too proud to say so.'

He felt his heart start to beat fast – a mixture of pride and adrenalin at the thought of the duties awaiting him that evening, patrolling the pier and the surrounding areas for any sign of enemy parachutist landings. This work was vital to the local security and Joe did his work properly, conscientiously. He could not understand why his wife was blind to that fact. She had swallowed all the stupid gossip among the neighbours in those early days of the war when the town's first branch of the Local Defence Volunteers had been set up in response to the ill-fated French campaign. It could boast several First World War and Spanish Civil War veterans among its ranks and its aim was to protect local civilians against the dreaded German invasion. Many of Joe's contemporaries, believed that they could potentially fight for a better world. A world without class privileges and without unemployment and deprivation. They had become increasingly frustrated by what they saw as government inertia and impotence in mustering, training and equipping this ever-increasing citizen army, this people's militia. And so, some of them took their own initiative and set up private training schools where they shared their own hard-won guerilla techniques with enthusiastic recruits eager to join in with patriotic zeal and take up the fight. The government had eventually reacted by stifling this enterprise and had set up its own official training programme.

Britain's last line of defence they may have been, yet they certainly were a motley crew with only elementary uniforms and too few reliable weapons to go around. In fact, when they were first set up, they had just the one rifle and five rounds of ammunition between twenty men. With weapons so scarce, it was generally considered doubtful whether their enthusiasm alone could offer any effective resistance against Hitler's hordes of highly trained, highly disciplined armies.

But Joe believed that the LDV did not deserve the epithet of "Look, Duck and Vanish". That simply was not fair. So, when Churchill re-badged them as the Home Guard, believing that the name Local Defence Volunteers was unlikely to inspire recruits, Joe had felt vindicated. Even so, it had done nothing to convince Sarah. And perhaps she had good reason to be sceptical and her cynicism was far from groundless. The War Office seemed to be without any clear strategy for deploying this militia of volunteers much beyond its original morale-boosting grand gesture.

Their equipment ranged from Molotov cocktails and the so-called Woolworth bomb, which was a crude lump of gelignite in a biscuit tin, to firing grenades using toy pistol caps and finally developing to truncheons and a clumsy form of bayonet fashioned from a long metal tube with a blade welded onto the end. All this looked to the general public as little more than a comical absurdity. A significant anti-invasion exercise on the beach had sought to quash any remaining doubts as to the purpose and value of creating a Home Guard made up of old soldiers and others who had never before experienced any kind of military discipline and who would have, in any event, faced a formidable and arduous mission.

'Well,' Sarah continued, 'All I'm saying is, I don't see *you* having the backbone to stand up to an invading army, Joe Cockington, that's all. What would you do, swat Jerry with your rolled-up newspaper? May as well do, for all the good you'd serve!'

Lilly sneezed loudly over Sarah's tittering and Joe left his wife's wounding remark hanging in mid-air rather than tackle her any further.

'God bless you, Lilly. Good night, Marilyn.' He turned to leave the room.

'Thank you, Joe. Good night.' Lilly sneezed again. 'Oh, excuse me.'

Suddenly, there was an urgent knock on the front door. Joe hated these unexpected intrusions.

'Well who's that now, come knocking at this time of an evening?'

'Oh that'll be Betty Ackroyd again. She's started baking for the WI and she's never got enough sugar.'

Joe opened the front door.

'Oh, evening Fred, my lad. What can we do for you?'

Fred Ackroyd wandered in looking lost and bewildered. He had made an effort to straighten his hair and tuck his shirt in for once. He took off his cap and was wringing it in his hands. His usual pallor was a shade rosier than Sarah was used to seeing it.

'Hello lad,' she said. 'What's up with you? We're all paid up on our deliveries for this week, I think.' Fred avoided her eyes.

'Er hello, Mr Cockington, Mrs Cockington...No, that's not what I've come about. It's er, it's...'

'Well spit it out lad. We're none of us getting any younger, tha knows.' Sarah said.

Joe raised his eyebrows so high, they disappeared under his mop of hair. He popped his cap on his head and marched out the door, yanking it shut behind him before any further interruptions could delay him.

'I'd like to have a word with Lilly, please.' Fred inched into the room.

'Oh?' Sarah asked, intrigued.

'Oh?' Lilly looked up.

Fred saw Lilly sitting at the table and his courage grew a little.

'Hello Lilly. I'd like to have a word with you...please...in private, like.'

'Well, I'm not very well, Fred. But alright.' Lilly left the table and moved across to the sofa. She sat down waiting for Fred to join her. But he stood there struggling like a fish out of water. Sarah was clearly superfluous here.

'Well, do excuse us, won't you. Come on Marilyn, we'd best do the washing up. In't kitchen.' She added pointedly, 'We won't be very long.'

Lilly offered Fred a cup of tea. Anything to put him at his ease. She admired Fred. He was a friendly face and she had always felt comfortable and relaxed in his company. Fred laughed nervously.

'Oh no, thank you Lilly. Bet you're wondering what's amiss, eh?'

'Well yes, you've certainly got me wondering. What is the matter, Fred? Is everything alright?'

Lilly had never seen Fred without his delivery boy's apron and the bicycle clips around his trousered ankles. She had an idea why he wanted so urgently to speak with her and a fairly good sense of what had brought him. He had left Mrs Bennett's shop yesterday morning under the cloud of an argument when Mrs Bennett had clumsily dropped a precious bottle of fresh full-cream milk on the cobbles outside the back door of her shop as Fred was handing it over to her.

The two of them had something of an altercation when she had resolutely refused to pay for the bottle of milk which lay smashed at her feet. Lilly knew that this would have to come out of Fred's next wage packet which she knew was unjust. She would certainly back the boy up if the matter dragged on any further.

But no, Lilly was wrong. There were in fact more important things on Fred's mind that evening as he tentatively approached her in that gloomy living room, still heavy with the aroma of the boiled mutton that had barely covered their plates that lunchtime. The soft light from the fireplace played on Lilly's cheeks, making her pale, watery eyes dance and sparkle gently and Fred thought that he had never seen her look so endearing.

Lilly sneezed uncontrollably.

'Bless you. said Fred automatically. 'Well, yes, it's just that I –'

Lilly remembered what Joe has said about 'coughs and sneezes'.

'You'd best keep your distance though, Fred.'

'Of course, I didn't mean to –'

'Because of my stinking cold, that's all. You don't want to catch my nasty germs, do you?'

'Oh, I see,' he said, noticeably relieved. 'I thought you were saying you didn't want me to, er...' He could see a lack of understanding in Lilly's streaming eyes although she was trying to hide it.

'Well, the thing of it is, Lilly...oh heck, I might as well just come right out and say it –'

'Yes, I wish you would.' Lilly blew her nose loudly.

'Bless you. Well, you know how things have been for me of late. Right bloody awful...for me and me Mam...since our Alan got shot down...Sorry for cursing.'

'That's alright Fred. I feel sad for you. I do really.' Fred warmed to her but still stood there, stiffly facing her.

'You've been such a good friend to me. A true friend. Just when I needed one. A friend, that is. Truth be told, I don't know what I'd have done without you.' Lilly blushed and paused blowing her nose.

'I haven't done anything, Fred. I just –'

'Oh no, you don't know the half of it! You don't know how much it's meant to me. Seeing you there in't shop every morning. Lighting up my world with your smile and-' Lilly felt the need to nip in the bud whatever it was that Fred was driving at.

'Now Fred, please don't get carried away. I'm only being friendly towards you. Anyone would have done the same.'

'Well, you see Lilly, you've come to mean such a lot to me. I'd say you are the reason I get out of bed of a morning these past few months.' His comments were left hanging in the air for what seemed to Fred a silent eternity.

The room had become uncomfortably stuffy to Lilly.

'Well, that's very sweet of you Fred. But perhaps, you're getting a bit ahead of yourself. You're just a bit mixed up perhaps.'

'No,' said Fred 'No I'm not. I know me own mind well enough and I'm come here tonight to ask you…' He braced himself. '…to ask if you would walk out with me sometime.' Now he was less sure of himself. 'If you wanted to, that is. I thought maybe next Sunday, we could have a stroll along the pier and I'd buy you an ice. I remember you saying how you liked the ices on the pier.'

Now Lilly understood.

'No thank you Fred. I mean I do like ices, of course, even in November. And it's very nice of you to ask me. But I'm afraid it won't be possible to walk out with you. I am married you know. You do know I'm married, don't you, Fred? And of course, I have Marilyn…' It was possible that Fred hadn't even considered the little girl. But he persevered.

'Oh, she can come too! Why not?'

'No, thank you Fred. I'm very flattered, of course I am, but I –'

'But I love you, Lilly!' Fred blurted it out as a desperate plea. At the precise instant that he uttered these words, Sarah and Marilyn entered from the kitchen. Their timing was impeccable. A cavernous silence pervaded the room. It was Sarah who broke up this awkward tableau.

'Well, now, I think you may have outstayed your welcome my lad,' she said.

Lilly stood up and moved towards the stricken Fred and put her hand gently on his arm.

'I'll see you in the shop tomorrow morning Fred, as usual. Go home now. Get some rest.'

Fred pulled himself together and stepped dejectedly towards the front door. He was awkward

and downcast. Lilly felt his pain and wanted to reassure him.

'I'll see you in the morning. Good night, Fred.' She closed the door after him without letting his disheartened expression upset her any more than it already had. Sarah would be no comfort or confidant to her tonight.

'Well, I hope you gave him short shrift, Lilly my girl? "But I love you" indeed! The great barmpot. Whatever were he thinking?'

'Oh, he's not himself, the poor lad.' Lilly felt nothing of Sarah's derision. 'He's struggling to come to terms with losing his brother. I feel so sorry for him.' She hesitated before going on. 'He's been writing me poems just lately. Pouring all his feelings into them. They break your heart, they do really. The lad's just a bit sensitive, that's all.'

'He's just a bit soft in the head if you ask me. Not that you don't deserve to have an admirer. You're a very attractive girl, Lilly, and don't you forget it. It's no wonder the young lad's sweet on you.'

Lilly couldn't help but let out a short laugh, in spite of herself.

'Oh, I don't know about that,' she said. 'What, with a big red nose and my eyes all streaming like this? I look about as attractive as a mouldy old kipper. Poor Fred Ackroyd... Well, well. What do you make of all that then, Marilyn? Best not tell your Daddy, eh! Best keep it just between us. I mean, I was only being a friend to the lad...'

She thought to herself as she later settled into bed how

Harry might react if she did tell him. Oh Harry, where are you, my love? You'd never believe what a bother we've got ourselves into here!' And that thought took her off into a deep dreamless sleep.

CHAPTER 11.

Lilly had let the customer come in, even though it was fully fifteen minutes past closing time. She knew it would make her late for tea and Sarah's fish, unidentifiable at the best of times, would be cold and congealed on the plate by the time she got home. However, she stayed on to take the gentleman's order and by the time she was ready to clear up and lock the shop, she knew she was already over half an hour late. She ran all the way home, nearly twisting her ankle twice and tripping melodramatically over an uneven paving stone. By the time she burst into the dining room, she was panting and coughing so severely that she failed to notice the chill that was hanging in the air or the sad, despondent look on both Joe and Sarah's faces. Only Rosalind's unusually fiery expression made Lilly stop in the doorway instead of dashing headlong for her seat.

'I'm sorry I'm so late. I just couldn't get away from the shop.' she gasped.

'You could have rang up to let me know, Lilly. You've always done that before.' Sarah never normally minded. She would always keep a meal hot in the oven. Everything seemed to Lilly to be out of kilter. A jagged sort of feeling pervaded the little room. Lilly was unnerved.

'Is everything alright? Is there something going on?'

'No, it's very far from alright,' said Rosalind. No-one else would meet her gaze. Lilly thought she looked pale and noticed her trembling ever so slightly. Perhaps she was cold. But it was her stare which seemed to freeze the air.

'You have a nerve to stand there as pure as the driven snow, a picture of innocence, oh yes, you have!'

'I'm sorry?' Lilly was discombobulated.

Joe cleared his throat and carefully placed his knife and fork down by his plate.

'Rosalind here seems to think that you might have been in her room, Lilly.'

'Excuse me, I can speak for myself, thank you. And I don't think, I know. It was her. She's always barging in there uninvited. That's how she came to know where I kept it all.'

Rosalind's voice was quieter now, calm and menacing. Lilly could feel a knot of tension in her stomach which she could not explain.

'What? Kept what? What are you saying exactly, Rosalind?' Lilly turned to Joe, but he was looking down at the pattern on the place mat in front of him.

'Rosalind believes that you have been into her room and may have taken some of her jewellery. I don't know how she – '

'She *did*. I know it was *her*. She's always going on about how she's short of money! I've heard her. We've all heard her. Struggling to make ends meet and all that. Oh yes, it was *her* alright.'

'Of course it doesn't sound like the Lilly we know,' chimed in Sarah trying desperately to appease the situation. 'I can see how upset you are about it, Rosalind, luv.'

Lilly remained standing.

'*She*'s upset? And what about *me*? You can't start making absurd accusations, based on no evidence at all. And I've only been once into your room and that was to take you in your tea which you all but threw back in my face!' Lilly was indignant. All this was utter nonsense. Marilyn was watching her intently. 'Now, I am sorry that you've misplaced your jewellery, but it has nothing to do with me.'

Sarah began to clear away plates and cutlery.

'Well that settles that then –'

'No, it's not quite as simple as that.' Rosalind stood up. 'I want Lilly to explain herself to the Police.' Joe put his hand on Rosalind's arm to try to restrain her as she was now bearing down on the hapless Lilly. This seemed to him to be rapidly becoming an impossible situation.

'But why on earth would I want to take your jewellery?' Lilly let out an empty laugh and turned to Sarah. 'I don't have trouble paying my rent, nor have I ever had. Correct, Sarah?' Sarah sat with pursed lips. 'So this insane accusation of yours is groundless.'

Lilly held out her hand to Marilyn as she looked straight into the eyes of her accuser.

'If you wish to discuss this further, with or without the help of the Police, you'll find us in our room.' She swept out through the door and, just managing to hold back her hot tears, she turned back to Rosalind.

'How dare you accuse me. Shame on you.'

And then Lilly slammed the door so hard that the whole room shook as if the lampshades, vases and ornaments all rattled in allegiance to her.

There was no sleep to be had for her that night or the next. Lilly rose early, even though it was a Sunday. There had been no mention of Rosalind who was assiduously avoiding Lilly but was keeping up her claim against her. This was the stuff of madness, surely! Lilly could not understand how everyone in that house, for a tiny seed of doubt had begun to take root even in the minds of June and Ethel, could turn so rapidly against her and take sides with the toxic Rosalind Trench. Lilly felt like an outsider in a way that she had never felt since first setting foot in that boarding house at the start of the Blitz. Where was the proof, anyway? So far, that basic detail had been conspicuous by its absence, although no-one seemed to care much about it. Perhaps that was why there had been no further threat of going to the Police. They would have laughed Rosalind out of the house. And yet, Lilly was far from out of the woods.

Sarah was the first one to meet her on the stairs that morning.

'Lilly luv, she means business.'

With just a frown and a shake of her head, Lilly followed the older woman down the stairs. It wasn't until they were in the kitchen that Sarah closed the door and motioned for Lilly to sit down. A brown paper bag sat in the middle of the little stained pine table.

'Well, luv, I'm afraid it does look bad for you.' Lilly sat motionless, waiting for Sarah to clarify.

'I were in your room cleaning yesterday while you were at

work and I found this under your bed. I pulled it out cos I'd not seen it there before. It's her jewellery.'

'But that's still no proof, Sarah! Surely, you know better than that. Anyone could have put that there. We don't have locks on our doors any of us, do we?'

'Well, she means to go straight to the police, all the same. And I'm sure none of us would want them coming to this house poking around and certainly Ethel and June won't want that!'

'And they will simply laugh at her and tell her to stop wasting their time. Why, I've no reason to take her things. Certainly not her jewellery. You must know that! And what's more to the point, you or Joe or anyone have just as much opportunity to get into her room as I have – in fact more so. Hasn't that occurred to you?'

Lilly was suddenly drained of all energy.

'This is insane. I would have thought you of all people and Joe should believe me and dismiss this whole business out of hand. Why do you give that woman so much house room?'

'To be honest, I don't know what to believe, luv.' Sarah gave out a deep sigh and straightened her headscarf. In her frustration, a sudden thought occurred to Lilly. It hit her with the direct force of a dart.

'What's this job of hers anyway?'

'What do you mean?' Sarah said.

'Well,' said Lilly. 'She never discusses it, does she? We only know that she's something to do with the Ministry of something-or-other. But what the hell does that mean?' Lilly leant forward. 'You know what I think, Sarah? I think she's nothing but a fake. A phoney. I do really. I wouldn't be surprised if she didn't work there at all. Nor anywhere like it for that matter! You remember that conversation we had the other day, before all this nonsense started? When we were having breakfast and you asked her what sort of day she had planned. You remember? She said something which I thought at the time was rather odd. She said "Why? Why do you always need to know what I'm doing?" Well, I thought that was rather uncalled for. And that thing of hers about always getting your surname wrong. I've always thought it was a bit peculiar. I think that's her way of asserting some sort of superiority over you. She does it as a kind of one-upmanship, do you see?'

Lilly let the idea settle and take root in Sarah's mind.

'Maybe it is some sort of top-secret war work she's doing...' Sarah offered, although she didn't really believe that anymore.

She was beginning to realise that she had been duped – they had all been duped. How could Sarah have been so blind to Rosalind's attempts to dodge or ignore the most innocuous of her questions about her work or social life? Her boss, her colleagues, who were they? Were they all billeted locally like her?

Then last Tuesday, June had asked innocently (or so it had seemed to Sarah) whether Rosalind had come across an older gentleman called Geoffrey Bramwell with whom she and Ethel had often been chatting in the pub and had struck up an acquaintance. It had transpired that he was working in the Civil Service, at the Ministry of Pensions over in Cleveleys and he had come up to Blackpool from London with the first lot in 1940. Administering War Service Grants he was, so he'd said.

'Terribly lonely he is,' June had told Rosalind then. 'Missing his wife something awful. But anyway, I said how we had a Rosalind Trench staying with us from the Ministry of Something Or Other and did he know you. But he said, no that couldn't possibly be the case, as there was a Rosalind Trench in his department who had been knocked down and killed in the street on her way home from work some three months since. Well, it can't be the same Rosalind Trench surely, I thought to meself, but then, it's not what you'd call a common name, is it? Trench...'

Rosalind had rapidly flushed an intense red.

'Well, there are thousands of us civil servants here, for goodness sake. The stupid man's quite mistaken!' Why had Rosalind suddenly become so irate? The matter was dropped, as June had neither the wit nor the insight to consider the possibility that this strange woman calling herself Rosalind Trench could possibly pose any real risk or danger. The notion of Fifth Columnists and all those dark spies lurking in alleyways was way beyond her comprehension and belonged only in films and cheap books, not in the streets of Blackpool, her streets...and why would someone posing as a spy in their house, threaten Lilly with calling the police anyway? It didn't make much sense to pursue that line of thinking, but Lilly was not going to let the Geoffrey Bramwell comment go unheeded. She persisted.

'I think you must ask her outright. Put her on the spot. It's about time we settled this whole business.'

Sarah sat upright.

'We could make some enquiries, I suppose. Call the Ministry switchboard and ask some questions. See if we can get through to her office or department or whatever. Is that the sort of thing you had in mind?'

Lilly thought about it for a moment.

'Or we could just *tell* her we've done that. See how she reacts. It would save us a lot of bother and might just prove what we've begun to suspect.'

'Yes, luv, flush it out of her. That's what we'll do!' Although Sarah was only too happy to have this awful situation done and dusted, she was not so keen on getting the Authorities involved in her domestic arrangements. Her eyes fell back to the pile of diamond earrings and the gold bracelets sitting between them on the table.

'Meantime, I'll return this little lot to Madam and tell her to keep them to herself. I am starting to wonder to meself where on earth she's got these from anyroad. What do you reckon? Oh dear, I am so sorry Lilly. Why I ever believed her, I'll never know. I said to Joe, I thought she'd most likely put these things in your room just to cause some right proper mischief. Although, for what reason, I'll never fathom.'

'Spite,' was all Lilly had to say.

It was only just gone four o'clock. Rosalind was home from work early. But even so, she was the last person to sit down to the evening meal. She habitually avoided meeting anyone's eye around the table and was as usual, reticent in joining in the scant conversation. The continuing rancour between she and Lilly had eroded everyone's appetite.

Knowing that right was on her side, Lilly had a burst of courage as she attempted to turn the whole situation on its head. Sarah was also ready to play her part.

'Oh yes, by the way, Rosalind,' Sarah began, 'I've been meaning to mention to you that as your landlady, I ought to have your daytime telephone number please luv. Just in case of an emergency and things of that sort.' Rosalind was a picture of placid contempt as Sarah laboured on.

'You do have a daytime telephone number, I take it? I mean they've given you a desk with a telephone and all the rest of it, I suppose?' As always, Joe was quick to catch onto what his wife was up to and was watching everyone's faces intently. Rosalind continued to chew her bread and margarine slowly without looking up. She fixed her gaze on the chipped little cruet set in the middle of the table, another well-used souvenir from a long-forgotten trip to Morecambe.

'I'm not obliged to give you my number, Mrs Crockington.' At least she's getting closer, thought Sarah.

'No, luv. But it would be a good idea, don't you think? Every one of my boarders does that.' Rosalind stopped eating.

'I don't... I mean I'm not at liberty...'

'No bother luv. I can get it from your switchboard in't morning.'

'No! Don't you dare do that.'

'No? Why not then?' Sarah had launched in and was not going to stop now. 'Is it because they'll not have heard of you there? No Rosalind Trench at the Ministry after all....is that it? You seem to have been lying to us all the way along, haven't you? Why have you lied to us? I've no idea why you feel the need to turn up here all full of airs and graces that, as it turns out, are nowt but a sham. Only you can explain that, but anyroad, you're no longer welcome in this house. So why don't you go and pack your bags and leave us all in peace, eh? I think that would be the best thing to do. Unless of course, you still want us to get the Police to come by?'

Rosalind rounded on her.

'What do you know of such things? You or anyone else

in this house, come to that? You don't have proper useful jobs, any of you. You just go on day to day living your petty, narrow little lives.'

'Now you stop right there, young lady.' Joe was on his feet. 'You know you've no business speaking in that way to any of us here in this house.'

He held Rosalind's gaze and leant in close to her.

'No good could ever come of this sort of thing, not for anyone and that's a fact. The whole lot of us should be ashamed of ourselves for ever having believed you and your wicked accusations against our Lilly. Especially at a time like this.'

Rosalind gave a short contemptuous laugh as she turned her icy stare towards Lilly.

'You think you're such a fine mother and wife, with your pretty little child here and her hair all fixed up in stupid ringlets.'

She was now sneering at Marilyn. The room fell silent. Then, with a scream of chair scraping on the wooden floor, Rosalind stomped heavily out of the room. Her exit, though welcome, was not nearly so thrilling as Lilly's had been several nights earlier, or so Marilyn thought.

When Sarah went to check the next morning after Rosalind had failed to appear at breakfast, all that was left of Miss Trench was her unmade bed, her latch key and the remnants of a deep red vegetable hair dye around the plughole of the little sink in the corner of her room.

None of the occupants of Sunny View would ever discover who Rosalind really was, nor that she'd had no fixed abode, no job, no family. The woman was simply drifting around the country, assuming different aliases and surviving by stealing from unsuspecting landladies and tenants, staying only long enough to work out a plan to rob the place and then making her moonlight flit before anyone could catch her in the act. She was talented in creating her own fake papers and ration books under her different names, but who had taught her to do that so effectively?

She would stroll about graveyards looking for identities to assume for herself. She had read in the local paper about a young lady of twenty-seven called Rosalind Trench who had been the unfortunate victim of a hit and run motor cyclist in the blackout and had died in hospital the following day.

She had not reckoned on Lilly or any of them turning the tables on her like that, unmasking her fantasy world of elegance and sophisticated delusion. But now she had gone, escaping from their scrutiny and had retreated back into her drab world of deceit and theft. Maybe, having raised suspicion of Lilly among the household, it had been Rosalind's plan to frame Lilly for her next theft. Who knew how long she had been at this game and who knew where she might turn up next or how long she could keep moving on undetected.

Maybe, thought Sarah, the house was full enough for the time being.

CHAPTER 12.

Was Marilyn pretending to be asleep? Was she trying to block out Lilly's restlessness? Lilly had had another of her dreaded Blitz nightmares. They were regular occurrences now. This time she and Harry had been sitting in their local picture house when the sound of the bombing raid was becoming so overwhelming that the audience was suddenly advised to make their way home as best they could. When they emerged from the cinema, the whole street was an inferno of burning buildings illuminating a jet-black sky like a huge red fireball. There was smoke and a horrible stench everywhere. Darkness lay beyond but not like night-time. Lilly could see the contours of the buildings and it was all very eerie and surreal. Bombs were dropping out of the sky at a fearful rate. Then, suddenly, Harry and Lilly found themselves inside a shelter in their back garden in London when a bomb hit and in the next moment, Lilly was gazing up at the open sky while a shower of acrid dust came raining down upon her. Harry could only move his body from his waist upwards because there were massive boulders resting on his legs. Lilly was pulling away the rubble and helped him to get free. Then they came across a woman's head. Lilly was smoothing her hair, clearing her nostrils and wiping her neck. She was patting her cheeks.

'Is that you Mum?' Lilly couldn't tell who it was because the woman's face was covered in thick black dirt.

'Yes, Lilly, it's me. I'm alright.' Oh thank God, Lilly gasped through her tears as she abruptly sat bolt upright, soaking her bed in a sweat of misery and distress.

For Marilyn there were to be no new toys or clothes. She was utterly remarkable, thought Lilly. She never complained about what she was missing out on. Though she had few possessions, being so young at the start of the war, the little girl was scarcely aware of deprivation and could not remember a peacetime Christmas or birthday. And yet Lilly also knew that Marilyn's capacity to cope with the disruption and separation from her father and the rest of the family in London was not limitless. She, like Lilly, was prone to bouts of anxiety and tension. Living for an unknown length of time in someone else's house had made it hard to relax or indulge in moods of self-pity. But Marilyn was becoming increasingly fractious and her nerves seemed strained. Lilly was startled to see how Marilyn's hands were often shaking now and she was restless with agitation, especially as she tried to drink her tea at the breakfast table before school. And there seemed to be no laughter between them these days. No girlish giggles and no more contented humming which used to get Marilyn into trouble with her nursery teachers back in London.

When Marilyn came home from school one afternoon, she wouldn't look any of them in the eye. Even Joe was disappointed to see her turn away from him when he launched forward from his armchair to ruffle her hair as he was wont to do on a daily basis. Normally it would make her giggle or at least smile to humour him. But today, she only looked at the floor, her lips pouting and she wandered unsteadily out of the room. Over her knitting, Lilly watched this uncharacteristic behaviour with alarm.

'Where are you going, young lady? That was rather impolite of you.'

A moment later Marilyn was back in the room but still with her head down.

'I've been sad all day,' she began as she slowly lifted her big sorrowful blue eyes towards her mother. 'Mr Nuttall let me go and lie down in the library corner where there's a bit of carpet and it's soft. He let me cry.'

'Oh Marilyn, were you crying again? And in front of the whole class. But why?'

'Don't know.'

'Come and tell me.'

With an effort, Joe extricated himself from his deep chair, its softness having enveloped him. He shot an I'll leave you to it kind of a look at Lilly, but Marilyn was already blurting out the whole story before he had managed to stand fully upright.

'Mr Nuttall thought I was sleepy, so he told me to lie down where it was quiet. But I wasn't sleepy at all. I was kind of twitchy and when he told me he didn't like my handwriting because it was not very neat, I wanted to run away out of the room because I really don't like it when he's not pleased with me. So he let me lie down till I felt better and was calm again. That's what he said.'

Here was a new challenge for Lilly to deal with. Rationing was preventing them all from getting enough decent nutrition. Sarah Cockington tried her utmost and was not unaware of her obligations to provide a reasonably healthy meal, despite the constant acute shortages of certain foods. Often they would all make a feast out of a hardboiled egg and a tomato with a slice of bread and sliver of butter or margarine if they could make it go around. Everyone in the house was concerned about Marilyn's weight loss and her palpable lack of appetite or energy. Lilly worried that the little girl might have contracted tuberculosis. Heavens, that ancient school building was always full of damp. It was not an uncommon experience among Marilyn's classmates.

Then one Saturday morning, Marilyn began weeping. She was inconsolable and she could not stop sobbing. Lilly grabbed her, shocked and impotent and took her out into the kitchen where it was cooler. Hysteria was taking hold of the child and she began to scream. She hit out at the cupboards then collapsed on the floor and began to rock herself steadily with her arms wrapped tightly around her grubby bruised knees. Lilly stood and stared down at her transfixed with alarm before bending down to throw her arms around the little girl and try to comfort her.

'It's alright, my Marilyn, really it is. Hush now. What's wrong. Can you tell me?'

Marilyn was silent for a moment and then the tears spurted again.

'Oh Mummy, I'm so lonely.' She buried her milk-white face in her arms. Lilly was choked to see her own little girl so distraught. She felt a pang of remorse. Was this her fault? She had let this happen.

'Mummy's going to make it all alright, just you wait and see...'

But how? Lilly looked around the room as if the cupboards and the chipped Butler sink might step forward to help them and show her what to do. Then June slowly opened the door as soon as she thought Marilyn had calmed herself.

'It's only natural that she should feel the strain, Lilly,' she ventured. Her uncertain voice petered out as she came towards them and helped Lilly to guide Marilyn to a chair.

'I must take her to see the Doctor as soon as ever I can this week.'

There was uncertainty about the availability and affordability of the local doctors. Their local hospital had become overcrowded and doctors taking part in the Emergency Medical Service had been relocated to where air raids had been most intense. As well as London, Coventry, Birmingham and Plymouth all needed more doctors and nurses and this had left Blackpool with a shortfall, so it was likely that poor Marilyn would have to wait.

This meant that they missed the onset of her subtle but insidious symptoms of St Vitus Dance.

Lilly was terrified. She finally managed to get her little girl in to see Dr Churngold as she trusted the elderly man to know what to do for the best.

'Doctor, has my little girl had some sort of nervous breakdown? I can't think what could have brought it on, really I can't. I thought she was doing so well you see.'

Dr Churngold was perplexed and initially dismissive. It was rare in his experience that such a young child as Marilyn should have contracted such an extreme neurological disorder as St Vitus Dance. He had seen cases in adolescent girls mostly, but Marilyn was barely five years old. That cut little ice with Lilly who had never heard of the condition before and was horrified by the symptoms she could see in Marilyn. Uncontrollable spasms and jerking limbs.

She was determined to get the right help from wherever it might be available. The Doctor merely prescribed bed rest for Marilyn and ordered Lilly to calm down around the child.

'Of course, I could give Marilyn sedation. That would be the best treatment I can provide for her. Otherwise, it's up to you to keep her settled and relaxed.'

'But she will recover, won't she, Doctor? My little girl will get over this awful disease or whatever it is?'

Dr Churngold tried to reassure her with the best of his knowledge.

'I hear that in America, they are treating this as a fever with a new experimental drug called penicillin. Of course, we won't have access to that over here and in any case, I wouldn't trust a new drug before it had been well tried and tested – and on older patients too. But you mustn't worry yourself, Mrs Stevens. In four months, six tops, I would expect your little girl to be right as rain. Now take her home and do as I suggest. Put her to bed and leave her in a cool dark room for as long as possible each day. Sleep is the best remedy really, you know. Very restorative. And I want you to keep a careful eye on Marilyn's temperature. Monitor it every day for three weeks.'

As Lilly took Marilyn's hand and ushered her out of Dr Churngold's room, the avuncular doctor remembered something else.

'Oh, Mrs Stevens, if you can, try to find Marilyn some jigsaw puzzles or simple board games to keep her mind occupied. Can you do that? Monopoly is my personal favourite, you know.'

'Yes, I'll try to do that. Thank you, Doctor. Goodbye.' Lilly smiled reluctantly at him. She wasn't convinced. She agonised about whether they should have stayed in London where at least they might have had access to a children's specialist, but she went out to find what she could. A well-timed visit to the bring-and-buy sale at the local church hall that weekend turned out to be lucrative for her. She handed in a whole pile of Picturegoer magazines (even though she had promised her sister Laura to keep them by for her). Miraculously she came away from the hall with a tatty but serviceable Monopoly set. It looked as though it had set its previous owner back a pretty penny. It was sitting there, waiting for her at the end of the large trestle table and Lilly could hardly believe her luck when she spotted it. This was her favourite game too. She and Harry, her mother and Laura would spend hours on Saturday afternoons locked in protracted and heated competition. Harry invariably won, his business acumen, so he liked to believe, being so much greater than all theirs combined. Now she would teach little Marilyn to play and, she hoped, this might give her some new skills to make up for so many weeks of schooling missed due to her illness. She hoped that the little players' tokens would please Marilyn: a modern iron, a sleek red sports car, a handsome white rocking horse, a steam ship, a shiny black top hat and a brown shoe which reminded her of the ones Harry would wear on Sundays. She also picked up a knitted jumper in pale yellow and a shaggy grey teddy bear which had lost its squeak but was still fluffy and soft and she knew it would bring a smile to the little girl's face.

There followed a period of extreme focus on Marilyn's health by everyone in the house. Lilly was infinitely grateful for the absence of air raids in Blackpool at that time to trouble the little girl's sleep, although within the house, peace came rarely. Sarah sometimes forgot about the child resting upstairs as she ranted and raved in her usual disordered bustle. Joe would try to shush her, but the impact of his remonstrations lasted only fleetingly. Ethel and June were anxious to see Marilyn recover and would pop their grinning faces around her bedroom door hoping to cheer and reassure her with little presents. They offered up their own rations to give Marilyn more to eat. Yet they still came and went at odd hours of the day and night and in their habitual charging about, they let the lavatory seat slam and doors bang. Exasperated, Lilly let her patience eventually escape her and on one occasion she whispered an uncharacteristic expletive into their bewildered faces.

'What's the matter with you? Are you both completely bloody mad? What do you think you're doing making all this noise?'

They apologised profusely and after that they padded about more quietly although Lilly could hear their stifled giggles through the walls and with clenched fists, cursed them to herself. Lilly could not relax and she indulged in a turmoil of guilt and fear for the daughter who was her whole reason for being. How did I miss the signs? I did this to Marilyn. I have given her this awful life, away from her family and I've made her live in this dreadful place... At times like this, Lilly wondered how she would ever find the capacity to carry on by herself. After everything that had happened since the start of the war, she seemed to be weakening now. If only Harry could see how far she had matured, how much hardier, more resilient she had become, he would be so proud of her. She mustn't disappoint him. She would find the strength from somewhere.

Then came the dreaded meeting with Miss Thora Eversley, Marilyn's headmistress. A frumpy triangular little woman with a moustache that was difficult to look away from and a stoop that made her seem far older than her fifty-seven years. Her diminutive size belied a fearsome hold on children and parents alike. Lilly had met her only once before at an end of term concert in which Marilyn had reluctantly taken part in the shaky school choir. Lilly had felt as though she were being admonished for having strayed into the part of the building where she should not have erred, but a number of other mothers had expressed the same feeling and Lilly decided that Miss Eversley was the kind of woman always best avoided.

Today's encounter Lilly would have gladly eschewed, but she had been summoned by Miss Eversley to discuss Marilyn's prolonged absence from school. Lilly felt the need of Harry at this moment. This was a burden that she never had expected to shoulder without him and she felt ill-equipped, unequal to this daily challenge and too weak in spirit to face it with assertiveness or confidence. Yet, there she was, in that stuffy, crowded study and the headmistress was staring intently at her from across her desk. It all seemed to take on an exaggerated immensity which made Lilly shrink back into her chair.

'It's not that I don't sympathise with the poor child's present predicament.' Miss Eversley began, once they were both seated and Miss Eversley had replaced her thick rimmed glasses.

Why won't she use the word, Lilly thought. It was a sickness that Marilyn had. She was sick. That was all. For goodness sake! She took a deep breath before she opened her mouth in response to Miss Eversley's relentless gaze.

'Yes, I understand that there are several other children across the school in similar circumstances. With similar symptoms, that is. It's all very disturbing. I understand that. But I'm afraid my little girl is rather out of sorts and it's just not possible for her to attend school for some time. You see, the doctor thinks that it might be a matter of a few months.'

Lilly was aware of her own difficulty or reluctance to come to the point. Marilyn was likely to need as much as six months at home. But she feared how the head mistress might blow up in her face at this idea.

'I simply wanted to let you know not to expect her back this term at least.'

'I see, Mrs Stevens. Thank you for making me aware.' The headmistress leaned forward placing her hands together neatly in front of her on the desk. Lilly sat back in her creaking chair and waited.

'But it won't do, Mrs Stevens. It won't do at all.'

Lilly was about to stand up and express her honest feelings in strong and direct words, her cheeks flushed with sudden anger and frustration. This was just the sort of reaction she had expected from this stupid old battle-axe. But Miss Eversley was only thinking aloud. She still had more to say.

'Of course there are ways around this, you know Mrs Stevens. Games and light recreation which Marilyn can do instead of her lessons - when she's having a good day, that is. She must keep up her maths and English whenever possible to do so. There are some excellent children's programmes on the Home Service these days. You do have a wireless set at home, I take it?'

'Oh yes, of course. That would be fine. Marilyn likes to listen to the wireless.'

'Well then, here are the titles of some programmes which I would recommend to you. They are very instructional, and I would expect you to find them easily if you tune in carefully.' Miss Eversley jotted down half a dozen programme titles and pushed the little piece of paper across the desk. Lilly picked it up gratefully, the wind thoroughly taken out of her sails.

'That's very kind of you, Miss Eversley. Thank you so very much. It's been rather tough on Marilyn, all this.'

'And on you too, I should say. I know how these things can be so very concerning, especially when the illness is so protracted like this.'

Lilly fought the flood of tears welling up so close to the surface.

The conversation came to an abrupt but decisive end as the headmistress stood up and, pushing back her immense leather chair, extended her hand wishing Lilly a 'Good day.'

Lilly felt as small as a child who had been scolded for some misdemeanour or other and she slunk away out of the office as quickly as possible in case Miss Eversley changed her mind and decided to put her on the black step.

'Oh and Mrs Stevens,' Lilly heard her say as she turned around to face her fate. 'You might pass on my good wishes to Marilyn and let her know that I'm praying for her speedy recovery. She is a lovely little girl and an excellent student. I have watched her come on in leaps and bounds. Such a shame that she has succumbed to this dreadful beast of a sickness.'

'Oh, I will pass on your kind regards to Marilyn. And thank you so very much.'

I got her completely wrong! Lilly reflected as she stepped smartly down the corridor and out into the cold air. She contemplated just how much this war had turned people from the cold-hearted pragmatism of their reputation into far more compassionate and accommodating individuals. Or perhaps it wasn't the war at all. Perhaps it had more to do with her lack of faith in the kindness of human beings.

Gradually, Marilyn began to recover and as Autumn gave way to the darker nights of Winter, she seemed to need less sleep and was eager to eat more and join the rest of the household at the table downstairs.

'Here she is, my little sleeping beauty!' crooned Lilly as she carried the still wobbly Marilyn into the front room one evening just as Christmas was approaching.

They had a muted celebration in the child's honour and Sarah persuaded each of them to give up their egg ration for the week so that she could bake a substantial cake. Marilyn had slept her birthday away in November, so Joe had suggested that they try to make up for it somehow.

This was an evening that Lilly had never expected to enjoy so much and she beamed as she watched the wan smile on Marilyn's face transform into the widest grin of delight. Sarah even managed some sugar icing for the cake, which was a dubious shade of yellow, although no-one seemed to mind.

CHAPTER 13.

83 Lansdowne Drive, Hackney, E8.

10th Jan 1943.

Hello Little Sis,

How are you and Marilyn?
Nothing much to report to you. Mother's chest is proper bad as you know this time of the year is always so difficult for her. I do worry. And coal prices have soared again – haven't they everywhere?

Anyway, I'm back to doing double shifts again now since the New Year. It's not too bad. It was fun while it lasted and I didn't mind at all working throughout the festive period. They rigged up a make-shift stage at the top end of the factory for us and a very elderly gentleman got up and started playing the harmonica. He was ever so good and we all had a smashing time listening to him playing our favourites. I thought of you, Lilly. You would have loved it too. Probably you would have started blubbering. I know how music makes you sentimental.

They made us a wonderful supper and laid on a menu to die for! We had Scotch broth to start with and that was followed with fried fish and chips with greens and then we had a choice of jam sponge or lemon pudding. And all washed down with limitless pints of beer which as you know is not on ration and so they positively encouraged us to help ourselves, although it was much watered down to go further and to stop us falling asleep at our benches I should say. But what a feast! I suppose you have fish and chips all the time up there by the seaside, but here it has become something of a real treat, although they didn't exactly pile up our plates, but never mind. The work I do is quite physically exhausting (have I already told you that?) so you will not recognise me when we see each other next as I have quite slimmed down and have never been so fit!

I do hope that you are getting to the picture house where you are? I saw a very good American film last Friday evening, just come out. It was called 'Star Spangled Rhythm'. Do try to catch it if it comes your way. It's quite an extravaganza!

All my love,

Laura xx

P.S. Tell Harry when you next write to him that they've dug up the football pitch in Turnbury Lane to make way for allotments! He'll have to pick up a pair of rubber galoshes instead of his football boots next time he comes home. Ha Ha.

'Oh, bloody hellfire, who's that now at six o'clock on a Sunday morning!' Joe had been sitting alone in the quiet of the early dawn, enjoying a cuppa and his beloved, three days-old newspaper from which he read every column inch. He had been savouring this rare peace and solitude. Beyond the gentle rustling of leaves outside, he could hear the distant clopping of hooves on the cobbled streets as the draymen went about their early morning deliveries.

Suddenly a sharp rap on the front door had ripped into this pleasant morning and put an end to his hard-won self-indulgence. Reluctantly he got up and went to open the front door. He gasped.

'Oh well, well, I never! Harry Stevens, as I live and breathe! You're the very last person I expected to see.'

Harry stood sheepishly on the doorstep, rubbing his hands together, trying in vain to keep warm. The collar of his great coat was turned up against his dark tanned neck and his army cap offered him little warmth against the cold January winds.

'Hello Mr Cockington. Sorry to turn up unannounced at this un-godly hour, especially on a Sunday…I took the milk train up from London, you see.'

'Come in, come in, son! The whole house is still asleep. The Missus was snoring her head off, so I came down for some peace and quiet. Otherwise, you'd have been stood there on't doorstep a good while longer for sure.' His laugh was kind and generous, just how Harry had remembered it.

He knew he'd done exactly the right thing to come here. He had always warmed to Joe Cockington and had the utmost respect for him.

'I did write to Lilly to tell her I was coming here on leave. She should be expecting me.'

'No son,' said Joe. 'I don't know as she's had any letter from you in quite a while now. She's been in one hell of a state not hearing anything from you and wondering what's become of you, like. Well, we all have....so it'll be one heck of a surprise for her.'

Harry was crestfallen.

'Oh dear, Lilly hates surprises.' He took off his cap while Joe began to rally round.

'Well, I'd best go and wake her – then we'll all have a nice cup of tea together to celebrate, eh? Oh, this is grand!'

But as Joe turned to go up the stairs, he spotted Marilyn standing on the landing looking down at the two men.

'Marilyn, guess who's here, luv!' Joe whispered up to her. He knew what a complex process this would be for the little girl who had not seen her father for so very long. Marilyn just stood there staring down blankly at them both, moving her gaze from one to the other.

'It's your dad. Yes, it is, it's your daddy home on leave to see you. What do you think of that then, eh? Come down and say hello to him. Come on.'

Harry held out his arms to her, with his heart in his mouth.

'Hello Marilyn, my beautiful girl.' But Marilyn was confused by what she saw and simply turned around and ran back into the bedroom. Harry was disconsolate. This was the one thing he had not contemplated as he rushed over sea and land to hold his beloved daughter in his arms once again. How could she turn away from him? The look she gave him was a bitter blow and he had no idea what to do. Is this normal? He contemplated. I suppose it must be, poor little lamb, she can't take it all in.

A moment later, Lilly came to the top of the stairs, hastily pulling on her dressing gown. She had curlers in her hair and was trying to focus.

'Harry? It can't be!' Lilly ran down the stairs and into his arms. Joe discreetly moved away into the kitchen, unnoticed by either of them.

'Oh, Harry! I can't believe it. Why didn't you let me know you were coming? I had no idea what had happened to you. When I didn't hear from you, didn't get any letters, I thought…I thought the worst, you know. Oh, Harry, it's been torment, it has really!' Harry could see that she was a mash of shock and delight. His own emotions were not dissimilar.

'But Lilly, I did write to you. I've never stopped writing. Why didn't you get the letters? Where did they go?'

'Maybe they've got lost somewhere. Oh, but you're here now. How ever did you make it back?'

'Well,' Harry started to explain an impossibly complicated journey, trying to make it sound like a Sunday drive to the seaside. 'We left Piombino fourteen days ago. Sailed into Southampton, then got on the train to Waterloo and I went straight over to Euston and caught the first train I could find up to Blackpool. I slept most of the way!'

'And how long have you got?'

'Nine days…It may be the last leave I get for a while, though. Just warning you, Lilly.'

'Nine days! Nine whole days! That's marvellous. Oh, where's Marilyn. Marilyn? Come down! Come down and welcome your daddy. Oh, she'll be just thrilled to see you.'

'Well,' said Harry with more than a little apprehension. 'She wasn't so sure just now. She's afraid of me, I think.'

'Afraid? Of you?' Lilly was anxious to reassure him that it was alright. It was normal. It would all come right. They just had to be patient with Marilyn as she inched her way down the stairs towards them, taking each stair with trepidation.

'It's only that she wasn't expecting you any more than I was. Oh, my darling, she's not seen a man in uniform before, well not close up, that is. She saw some soldiers the other week, when we were walking along the pier and she turned to me and she said "Is that what my daddy looks like when he has his uniform on?" And I said "Yes, that's right. Only, your daddy's much more handsome," which of course you are.'

Lilly saw at once the silver glint of Harry's tears and she

wanted to cry with him. She wanted to hold him and sob with him. But instead, she sought to deflect Harry's attention away from Marilyn while the little girl – and all three of them - adjusted to this sudden change in their circumstances, confined as they were, this little family, in the cramped space at the bottom of the stairs.

'Oh, my hair. Look at the state of me! Oh Harry, how could you just turn up here and get me out of bed looking like the cat's dragged me in from the back yard!'

Harry just gazed in wonderment at the beautiful woman in his arms. He hadn't held her for nearly three long years.

'My darling, you're still as beautiful as the day I married you!' Then he picked up his beloved child and was thrilled beyond expression as he allowed himself to believe that she was slowly beginning to warm to him.

'There now. How's my own little Marilyn? My, how you've grown. He struggled to clear his tight throat. 'She's looking more like you, Lilly.'

'Well, she would, wouldn't she!'

Harry was transfixed.

'She's a credit to you Lilly and no mistake!'

Joe was keen to usher them into the room before they woke the rest of the house.

'Er, excuse me folks. I've made a pot of tea for you both. Come and get it while it's hot… and while you can still get a word in edgeways. The missus will be down presently and she'll want to know everything about you.'

It was too late. They could hear Sarah stomping down the stairs.

'Well now, who's this? Harry Stevens? What a surprise! What are you doing here?'

'Hello Mrs Cockington. I'm here on leave and I am sorry, it seems that no-one knew to expect me today.'

Lilly wished with all her heart that she'd been there waiting at the station to meet her husband from the train. She would have put out the bunting for her Harry! Oh, but he would have thought that too daft and told her to save it for when the war was finally over…She barely heard Sarah wittering on.

'And it's *Sarah and Joe* - none of this formality. By heck, but it's good to see you! And how are you going on, eh? You fair gave this poor girl of yours a fright when your letters stopped coming. We were all worried sick, weren't we Joe, eh? Have you put the kettle on for these poor kids, have you?'

Joe pointed to the pot there on the table and then went to the kitchen to fetch her a cup. Sarah thought they'd be wanting some nice hot breakfast right enough. And she was eager to hear what plans they might have. What was there to do in Blackpool…in January? But Lilly's mind was on more immediate matters.

'Oh, but where will you be staying, Harry?' she muttered.

Harry looked about him uncertain of what to say. Sarah was right there to the rescue.

'Now don't you worry about that. You can all squeeze in together. Nice and cosy, like. And Joe will be glad of a bit of male company for once. He might feel like pulling his finger out a bit more around here then…'

Joe returned with a cup in his hand. Before he could answer, Harry jumped in.

'That is so very kind of you, Sarah.' He handed Sarah his ration book. 'Thank you, both of you. I knew I could depend on you for your hospitality. You've been a lifeline for Lilly and Marilyn. Especially a couple of years back when we lost the house in Forest Gate and everything…I just knew we could depend on you-'

'Now then,' Sarah shushed him. 'We'll have none of that nonsense. It was what any human being would do for another. Besides it's been a real treat for us having Lilly and young Marilyn around the house.'

'You must meet our other two boarders,' said Joe. 'Two young lasses, June and Ethel. They'll be, er, sleeping late just now, but you'll see them presently.'

Lilly was ecstatic.

'Oh Harry, nine whole days! It's like a dream!'

Harry was keen to make the most of their precious time together.

'Well now, I was thinking on the train, that maybe we could all pop up to Morecambe while I'm here. I can hire a car.

What do you say?'

Lilly was all for it. It was a marvellous idea, except that the car of course was out of the question.

'The bus will do us fine. And Marilyn will love it,' she said decisively. 'When? When can we go?'

They decided on going the day after tomorrow, if they could arrange it, leaving straight after breakfast. Sarah began her raucous laugh.

'Morecambe in January. Very bracing, that'll be. Well, at least you'll not be bothered by the crowds.'

Joe was chuckling too as a thought occurred to him.

'We went to Morecambe for our honeymoon back in 1923. Aye, we had a fine old time. You were as pretty as a picture in them days, Sarah.'

'Don't be so soft,' said Sarah with a slap on the table that made the tea pot lid rattle. 'These young'uns aren't going to be interested in our honeymoon, all them years since!'

But Lilly and Harry were interested and persuaded the older pair to tell them about it. All about how it was August and they had hired a little car and set off to the lovely little guest house just off the seafront, although Joe had forgotten the name of it...

'Her poached eggs are what stick out in my memory,' Sarah began with a pensive smile. 'Lovely and runny they were..."

'And we did plenty of walking along the promenade –'

'Well, it's not so easy to do these days is it? Poached eggs...'

Harry and Lilly glanced at each other. Their hosts were evidently travelling in parallel down memory lane.

'I do recall how choppy the sea was!' said Joe.

'Strolling through the streets, popping in and out of all them lovely shops...' recalled his wife.

'And I remember we stopped to listen to that brass band concert in the open air one evening after our tea. It were over t'road from the old Winter Gardens...Oh let me see if I can fetch that photo album. It's in t'drawer, in't it?' Joe was off to the sideboard.

'I remember that was the evening when you burnt your fringe on that candle, Joe, remember? When were sitting ourselves down to the table in that fancy restaurant. It were so embarrassing! It were supposed to be a romantic table in't corner just for us, like. And when we got there, the waiter, he held out his hand – I can still see 'im now – to take Joe's overcoat from him to hang it up and me daft husband 'ere, he thought the man were just being friendly, so Joe shook his hand instead. He had no idea, honestly! And don't you go rummaging in that drawer again for Pete's sake. You'll have the whole lot out on't floor! Joe!'

The moment was over.

'Yes, well, it sounds like you both have lots of fine memories,' Harry said quickly. 'Perhaps we can make some of our own. What d'you say, Lilly? I'll arrange it all. Don't you worry about a thing. It'll be just like we used to do...before the war.'

Lilly was choked and her tears began to sting her eyes.

'Yes alright,' she said, 'I'd like that just fine.'

It was the very best of times, better than anything Marilyn had ever known during her stay in Blackpool. Harry was always making her laugh. He was always happy and tender and she quickly came to adore him. Marilyn had no concept of the brevity of time or how desperately painful it would feel to say goodbye again when it was time for him to leave them. As for Harry, it was nothing short of a miracle that there he was, after all he had been through in Italy, strolling along the Promenade here in Blackpool arm in arm with his two beloved girls, Lilly on one side and Marilyn on the other with her hand in his, stuffed deep into the pocket of his great coat to keep cosy and warm. I've got myself a beauty on each sleeve right here, he beamed. He wouldn't have been at all surprised if every passer-by had stopped to congratulate him on his good fortune.

The undulating sea was an inhospitable brown-grey and as clouds amassed above them dark as a new bruise, they strolled on obliviously, chatting and giggling. They shared their stories of recent events and Lilly recounted how she had tried to help the poor man who was having a heart attack right there on the Promenade a few short months earlier, how she had watched him being led away into the waiting ambulance and how she wished that she had known what had become of him. And then they just looked deep into each other's eyes, as if they could hardly believe that they were in one another's presence, afraid that this was only a cruel dream that would suddenly burst its golden bubble and rouse them back into grim reality at any moment. But no, this was better than a mere dream and the weak January sunshine gave everything a positive hue and made them blithe and carefree. They found a bench and sat down, the three of them. Marilyn's hand still tucked inside his pocket.

'Tell me, Lilly dear, what's it been really like for both of you here in Blackpool? You always put on such a brave face in your letters. I want to know how you really live and what you have had to put up with.'

Lilly thought carefully before she responded. There was so much to say and so much she couldn't share. About her anguish every time she heard the news bulletins about casualties in Italy or Africa, or wherever the hell Harry was supposed to be at that moment in time. About how she had been living in constant suspense, wondering whether he was alive or dead. About the terrible tension she felt waiting to hear from him and not knowing whether each letter would be his last. About how the long wretched days stretched out before her...He had given her a chance to indulge herself in woe and self-pity, but this wasn't really the time for that, was it?

'Well, I can tell you one thing for certain, it's not like living in the East End. I mean imagine if we'd stayed there!'

Harry sat back and looked straight ahead. He didn't care to imagine it.

'That's why I urged you to leave in the first place. I never shall stop thanking the Gods who wanted me to write that letter to you. It's the best thing I ever did in my life. Aside from marrying you, that is.'

She brushed his kisses away.

'Not in front of Marilyn. And Sarah Cockington would call you a soft beggar Which of course you are!'

'But I just wanted to-'

'No Harry let's not. Not here, or else I shall cry again. You know what a silly little fool I am. Let's just enjoy ourselves while we've got the chance! C'mon let's go and play on the pier, What d'you say to that, Marilyn?'

The same amusement centres on the piers were still thriving that Lilly and Harry had fondly remembered from their pre-war holidays and were drawing many eager customers to their freak shows and shooting booths. Lilly astonished both Harry and Marilyn and startled several bystanders with her shooting skill and excellent aim. Her focus and determination to shoot accurately won her a stack of cheap and gaudy but well-earned prizes. She recalled with a sharp pang in her stomach the large celluloid dolls that Harry had won for her on their Blackpool honeymoon and which she had kept in their little East End flat now destroyed in the Blitz of 1940. She wished she had left them in the attic at their Edmonton house until they could get back there when this awful war was finally over.

Harry was enjoying watching the many new Airforce recruits marching up and down and he noticed how green they looked, how fresh and eager. He admired their enthusiasm and the look of pride and purpose etched into their faces as they focused on their task and he recalled feeling that way himself during his own early training, enveloped in physical courage and an illusory patriotism. Lilly, meanwhile, watching the new air force recruits, simply felt grateful that her Harry had enrolled in the army where perhaps he had a greater chance than his Royal Airforce counterparts of keeping his head down and making it safely through the war.

Although she had become hardened to the BBC wireless announcements relaying news of some impressive battle in the skies ending with the soft codicil, 'one of our aircraft is missing' or 'a number of our aircraft failed to return', she felt wretched for the poor mothers, wives, sisters, sweethearts who must be scouring the daily newspaper columns for the lists of British planes lost. So many of them...

The airmen were attracting the attention and curiosity

of many of the town's visitors and locals alike, whose scrutiny and idle observation irritated the harassed non-commissioned officers as they doggedly attempted to ignore the hordes of onlookers. They barked their commands at the energetic squads as they attempted what according to Harry was known as a "feet-astride-jumping-arms-upward-raising". They looked self-conscious and Lilly thought they must feel as though they were the chief entertainment in the City Zoo.

They stopped to gaze at the sparkling sea, their arms perched on the cold handrail which Marilyn could not yet reach. Lilly felt a stab of guilt that this moment seemed so perfect and blissful. Her thoughts turned to her mother and sister back in London.

'I had to laugh when Mum rang me up to tell me all about their terrible weather over Christmas,' she said to Harry. 'I mean, the line was awful as always, so I may have mis-heard her, but she was having a good old rant about how it hadn't stopped snowing for days there in London.'

'Oh yes, they had a White Christmas there after all,' said Harry. 'I bet Laura was pleased?'

'Well,' said Lilly. 'Not that she saw much of it while she was cooped up in that awful factory, but yes, the snow lasted six weeks, apparently. Mum said the lads coming home to Blighty on leave were lucky to make it to London, what with all those abandoned vehicles littering the roads. She said some of them got stranded and had to stay the weekend in Dover! And in London, Mum said they'd had no post, no rubbish collection - and no coal deliveries either. Their delivery lorry broke down apparently and, due to the snow, they couldn't get the right tools to fix it for ages. I don't know, everything's so cheap and shoddy these days. Mum doesn't complain though, well she never does, does she? Not really. I told her to keep plying herself with hot toddies to thaw herself out!'

Harry was lost in thought.

'Just imagine how you'd have felt if that had been me stuck in Dover. Cor blimey! I'd never have heard the end of it!' He chuckled as Lilly punched him softly on the arm.

The following day a reluctant Marilyn had to go to school. The morning was full of rare winter sunshine, which although did not carry with it enough strength to warm their bones, at least it inspired Lilly and Harry to take a robust stroll around the beautiful Stanley Park where they had spent many happy hours on their holidays before the war. Lilly looked about her, full of wistful melancholy.

'Oh, what a great pity it's not June or July, Harry,' she said. 'I just love to see this park at that time of year, when the roses are in full bloom. It makes quite a picture doesn't it!'

Through the barren trees surrounding them on both sides of the footpaths, they came upon the recently opened café built in the modern Art Deco style. They both gasped when they saw its tall, impressive splendour.

'Well now, this is new since we were here last,' said Harry. 'Cost a pretty penny, I shouldn't wonder! Come on, I'll treat you to a hot cup of tea inside.'

They reminisced as they took in the circular Italian Garden at the centre of the park with its marble fountain and four marble seahorses which always made them giggle. Then they visited the bandstand which still seemed to retain the echo of famous brass bands that had performed there in years gone by. They reached the clocktower and turned towards the cricket grounds, neither one of them wishing to leave the peaceful atmosphere of the park.

'Remember the celebrity charity cricket match we watched that time, Lilly darling?'

'Yes, and we couldn't recognise any of the celebrities, could we?'

After they had visited a war artists exhibition which had seemed to them too full of gloomy paintings of battle ships and Lilly had bought some more amusing picture postcards for Marilyn, Harry took Lilly to a lunchtime concert at the Assembly and Concert Room in Talbot Road, something they had always loved to do since their courting days. The Orchestra was made up of Royal Air Force musicians and while they were vigorously playing Smetana's Overture to the Bartered Bride, Lilly's mind wandered and as she gazed up to the ceiling, she noticed the cracked plaster and filthy fanlight windows. *Such a shame*, she thought.

'After you, Mrs Stevens..." Harry took off his hat reluctantly as they all came into the cabbage-smelling hallway from the icy evening outside after they had gone together to pick up Marilyn from school, much to her delight.

Harry felt the perishing cold cut right through him. It had been a constant struggle since he had left the heat of Italy behind.

'I swear Piombino must be the hottest place on Earth. Never mind North Africa. It has nothing on the heat of Piombino –'

'You name dropper! You're just showing off with all your gadding about. You're trying to make Marilyn and me jealous with all these fancy place names.' Lilly had never seen her husband looking so tanned before.

Harry paused. There was something on his mind which had been festering for a several hours now.

'Yes, well, talking of *jealous*,' he began cautiously. 'That reminds me, you know Sarah Cockington wasted no time in telling me that you have a secret admirer, Lilly dearest.'

Lilly felt her cheeks reddening. What was it, anger? Embarrassment perhaps.

'Oh, for goodness's sake! That woman has too much to say for herself. She ought to keep her mouth shut instead of stirring up trouble like that.' Lilly didn't care whether Sarah was about to overhear her comments. She would nip this one in the bud. 'No Harry, there's no secret admirer. Nothing like that at all, please don't be so daft.'

'The Lady doth protest too much!' Harry laughed. 'I heard that the young man apparently professed to you his undying love.'

'No! He did not. It was just that, well he got a little carried away, that's all. Poor Fred Ackroyd. He's just got himself a bit mixed up in his head.'

'So, who is this Fred Ackroyd, and what does he want with my wife?' Harry couldn't fight the urge to tease her.

Lilly wanted Marilyn out of the firing range. She

suggested that the little girl go and play in their room. Watching her go obediently up the stairs, Lilly turned to Harry and began to explain calmly how Fred was Mrs Bennett's delivery boy and how he popped into the shop most mornings. She wanted to convey to him how awful it had been when Fred's twin brother Alan was reported killed in action last summer over in France and how Fred had taken it very hard as they had been so close. She wanted Harry to understand that Fred had failed his medical on account of his bad asthma so they wouldn't take him into the Forces. It was somehow important to her to make Harry understand what it was like for young Fred and how he'd started pouring his heart out to her over a cuppa and even written her poems. Very good they were. Very powerful. And then when he popped round that evening to tell her that he thought he might have feelings for her, of a sort... well, like she said, he'd got a bit mixed up, that was all. But of course, she had put him straight and now it was all fine. She wanted Harry to understand. She waited. Harry thought about it for a minute.

'You're sure you didn't encourage him? You know, lead him on? Poems indeed!'

Lilly was dumbfounded. What did Harry mean? Still he blundered on, seemingly in his own private train of thought as he turned away from her taking off his hat and coat.

'Yes, yes you hear about it all the time, in the papers and in the films....and the lads are always getting these 'Dear John' letters.... Blimey, you don't expect it to happen to your own wife!'

Lilly couldn't work out whether he was joking or not. She hated his teasing and she never knew how to play this game of his.

'What are you getting at Harry, I want to know!'

But Harry persisted.

'You know well enough, my sweet. And of course, there you are, pushing thirty. Not so young as you used to be...'

Lilly stood there, open mouthed in horror.

'Are you accusing me of, of –'

'Yes, that's right,' said Harry without so much as a blink to help orientate her.

'You can't even bring yourself to say the word can you! Alright I'll say it for you. Affair. That's what you've got yourself into. An affair. Oh yes, as soon as my back is turned.'

'I'm not even sure if you're joking or not. Harry! Are you joking?' She was becoming tearful. 'Don't tease me. You can't seriously be standing there accusing me of having an affair with Fred! When I just told you how it was. What had happened. Say you understand how it was. Harry –'

She couldn't see the usual glint in his eye. His mischievous expression.

'I can see very clearly how it was...'

This wasn't a game anymore, or was it?

'Don't you stand there accusing me, Harry... And if you think we're going to Morecambe now, after you've just accused me of-'

Joe was at the top of the stairs.

'Oh hello, you two. I thought I could hear your voices. Have you had a grand day out together?' He marched down the stairs in double quick time as he spoke and didn't linger on his way to the kitchen. Harry and Lilly just stared at each other. Harry was subdued.

'Sounds like this Fred Ackroyd boy has had a lucky escape. What with your terrible moods...' He attempted a chastened grin. This usually won her round.

'I'll thank you to be more respectful to me, Harry Stevens.' But then Lilly relented. 'Oh really, I don't want to spend our precious time together arguing about Fred Ackroyd. Haven't we got more important things to be doing?'

She moved towards Harry and they embraced, their familiar affection for each other restored. This was silly and not at all like either of them normally behaved. But these were no longer normal times. Just then, the front door opened and Ethel came in.

'Oh evening,' she said airily. 'Had a nice time out and about? Want to share a nice hot pot of tea? I've bought an iced bun for Marilyn. Is that alright with you? I know how she loves them.'

Lilly always felt she was in the younger girl's debt. Her

generosity was limitless.

'Oh Ethel, you are always so kind. But you mustn't go using up your precious coupons on that child. I'll just call her down. Marilyn!'

Marilyn came coyly downstairs. She was still puffy-eyed after the three of them had been to see the new Disney film, Dumbo. Most of it had gone over her head, thankfully. But she was terribly upset by the film and Harry reckoned that it was the powerfully emotive music that had got to her. Marilyn had cried and cried. They had to stand outside the Odeon for a full 20 minutes while she had got it out of her system. People were staring as they went past. How embarrassing! Then the only thing that would cheer her up was the promise of a fruit juice at the Winter Gardens. But when they had got there, it was just closing for the day.

'Hello you!' Ethel chimed as soon as she spotted Marilyn at the top of the stairs. 'Come with me young lady and see what treat I've got in store for you.' Ethel smiled softly as she took Marilyn by the hand and they went into the kitchen together.

Harry and Lilly still felt awkward. Lilly realised that she hadn't even taken off her coat.

'So, you said you might not get leave again for a while?'

Harry gently kissed her forehead.

'No, I don't think so. They're sending us further afield this time. I can't give you any details of course.'

'No, no of course not.' Lilly was trying to be stoic. 'It's just a shame that's all. It's hard with you being so far away from us.' She knew that Harry was just doing his bit for the war effort of course, but still…

Harry lifted her chin with his forefinger and smiled down at her.

'By the way, I saw a lovely cottage in a magazine that somebody had left on the train from Southampton. It was somewhere like Sussex, or Surrey maybe. Can't remember. But it did remind me of that little place on the coast that you'd set your heart on back in '38. You know the one?'

Lilly remembered it. Thorpe Bay. It had that pretty garden with the weeping willow tree. Yes, oh well. That was a million miles away now.

'One day my darling, one day soon,' he said. 'We'll go back and find your dream house.'

'Oh Harry, will we? Will we ever get our lives back again?' It seemed impossible to her.

'Of course we will. The war's already gone on for two years. This time next year, it will be a distant memory and we'll all be back to normal, I reckon.'

It was enough to set Lilly's heart fluttering.

'What I wouldn't give to have my own place again! Somewhere for Marilyn to call home. With our own back garden for her to play in. And all the mod cons…'

Harry held her tightly in his arms.

'Well, keep that dream alive in your heart and then when this stupid bloody war is finally over and done with, I'll come back for you both and we'll start planning again. Perhaps we can move out to the seaside, to Margate or Dover. What do you think?'

'Or Westcliff-on-sea! Oh Harry, that would be fine, just fine.' The moment was theirs and theirs alone.

CHAPTER 14.

Lilly came bursting into the room, still in her dressing gown, eager and excited to be going on her trip to Morecambe. She threw open the curtains and reacted in horror to see thick snow on the ground.

'Oh no!' She gasped. 'Oh, I don't believe it. They didn't forecast snow in the papers, did they?'

It was not often that they would see snow in Blackpool. The salt in the seaside air would usually ward off the icy weather, but this was an odd exception, an unlucky twist of fate and it dashed Lilly's hopes. Marilyn wandered into the room.

'Oh Marilyn, sweetheart, mummy's afraid it looks like we won't be going to Morecambe today.' They both looked out of the bay window. To Marilyn the snow was a marvellous sight. It seemed to her as if an infinite number of minute diamonds had been pressed into its blue-white surface. But its sparkling brilliance was lost on Lilly who saw the snow as an immediate, immovable obstacle to her simple wishes.

'We won't be going anywhere by the look of it. Look at all that snow. The whole street is covered with it. Oh Harry, why did you have to get leave in January, honestly.'

She sighed and sat down heavily on the sofa with Marilyn. But then stroking her daughter's hair, Lilly checked herself. She shouldn't be so ungrateful. At least they were all together.

Harry came jauntily into the room.

'Well, that about puts the tin lid on our little trip, ladies. Sorry old girl. Looks like they've shut off the main roads out of town. Even the trains won't run in this lot. I am sorry.'

Lilly knew it wasn't Harry's fault. He hadn't rung up God and asked for this snow any more than she had. They would just have to make the best of it today and perhaps it would clear in a couple of days. Perhaps.

'Anyway, let's start by stoking the boiler, eh. You sit down and I'll go and put the kettle on.'

'It won't suit you, madam.' Harry winked at Marilyn. Lilly rolled her eyes at this ancient joke. She had heard it so many times before. Harry, her Harry, romantic, clever, demonstrative, artistic Harry. Only he could raise her spirits today.

But before she could reach the kitchen, Sarah bounded in from there waving a letter in her hand and nearly knocked her over.

'I've some exciting news for you and Marilyn, Lilly! Anyroad, it'll cheer you up and put a big smile on your faces! You'll never guess what, I've a new lodger coming here on't 25th of April, Easter weekend. For the whole of the Summer. And he's an actor, well a comedian at any rate. He's coming all the way up from South Wales, so he says 'ere.'

June came into the room just at that moment and Sarah's announcement stopped her mid-way through an indulgent yawn. She was enthralled.

'Ooh a real-life comedian! Under our roof! Just think of it. What's his name?'

Sarah pretended to forget and searched her letter for the name.

'Oh now, let me see, he's called Victor Norman. By all accounts he'll be here for the summer season at the Hippodrome. Five months. How marvellous, eh!'

Of course she was thinking of the money.

June had never heard of him, but still... how romantic! A real-life celebrity here in their house...for all those months.

Sarah went over to the wireless to seek out some jolly, heartening music to mark the change in her fortunes. She was right, her news did cheer them up. And it put a big smile on Marilyn's face too, although she had no idea why.

It was late. The clock chimed 2.00am. Harry and Joe were trying their best to be quiet, but they had been drinking hard at the near-by George Hotel and had made quite a night of it in a number of other local pubs after that. Harry was giggling like a silly child.

'Shh, don't wake the whole blinkin' house up!' He whispered loudly.

Joe was laughing now.

'No, no we don't want to do that. Don't want to wake the lioness now do we!'

'Is that your lady wife you're talking about?' Harry pretended to be shocked. 'She's a good woman, your wife. Got a good heart.'

Joe stood up straight to consider this.

'Aye, that she has. Mind you, she uses it sparingly.'

Harry started his schoolboy giggle again. He nudged Joe's elbow.

'Eh, eh, what about that barmaid at the George, eh? Cor, strewth, what a figure! Ho ho, blimey!'

Joe was feeling utter contentment.

'I'd say! Oh, but by 'eck, I had a right grand night out tonight Harry, my lad. Thank you for your company. I'll miss you when you've gone back.' He suddenly knocked over a lamp. 'Oh 'eck!' Now look what I've done.'

'Shh, be careful, you clumsy bugger!' Harry was laughing as he tried unsuccessfully to restore the lamp into position while Joe pulled him up by his braces.

'Oh, just leave it where it is. I'll see to it in't morning when-'

'It *is* the morning!' Harry blinked hard. They both fell about laughing at this just as Lilly entered in her dressing gown.

'What in heaven's name is going on down here? What time do you call this?' She stooped down to retrieve the broken lamp and seethed as she looked at it.

'Oh...did you just do this? I don't believe my eyes. And you, Joe. I've never seen you in such a state as this!'

'Sorry Lilly, luv.' Joe looked at her innocently. 'We were just coming up to bed. I hope we didn't wake you?' Lilly was incredulous.

'Of course you woke me! I'm surprised at you both, honestly. Look at the state of you.'

'Now, Lilly,' said Harry decisively, or so he thought. 'Don't you go getting your curlers in a twist!' He giggled again. 'You were quite happy earlier this evening when we said we'd be back late. "Are you sure you don't mind, Lilly?" I said. "No, no" you said. "You boys go and have a nice evening together," you said. "Enjoy yourselves." And so we did, didn't we, Joe?' Harry was pleased with himself. But this just riled Lilly even more.

'Yes, but I didn't expect you both to come back home drunk as Lords and behaving like a pair of...of idiots! And you can forget our trip up to Morecambe in the morning.' She turned to leave.

'What? Why? What are you talking about?'

But Lilly was adamant. She could hardly see Harry getting up at 6.00am for the rickety old bus and then sit on it all that way without being violently sick. His face would be greener than his uniform!

'Oh Harry, how could you! You knew we had an early start in the morning. How could you let us down like this! You make me so fed up sometimes, you do really! Now let's get to bed.'

She stormed out, leaving a chill draft hanging in the air which sobered the two men up like an icy shower. Harry looked down at his shoes.

'Well, that's that then. I'm in the doghouse tonight and no mistake!'

'Will she forgive you, d'you reckon?' Joe asked Harry.

'Oh Lilly? She'll be fine. Right as rain in a week or two.'

But then Harry remembered. He only had a week and then he would be leaving to go back on duty. He shook his head, more to clear it than anything else.

'Oh blimey, I'd better go upstairs and try to patch things up. I am a fool.' He paused. 'I love that gal. God knows I do. And I'm not going to leave here before I make it up to her.'

'Aye, make it up to her,' Joe echoed. 'That's right, Harry lad, see that you do, eh?'

This time she made certain that she would see him off at the station. Lilly's dread of that moment when Harry's train would pull away and leave her standing forlorn on the platform had hung around her heart for the entire time they had spent together in Blackpool. Yet these final thirty minutes on the platform at least afforded them some extra time alone, as alone as possible amid the raucous throng of uniforms enveloping them.

It was just as well they had arrived ahead of time, as they had only just located Harry's train on the departure board when they noticed that it was now due to depart fifteen minutes earlier than originally scheduled. Lilly was exasperated.

'Oh, Harry, why ever have they done that?'

Harry muttered a few expletives to himself as he looked up at the board.

'Good job we didn't decide to go and sit in the café for one last cup of tea together. Can you imagine how awful it would have been to have to run like mad things all the way over to this platform? We never could have made it. There'd have been all hell to pay if I'd missed this train!'

'Perhaps it's just as well it's earlier than we expected,' Lilly said as she stared down at the ground. 'It's better this way I think. Only the briefest goodbye. There'll be plenty of time for tears after you've gone.'

'Now then, we'll have none of that. Chin up my girl.' Harry lifted Lilly's delicate face and held it softly in his gloved hands.

'Have faith in me to keep myself intact till we're together again. Please be strong for Marilyn.'

'Yes, I will. Of course I will.'

And then the moment came when he must take his seat on the train. It was not a window seat and she could hardly see him waving to her through the film of grime caked onto the window. The whistle blew. It was shrill in her ears and she stared blankly at his train as it trundled away from her into the cold mist.

She turned and staggered back along the platform to the station concourse. No need for stoicism now. She let the tears stream down her cheeks and she thought she might collapse under the unbearable sadness of it all.

CHAPTER 15.

*'Sunny View', Keswick Road, Blackpool, Lancs.
2nd May 1943.*

Harry darling,

I do so hope that this letter finds you well. Thank you for your last letter. It was worth the long wait! It did make Marilyn and me laugh out loud! I'm glad to hear that your journey back to your base was in the main uneventful, apart from the cheese scone incident at the railway café!

We go on here as normal. The big excitement is that Victor Norman, our comedian from Wales is here with us now and has made quite an impression on our little household. You remember Sarah getting his letter and telling us that he would be staying with us for the summer season? Well, he's quite a character and he runs rings around Sarah, if you can imagine such a thing! I'm sure you would like him ever so.

Please don't berate me for not writing much detail about my aches and pains. It's all normal for someone in my condition... It's all far too dull and boring for you to have to read about. So instead, I have some news that will blow your socks off! ...There's no way to soften the blow, to bolster you up with a brandy or to make sure you're sitting down first.... But, Darling, we're having twins. Twins! Dr Churngold was very sweet about it. He said he was absolutely sure and he wished us double congratulations!

I do hope you're alright with this. We never wanted Marilyn to have to grow up as an only child but to have a brother or sister instead whom she could boss about and torment, but this is a double dream come true!

Please write back to me just as soon as ever you can to assure me that you are as over the moon about this as I am.

Marilyn is getting on well in school, I'm happy to report, though her poor spelling continues to concern me. She did own up to being smacked by the teacher at lunchtime yesterday for licking the custard out of her bowl. I ask you! Where did she learn to do that? I was rather ashamed of her. By all accounts, the bowl went flying across the dining room. She is of course so very excited about the babies and sometimes I wonder how she'll manage to wait until they arrive in the Autumn.

Anyway, darling, your little monster sends her fondest kisses to you. Keep yourself safe and well.

As always, your loving wife, Lilly.

CHAPTER 16.

The curtains were drawn tightly in the front room. They were a cosy group, each with their own disparate thoughts and brought together around the table contemplating their steamy cups of Ovaltine. Sarah got up from the settee to join Ethel in a game of cards. It was Gulliver's Travels tonight, their favourite. Only Joe broke the silence with his incessant fight with the drawer of the dresser as he searched in vain for the luminous blackout badges he had bought last week for everybody in the house to keep safe. They had cost him tuppence a piece from the general store and he could feel himself break out into a cold sweat in case he'd lost the lot of them.

'I swear Joe, that drawer is going to collapse with the weight of all your junk!' cried Sarah. Joe's insistence that it was all useful stuff was what piqued her the most. June was curious.

'What does he keep in there anyway, Mrs C?'

'The Lord alone knows! I'm sick to death of looking at it.'

June was humming quietly to a song which wafted out from the wireless as she wrapped Marilyn's long brown hair around some rags very carefully to make beautiful curly ringlets in the morning, while Marilyn was reading her New Vimto book and muttering its slogan softly under her breath, knowledge is power...though she didn't understand what that meant. The ringlets ordeal had become their weekly ritual and all the teachers at school complimented Marilyn on her voluminous head of curls. Even the little boy who was selling his brother's sweets rations for exorbitant rates, a pint-sized black-market racketeer if ever there was one, had stopped to whistle appreciatively at Marilyn as she passed him on her way to the girls' lavatories. She ignored him of course but she was shocked all the same.

Lilly was in a particularly fractious mood. She had allowed herself to be drawn ever deeper into a restless whirlwind of activity all day but had now taken Sarah's stern advice and had sat herself down in a concerted effort to steady both her nerves and her racing mind.

She was eagerly re-reading Harry's letter. In it, he was excited to tell her all about his brother-in-law, Richard who was his Best Man at their wedding. They had been the best of mates for years and they were inseparable. When Harry had been released from his management job to go into the Army, Richard could not wait to realise his own long-held ambition of joining the Royal Air Force, only to be thwarted by his colour-blindness. Now, however, determined to do his bit and encouraged by Harry, he had just been accepted into "intelligence". His duties were classified and his family knew never to ask about his wartime duties, or even about the contribution he was about to make to winning their victory.

Lilly took out a hand-drawn picture and studied it carefully before showing it to Marilyn. It was a portrait which Harry had drawn. Lilly had always admired his talent as an amateur artist, although he himself had never made anything of it. Harry would sit for hours with his pencils and a bit of old paper or cardboard and draw the most extraordinary images. Buildings that caught his eye, or film stars mostly. His talent lay in capturing the minutest detail and recreating it in a beautifully nuanced copy. And this precious picture in her hands now, this was little Marilyn. He'd taken her photograph on her birthday and kept it in his breast pocket. They all agreed that it was just marvellous.

'Are you a tight-knit family, Lilly?' June asked.

'Not really, no.' Lilly thought carefully before she went on. 'I'm not that close to Harry's sisters. They're alright, but I don't really see eye-to-eye with them. They don't seem to want to keep in touch. And his parents both died in '37, about a year after we were married. It's a shame that they never got to know Marilyn and won't see these two babies...'

Suddenly Lilly felt a sharp pain in her stomach.

'Ouch! Sorry. They're fighting in there again! A pair of footballers I'm having, I reckon,' she said. Sweat was breaking out across her forehead. Sarah looked at her closely.

'You ought to be more careful, luv. Maybe you've overdone things again today.'

'But it's been so hectic in the shop all day!' Lilly replied, brushing the hair from her forehead.

'The customers do get so very frustrated and angry at the clothing restrictions and having to do without. As if it's my fault! You know, one woman has been trying relentlessly over the past two weeks to buy an overcoat for less than the required sixteen coupons. She went and collapsed in a heap of apoplexy today when she couldn't have her own way! And then of course, suits can only be single-breasted to save on work and on cloth, as you know. This afternoon, I had to remind a very aggressive elderly man that he was only allowed to have a maximum of three buttonholes in the front of his suit and no buttons on the cuffs of his shirts. Then, when he angrily waved his walking stick in my face, well I stepped forward, calmly told him that I was only doing my duty and that was no way to speak to a lady.' June chuckled at the scene Lilly was describing.

'Why didn't you just tell him to leave the shop?'

'Well, I wanted to say, "kindly leave sir, or else I'll call a policeman", but my courage didn't stretch that far. Mrs Bennett would have my guts for garters – quite literally – if she caught me throwing a customer out the door!'

Deciding that she needed to cheer herself up, Lilly had popped into Woolworth's on the way home from the shop and after collecting Marilyn from school to pick up the new issue of Picturegoer magazine as a treat for them both to look through that evening. Its pages were filled with glamorous stars and their radiant smiles. Beautiful people, enchanting names, Katherine Hepburn, Ginger Rogers, Leslie Banks, Lionel Barrymore. They inhabited another world and Lilly thumbed each page with a kind of reverence and fascination. Lilly would read the articles out loud to Marilyn who delighted in listening to what seemed to her to be fairy tales from a mythical place called Hollywoodland where ladies wore striking gowns of impossible colours that she had never seen anywhere else before and where the men were dashing soldiers or brave cowboys. Lilly had brought with her from London the Daily Express Film book, her birthday present from Harry in 1935. There was not an article nor inset picture in that book that she could not recall from memory or recite by heart. It brought her comfort and escape. Its stiff faded gold covers also served as a flower press for her roses at the end of each summer. It was one of her prized possessions.

As always, they had been waiting ages in the queue at Woolworths. Everywhere was so crowded in town these days. Then Lilly had turned around and Marilyn was nowhere to be seen. Lilly asked the people in the queue behind her if they'd seen her. She had obviously wandered off. Lilly had started to panic. As she turned a corner at the back of the shop, there was Marilyn, holding a lady's hand who was about to make an announcement on the Tannoy. Lilly said, "Marilyn, where did you get to, young lady?" The woman told her that she had found her roaming around the toy shelves and was about to report her as lost.

'She'd only gone about ten feet away from me!' Lilly explained as she replayed that tense moment out loud. 'Honestly, I didn't know whether to laugh or cry!'

'That's priceless! Oh Marilyn.' Ethel laughed.

But Lilly didn't hear her. She winced again with an intense searing pain.

'You must excuse me please, I'm feeling a bit queasy. I might just turn in. I'm going to put my hair up in curlers and then try and get some sleep. It's been quite a day.'

June tried to help her up the stairs, but Lilly didn't want any fuss, not even to let her carry her glass of milk up for her. June followed her out the room anyway as Lilly and Marilyn said their laboured goodnights and left the room.

'Well, you sleep tight, the pair of you,' said Sarah. 'And Lilly, no more nightmares about poisoning your babies!' Ethel looked up.

'What was all that about her poisoning her babies?'

Sarah began to explain. Evidently, Lilly had been having recurring dreams about the twins. Last night she had woken up in a sweat because she had dreamt that Harry had given the twins surgical spirit instead of gripe water.

'They were in a right tizzy because they thought he'd

poisoned them.'

Ethel laughed.

'Well, the poor little'uns certainly would have had one hell of a hang-over in the morning!'

Suddenly, they heard Lilly scream from upstairs. It was a terrible, visceral scream. June burst into the front room in a panic.

'It's Lilly!' June could hardly get her words out. Sarah was on her feet in an instant.

'Has she had a fall?'

'No, no! She's having the babies, I think. Oh, Mrs C, do come quick, Lilly's in an awful bother. Her babies are coming, they're coming fast!'

Joe grabbed the phone to ring for Dr Churngold. Then he thought again and decided they had better get her straight to hospital.

CHAPTER 17.

'If carrots are so good for your eyes, then why do they hurt so much when you try and stick 'em in? Eh, Mrs C?'

Sarah forced a polite grin as she peeled the last of her meagre pile of potatoes and carrots in readiness for the evening meal. Her newest lodger had taken to following her around like a new-born lamb as she moved between the kitchen and dining room table. Finally, they sat down to join Joe and have a cuppa, a chance to get to know a little more about each other.

Victor Norman was a welcome addition to their household. The comedian from the South Wales valleys was originally supposed to be staying with them for the summer season. But due to the unexpectedly warm and prolonged autumn weather in Blackpool and the enormous crowds it had attracted, Victor had been asked to extend his run at the Hippodrome. He did not need asking twice! He was thrilled.

Sarah had been more than a little disappointed by his shabby appearance when she first opened her front door and saw him standing there on her step. As she ushered him inside, she inspected him closely, not hiding her scrutiny of the grime mark around his collar and his frayed cuffs. She also noticed his ill-fitting trousers and she found it difficult to put an age to him. he was clearly past his best. He was overweight and with his receding hairline and slight stoop he could have been anywhere between forty-five and sixty. She thought him rather cocky and too full of beans. He seemed to have literally got his feet under the table in no time at all, but Sarah was happy to put up with his lousy jokes at breakfast-time, his ceaseless chatter and niggling good humour. After all, she shared his excitement about the easy money that his work would be bringing in.

'Oh yes, you see Mrs Cockington, a Pro can't fail at Blackpool! Not these days. It's regular work. Good money too. And the whelk-and-belch crowd laugh at anyone - and anything - that moves, honest to God!'

'The whelk and what?'

'Belch, Mrs Cockington. You know, they're none too bothered about what they're watching. They just want good solid entertainment. Oh yes I can tell you, it's good to know I won't be starving for the rest of this year.'

Joe was reaching back into his memory to that evening a decade or so back when he and Sarah had walked the length of the South Pier to see old What's-His-Name, oh who was that comedian they used to go and see…?

'So many times, we'd get proper soaked getting to the theatre, d'you remember, Sarah? Oh aye, I thought we'd never get there. What with my bunions and your…ah, yes of course, it were old Harry Korris.' Joe chuckled in remembering. 'They call 'im the Falstaff of the South Pier on account of his being built more for comfort than speed. Ah yes, you remember Mother! Oh we do like 'im.'

Victor humoured his host but was quick to get the conversation back around to himself.

'Oh, there you are, yes,' he said in his broad Welsh accent. 'You can't beat the old-timers. Now, these seaside summer seasons, the decent board and lodgings we can afford and the sunshine, they bloody-well beat the cramped railway compartments, unreliable theatre managers and grimy old digs I put up with for the rest of the year, they do! Er, that's when I'm actually in work, mind.' He paused and looked down at the table. Victor was straying into territory into which he was not yet ready nor willing to delve in front of them.

'Anyway, as I always like to say, on a clear day on the pier, you can see the ocean. And on a windy one, you're in it, eh!' Victor laughed heartily and Joe laughed along with him.

'Oh yes, very good. You're not wrong there, lad! Well now, tell me, there must be a lot of camaraderie among you comedians playing all them theatres across town?'

Joe had hit the right chord there. Victor lived for his get-togethers with his fellow comedians for coffee most mornings to have a good gossip, usually at the Savoy or the Winter Gardens. There was always a lot of laughs.

'A big happy family, we are. You see, I don't have much family of my own. Not since my dad was killed at the start of the Great War and my mam and two young sisters were all carried off by the Flu in 1919. Very sad it was...' His steady voice faltered for a moment, but yes it was a fact, there was nowhere quite like Blackpool for Victor. It was a life which Joe was struggling hard to imagine.

'Is this all you've ever done in your life, Mr Norman? I mean to say, surely there's some other line of business or trade you'd have tried –'

'Please call me Victor. Vic, they call me around here, they do. Actually, it's a very good question, that is. Well, you see, my dad was the last in a long line of fiercely proud miners and he forbade me to do anything with my life except to follow him down the mine, you see. So, at the age of fifteen I upped and left home. When I got the job of 'Opposite prompt and Line Boy' for just thirty bob a week at the New Theatre in Cardiff, I was so thrilled that I'd made it into showbusiness and nothing could stop me! But then my dad found out where I was working and paid a bribe to the theatre manager to give me all the worst, most horrible jobs to try to discourage me and make me want to give it all up and come running back home with my tail between my legs. Of course, I did all them jobs without any complaint, didn't I!'

'So tell me then,' Joe asked, captivated by Victor's history. 'What's it like to be stood up there on the stage in front of all them hungry crowds, eh?'

'Well, that bit's alright. Nothing to fear there.' Victor scratched his head. 'But it's when the lights first go down, that's what I hate the most. I never have liked the dark. Not me. Since I was just a nipper, I've hated the dark, I have. Dread it every night. And when I'm alone on that stage, sometimes I think I'm going to pass out from trembling so much.'

Victor tried to laugh at himself.

'I'm such a great oaf! It's twp, stupid, you know? Dumb! But then, when the lights come up and my act begins with all the music and the applause, well that's a kind of magic to me, that is...'

Sarah broke his spell.

'Oh, you'll get along well with our young Marilyn then,' she said. 'That little lass is another one who dreads the dark, every night. She never seems to get to grips with it, does she Joe? Cries her eyes out, she does and that's a fact. It's miserable for her. It was them air raids in London when she were nowt but an infant. It must have had an effect on her...'

Victor seemed not to hear her.

'D'you know, I found a palm reader on the pier just the other day. She certainly got the measure of me, right enough...' Victor noticed how the Cockingtons had the same habit of raising their eyebrows in almost perfect symmetry.

'Well, yes I know what you're thinking, but it was raining when I found her and besides, the pubs weren't open yet so it was a blessing to get in out of the wet. Anyway, believe it or not, she could tell what was on my mind. She said she could see that I was affected by something that was...I dunno, bothering me I suppose. *"Something vast and very dark",* she said. She told me I must overcome whatever-it was while I was here in Blackpool.'

'What are you talking about, Victor?'

'You see, Mrs Cockington, she'd picked up on it straight away, she had. Honest to God. As soon as I'd told her I was a comedian. You know what she said to me? Not that I held much store by any of it when she said it of course, but still, she said to me, *"There's no point in dreading what you can't avoid. Best to stand up to it and not let it beat you."* That's what she said, I swear to you. So that's what I'll do. Only...'

'Only what?' asked Joe. He was not keeping up.

Victor had allowed the Cockingtons into his secret, carelessly and without intending to. He might as well tell them everything now. His mind had strayed back to last summer, just at that moment when he was about to begin his act on stage at the Glasgow Empire.

'I know my routine like the back of my hand, you see. I've done it a hundred times before. Only this one particular night, I got so windy when they turned down the lights, that I collapsed in tears. I swear I don't know what came over me. I felt like I was trapped in a dark tunnel and I couldn't breathe. It was horrible! The crowd was no help. They just started jeering at me. Never gave me a chance to recover myself. So, before they started throwing stuff at me - 'cos they often do that, you know, don't ask me why - I just ran for it. Got clean away, like a scalded cat on skates. Terrible it was! I could never go back there now. Not after that. And all because I hate the bloody dark. Honest to God, a man of my age.'

Joe was growing impatient.

'Well now, you never know, once this war's over, you might be topping the bill yet.'

'Oh, not me, Mr Cockington.' Victor was back in the present. 'No sir! Most acts dream of topping the bill, but years and years of hard grind have taught me to be a bit canny. Those headline acts, they have all the pressure to pull in the crowds. But the likes of me, little Victor Norman, further down the bill, well it's not up to me how many tickets get sold, or whether the show gets good reviews or bad. All I have to do is to stick to what I know. It's far safer that way, I reckon. D'you see?'

'Oh well, you'll not hit the big time with that attitude, now will you! I were hoping to sell your autograph when I need me old age pension. But only if you become rich and famous, like George Formby. We like 'im, don't we Joe?' Sarah got up from the table.

'Anyroad, it's all very interesting talking to you Victor, but you'll have to excuse me now while I get on with the tea, or else I'll have a house full of hungry boarders on me hands.'

Victor stood up too. He would have to rouse himself and get ready to face the crowds.

'Thanks for the cuppa – and for the chat.' He said carrying his cup and saucer to the sideboard. Joe gently blocked his path.

'Rather you than me,' he said to Victor and looked him in the eye. 'Do you know what I'm wondering, though? I'm wondering why a young fella in your position with no missus and no kids to worry about, why he's not in uniform. You know what I'm saying? Why is that, exactly? If I may ask you Victor?'

Sarah did not miss a beat.

'That's a bit rich coming from a lazy beggar like you, Joe Cockington! Anyroad, don't be so nosy. He must have his reasons. Don't you luv? Don't you have your reasons?'

Victor laughed, a full, hearty belly laugh. They couldn't tell, but the fact was, he was not so much the 'young fella' as they might think. At nearly fifty-four, he was beyond the call-up age.

He had managed to keep a low profile and had come through without a scratch so far. He must have led a charmed life. He hadn't wanted to spoil his run of luck, so he had tried to get into ENSA to entertain the troops. He could just see himself out there in North Africa or in the Mediterranean in front of all those soldiers. Just like Tommy Trinder! No darkness to suffocate him there, just thousands of smiling faces, appreciating what he was doing for them.

But it hadn't happened that way. He got lumbered doing a stint as a Bevin Boy down the mines instead in 1939. Down there in that dark hell hole! It was without doubt the worst experience of his life. He had only to close his eyes and he could still feel the way his flesh would creep that first time he went underground, still feel the sudden seventy feet per second plummet all the way down. That's what the regular miners had called the "initiation drop".

'Oh don't you worry, Mr C, I've done my bit alright. I was conscripted to work down in the mines, would you believe. Luck of the draw it was. No wriggling out of it. And the irony was not lost on me. Oh, how my dad would have laughed at the poetic justice! I couldn't believe it when I registered for my National Service and the fella said to me "Bad luck son, you've been balloted to go down the mines, you have". I told him, "You're kidding me. I'm not going down there!" I did try to object, you see. I really didn't want to be sent down them mines. But hardly anyone had their appeals allowed and of course, they threatened us all with prison if we continued to refuse to obey the Directive.'

'Anyway, then the training started and so there I was, see, all kitted up and ready to go. They got us into them cages to take us down, all packed in there we were. They told us to bend our knees, said it would hurt less. Then I remember the regular miners yelled out "Alright, let 'em go!" And they just let us drop to the bottom. All nine hundred and eighty-five yards down. It made my nose bleed and I thought my ear drums were going to burst. But just a joke it was, on the part of the regular miners. Some joke! Honest to God.'

He was on a roll, thought Joe. A more comprehensive answer to his question, he could not have asked for.

'Alright,' he said to Victor. But at least you didn't have to go around in uniform all the time, eh? You had that freedom at least-'

'No, Mr C, you don't understand. Let me tell you, that was the trickiest part of all, it was, you see, because being of military age and in civilian clothes, we were often challenged by the public who reckoned we were conscientious objectors or draft dodgers, or even worse, I was sometimes stopped by the Police who suspected me of being an enemy agent. And there was resentment too because those mining communities are very close knit of course and the locals hated us for taking their men's jobs who were away in the forces. They told us to clear off and go home. It was no picnic being a Bevin Boy, let me tell you! Not a happy set up at all. But still, my dread of those dark airless spaces where I was working only fuelled my dreams further and I lived for the day when I'd be free to pick up my theatrical career where it had so abruptly left off.'

Oh yes, Victor felt that he had had done his bit, alright. But could the Cockingtons ever truly understand, he wondered, these two strangers, veterans of another war?

Joe considered what he'd told them for a moment as he puffed gently on his pipe.

'It would have been far better surely if the regular miners as you call them were told to stay put and carry on mining as a reserved occupation and let the other lads like you go off and do the fighting.'

'The Government always get things muddled up,' said Sarah.

'The fact is,' Victor explained, 'I'm too old to be of any use to them anymore. So, I've chosen to entertain the troops here at home, as you might say.' Joe's eyes twinkled.

'The whelk and belch brigade?'

'There you are, exactly sir!' Victor laughed.

'Well, of course, there's always the Home Guard, you know. Three evenings a week and Sunday afternoons. I could introduce you to the-'

'Ah no, no, I don't think that would work, see I'm on stage every evening and then there's the Matinee on Sundays-'

The phone rang. Joe went to pick it up.

'Saved by the bell, eh!' he grunted to Victor, thinking that this conversation was not over yet.

'Hello, Sunny View Guest House... oh hello Lilly luv! How are you going on...? Eh?' Joe gasped and his hand shot up to his forehead.

'Oh Lilly, oh no, no! I'm so sorry luv... No, no you won't get a taxi home. You just sit tight and I'll be up to the hospital directly. Oh, what an awful shock for you. I'm so sorry.' He slowly replaced the receiver.

'What is it Joe?' Sarah asked.

'It's our poor Lilly. I'm afraid she's lost them twins of hers. They were stillborn... I'm just going to go pick her up and fetch her back. Be kind to her when she gets home, Sarah. She's had a terrible time of it.'

'The poor luv. You'll have to excuse us, Victor. That's our boarder from London, Lilly Stevens. Oh, the poor mite. She were so looking forward to having them twins home. She'd set her heart on having some company for little Marilyn. What a shock! Oh where's me smelling salts! I must get me smelling salts, Joe!'

It was early in the morning nearly a fortnight after Lilly had come home from the hospital and the curtains in the dining room were still closed. At the breakfast table, everyone was watching their step around Lilly who was still very fragile, both physically and emotionally. Joe had an idea and turned to Victor hoping to lift the mood.

'Well, I am glad we got to see your show at last, Victor, my lad. You'll be packing up to leave next week, won't you?'

Sarah caught on.

'Oh, and we did laugh,' she said. 'You were ever so funny, Victor. Wasn't he Joe? Bless your heart. I were right proud of you!'

'Oh thank you Mrs C. Very kind you are. Diolch yn fawr i chi, as we say in South Wales...'

Sarah had wasted no time in telling everyone sitting in her row in the theatre stalls that she was Victor Norman's landlady. Talk about shining in the reflected glory! For Lilly's sake, she went on,

'And that stupid woman with the laugh sitting behind us, you remember, Joe. The one who laughed like she were laying an egg!'

'Aye, and it sounded like a square egg at that!' Joe laughed weakly.

'A square egg! Honestly. Here luv, let me pour...' Sarah gently took the tea pot out of Lilly's unsteady hands. Unwisely, as it turned out.

'No I can manage, really I can. Please don't fuss around me!' Lilly hissed at her.

'Of course. Just as you wish, luv.'

'I'm sorry, I didn't mean to snap at you like that, Sarah.' Lilly said as she got up from the table and took her plate and cup into the kitchen. Then they heard crockery crashing to the floor. Sarah knew that these were her last and the chances of finding replacements in the shops was practically zero. Much of her crockery, handed down to her by her mother and aunt, was chipped and dented but they all pretended not to notice in their stoic response to the shortages.

'What the -'

'Leave it. I'll see to it, Sarah.' Joe rushed into the kitchen and brought Lilly out with his arms arounds her, comforting her as she wept.

'I'm so sorry, I don't know what came over me...it's my nerves.'

'Well, you just come and sit down.' Sarah guided her towards the settee, but Lilly stood stock still at the head of the table. She didn't even notice Marilyn staring at her, or the turmoil of tears trickling silently down the child's own cheeks. Had any of them stopped to find out how Marilyn was coping with this tragedy or with the sight of her mother so distraught? Had any of them taken the time to explain to the little girl why her baby siblings had not come home? She was still waiting to see them, to play with them.

She had waited up all night and even sat by the bedroom window looking down the street in case they turned up in a taxicab, her mother being too weak to carry them home in her arms. She couldn't understand why the grown-ups were all so sad. She wished that she could have her daddy close by to explain it to her and make it all come clear. But he hadn't come home to her either.

All any of them wanted to do in that house was to help Lilly, to comfort her and restore her strength.

'Lilly, you've been through so much,' said Ethel, feeling her pain and almost in tears herself, so much affection she had for Lilly. 'And we've not been able to help you like we'd want to do. I can't even begin to imagine what it's been like for you since that night last week when... when the babies -'

Sarah chided her.

'Shh now Ethel. Lilly doesn't want to be reminded of it.'

But Sarah was wrong. Lilly very much wanted and needed to talk about it.

'Well, you know when my waters broke so violently, I thought I'd given birth there and then. Of course I hadn't, obviously. You know, later in the hospital ward, they didn't make me register the birth, luckily. That would have been so horrible. I just can't imagine having to register a birth and a death at the same time...They took my babies away from me. They said they would take care of everything. You know they don't make room for stillborn babies in the cemetery. So, they put them in with an adult corpse. Any dead body would do. A stranger's coffin. That's where they put them. They never told me who it was...' Lilly looked down at her handkerchief. She had twisted it around her fingers so tightly that it was starting to fray. Her fingers had turned white. 'And that was that. They told me to go home and rest quietly. I never met my babies, never got to hold them in my arms, never got to tell them how precious they were. But they were mine and I miss them! I failed them, I know I did. I feel so ashamed. I failed my babies. What did I do to make this happen? You know, I never used to believe in a broken heart before now, but...' She looked up, imploring them. 'Am I over-reacting, do you think? Am I?'

They were stunned. This raw emotional display was totally beyond their comprehension and nothing like Lilly's usual cool reserve. It was June who reached out to her.

'Oh Lilly luv, come and sit down, please. Put your feet up. You'll feel so much better.'

'I don't want to *feel* better!' Lilly shrieked. 'I don't want to feel *anything*.' She wanted so badly to feel only a numbness. A nothingness. 'I'm fine, really I am. There's nothing more to say. If you'll just excuse me now, I need to get on.'

Lilly hurried out of the room and up the stairs. The others looked at each other, bewildered. There was a heavy pause which none of them knew how to break.

'Well, I reckon we could do with some of your jokes right now, Victor Norman, awful though they may be. Just to give us summ'at to laugh at.' Before Victor could respond to that, Ethel came up with an idea.

'Perhaps we could take Lilly out to see your show one night before you leave, if she's feeling up to it, of course. What do you say, June?'

Joe thought that was a grand idea and urged them to make a plan as he set about clearing away the breakfast things. Ethel busied herself too.

'I think I'll just go up and look in on Lilly,' she said and turned to Victor. 'Just to make sure she's...well you know. Will you watch the little'n for us, please Victor?'

Victor was horrified at the prospect of having to watch over the little girl. Making kiddies laugh was certainly not within his repertoire. But this little girl was different. He knew that she had something special about her.

They had already found a bond between them, based perhaps on their shared dread of the dark. If he could help her in any way, of course he would. Victor and Marilyn were sitting opposite each other at the table. Such a contrasting pair they made too. Victor the world-weary comedian stuck in his rut of mediocrity and disappointment, but to whom they had all turned that morning to cheer them up with his unfailing humour and cheeriness. Marilyn, a little girl lost in a mire of confusion and sorrow. She was shy with him, hardly having said two words to him since he had arrived in that house. She certainly was not engaging with him now. Pointing to her teddy bear, Victor asked,

'Is that your friend? Handsome chap, isn't he? What's his name?' Marilyn said nothing but just looked down at her lap. Victor felt the need to persevere.

'Mm? Well, let's call him Freddy. Freddy the Teddy, what do you think, eh? You know why little Freddy isn't saying anything? Well, it's because the curtains are still closed, isn't it? Why don't you go and open them, bach!'

As Marilyn did so, she left the teddy on the table. Victor set it in position so that the early morning sunlight streamed through and shone on it as a kind of spotlight. Victor brought the teddy bear to life. He started performing with the bear as a ventriloquist and dummy. Marilyn was unsure at first, but she soon started to giggle and enjoy the 'show'. Victor put the teddy to his ear and pretended to listen intently. This wasn't so bad after all, he thought.

'What do you mean you want to do a little dance for Marilyn? Oh well, yes, go right ahead. Be my guest.' Victor switched on the wireless, luckily just as a happy song-and-dance number was in full swing. He moved over into the living room and began performing a little dance routine with Teddy on the back of the sofa. Marilyn followed him and sat down on the sofa to catch a closer look.

'Teddy looks forward to the sun coming up every morning because he knows that when the curtains open and the light shines in, it's time to play. You see, he knows that the dark is only the short time between happy playtimes. And when he remembers this, he's not afraid of the dark anymore!'

Victor carried on with the song and dance routine while Marilyn fell about in a fit of giggles.

'You're a funny man!' she cried as she rolled over onto her

front and buried her face in a tatty pink cushion.

'Perhaps I am. Thank Christ for small mercies!' Victor applauded himself.

CHAPTER 18.

Another new routine quickly established itself for Lilly and Marilyn. In that hurried fashion that only a wartime expediency can necessitate, people were wistfully putting their past lives and habits on hold with a quiet though reluctant understanding that life was transformed forever, hurtling blindly towards an uncertain future.

Mrs Bennet took Lilly back on with a surprising and uncharacteristic eagerness. Lilly had only half-expected to get her old job back now that she was not to be a nursing mother with new babies to care for.

'Why, of course you must have your position back, Lilly Stevens, my poor dear!' She swooned. Lilly was surprised by her expression. Her usual rock-like countenance, complete with its fissures and crannies, now took on a softer blend of pragmatism, tinged with sympathy and relief.

'I can't tell you how sorry I was to hear your sad news. I am sorry for your loss. Here, come in and sit yourself down luv, do please.'

Lilly was glad of the seat. Her legs had been trembling with fear of rejection or some other, vaguer kind of dread.

'I would offer you a cup of tea, only that Ackroyd lad hasn't been round for the last two mornings so we've no milk.'

'Oh, I'm sorry to hear that. Is he alright?' Lilly asked tentatively.

'Well, how should I know? I never asked. Evidently sommat to do with his chest. As soon as we get a bit of Autumnal fog, you never see hide nor hair of the lad. He's not the most reliable character, now is he!'

'Oh, but he has the most appalling asthma...' Lilly's voice trailed off into her own thoughts. She must call on the Ackroyds soon. They had had their own share of misery while she had been absorbed with hers.

'I won't beat about the bush, Lilly,' Mrs Bennett's shrill

voice brought Lilly's attention back to the matter in hand.

'That young Molly Chambers who I took on to replace you, well, let me tell you, she's next to useless, really! Late most mornings, rude to my customers. Well, I was on the brink of giving her notice. I thought that she might have sommat about her, having done a stint at that big factory, but no, she's turned out to be a bit of a disappointment, I have to say. But your stepping into the shop today, well, it must be some sort of a miracle, if you believe in such things. So then, luv, when can you start?'

The swiftness of her decision took the wind out of Lilly's sails. She hadn't been expecting this lucky outcome, so she was completely unprepared to talk details.

'Well, I can start next Monday.' she said without thinking. 'How would that suit you, Mrs Bennett?'

And so, it was all arranged. Out went the poor witless Molly, thankfully a couple of days before Lilly started back in the shop. No embarrassing resentful glances needed to be exchanged. Lilly simply took up again the button-hole-making life that she had so readily given up six weeks before her babies were due. She had dreamed then of a new life of domestic bustle, but here she was again, a small but full circle. With a deep sigh, Lilly put on her apron and settled back into her tasks, hoping that the recent surge in demand for new clothes as folk were now daring to anticipate the tide of the war turning in their direction, would mean that her working hours would fly by.

November 19th 1943.

My darling Lilly

How are you and Marilyn? I hope you are getting stronger by the day and how I wish I could be there by your side to aid your recovery, my dearest one.

All's well here. I am sitting perched on the edge of my bed barely able to contain my excitement. I have a plan for when this dreadful war is over and I will return home to you both. I want to share this with you now and I hope you will love it as I do!

As soon as ever I get back home to Blighty, I want to set up my own business using my design skills and artistic flair that you are always reminding me about. I want to make beautiful gowns and I reckon there will be a good market for these before too long. Ladies won't be happy to put up with make do and mend or clothing restrictions for ever and you tell me that patience is wearing thin already (excuse the pun.) Simple as that.

I think if we sell our house in Edmonton and move back to the East End or what's left of it after Jerry's had his field day, we'll have a little bit of profit which I shall invest into getting us going. On top of that, I will apply for a loan from the bank. We can source the material for a good price and sell our gowns overseas. I hear that Sweden and Denmark etc will be good markets and that's just for openers. We will have fun trying our luck. It will be jolly hard work of course, but if you will have faith in me to make a good go of things, I will promise you that I will give it everything I have. I will work hard at it and of course, we will need to be adaptable and self-disciplined but I promise you I won't let us starve!

I will also need to take on some staff eventually if things do take off. Maybe a couple of seamstresses and a cutter, but most of the business, I can take care of myself.

Oh my darling, I have often been wondering about what Civvy street will look like for me and here is an opportunity which I can believe in and I should grasp it with both hands. Do let me know your thoughts on this please. Can you picture yourself as the wife of an accomplished businessman, surrounded by the spoils of our success? Dripping in jewellery, wrapped in beautiful fur coats and seated in a big flashy car!

Oh well, back to reality for now. I will have to get on with my boot blacking, but my dreams are vivid and full of possibilities for our bright future all together.

Please kiss my beloved daughter for me. It breaks my heart to think that I will be missing yet another of Marilyn's precious birthdays tomorrow, but I will be there in spirit and wishing her many, many happy returns.

As always, your ever-loving Harry.

One cloudless afternoon as Christmas beckoned, Marilyn was off school. She and her classmates were now crammed into large classes comprising children from all over the country as evacuees, refugees and the children of civil servants uprooted from their homes sat knee to knee with local children. Desks, stationery and books were in short supply. Older teachers had been brought out of retirement to support the over-stretched staff and help with the pressure of increased class sizes. To Marilyn, her teacher Mr Hamilton seemed ancient and decrepit. He always had spittle gathering in the corners of his mouth and he would leer unblinking at her as if he were searching desperately for some excuse to chastise her. On this particular day, Mr Hamilton had suddenly been taken ill in front of the class.

Just before collapsing, he had been led away by the school nurse who had been summoned by an enterprising young boy with the presence of mind to call her.

This incident added yet another pressure to the hectic management of the school day and no-one in charge stopped to acknowledge the potential shock or distress it might have caused the children, except that the class was then dismissed mysteriously for the rest of the day.

Marilyn decided not to go home. She preferred to see if Lilly would let her stay with her and watch her at her work. She had run all the way to the shop and Lilly hadn't the heart to turn her away, just as long as she would sit quietly and behave herself. She asked Mrs Bennett if it would be alright and the old lady agreed, knowing that it would be a small price to pay if it meant keeping Lilly from leaving early. Now Marilyn had put the curious incident at school to the back of her mind as she swung her legs on a high stool watching Mrs Bennett's customers come and go.

She had long finished her glass of rosehip syrup, a treat that Mrs Bennett kept in especially for the little children who visited her shop. There's lots of vitamins and goodness in that glass! She would always say as she handed over the tiny whiskey tot of the sweet sickly pink liquid to the eager child.

Marilyn wondered whether it was in fact one of the

old lady's thimbles that she was drinking from, but she knew better than to grumble. It was exciting to have a glimpse into this other world that belonged to her mother and she was impressed by the bustling busyness and all the accoutrements of Mrs Bennett's shop. She had listened carefully to all the stories and weary anecdotes that Lilly would bring home and share at tea-time. Now Marilyn was actually there. It was all so exhilarating.

'Let's have a cuppa, eh Lilly? How about you Marilyn?' Mrs Bennett was speaking to her as an adult and she was flattered.

'There's no milk again of course. Lilly, would you be a pet and pop over the road and fetch us some? Take a thruppenny bit out of the till and here's me ration book. Ta, ever so, luv.'

'Will you watch Marilyn for me then, please?' Lilly was glad to have an excuse to get out of the stuffy little shop and get some refreshing air on her face. She cupped Marilyn's little face in her hands.

'Be a good girl. Mummy won't be long.' Marilyn felt the warmth of Lilly's fingertips and looked straight into her mother's beautiful blue eyes. She nodded. She was happy in the company of Mrs Bennett and she squeezed her teddy for extra reassurance. She carried him everywhere and even hid him in her school bag so that he was never far away from her. This was Freddy the Teddy as Victor Norman had insisted on calling him, but Marilyn was too shy and polite to put him right. Actually, the teddy's real name was Nanook. Her daddy had bought him for her in Blackpool when he came to stay with them on leave that last time. The bear was covered in soft shiny grey fur and made a comforting cooing sound when rolled back and forth. Harry had christened her teddy bear Nanook of the North as he thought that was fitting, given that the bear came from Lancashire, which always seemed like the frozen North to a Londoner. The subtlety of this reference was totally lost on Marilyn until she was much older and able to understand her father's offbeat humour, by which time she had passed the threadbare, voiceless Nanook on to her own daughter.

A moment after Lilly had disappeared out of the door,

an unfamiliar young woman crept gingerly into the shop. Marilyn noticed how Mrs Bennett seemed to bristle and smile simultaneously as soon as the tense young woman stepped up to the counter, impervious to the presence of a young child sitting there.

It was Molly, her erstwhile assistant. She was a scrawny, tatty girl of about eighteen and with deep-set eyes and cracked lips. Molly had not been inside the shop since Lilly had replaced her some weeks back.

'Hello, Molly, luv. How are you? How are you going on now?'

'Oh, so you've heard then, have you Auntie Charlotte? I wondered how soon it would all get spread about.'

'No, no, I only know that you had some bother the other evening. I don't know exactly what went on. You've been unlucky, so your mam has told me.'

Marilyn understood nothing of this conversation and thought perhaps the two women were deliberately speaking in riddles in that frustrating way that grown-ups had when they were trying to protect her young sensibilities. On this occasion, she did not have to wait too long to fathom out what exactly had befallen Molly, the odd young lady standing awkwardly across the counter from her.

'Hah, oh ay you could call it unlucky. I dunno, maybe it could all have been avoided. But I were so tired, you know?' sighed Molly Craddock. 'Otherwise, I never would have done it, like. I mean, I had just finished an eleven-hour shift, for goodness' sake! I'd been sitting there in Reception for three quarters of an hour, waiting for me driver to take me home.'

'Yes, I'm sure you were tired.' Doubts began to creep into Mrs Bennett's mind. She had known Molly since her birth. She was family. It was her opinion that her youngest sister had married way beneath her twenty years earlier and was now supporting a layabout husband, a slacker who hadn't even been called up and four young daughters, none of whom could settle to anything much.

This fact Mrs Bennett had always been determined to conceal as she was embarrassed and offended by these relations of hers. She looked down on them as nothing better than lower class riff raff. Not a single book in the house, she would lament. No education and certainly no desire to make anything of themselves. Bad news they were, she often thought so. Couldn't trust any one of them. Was Molly the best of bad bunch?

But still, she wanted to hear what the girl had to say for herself. Might be amusing. Molly leaned on her threadbare elbows letting the polished counter in front of Mrs Bennett take her weight and the old woman was vexed by the black dirt under the girl's fingernails.

'I fell into conversation with the security guard at the front desk, you see,' she began.

'Listening to him rabbit on about bream fishing in Chorley before the war. He'd even shown me his holiday snaps from Morecombe int' summer of '39 and I'd feigned an avid interest. But you know, I'm glad I had done that, Auntie Charlotte because he remembered me later, when I rang him up to tell him what had happened. When I wanted to warn him, in case there might be others that night. And when I needed him to recall a face. He were ever so kind to me, he were.'

Even though she had wanted to help the girl, to try to give her a helping hand by offering her a job in her shop even though she had known it would be a disaster, Mrs Bennett cringed each time Molly called her Auntie Charlotte. It made little difference to her that Marilyn was avidly listening.

Without warning, the young woman broke down in a mess of tears and anger. Marilyn looked squarely at Mrs Bennett wondering what was going on, but the old lady simply stepped forward and put her hand tentatively upon the Molly's shoulders.

'There, there now shhh. It's a shame. But it could have happened to any young girl in your position, you know that.'

Having been so unceremoniously dismissed from Mrs Bennett's employ once Lilly returned to the shop, Molly Craddock had soon found work again as a machinist at Squires Gate, a large Government-owned factory built during the war for production of the mighty Wellington bomber and at its peak it was turning out some one hundred bombers each month for RAF service. Its role was invaluable in helping to turn the tide of the war and secure victory for the Allies. As many as ten thousand men and women were employed there.

The factory was a national asset and played a very considerable part in providing full employment for the people of Blackpool and the surrounding area.

'I don't know, I'm sure! You young women working around the clock, finishing your shifts at all hours of the day and night. It's not right!' said Mrs Bennett. 'It's not right making women walk about in the blackout. These factories must realise that they're becoming easy targets for devious criminals and drifters, don't they?'

This war had given rise to reported crime in England by almost sixty per cent. Joe had noticed with increasing alarm just how frequently the newspaper headlines were proclaiming murder, rape, robbery and burglary all of which were flourishing in the dark and the chaos of the blackouts. People were hurrying about their business in a state of relative panic. Even in Blackpool, where such a thing was unheard of before the war, women young and old would now walk about looking over their shoulder.

Molly had decided not to walk home from the factory by herself that particular dark foggy night. *Only a fool would risk a mugging or worse on such a night as this,* she thought to herself. She had asked the factory security guard on the door to telephone for a taxicab. She felt much happier waiting with him in his warm, smoky little office.

Molly regained her composure, moved away from Mrs Bennett's well-meaning grasp and went on with her story.

When the taxicab driver had eventually appeared, wandering in from the cold December night through the revolving doors, he stood there in front of her in his dirty jacket – that's what she could recall most vividly, his jacket. No uniform like the others always wore. And no ID number on him either. Just an arrogant, brassed-off expression on his face.

'Looking up at him from where I sat, I knew instantly, of course I knew, that I shouldn't move from the spot, but then it was getting late and I was so tired.' She allowed herself a hearty blow of her nose into a ragged handkerchief. 'He told me that he'd only joined the taxi firm last week and they hadn't got around to giving him his ID badge and all that. He offered to show me his driving licence. Well, I'd never seen one of them before, so I didn't really know what I was looking at when he thrust this grubby bit of paper in me face!'

'Alright then,' said Mrs Bennett. 'So, you followed him outside, did you? And then what happened?'

'Yes. It didn't seem to matter to him whether I followed him or not.'

Mrs Bennett stopped her.

'Was it even a proper taxicab?'

'No, no, it were just an ordinary car. Don't ask me what make. But it weren't any kind of taxicab, no.'

Molly was reliving every detail there in that little shop. Marilyn wondered how long her mother would be with the milk. This story seemed to be taking on epic proportions. Would there be a moral or lesson at the end of it perhaps? She wondered. Molly continued to draw them both into an intriguing account of what had apparently happened next.

Outside on the busy road that night, the cold air had cut through her. She would be so glad to get home. Molly had got into his car and he had climbed in to the driver's seat saying nothing, ignoring her. He had slammed his door looking straight ahead of him as he asked her where it was they were going.

'Lowther Gardens, please,' she had told him. 'It's in Lytham, just beyond Fairhaven Lake. Can I suggest that you –'

But then he had turned round to her and all of a sudden, had become really angry.

'You don't bloody suggest anything, luv! I'm driving, not you, see? You don't start telling me how to do my job. You just sit there and shut up! Got it?'

Molly was totally stunned and winded by his outburst.

'I beg your pardon? she said. 'I wasn't meaning to tell you-'

He bellowed at her again.

'Just shut up!' he shouted. Molly could hear the revving of the engine as the car began to pull out into traffic. Her heart was thumping. But he'd only just begun.

'You have it easy, don't you. With your simple job at the factory. You've no idea what it's like for me. Not a flamin' clue. No job, no cash and stuff to get for the kids...This close to Christmas, there's not much hope of getting work either, just a lousy bloody cabbie job for a mate...what a way to make ends meet for an army reject.'

'I'm very sorry to hear that.' Molly had felt like a tiny, scalded child, but she was also indignant. 'But what's it got to do with me?'

'What the hell would you know about it?' the driver went on. 'I don't want to hear a flamin' word out of you. Got it?' He had lit a cigarette.

'You won't mind if I smoke?' His laugh was vicious. 'Of course you won't,' he said.

'Look, why in hell are you doing this? What is your problem?' Molly cried at him, but the driver had just laughed at her again.

'My problem? My problem?' was all he had said.

At this point, Molly had not known what she should be thinking or feeling or saying. She had just sat there on the back seat of his car and waited. She could hardly find her voice, but then she had begun to panic as she looked out the window.

'Where are we going? You're taking all the wrong roads! Listen to me!'

But the driver was having his fun. Surely Mrs Bennett could understand how it was.

'Not listening, luv,' the driver was still laughing at Molly in his rear-view mirror.

'Stop the car! Stop the car!' Molly had screamed, knowing how unwise this was.

'What did I tell you just now. Shut up!' The driver was obdurate, even though Molly was screaming at him.

'You need to let me out here. Now! You hear me! Now! You pig! What's the matter with you? What are you trying to do?'

'I'm not gonna let you out here, luv. We're nowhere near where you live, are we?'

'I'll walk the rest of the way from here. Thank you. Just

stop here and let me out of the car.'

The driver said nothing.

'Don't ignore me. Let me out of the car!' But there was no reasoning with him. He was totally mad, in all senses of the word, Molly had reckoned.

She had realised that all the streets were deserted. No-one to see her banging on the car window. Then he turned into a side street and she could hear the tyres screeching as his car took the corner. He slowed down. Molly had had no idea in that blackout where on earth they were.

Then she saw them in the dim moonlight. A row of scruffy, tumble-down garages. Her blood had run cold. She wanted Mrs Bennett to imagine it. Molly had thought, Oh my god! This is it. Of course, he's going to attack me now. Or kill me…

She was powerless. Utterly without any control of the situation. It was the oddest feeling, that. To be completely at the mercy of a total stranger. She had felt her heart pounding, almost choking her. Her sweaty hands were gripping the seat. A cold veil of panic had closed in around her as she had sat there. Molly's breathing had quickened and she had felt her throat go as dry as the desert.

Fight or flight - although neither option was available to her at that moment, only inertia. She had wanted to cry, but no tears came.

She had started to think *why me?* But then she had thought, *why not me?* This could be anyone, couldn't it? Molly saw the driver looking at her in his rear-view mirror. He said nothing.

'Foolish, when you think of it. Foolish to get into his car in the first place.' Marilyn now saw Molly's eyes fill up with tears again.

'But then look, who of us ever ambles through life without ever doing at least one foolish thing, eh?' cooed Mrs Bennett. She knew she was right.

'Oh yes,' said Molly. 'Just one foolish act and your whole life can change forever…' She went back to her story.

Suddenly she had realised that they had turned into her street. She could see her block of flats. How they had got there, she had had no idea. He had stopped the car. He had decided he'd had enough fun with her, she supposed. The car had pulled up and stopped.

'I hope you don't expect me to pay you for that!' Molly had blurted out at him. It was daft, she knew, but then as she had got out of the car and had slammed the door, Molly was aware of the driver saying something in retort, as she had dashed across the road to her front door.

Then suddenly his car had revved and was mounting the kerb at speed behind her. As soon as she had realised what was happening, Molly dived into a hedge.

'What the hell!' She had screamed, but she got swiftly to her feet in time to see his car speeding off away from her in a great cloud of smoke and dust. Molly could not believe it. What was he doing? He was driving down the wrong side of the road!

'Oh my god,' she thought. 'Who is he going to pick up next?'

When she had tumbled through the front door of her flat, she had rushed down the hall in a state of distress. She slammed the walls, trying to catch her breath. Then she went back down to the communal telephone by the front door to call the factory front desk where she had been sitting just a couple of hours before. Yes, the same security guard was still there. He remembered her and he recalled the man who had picked her up.

'Why, has summat happened, to thee, lov?'

He had no idea! And then, as she was trying to explain to him what had happened, Molly just had to let the tears come. She couldn't help herself. It was a blessed relief.

'So you've been down to tell the Police, I take it? Didn't they want you to press charges? You did go to the Police?'

'No, what's the point Auntie Charlotte, eh? It would probably never come to court. I mean, he didn't harm me, not physically. And I reckon as it would be my word against his. Besides, he knows where I live.'

The security guard at the factory had complained on Molly's behalf to the cab company but apparently, they had told him that the driver, whoever he was, had said that he'd only wanted to "give her a fright". Like the whole thing had been some sort of a game for him. A bit of a laugh, she supposed.

'I'm sorry, I didn't mean to tell you all this, not with the little girl sat there, ever so quiet, like. You're the first person I've mentioned it to, Auntie Charlotte. Can you believe it? I've not uttered a word about this to anyone else.'

'Why ever not?'

'I dunno. I've just felt so… oh, I don't know,' she sighed. 'But I can tell you this though, I'll not ever use a taxicab on my own at night. Not ever again. Just not worth taking the risk, is it? I mean, was it worth taking the risk that night? Perhaps that's the point. That was the daftest thing of all. Wasn't it, eh?'

And then she said something which made Marilyn sit up and take notice, something which shaped her nightmares that night.

'The thing is, Auntie Charlotte, it seems to me that there's no fear like when it's dark and you've no control over your own fate, is there?'

And with that, Molly swept out of the door just as Lilly was returning with the milk. It seemed to Marilyn that her mother had been gone for ages. Perhaps it had been ages. Time was often distorted as new ideas, images and possibilities crowded together inside her young mind.

'Who was that?' Lilly asked breathlessly.

'Oh, that was young Molly. You've never met that lass have you! She's fetched up at yon Squires Gate factory now,' said Mrs Bennett. 'And she got herself in some real bother t'other evening, or so she says. But, you know, nothing in that story of hers rings true to me. I wouldn't be at all surprised if she's made the whole thing up!'

'But why would she do that? Why would she waste your time in telling a whole pack of lies?'

'Oh, because that lass is lonely. It's attention-seeking, that's all. I feel sorry for her actually. She's what you might call delusional. Aye, that's the word for girls like her. De-lusion-al.' Mrs Bennet let the word creep around her tongue like thick cream.

'She always has been an attention-seeker that one, you know. She makes up stories to get attention. But I can see right through her.

I mean, how can a girl like that afford a taxicab these days, I should like to know! And honestly, as if sommat like that would happen here in this town.' Lilly frowned. Had Mrs Bennett forgotten that she'd been out of the shop during this whole taxi story? And Lilly was too busy to stand there listening to her recounting it all to her.

'She let the girl call her Auntie! So, was that her niece, then?' whispered Marilyn in Lilly's ear.

'Too far-fetched,' Mrs Bennett was still wittering on. 'Didn't make much sense to me. Never heard such an unlikely melodrama in all my life! And that wretched girl didn't even stop to buy anything! I do wonder why on earth she should want *me* to know.'

Actually, Mrs Bennett knew why. Molly couldn't tell her own parents what had happened in that taxicab for fear of her father's reaction and the ensuing brutality. She dreaded him more than the taxi driver.

'Perhaps she knew you'd understand. She obviously felt she could trust you.' Lilly suggested.

'To hell with that family!' muttered Mrs Bennett as she launched off to the back of the shop.

CHAPTER 19

Christmas was around the corner at last. A very modest Christmas tree stood forlornly in the living room corner, emitting only the slightest expression of yuletide cheer. Sarah was sitting alone on the sofa clutching a letter in her hand when Lilly and Marilyn burst in carrying their meagre groceries. Marilyn was grinning from ear to ear and could hardly contain her excitement at the prospect of having the two-ounce ration of sweets raised to three ounces in time for the holidays. Such simple pleasures were the minimum prerogative of every wartime child.

'Hello Sarah. Look at us, we're a right pair of busy bees today. We've been all over town looking for a new hat for madam here, but could we find anything she liked? And when we finally found one that I thought would suit her just fine, they didn't have any more of her size in stock. Goodness knows, there's so little choice of anything anymore, isn't there? I might as well have a go and make something myself.'

Lilly finally noticed that Sarah was sitting there in a daze. She realised with a shock that she had been crying.

'Are you alright? You don't look too good. What is it, Sarah? You look like you've just seen a ghost.' Lilly gently sat down next to her. 'Marilyn, why don't you take off your coat and go into the kitchen and fetch yourself a glass of milk, there's an angel.' Then she turned to Sarah.

'What is it?'

Sarah handed Lilly the letter which she had been clasping tightly.

'Here luv, you have a read of this,' Sarah said without looking up. 'I found it at the back of his wardrobe this morning. It were sticking out under some old shoe boxes. Lord only knows how long it's been there...I don't know why he never showed it me before. I never had any idea.'

'Joe you mean?'

'Aye, of course. It seems he were a war hero. In't last war.

A proper war hero. My Joe...go on, read it. Read what it says there.' Lilly took the letter and started to read.

Bolton, Lancs.
December 19th 1921.

Dear Mr Cockington,
It is with much sorrow that I write to tell you that my beloved husband, William Moran has passed away peacefully after bravely combating tuberculosis..."

Lilly paused and looked at Sarah uncertainly.
'Go on, luv.' Sarah said.

I know only too well how much we owe to you for your unselfish act of kindness that day in December 1915 when you saved my William and your other three comrades in France as that dreadful green-yellow cloud of chlorine gas came drifting across the field, engulfing you all. Your swift action to drag them back to the shelter of the trench, covering their mouths and noses with a damp cloth, reduced the effect of the gas and saved those men's lives. William never, ever forgot how much he owed to you and his gratitude never dimmed. To him, you were always a hero of the greatest order.

Whilst it is so tragic that we have lost William at so young an age (he was just 29) we were, thanks to you, blessed with those six extra years together during which we have had two wonderful daughters, Amy the elder and little Josephine, whom we named after you. May God bless you and keep you safe.
Yours sincerely, Margaret Moran.

'Well I never,' said Lilly as Marilyn returned from the kitchen.

'Ay, and that's not all. Look what else I found.' Sarah opened her hand to reveal a war medal. She was at a loss to understand why Joe had never mentioned any of it to her, nor to anyone else, as far as she knew. Turning over the medal in her hand, she read its inscription again. A medal for "*Bravery in the field. Awarded for gallantry*".

Lilly looked at Sarah for a moment.

'Well, are you going to let him know you've read this

letter? Maybe he's forgotten he had it. Or at least, he wants to forget about it perhaps. Did you know he'd been gassed in the Great War?'

'Yes, yes of course I did, although I never really knew much of any detail. Joe won't talk about it, not to me or to nobody. He has this terrible chest and his eyesight's never been very good. That's why they laid him off from the Railway after the war.' Sarah said with an undertone of bitterness. 'He were invalided home in 1915 after that awful gas attack and he were convalescing for several months down in Kent. In a sanatorium. Tunbridge Wells it were. The air apparently was good for him down there. Although surely not as good as the sea air here in Blackpool, I thought at the time. I couldn't get to see him till they sent him home the following August. Then he were passed as 'unfit for combat'. And he thought he were nowt but a failure. A write-off. He were devastated, Lilly. You know how the young men were back then. Or perhaps you don't remember, you'd have been too young. So eager to go and fight, they were! No matter what they were going to face. He never did speak about them trenches, nor his pals and certainly not this.' Sarah carefully took back the letter from Lilly.

'What should I say to him, lov?'

Lilly believed that it was a very private matter between Sarah and Joe. She did not want to intrude.

'After all these years!' Sarah went on, to herself. 'And all them times he's let me ridicule his Home Guard shenanigans. And when I go on at him for being lazy and weak, he's never let on about what happened back then...Oh Lilly. I feel so awful.'

Lilly squeezed Sarah's hand and smiled.

'Well, you know now. And you shouldn't feel awful, you should feel proud of him. And you are proud obviously. We'll leave you to your thoughts. Come on then, Marilyn. We've got some Christmas wrapping to do upstairs in our room. Shall we make a start on those paper chains, eh? We're using up some of Joe's discarded newspapers and painting over them. Very enterprising, don't you think? Come along madam.'

Marilyn skipped cheerfully out of the room and clomped noisily up the stairs.

Once again alone, Sarah allowed herself a heavy sigh of pride and just a tear or two. Something else was troubling her. What kind of humiliation might Joe be hiding away along with that medal?

'Oh Joe, you daft beggar. Why did you never tell me you'd saved all them fellas' lives?' She said out loud as she stared down at the medal.

At that moment, Joe entered, jovial as ever.

'Now then Mother, you'll never guess what, the Rotary Club have asked me, nay presumed, that I'd play Santa again on their Christmas float and at the Orphanage. I expect I'll have to say yes. I always do.'

Sarah pulled herself up sharp.

'You never fooled young Marilyn last year…'

Joe chuckled.

'Well, no. She's too bright, isn't she? Look, there was a bit of her tracing paper on't floor by the stairs. Marilyn must have dropped it on her way up. I'll fold it away in me drawer here. It's only flimsy. Won't take up much room. Are you alright? You don't look so clever.'

Sarah was about to tell him there and then what she'd found, but she thought better of it and turned away from him, carefully putting the letter and the medal in her apron pocket.

'I'll fetch you a hot cup of tea. Get your circulation going a treat, that will.'

'Ah, that's my girl.' Joe opened the drawer of the dresser to put the small flimsy piece of tracing paper away. As he did so, the bottom of the drawer suddenly gave way and the whole lot crashed loudly to the floor. Sarah and Joe just stood there and stared helplessly at the contents strewn all over the rug, saying nothing. Then they looked from the floor to each other and burst into an inexplicable fit of giggles.

'Well, I hope you're pleased with yourself, Joe. You great barmpot! What did I keep on telling you about that drawer!'

Lilly came downstairs and entered the room excitedly waving a letter in her hand.

She had just noticed a letter from Harry waiting for her on her dressing table. One of the girls must have picked it up that morning and put it there for her. They were always kind like that.

'Oh dear, what's happened here?' Lilly gasped looking at the mess. 'Are you alright? I've had his letter! I just came down to see if you'd let me read it out to you both?' Lilly knew what their answer would be.

'Why don't you do that, luv,' said Joe as he busied himself on his hands and knees picking up the debris from the floor. Lilly sat on the arm of the sofa and began reading.

November 30th, 1943.

My Dearest Lilly and Marilyn,

I hope this letter finds you both hale and hearty. Well, my darlings, we are on the move again, although where to, I cannot tell you, of course as you know. But I can tell you that our BLA unit is about to be joined by several forces from other countries, mainly Canadians and Poles so far. All decent enough chaps by the look of them.

There was much excitement in the barracks last week when we Brits received a pair of pyjamas each as part of our kit. This is a real perk and one which has never been provided to us rank and file servicemen before. Just what is needed on these cold Autumn nights. Are they softening us up, I wonder?

I feel we are gaining the upper hand all the time and this latest push might just do Jerry in the eye! I heard the other day how Herr Hitler is mobilising children over the age of 10 to fight in the war. Imagine that! By all accounts, boy soldiers as young as 15 have already been captured in the front lines by Allied troops. You have probably heard that the Nazis are suffering heavy losses on all fronts and are looking desperate now, especially after Italy's surrender in September.

Thank you for your last letter. Sounds like these past three years have turned you both into a proper pair of Northern lasses for sure! Will I be able to understand you when we meet again?

I will write to let you know directly I get my next leave. Until then, take every care of yourselves and look out for each other.

With Everlasting love, your loving Harry.

'Well that's grand, that is!' cried Joe. 'You must be right proud of him, with all that he's doing.'

And with a knowing look to Sarah, Lilly smiled.

'Well of course I am.'

CHAPTER 20.

'Sunny View', Keswick Road
24th December.

Dear daddy, I wanted to say Happy Christmas to you! May all your wishes come true.
Your loving Marilyn xxx

'Now then ladies, I were thinking,' Joe began, removing his pipe to raise his smeary glass, 'Life has to go on. I mean to say, war or no war, you can't let them idiot Germans take away our will to live. After all, it's Christmas day, the one day of the year when we should try to forget that there's a war on.' He took a big swig of beer and before his wife could jump in to rebuke him and ruin the atmosphere that he was bursting to create, he went on, 'We should celebrate life and remember how blessed we are in this household of ours. So, we're gonna have ourselves a party right here in this house!'

It was a declaration. Lilly noted beneath his jovial smiles his steely determination to make the best of their situation. What she wasn't prepared for though, was the paper dart board with a picture of Hitler bending over to show his backside beneath the slogan "Make him touch his toes boys!"

'Wherever did you get that from?' she gasped.

'The lads up at the allotment got hold of 'em. A job lot they had. I couldn't resist it. Been keeping it by for today.' Joe looked like a little naughty schoolboy. To Lilly, he seemed suddenly to have lost twenty-five years from his face. Ethel and June laughed so much that their sides hurt. They hadn't laughed like that since Victor Norman had taken his leave of them, finally moving out after his extended contract had finished. They all missed his clomping about the place. He certainly would have appreciated Joe's Hitler dart board.

Christmas dinner for the six of them stretched Sarah's limited culinary capabilities to their full extent, no matter how cheerfully she set about creating something out of the scant supplies in front of her. Not blessed with the widest imagination at the best of times, she scratched her head trying to work out how to substitute the Christmas turkey with the few vegetables she could lay her hands on together with their own garden produce which amounted to four potatoes, half a dozen undersized brussels sprouts, three carrots and an onion. There was hardly any meat in the shops now of course and what there was, came with a heavy price tag. No chance. They would just have to go without this year. Lilly chose not to share with them the contents of her last letter from Harry in which he had unwittingly tortured her with the details of his Christmas dinner at what was called the Spokes Club. She had licked her lips at the thought of it: baked rabbit stuffed with parsley and celery, candied carrots…no! It was too much.

'Before we all tuck in,' exclaimed Joe, 'I think we should drink a toast to our boys overseas as a token of our pride and gratitude and especially to young Harry Stevens. Perhaps this time next year, we'll be at peace and sitting around the table all together again.' Before any tears started to flow, everyone cleared the lumps in their throats and raised their glasses.

'To absent friends!' they chorused. The string of 'make-do-and-mend' paper lanterns and paper chains brought a splash of colour and looped above their heads, courtesy of Marilyn who had worked diligently for several days, cheered the gloomy little room.

When they had all finished their Christmas meal, with some relief that it was over, they then turned their attention to opening the Christmas presents which had been parked optimistically under the modest recycled Christmas tree, salvaged from the last twelve Christmases.

Lilly was dreading this moment. Christmas had become more painful and austere as inspiration for what they might be able to give to each other had dwindled with each passing year.

Sarah, Ethel and June's gifts could be easily arranged as she had been saving her soap rations for several weeks and knew that this would be a much-appreciated gift. Lilly was overjoyed when she came across a presentable second-hand garden fork for Joe at a near-by jumble sale in September and had hidden it under her bed knowing full well that Sarah would spot it but she had thankfully kept the secret safe. But it was for Marilyn that they all wanted to be as creative as possible.

Conscious of how her simple toys had been so important in restoring the child's health and confidence when she had fallen ill, they all set about saving a variety of odds and ends, scraps of material and wire from clothes bales from Lilly's shop, canvas, wood, screws and nails from Joe's allotment plus an array of bottles, match boxes and cartons which Ethel and June had purloined from their gentlemen friends, about which Lilly preferred to know as little as possible. She now presented Marilyn with a pretty respectable doll sitting on a doll's horse and cart, complete with leather reins for the horse.

'Oh, mummy it's grand. I love it! Thank you Thank you!'

'Best eightpence I ever spent, that's for sure!' Lilly declared to Sarah as she beamed with pride watching Marilyn's face light up in the reflection of her new toy. The pamphlet she had sent off for called "Improvised Toys for Nurseries and Refugee Camps" by Nancy Catford had proved a treasure trove of information and easy to follow tips for crafting toys that she knew Marilyn would delight in. Lilly was adept at creating garments from patterns and had often created elegant designs of her own to fit Marilyn's favourite dolls. It was an easy step for her to progress into making small toys and she had relished the quiet moments away from the rest of the household once Marilyn was asleep when she could beaver away to fashion the new horse and cart. It had restored her own peace of mind too, in no small way.

New Years Eve celebration had become a mocking shadow of its former self during those dark war years. But in the Cockington's house there was a growing optimism, a spark of energy that began with Ethel and June's boundless excitement and caught light around Joe, warming his imagination as to what the new year, 1944 might bring. Even Sarah could not help herself and then it was Lilly who had finally broached the subject one dark evening in early December.

'You know, it wouldn't be a bad idea if we all stayed home together on New Year's Eve and had a bit of a do. What do you all think?'

'You mean party games and beer?' said Joe as his eyes alighted on the sideboard wherein stood a paltry array of bottles awaiting permission to disgorge their alcoholic treats. 'Why don't we get old Betty Ackroyd and Fred if he's kicking his heels and has nowt else going on. That'll cheer them both up a bit.'

And so they gathered all together, for the first time in several months, in that modest little front room and Marilyn joined them to see in the New Year. Lilly allowed her a small amount of diluted rum in a whiskey tot glass. The drink went straight to her head of course and she felt a funny sort of giddiness which was not unpleasant but which the child supposed that if she were to mention, the drink would be taken away from her immediately and she didn't want that, so she said nothing and let the feeling wash over her. It was a happy and comforting scene. There was laughter and good will a plenty.

'Come on now everyone!' cried Ethel. 'We've got a couple of hours before midnight comes, so how about some party games, eh? Mr C, you promised us, remember!'

Joe scratched his head, dulled in his thinking after his third bottle of beer. Lilly stood up.

'My favourite game is one which Harry and I used to play with his mum and dad and sisters. It's called *Who Am I?* You have to guess the answer to a riddle. It's a real hoot, really it is!'

'Ok then luv. You take the floor, why don't you.' Sarah's competitive streak was heightened by the party atmosphere. She sat upright, ready and alert.

Lilly was suddenly the centre of attention. She nervously collected her thoughts and began to recite Harry's own favourite riddle.

'Alright, so who am I?' she began as she cleared her throat and took a deep breath.

I reach for the wings but I do not fly,
I sometimes fail, but I always try.
I live life vicariously, cry tears you may or may not see.
I work in darkness and in light, the same routine night after night.
A whole, made up of many parts,
I aim to touch and warm your hearts.
A wealthy life may never be, though riches are surrounding me.
Reviews, revues, my daily life, to some, this seems like endless strife.
I throw my voice into the void.
My work when done, I hope, you've enjoyed!

Lilly looked around the room.

'Well, any ideas?' She sat down, her heart thumping in her chest as so many family gatherings in other small front rooms a long way off filled her head. Joe took a gulp of beer.

'Very good Lilly. I'm sure I don't know!'

'I think you're an actress. A stage actress, is that right?' June was wide eyed with delight. 'The same routine night after night, Reviews, revues...oh and I throw my voice and all the rest of it. Is that right?'

Sarah glared at her.

'Well, yes of course,' she said. 'I can see it now. That were an easy one, Lilly. Just to start us off, like.'

'You have a go now then Mrs C,' June giggled and gently nudged her landlady. Sarah thought quickly and her eyes flickered around the room until an idea struck her and she was on her feet.

'Okey Dokey, listen carefully to this. Who am I then:

I look over your house in a critical way,
I inform you that kiddies are coming to stay.
You'll not be dismayed if you've had boarders before,
But you really can't guess what I may have in store.
A day or two later I'm back on your step,

A child in tow by the scruff of his neck...

Sarah paused.

'Oh, I can't think of no more rhymes! But you can guess the answer. It's a Billeting Officer, you see.'

'You're not supposed to give us the answer, Sarah!' Joe said and tutted loudly.

'Oh I'm a barmpot, aren't I!' Sarah's cheeks flushed partly from embarrassment and partly from the generous refills of beer flowing regularly into her glass from Joe. Then Lilly turned to Betty and Fred, as she realised they had hardly spoken for much of the evening but had sat quietly observing the jollity and mirth as though they were watching a play from the back of a theatre.

'Won't you take a turn now?' she asked them. 'Fred, you show us how to make a clever rhyme, why don't you?'

'Him?' snorted Sarah through a fug of smoke and beer fumes.

Betty gently nudged her son to stand up and though his face was scarlet and his hands were shaking, a flash of inventiveness inspired his imagination.

'Well then, here's someone you might all know...

I'm a strict old battle-axe with needlework skills
I own my own empire of fashions and frills.
You may bring your old garments for tricky repair
No matter how complex, I won't turn a hair.
But coax me to smile or urge me to thaw,
Then I'll give you short shrift and I'll show you the door!
In my well-ordered province, my shrill voice dictates
But I shift my stout frame when a posh patron waits.

Lilly looked at him askance in mock astonishment and pretended to be scandalized.

'Could this be my esteemed employer to whom you refer?'

Fred simply grinned sheepishly at this jibe at Mrs Bennett and suddenly as the room applauded him, he was having the time of his life.

And so this game went on until everyone had had a go and there was much laughter and leg-pulling, through all of which Marilyn slept soundly, oblivious to the racket. Then it was midnight and they all cheered in the new year and started gamely to link arms and sing Auld Lang Syne until they realised that none of them could recall any words beyond the first few lines. They sent Fred, the traditional dark-haired man, outside to bring in the new year with a lump of coal snatched from the grate. Then with more giggles, they slurped back the last of their drinks and slumped into their seats, nobody wanting to be the first to break up the party. It had been a very pleasant evening and one that was to linger long in the memory.

As she passed round the tea and cocoa, Lilly was already penning a letter to Harry in her head, her first of the New Year 1944. She ached to lift from this modest little room a taste of their spontaneous joy and convey it to him across the miles.

BLA Spokes Club
January 1944

Happy New Year to you, my precious little darling Marilyn.
Your daddy misses you every day and wishes you a healthy and joy-filled 1944. I hope you learn your ABC by the time I come home to you.

Maybe this year we will see peace in the world and I will be able to be with you and Mummy again. God willing.

Mummy's letter, waiting for me in my billet first thing yesterday morning, cheered my heart so.

I was happy to hear what a lovely lively time you all had at 'Sunny View' over Christmas. I haven't heard your mummy enjoy herself so much in ages! Our Christmas here with all the chaps was a more sombre affair as we had to be well-behaved in front of our superior officers etc. We all made the very best of things and I was the most buoyed up when I received your lovely presents. The socks you knitted all by yourself and the little poem you wrote. I can't tell you how happy that made me feel and I will keep it safe with all your other letters. Please send me another poem as soon as you can think one up. You have a lovely way with words, my precious darling.

Now then, as I kiss your picture every morning and every night – the one with you as a little toddler sitting on mummy's lap – taken on our deckchairs in Edmonton during your first summer – I marvel at how beautiful both you and your mother are and how lucky I am to have you two in my life even though we are so far away from each other.

I write to you today because my dearest one, I am going to be transported to another part of the country and I may not be able to write to you and Mummy again for a little while. But please don't be worried or miss me too much as I will be quite safe and happy working hard amongst my great pals and having lots of laughs in the process!

Tell mummy that I adore you both. I send you lots of love and ask you to be a big girl and help mummy when she needs you. We are both so proud of you.

With my everlasting love to you both,

Your loving Daddy.

'Happy New Year to you, Miss Chadwick, how lovely to see you this fine morning!' Mrs Bennett was always thrilled to see her more genteel customers in the shop. It was flattering and most gratifying to see them return and she would bend over backwards to make them feel at home.

'How do you do, Mrs Bennett.' The lady in front of her was one of the town's more esteemed citizens. She was a pillar of the community and a mainstay of the church choir. She was a tall, upright woman in her late sixties with a shock of silver dashing across her dark auburn hair.

'Actually, it's the young lady, Mrs Stevens with whom I have come to speak this morning, if you please. I'm afraid I don't think we have been introduced –'

'Oh yes, I shall call her for you, with pleasure.' The obsequious smile had already drained from Mrs Bennett's face as she swept out to the back room where Lilly was working quietly with her head bent over a gigantic raincoat.

'Madam Well-to-Do out there has asked for a word with

you, Lilly. Better go and see what it is she wants.' Mrs Bennett spoke in a barely audible hiss.

Lilly had no idea what her employer was talking about, but she obediently dropped the coat onto her bench and sidled past her into the shop.

'How d'you do, Mrs Stevens. Miss Chadwick is the name.' She thrust her gloved hand towards Lilly's enquiring face as though she were intent on swatting a fly in that space between them.

'I have been tasked by our Vicar, the Reverend Christopher Park to expand our soprano section of the choir at Holy Trinity Church. Goodness knows, we have enough altos to sink a battleship these days, but at the lighter end of the spectrum, by which I mean the younger ladies who can possibly make something of a top B, there is a distinct dearth. So many of them seem to have been spirited away to the factories and other such war work in the evenings. I myself can make a passable effort of Vivaldi's Gloria, but I rather need assistance – and you may be just the young lady to help us out!'

A host of thoughts suddenly jumped into Lilly's head, but none of them enabled her to grasp exactly what this lady was wanting of her.

'Me?' She blurted. A giggle was looming up in her throat. Then a long bottled-up memory suddenly reignited in Lilly's mind.

'You are asking me to join your church choir? Is that right?'

'Well yes, please. You might care to consider it. We've not had the pleasure of seeing you in Church but –'

'No,' Lilly retorted quickly. 'I'm afraid I'm not a regular church goer, not since –'

'Well, you would find us a friendly lot. We would make you feel most welcome.'

Lilly was at a loss for the right response, while Miss Chadwick would not let up.

'Oh, I can see that you are in two minds, Mrs Stevens, but you know, the choir has been battered and bruised somewhat and we so very nearly had to abandon it altogether last year when the blackout restrictions made our evening performances so problematic. And now the Authorities are threatening to commandeer our hall to house the expanding ARP unit. It really is a losing battle, but one must hold one's nerve, don't you agree?'

And then in a warmer tone, she stepped forward towards Lilly and added,

'Do you have any family with you here in Blackpool at the present time? You don't mind me asking?'

'No, of course I don't mind you asking. I have my little daughter Marilyn with me. She's not long turned six years old. The rest of my family is still in London. My husband is in the Forces.' That phrase always filled Lilly with a mix of pride and regret bringing a lump to her throat which she could not hide even from strangers.

'Well,' persisted the older lady. 'If your family is so far away, why not come and be a part of ours, at least for the Duration? And we really do need you, my dear.'

Lilly was amused by this invitation, so totally unexpected as it was.

'I'm rather taken aback, I must say. And I'm flattered - if a little intrigued, Miss Chadwick.'

'Oh jolly, jolly good! Then you will come along? We meet on a Friday evening at the Holy Trinity Church, South Shore. In the church hall, that is, seven thirty sharp.'

'But don't you want to hear me sing something first? I might be completely tone deaf as far as you know. I might be the last thing your sopranos need!'

'Oh no, no, I have no fear of that. You come highly recommended, my dear.' And with that air of mystery, she turned and elegantly made for the door.

'By whom, may I ask?'

'Ah, now that will be my little secret. Well, the Reverend will be so delighted and I will have done my duty by recruiting you. We shall look forward to seeing you next Friday. Oh and why not come along a little earlier, say around seven and take a cup of tea with us. I bring my own biscuits when I can get enough rations together.'

She chuckled and bustled away out onto the busy street,

letting in a piercing blast of noise and freshness into the little shop. Lilly was dazed. That sort of thing had never happened to her before and she was very tempted to take up Miss Chadwick's invitation. She could make it work if she could perhaps leave Marilyn with Sarah and Joe to look after. It would only be for a couple of hours. Or perhaps she could take Marilyn along with her. It might be a novel experience for them both. She would ask the child to decide, oh assuming that the Cockingtons would be willing, of course. Perhaps she was taking advantage of their kindness too much already.

Besides, who did she think she was, putting on airs and fancying herself as a soprano in a church choir! Her mother would scoff. She would always scoff at Lilly's creative inclinations, just like when she wanted to study the piano or take up amateur dramatics in the local church hall. And Harry always said she sang like a strangled frog, but that was unfair. Wasn't it just his way of keeping her feet on the ground when he thought she was getting too far above herself? He saw that a comment like that would always hit home. But maybe he was right. He knew her better than she knew herself in so many ways. If she had any real talent, he would have recognised it for sure. Perhaps she wasn't as proficient a singer as she would like to think. She hadn't even seen sheet music since she was in school. Oh no, it was all too daft, really!

Lilly sighed and shuffled reluctantly back to her waiting raincoat, a sombre reminder of her workaday reality. She sat down to re-thread her needle through a mist of tears which stung her eyes and made her hands shake, thwarting her efforts.

Ethel insisted and so Lilly thought she must know what she was doing.

'But I don't want to look like old Mrs Mopp, Ethel, my dear!'

'Lilly, I promise you won't. You'll look like the belle of the ball, you will. Now sit still and let me transform you back into a modern glamourous lady!'

'You know there's the South Shore Charities Association Welfare Ball next Saturday,' June piped up.

'Oo, there's a right mouthful!' said Sarah. 'How much do they want for the tickets, then, eh?'

'Five shillings a piece. Bit steep if you ask me.'

Lilly was hardly listening as June and Ethel were chattering away full of excitement after they'd been to the pictures that evening and had come home determined to show the rest of the household the latest in hair fashion. They took Lilly's headscarf and turned it into a turban over the victory rolls they had already shown her how to make.

It was all very quick and easy and Ethel was pleased with her handiwork, while Lilly, as she inspected herself in the mirror over the fireplace, was uncertain as to whether this new look was more suitable for the kitchen floor rather than the dance floor. And anyway, she had only come downstairs to seek Joe's advice.

'Well, I think you should go. Yes, I do. It's a wonderful idea, Lilly.' There was no doubt in Joe's mind. And no hint of absurdity or sarcasm in his face, though Lilly searched earnestly for it.

'You think so?' she asked him. 'You really think so? Oh well, I would like to give it a try, I must say. I haven't sung in a choir since school. I've just never had the time to join a choir since then.'

Lilly had enjoyed the choir days of her youth and had sang her heart out. It was always an uplifting experience which made her feel proud and joyful.

Her parents had never seen her sing. They had never shared in this part of her childhood experience. They had turned down any opportunity to watch her sing alongside her classmates. It was as if this was an activity belonging to a different world from which they felt themselves excluded. An alien world. Lilly understood, but at the same time, she didn't understand. She tried in her childish way, to form a bridge for them to cross, but they saw life through a different paradigm in which young girls didn't sing sacred works for pleasure, but instead went out to work in factories or shops and paid for their keep. Girls just like her sister Laura. Besides, her mother said, they would only show her up. They wouldn't have the right words to say or the right clothes to wear.

As much as that didn't matter a jot to Lilly, she accepted their reasons and rebuff. So she sang to an audience of strangers, a sea of faces and none of them there for her.

'Oh, I don't know I'd be so nervous! And I haven't a thing to wear –'

'What a load of hogwash! There's a war on. You don't need to look like Vera Lynn, for heaven's sake.' Joe leaned in towards her, crushing his newspaper under his stomach as he did so. His armchair squeaked.

'And I'll tell you sommat else, my girl. Life's too short these days for may-be and oh, I don't know. You take it from me.' And then he sat back with a look of satisfaction across his face as if that was that. He had said his piece as Master of the House and his word was final.

'Oh well, if you insist, Joe,' said Lilly. 'I'll give it a go, just because you say I ought to.' She sat back in her own armchair and clenched her fists with a sense of excitement and apprehension. Who would have thought it! Lilly Stevens, soprano in a Church Choir. And all because the war had carried the young ladies with proper beautiful voices away to take up occupations far from home.

It was getting late. She should go up to bed. She could hardly wait to get her head on the pillow next to Marilyn's and dream all night long of singing like Vera Lynn.

CHAPTER 21.

'Sunny View', Keswick Road, Blackpool, Lancs.
21st February 1944.

Dear Daddy,

Happy birthday. I miss you and I can't wate to see you again very soon. I baked you a cake with my rations but I had to eat it all up because you are not here and we don't want to waste anything. Don't worry, it was not a very big one. Mummy told me off today because me and my frend Ronald spoak to some men on the Golf Links which is next to our school. I didn't know who they were and they spoak funny. Our teacher Mr Nuttall told us that the men are from Italy and I thought they might know you as you have been in Italy for the war. They seemed like very happy men. I asked Mummy why they are here and not in Italy but she said they are here because we need to keep an eye on them, but I don't understand what she means. Must go now as its my tea time. Bye Daddy.

Lots of love and kisses from me and mummy. Marilyn.

The remarkably bright winter days gave June and Ethel an impulsive premature sense of Spring peppiness and energy. They decided to go on a spree that Friday evening. The tiny Mitre public house was their local favourite. They were known there and they liked its intimate convivial atmosphere. As soon as they stepped inside, a warm sea of smiling faces would always greet them. The smell of beer and sweat pervaded the little public bar. Its focal point was the ancient upright piano standing faithfully against the wall which was rarely left untouched. Its out-of-tune keys were worn and yellowed from the enthusiastic bashing of regular spirited players and it propped up beer glasses and energetic singers alike. Young and old, the regulars gathered here every Friday night at the Mitre to forget their work-weary week, ignite some energy into their gloomy lives and lean on each other with the camaraderie of an old soldier's regiment.

'Ever get the feeling we're being watched?' June giggled as she and Ethel sat perched on their bar stools. The girls lived for their Friday evenings, chatting and laughing with the other drinkers. A variety of men were gathering around them, some in uniform, others from the Civil Service, often lonely souls looking for companionship so far from home.

Ethel surveyed the room. She could see a young dark-haired man smiling gently at them from where he sat alone at a table under the window. As soon as she caught his eye, he rose slowly from his seat and sauntered casually over to them.

'Aye aye, here we go, June,' she said. 'Look who's on his way over to us!'

'Good evening, ladies, Pascoe's the name. Jerome Pascoe. May I have the pleasure?' His name made the girls giggle even though they knew they were being impolite. If Pascoe was particularly struck by how June appeared to him to be a fast drinker for such a chit of a girl, he certainly did not let this show.

'Where are you from, Soldier?' asked June.

'No, ma'am, I'm no soldier. I'm just an aircraft mechanic and I'm from Albuquerque, New Mexico. Have you heard of it?'

'Can't say as I have, but I'm guessing that's in America somewhere?'

'It sure is ma'am. The Land of Enchantment, is how it's known back home, on account of all the fine scenery we have there around us!'

Emboldened by this initial exchange, as well as the three whiskeys which he had consumed by this point in the evening, Pascoe was now sidling up to the two young girls and immediately, as Ethel had remarked later, homed in on the hapless June who was always so readily drawn into a conversation.

He was calm and sociable and his wit came easily to him that night. He was also rather free with his hands, thought Ethel. After June had laughed at his third wise crack, Pascoe slipped his right arm around her shoulders.

In spite of their better judgement, June and Ethel both laughed a lot and June was soon smitten with this tall, dark and slick American. Suddenly, June had an idea.

'Have you ever walked along the front, over to the Metropole?'

'No, but I sure would like nothing more than to stroll with you along the Promenade under the stars. Seems to me that it would be a pleasant thing to do.'

Ethel thought that he was a bit too self-assured actually and tried to give her friend her most subtly raised eyebrows in an expression of caution.

'Okay then, well, if you ladies will excuse me one moment, I'll just go find the bathroom.' Once free of him, Ethel leaned in close to her friend.

'I think he's a great deal too forward for his own good, that one, if you ask me.'

But, enjoying the attention, June seemed not to mind his familiarity and her laughter lit up her face. She thought he was the most romantic man she'd ever met. She couldn't wait for him to come back so that they could go off together.

'You don't mind, do you Ethel?' she whimpered. 'You never know how long you've got with these fellas while they're over here. Imagine me going with a real live Yank! What would me dad say if he could see me now!'

'Plenty!' said Ethel.

'But surely you can't help but agree wi' me that life is short!' June exclaimed. 'And so why shouldn't we seize the moment with both hands, eh? Plenty of other girls have met GIs across Blackpool, haven't they? You know, I were talking to a young woman in the queue for the baker only t'other week. And she were describing to me in minute detail how she had been going steady with a young GI corporal whom she had met at the Winter Gardens New Year's Day festivities. Evidently, he'd told her that he were looking for his Sergeant and asked her if she's seen him about anywhere. Sounded to me just like a typical boy meets girl ploy, but after a while they decided to get a coffee and they spent the rest of the evening together. When she brought him home to meet her mam and dad, this GI fella had brought some cigars with him for the dad and chocolates for the mam which impressed them all no end. You've heard how these Yanks are always very generous and this one just charmed them off their feet when he turned up for tea in his dress uniform. She said she supposed that he were also eager to please and to adapt, like, being as he's so far from home an all that. So why, then Ethel, shouldn't you and me have some of that excitement and glamour too? Aren't the Authorities always going on about how we ought to be a little more friendly towards the Yanks? We don't want to be cold prudes to these poor young fellas the way that so many of the other locals are, now do we?'

Ethel couldn't help but see June's point of view, despite her instincts. She was struck by their smart gleaming Government Issue uniforms and the contrast with their own increasingly shabby clothes. But the distinction wasn't only sartorial. The Americans seemed effortlessly to exude the kind of glamour with which June and Ethel were besotted and no wonder, they had come from a land of relative plenty, their pay outstripped their British counterparts and their supplies were abundant including copious chewing gum, cigarettes and ready cash which they spent conspicuously around Blackpool's many hostelries. Ethel had to admit, both to herself and to June, that the excitement of meeting the GIs up close was indisputable.

Several other drinkers in the pub that night noticed this couple as they began their fateful flirtation. They made a strikingly incongruous pair. The Yank looked so smart, while June looked shabby. That was what they told the Police.

Pascoe hot footed it back from the 'bathroom' and promptly whispered something into June's ear. She grinned and readily agreed. Putting her hand on Ethel's arm, she said without a hint of embarrassment or demure that she was going to show this fella a bit of Blackpool. Then without waiting for Ethel to finish her response, they boldly walked out of the Mitre pub and headed off towards the tram shelter at North Promenade.

It was the last time Ethel would ever see her best friend. If only she had stayed by her side. Had she known what few precious minutes remained to June, she never would have let her walk out of those saloon doors.

CHAPTER 22.

It was seven o'clock on the dot. Lilly stood still facing the imposing blue wooden doors of the village hall. A harsh chill was descending around her and she could not linger long outside. She was nervous. This was all so new to her and she suddenly felt very small and alone. Keep going, keep going, she said to herself. This is the right thing to be doing. Inside the hall, she could see no-one. A fleeting panic swept over her. Had she got the wrong evening? She let out a timid 'Hello', hardly expecting anyone to answer, but then suddenly the shutters snapped open in front of her and a small kitchen was revealed in which stood the vicar wearing an apron over his vestments and the elegant Miss Eleanor Chadwick rapidly wiping teacups by his side.

'Young lady, you made it. You decided to come. Oh, I am so pleased! You shall have a nice hot cup of tea. Do come on in.'

Lilly dumbly followed her into the kitchen. She took the not-so-hot cup of tea from the counter and drank it down in one, as if it had the power to give her the courage she so badly needed to get through the next couple of hours.

'Please call me Lilly, she said weakly.' Then the vicar held out his hand to greet her and she was grateful to take it, a lifeline to a drowning swimmer.

'So lovely to meet you, Mrs Stevens. You are most welcome.'

In no time at all, other choir members started to fill the hall. There was a good ten minutes of chair scraping and chatter while Eleanor Chadwick valiantly introduced Lilly to as many fellow choristers as she could while thrusting a copy of sheet music into her hands and ushering her to a seat which someone had set out for her in the third row from the front. She sat down quietly while her two neighbours were evidently having a heated conversation about the benefits of Anderson shelters.

'...My Graham said he had to dig four feet down. But we'll be safe now if a five-hundred-pound bomb lands as much as twenty feet away from us. Just imagine it -'

'Ah yes, but what about those poor lassies we read about who were buried alive in their shelter? Imagine that! No, no, I still maintain that we're far better off taking shelter under the stairs, should the need arise. No flooding and a great deal warmer I'd say!'

'I just keep my shelter to store me carrots and spuds,' piped up a third lady.

'But won't that attract the rats though, eh?'

Nothing to add to that. Lilly looked about her. She caught the last few words from the ladies behind her who were bemoaning the quality of underpants these days.

'...And they have the cheek to ask for four coupons and they're not even fit for scarecrows!'

'And what about all those unscrupulous mothers keeping their kids off PE just so that they can put on weight and then qualify for extra clothing coupons. It's going on, you know and it's dishonest, that's what it is...'

Others greeted her with a reserved smile, some were all too pleased to meet her, while others barely hid their surprise and disdain at seeing a new face in their midst – and one so very young. Lilly looked around the room and realised that she was easily the only female under sixty-five.

A loud tap tap tap of a baton on a music-stand made Lilly jump out of her skin. The Reverend Christopher, as he evidently like to be called, was eager to make a start.

'Good evening Ladies and Gentlemen. So nice to see you on this warther wainy evening.'

Lilly noticed that he had difficulty in rolling his Rs which made her smile quietly to herself. She would note all this down in her next letter to Harry which was rapidly forming in her head.

'We are thwilled this evening to intwoduce our new sopwano, Mrs Stevens. Do please stand up and take a bow, Mrs Stevens.'

Lilly's legs suddenly turned to lead and she could hardly lift herself off her chair. She waved briefly to the ocean of faces which had turned to her. Still the same stoney expressions – obviously they would need to take their own time to warm to her. She quickly sat down again while the heat in her cheeks subsided.

'Now then, let's go fwom the top if you please, Chwoir. Mrs Stevens, if you are unfamiliar with the Vivaldi Glorwia, please just listen and join in when you feel good and weady.'

More scraping of chairs, a good deal of throat-clearing and the assorted bunch of choristers stood up and readied themselves to start. A wizened old gentleman sat at the piano in the corner and bashed out the introductory notes. As she stood up, Lilly was horrified to realise that there were two rows of very tall, dishevelled women whose generous proportions and shabby but large-brimmed hats completely obscured her view of the vicar, elevated though he was on his podium. She tried in vain to catch a glimpse of him through the tiny gaps between these ladies, but the gaps were fleeting and she knew it was hopeless to try. Claustrophobia and panic seized her and she sat down again. It was no good, she would have to try to move to the front row somehow.

When the evening was over, Lilly took a deep breath as she approached Eleanor Chadwick who stood with the Vicar at the door giving the impression of a hostess waving off guests from a formal dinner.

'Well, my dear and how was it? I do so hope you enjoyed?'

'Um, I'm afraid to say,' Lilly began, 'I'm rather too short to be sitting so far back. Would it be possible for me to sit in the front row, do you think, just so that I may see the Reverend wave his stick, er sorry, I mean his baton? It would be ever so much better, I'd say.'

Eleanor Chadwick looked at the Vicar and he looked back at her as if Lilly had just suggested something despicable, unspeakable.

'Oh my dear, the ladies in the front row wouldn't like that. No no, not one little bit. You see, they have been here for many years, some of them over thirty-five years in fact. And they feel they have earned the right to stand in the front row. You do see how it works, don't you, my dear? You have to *earn* the right…'

Sarah was vexed that they were still waiting for June to join them as they sat there around the table ready for their breakfast. The tea was stewing and cooling in the pot.

'And where is young June this morning! I take it she's not still in bed. Ethel, didn't she come home with you last night?'

Ethel was already feeling a strange sense of apprehension that she couldn't yet put into words. She had woken with a start in the small hours and, realising that June had not yet come home, had felt a heady mix of annoyance, amusement and envy together with a tinge of guilt at having let her friend walk out of the pub like that with a stranger and without her. It wasn't as though this was the first time that either one of them had stayed out all night. It wasn't likely to be the last either with the way things were looking up for them. So what was there to worry about? But in front of Sarah, Ethel was trying her best to appear simply affronted.

'Don't look at me, Mrs C. I'm not her chaperone, am I?'

Sarah wasn't going to let this impudent young girl get the better of her this morning. She leant heavily on the table and looked Ethel in the eye.

'No, but you were both out together last night, weren't you? Didn't you spend the evening in that awful little pub you both love so much?'

'Yes the Mitre, and there's nowt very much wrong with it actually. It's right cosy...but anyway, we met a young lad there, didn't we. And he were really charming. We were a bit taken aback when he came over to us, all brazen like. I think he'd already had a few - if you know what I mean. Anyway, guess what. He was an *American!*'

Sarah was unimpressed. There were Americans on every street corner these days, it was no big deal!

'What were his name then, this American?'

Ethel smiled wistfully.

'He called himself Jerome Pascoe if you don't mind! I reckon he was only about twenty-two or twenty-three. Bit young for my liking, but you know June's not so fussy... Anyway, this Jerome fella says he's an aircraft mechanic.'

Around the table, everyone waited to hear more. Ethel went on.

'And,' she said in a terrible mock American accent, 'he said he just loves our Blackpool nightlife! Anyroad, the last I saw of them was when they went off, out the pub hand-in-hand for a stroll along the Promenade under the stars...'

Sarah was not surprised by June's behaviour, knowing these young women as well as she did, but she couldn't help her quickening pulse and thought, the stupid girl, she'd only just met him!

'An American,' Ethel persisted. 'A Yank. Looked just like Gene Kelly, he did an' all...'

Suddenly they heard a sharp knock at the front door, very loud and insistent. As Joe opened the door, he recognised the policeman standing there with his hand on the wall. He seemed drained of energy and colour as though he had just come from a very long night shift.

'Hello, Officer Brathwaite, what's amiss with all your banging on't door? Looking for

someone?'

PC Braithwaite was in his early seventies, brought out of retirement to cover the shortfall in younger officers for the duration of the war. In all his long years of service, he had never had to deal with such a horrific incident. Joe noticed that he was unsteady on his feet and struggling to make himself heard.

'Please excuse the intrusion Mr Cockington, but are you the landlord of a Miss June Hetherstone?' Sarah was at the door, needlessly elbowing her husband out of the way.

'I'm her landlady. What is it, Officer?'

'May I come in please, madam?'

'Yes of course,' said Joe as he stepped aside to let the policeman in. PC Braithwaite panted loudly at the effort of stepping over the threshold. His world-weary tread was laboured and he seemed to take an age to state his business. He delicately removed his helmet as he stepped into the hallway.

'A young man by the name of Gordon Trubshaw informed us last night that he'd made a rather grim discovery in one of the air raid shelters in the colonnade on the seaward side of the Metropole Hotel. I'm afraid, it looks like a young lady may have been strangled to death and the young lady evidently was a Miss June Hetherstone. Her handbag with her name and address was found near where she was, er lying-'

They all heard Ethel screaming from the breakfast table.

'No! No!! It can't be June! She wouldn't let him do anything to hurt her!'

'Get me my smelling salts, Joe, quick!' demanded Sarah as she ushered PC Braithwaite into the front room. 'This young lady is Ethel Scott, Officer. She's June's best friend. They were out together last night. Tell him Ethel. Tell him what you were just telling us.'

PC Braithwaite shuffled over to where Ethel sat winded at the breakfast table.

'Now then, Miss Scott, I'm PC Braithwaite. I'll need to have a talk with you please. You may be the last person to have seen Miss Hetherstone alive yesterday evening. Could we go somewhere in private, like? And then you can tell me what you might know about what went on last night?'

Ethel started shaking uncontrollably, she was white with terror.

'Well, I don't know –'

'Of course you do, my girl!' Sarah urged her. 'You go on into the kitchen with the policeman here and tell him everything you remember about June and this...this young soldier of hers.'

'He were a *mechanic*...'

PC Braithwaite ushered Ethel into the kitchen.

'Come on miss, this way. Excuse us, would you please.' He negotiated his way around Sarah who was eager to join them in their discourse.

'I told her that all her silly giggling would land her in trouble one of these days. I did, I told her.' Sarah didn't know what to do for the best. 'Shall I make us all a fresh pot of tea?'

'Sarah! This is not a social visit for crying out loud!' Joe protested, remonstrating her.

'Well, I hope they don't waste any time in finding this

American and when they do, they should hang him, proper!'

No-one else knew what to say. They were stunned beyond words.

CHAPTER 23.

A fortnight later, it was Joe's birthday. In a sober mood, Betty Ackroyd had come in to join them all as they sat drinking tea and she offered them a meagre cake. It was a subdued affair and nobody felt much like celebrating. Betty had brought Marilyn a little present too.

'Here you are my pet, look what I've made for you.' She held up a little octopus made of grey wool which she had fashioned by plaiting the eight legs, around the bottom of which she had tied blue and white wool. He had matching light blue and white wool tied around his neck as a fetching scarf and his head was made from the unplaited end of the wool bundle onto which were stitched dark blue eyes and a red mouth. His hair was somehow curled into tufts so that the little creature had the look of a startled Stan Laurel. Marilyn was thrilled with him and as she inspected him more closely, Lilly proclaimed that he should be called Oscar the Octopus. Marilyn became very attached to Oscar and carried him everywhere. At night Lilly found him snuggled across the little girl's neck to keep her warm and to comfort her as she sought the kind of pleasant dreams which were eluding everyone else in that house.

There was a sudden knock at the door. Two police officers were standing on the doorstep. One was PC Braithwaite again and the other was a tall urbane and imposing man in plain clothes. He was in a hurry.

'Good morning, madam. My name is Inspector Pennington. I'm from Scotland Yard and this is my colleague PC Braithwaite from the local constabulary, whom I believe you already know. We're investigating the death of your late tenant Miss June Hetherstone.'

Sarah gasped.

'Oh Scotland Yard! Well, well, you'd best come in, gentlemen, hadn't you. This is my husband Joseph Cockington. This is Mrs Stevens, another boarder of mine and her daughter. Oh and this is Mrs Ackroyd, our neighbour from two doors down.'

'How d'you do,' said Betty reverently as Pennington lifted his hat to her.

'How do you do, madam.'

Lilly decided to take Marilyn upstairs to their room so that the others could talk to the policemen in more detail as required. They wished her good day as she edged past them and left the room.

Without any further delay, Pennington sat down and got out his notebook and pencil in what Joe thought was in that same business-like manner they always acted in the films.

'Now, I won't take up much of your time this morning,' Pennington began with the weakest of smiles, without acknowledging the birthday trappings which were plain to see. 'But as you may know, we've been drafted in to assist the Blackpool police. We expect to be able very soon to carry out a large-scale identification parade. We want Miss Ethel Scott to come along as a key witness. If we have our man, she's sure to pick him out.'

Oh, poor Ethel won't like that one bit, thought Joe. And as if he could read his mind, PC Braithwaite leant forward to Joe.

'It's got to be done sir. Whether the young lady likes it or not. Where is she, by the way? Where can we find her?'

Ethel had just popped out to the shops with Sarah's meat coupons. She was due back any minute. Evidently, the butcher only had scrag end these days and she was not one for standing around queuing, especially not just for a bit of old scrag end. It seemed to distress her something shocking, waiting around in a Butcher's queue.

'As I was saying,' Pennington continued, 'We know from Miss Scott's original statement that this American had befriended Miss Hetherstone during the evening of 25th February...'

Betty wanted to add some of her own insight here.

'If you ask me, I reckon as June were no more than an inoffensive little thing, if a little shabby and not very bright. But she did like to socialise with the gentlemen, well, didn't she Sarah...?'

'That's not really the point, Betty. Go on inspector, do, please.' said Sarah, wishing her neighbour would take her cue and go home.

'Well,' said Pennington, 'It's my belief that we'll find the man who was last seen with Miss Hetherstone easily enough. We've got our men all over the American airbase. There aren't so many places he can be hiding. He's most likely staying in a local boarding house around here. There's already a number of landladies over in Lytham Road who have come forward saying they have American soldiers billeted with them. It's just a process of elimination, you see.'

Joe was watching Pennington closely.

'What will happen then, Inspector…once you've done all of your eliminating?'

'Well of course, once we have our man, the matter will then have to be handed over to the US military. In the fullness of time.'

'Oh, I see.' Joe said. There was nothing else to be said. It was all so much to come to terms with. PC Brathwaite could see how they were struggling to make any sense of what had happened.

'There'll have to be a Court Martial, most likely at Blackpool police station.' He paused to exchange an awkward glance with Pennington.

'But there is just one thing we'd like to ask you please. Did Miss Hetherstone, by any chance ever suffer from…epilepsy?' His question seemed to come from nowhere and was met with blank faces around the room. Joe was getting ever more confused.

'Well, she never had any fits or nothing like that while she were under this roof, if that's what you're asking. She didn't, did she, Sarah?'

Sarah dismissed it out of hand.

'No of course not. Of course not. And anyroad, who'd ever heard of anyone dying from an epileptic fit? It's a bit of a leap, if you don't mind me saying so, Inspector.'

'Well, now, I would say that's a matter for the Inquest to resolve. They'll decide whether the poor girl died from natural causes or by human hand. We're just trying to keep all our options open, as it were. Either way, we'll find our man easily enough. The Yanks stick out like a sore thumb around these parts. It's just a matter of time, I'd say. Anyway, we need to press on. I'm afraid we can't wait any longer for Miss Scott to return.'

PC Brathwaite instructed them to let Ethel know that the police would be in touch with her in due course. He added that she shouldn't have any cause for concern. It was only her duty she was doing, after all.

'Yes of course, Inspector,' said Joe solemnly. 'We'll see that she knows what she's about. Thank you for calling round to keep us informed.'

Once the two Policemen had left and he had closed the door after them, Joe scratched his head and was at a loss.

'Well, ladies, what do you make of that! Epilepsy, indeed. I mean to say, whatever will they tell us next?'

It was such a cruel irony, thought Joe, that for the duration of the war so far, Blackpool had escaped the Blitz mostly unscathed. No-one had ever lost their life in the air raid shelter on the promenade at Princess Parade. Why then should June have to be the only one?

After all they had lived through, June had to die not from the actions of the German Luftwaffe but at the hands of the U.S. military. And so Joe followed the press coverage of June's case as it gathered salacious momentum in the newspapers. Much of what he read he vehemently disagreed with. How dare they disparage June so publicly, especially to damage her reputation in this way, he thought. He was helpless, a mute bystander as the chaotic and mis-handled trial progressed.

A surprising amount of detail came forward enabling the press to piece together the fateful final hours of June's life. The papers described in cynical detail how, having left the pub, this unlikely pair, June and Pascoe, had walked off the broadly lit promenade and sauntered towards the air raid shelters by the Metropole Hotel which were incorporated into the colonnaded walkway that also formed the retaining wall for what was later to become the Metropole Hotel car park. Both had already consumed more than their usual limit of alcohol and they were smoking heavily. No-one had taken much notice of them as they made their lolloping, drunken progress through the dense night air. No-one had heard them as they giggled and flirted together, Pascoe's arm clamped around June's slim shoulders. They had almost stumbled twice but this had only added to their reckless joy in each other's company.

It was here among the air raid shelters that later on in the evening, two servicemen and two civilians intended to bed down for the night. After shoving the door open, then entering and lighting a match, they had discovered a girl's partly clothed body by the doorway. It was a grim sight, that first glance. Most of the clothing was missing from the body and she was wearing only one shoe. The discovery had caused a flurry of anxiety and morbid excitement among the locals as soon as daylight had broken through, but the shelter was quickly locked up to thwart the shameless sightseers.

On the 9th of March, the police announced they were searching local boarding houses for "an American airman or soldier with high cheek bones, dark beady eyes and good teeth". The following day a large-scale identification parade was carried out at US Air Service Command. It didn't take long for the police to establish Jerome Pascoe as a person of interest in this case. He was traced to his base at Warton, about eight miles south-east of Blackpool and taken in for questioning. Witnesses identified Jerome Pascoe with little trouble or hesitation. The Inquest had concluded that June died from asphyxia due to manual suffocation. There were cuts on her face and a large area of bruising to her skull.

Joe had made sure to keep that section of the newspaper out of the way of anyone in the household. The ladies shouldn't have to read these terrible details. He was shocked enough himself and could not contemplate how the others might react to them. The newspapers were dedicating an increasing number of column inches as the trial progressed, but each day, Joe ripped out the article and swiftly screwed it up into a ball and threw it into the fire.

He wished that the eager flames could obliterate the harsh condemnation of June's character whilst somehow purging the household of its grief and shock.

One morning Lilly was about to clear out the grate to make up a fresh fire, just to take off the chill in the room. As she knelt down, she noticed a picture of a man staring back at her from the newspaper which Joe had not fully scrunched up. It was a familiar face, although Lilly could not place where she had seen it. She picked up the ball of newspaper and uncrumpled it to get a better look at the article. It described how Jerome Pascoe had been seen by a man called Kenneth Winchmore, a resident of Abercorn Place, Blackpool who had heard a stifled scream some distance away as he was strolling past the colonnade. Just as he had gone to investigate, Pascoe had apparently run out in front of him. Mr Winchmore had tried but failed to apprehend him. Due to a weak heart and being somewhat advanced in years, Mr Winchmore could not give chase. He had however, obtained a good look at the dishevelled, desperate appearance of Jerome Pascoe in the light from the stars and this was sufficient to be able to identify him as the perpetrator of the heinous crime against Miss June Hetherstone...

Where had Lilly seen this man before? She knew she had met him but could not recall a conversation. She stared more intently at his gaunt, monochrome face.

'Oh, my goodness me!' Lilly gasped as she sat back on her heels. This was the man she had helped on the promenade a couple of years back. The man having the heart-attack. At last, now she could be certain that he had survived that day, that he had lived.

She had so often wondered how he had got on and what had become of him after he had been carted off in that lumbering old ambulance. Despite the circumstances, she could not help but feel a sense of pride that she had assisted that day in his recovery, perhaps just so that he could go on to play his small but pivotal role in bringing June's murderer to justice. *How strangely the world turns,* Lilly thought.

The matter was finally handed over to the US military. Pascoe admitted being in the shelter with June. He denied killing her, despite blood being found beneath his fingernails, although no-one bothered to ascertain whether or not it was actually June's blood. In late April, at a Court

Martial set up at Blackpool police station, Pascoe's defence set out to prove that June may have died from an epileptic seizure, based on the one witness who had claimed to have seen June frothing at the mouth in the pub one evening. A landlady from Lanark Avenue had come forward claiming to have seen Miss Hetherstone coming away from the Doctor's surgery the week she died. Neither the lack of any sound evidence of this, nor the fact that June had had no medical history of epilepsy, had deterred the Court.

Another witness who claimed to have seen June trembling and frothing at the mouth one evening a few months previously was a local landlady who also asserted that June frequently came to her house late at night with a soldier.

'All the American soldiers at my house have behaved so well and I just want to help the boy,' the landlady said, indicating Pascoe. 'It is such a shame that his life is to go for so worthless a girl. Another half a dozen ought to go with her if you ask me.' Her comments caused an uproar in court.

'Turn her out!' shouted a voice from the back of the room.

Jerome Pascoe was cleared of murdering June but was found guilty of her manslaughter. He forfeited all pay and allowances, received a dishonourable discharge and a sentence of ten years hard labour. His motive was never fully clarified, leaving in his wake a plethora of theories and speculation. In seeking to preserve a strong united allied war front, the incident was clearly a humiliation and an irritation to both US and British authorities.

That was the end of the whole terrible business. Life for the good people of Blackpool went on as before, the more compelling priorities of wartime reclaiming their attention and the gruesome aspects of this tragedy captivated them no longer.

Except for the household of Sunny View, where life could never be as lively and cheerful as it had so recently been. The gap left by June's absence would be felt keenly though the house for many months to come before life could gradually creep back to its normal routine, battered as it had been by such significant catastrophe and upheaval. For Ethel Scott it was a struggle to manage her daily existence and she would never get over the loss of her dear friend.

Whatever horrific fate had befallen her in those air raid shelters, poor young June Hetherstone was finally laid to rest in an unmarked grass grave in the Roman Catholic section of Layton Cemetery in Blackpool with nearly a hundred mourners present. They comprised casual friends and acquaintances, distant relatives who had journeyed from far afield, but mostly they were random strangers drawn there by unchecked morbid curiosity. An incongruously ornate wreath adorned her grave from the landlord, staff and friends of the Mitre public house where June had waved her last joyful goodbye.

At June's funeral wake, several mourners were milling about, filling the Cockington's small front room. Most of them had simply strolled through the open front door in search of scant cake and tea. Betty Ackroyd had brought Fred along evidently against his will and he blushed a permanent and conspicuous deep crimson whenever Lilly was within six feet of him. The occasion had made Betty particularly weepy and had given her the opportunity to re-live her own grief for her son Alan, whose uniformed photograph she shared with anyone whom she was able to trap inside her maudlin little web.

Fred stood by his mother's side all throughout the afternoon lacking the confidence to walk about the room lest he should be required to enter into polite conversation beyond his capacity. He had written another poem and left it in his usual place for Lilly to find underneath a book on her workbench in Mrs Bennett's back room. Its tone was angrier than his previous poems which had unsettled Lilly. She had not seen him all week to try to discuss it, but she appreciated his gesture and felt that this was his way of offering her some kind of solace at this dreadful and disorienting time.

Bad men batter, bruise and blister
Raging rows, go cry to sister
Bad men rile, rouse and rattle

From lifelong love to daily battle
But bad men, mean, move and muster
Decide and act with verve and lustre
And for this alone, she'll fall again
Because after all, it makes them men
Good men gently ease along,
With charm and grace not labelled strong.
But all this consideration breeds
Is the kind of love no woman needs.

Victor Norman had been on his way to Newcastle when he had read about poor June in the papers. He had wanted to get back there to the boarding house to try and give some comfort and support to young Ethel and the rest of the household. He had always found the two girls so full of energy and a determination to live their lives to the full in spite of the harsh reality of their way of life, the truth about which he had soon guessed. And on this saddest of days, he was without any ready wit or humour. Stripped of his funny-man persona, Lilly thought that Victor Norman had aged considerably with his thinning hair and extended waistband. He was speaking at length to PC Braithwaite who was still wearing a constant look somewhere between exhaustion and embarrassment.

The tall gaunt policeman had said frequently to the room that he had only dropped in to pay his respects and now he ought to be on his way. Despite this, he had gulped down three cups of tea in the twenty minutes since his arrival.

Leaning up against the door frame, Lilly was watching them all, willing them to drink up and go home. She suddenly felt like an outsider, an interloper with no right to be there amongst them. As she stood alone feeling isolated, an unexpected homesickness overwhelmed her like an old adversary suddenly reappearing after having kept a low profile for so long in the dark shadows. Joe came to her rescue.

'Here you are Lilly luv. Here's a nice cup of tea to warm your bones.'

'Thank you, Joe. You are kind.' Lilly sighed. 'Poor June.

I can't get over it. She was just so young. I suppose he's repenting what he's done, that Jerome Pascoe. Do you think so?'

'I bloody well hope he is! But I'm sure I don't know what makes these Yanks tick. I just hope the authorities have done right by our June.'

'At least she got a proper Catholic burial,' said Lilly. 'I never would have guessed that the girl was so popular. There must have been over a hundred friends and relatives there at the church. I'm glad to see the Police kept the public at a respectable distance... I'd say it's a blessing that June's parents aren't around to see this, Joe. I do really.'

'But honestly,' Joe confided to Lilly, the heat rising in his face. 'I can't fathom it. After everything this country's been through, that it should come to this. I mean to say, is this what we've all been fighting for these past five years? So that some mindless Yankie hoodlum can come over here to our town and do such a despicable thing to a defenceless young lass?' He paused. 'How's young Marilyn taken it all?'

Lilly was grateful that Marilyn was too young to understand what had happened to June. And she had no intention of telling her any of the details either.

'I know how much she's missing her Auntie June. She was always so kind to the child. They adored each other.'

'We'll all miss June, that much I do know.' Joe continued shaking his head sadly. 'But I really can't fathom it. This sort of thing just doesn't happen round these parts.'

Lilly looked up at him sadly.

'Well Joe, I'm afraid it has.'

It was such a perfect summer's day. They sat around the wireless and not one of them dared to speak. It was all too fantastic. It was too much to hope for. It was time. The BBC had said so.

"D-Day has come. Early this morning the Allies began the assault on the north-western face of Hitler's European fortress. The first official news came just after half-past nine, when Supreme Headquarters of the Allied Expeditionary Force issued

Communique Number One. This said: Under the command of General Eisenhower, Allied naval forces, supported by strong air forces, began landing Allied armies this morning on the northern coast of France".

83 Lansdowne Drive, Hackney, E8.
23rd June 1944.

Dear Lilly and Marilyn,

I hope all's well with you both?
You have no doubt been hearing all about this V1 flying bomb they're sending our way now and I wanted to write to you as soon as possible to put your minds at rest that we're both alright, Mother and me. A bit startled by it all, and it makes you want to just throw in the towel and give way to panic. Although I must say, I don't let on how I feel to Mother or else it would get her down. She would say, and quite rightly, that if we all give in to panic, then we play straight into Hitler's hands. So, we must hold our nerve.

There are around one hundred V1s coming over us every day now and as you can imagine, thousands of casualties. The school near us was bombed out last week, but thankfully all the kiddies were safe in their shelter. I saw one of those strange pilotless V-1 monstrosities landing over the rooftops nearby yesterday evening. It was travelling at lightning speed with flames belching out of the back of it. To see it so low, roof-height, I will never forget it as long as I live.

Everyone in the whole factory had to get down on the floor under the work benches and desks. There wasn't time to get to any outside shelter, you see. Some of the younger girls thought it was great fun. But my heart was in my mouth because of that horrible silence after the engine stops. You just have no idea where the thing is going to land and go off. Did you hear about that terrible tragedy on Sunday morning at Wellington Barracks when a V-1 landed on the Guards Chapel during a service? I think over a hundred people may have lost their lives. And then on Wednesday, they destroyed Clancey Street with a single bomb!

But, my dear, on a cheerier note, I remember what an awful time of it you had with that woman called Rosalind who came to stay with you some time ago and I did want to let you know, if you hadn't already read about it in the papers (I know how bad you are at keeping up with the news) that they've caught a young woman as she was trying to steal from a bombed out block of flats in Camberwell about a fortnight ago. They said that she had been roaming about the country and she had admitted to having robbed houses all over the place, including Blackpool. They said that she had assumed lots of false names including that of Rosalind Trench! Can you believe it? She will appear at the Old Bailey court. You know how the Authorities take a very dim view of looting and thieving these days and I expect that they'll make an example of her to stop others who might be taking advantage of the chaos during the air raids and blackouts, especially when they hamper the rescue efforts of the emergency services. Anyhow, isn't that a turn up for the books! Fancy you having met her. Although, I hope this news doesn't bring back too many unpleasant memories for you.

Sorry that this has turned into such a gloomy letter. I'm not feeling quite on top of things and I suppose it's because I'm feeling the effects of all these years of bombing raids! So I will pause here and push off for now.

Write back soon. Mother sends her love to you both.

Laura xx

It was an intensely warm morning when Marilyn was playing with her dolls outside in the back garden. She was miles away, daydreaming of how she was going to teach her dolls to wash up all the teacups and saucers when suddenly she heard a tapping from above her head. Sarah was trying to get her attention from the upstairs back bedroom, only the window was stuck fast and she couldn't get it open. She was beckoning the child to come up. Marilyn obediently though reluctantly left her game and ambled back into the house.

'Here you are luv. I was wondering if you'd like these. Why don't you try 'em on for size?' Sarah was standing in front of her giant wardrobes which to Marilyn seemed so vast that they threatened to swallow her up. Sarah had several cardboard boxes open on the bed from which had spilled out a modest array of children's clothing over the faded crimson counterpane.

'Do you like 'em, luv? Try 'em on for me, why don't you, eh?' Sarah's voice was unusually soft and as Marilyn's gaze moved between the bed and Sarah's face, she noticed the red rims of Sarah's eyes and the screwed-up tissue which she was clutching in her hand.

'Are they for me? I've never seen so many clothes in one heap before!'

'They belonged to my little girl. She were called May. 'Sarah turned away as her voice trailed off.

'What happened to her?' Marilyn was uncertain whether to ask any questions at all.

'It were diphtheria. Terrible disease that were. She were just turned nine, that's all the time we had with her. Anyroad, I don't know why I never thought of it before, but if they fit you, you might as well make good use of them. Probably a bit big on yer as you're so tiny, but you'll grow into 'em I'm sure. God willing.'

Marilyn was unsure about whether she wanted or ought to take the dead girl's clothes. What would her mum say? But she acquiesced and tried on a couple of skirts and blouses. They were clearly outdated but Marilyn had hardly any sense of what fashionable little girls were supposed to look like. Indeed, all her clothes these days were pre-worn and she knew no different. And her mum was only too happy to accept cast offs from others. She would surely be over the moon about all these!

But Lilly was appalled.

'How can you put upon the child and embarrass her like that Sarah, honestly!' was how Lilly reacted when Sarah broached the subject as they washed up together that evening.

'I reckon you're being a bit unreasonable, Lilly. I only thought they should be put to good use. No value to anyone in them sitting in boxes in me wardrobe, is there? Besides, I thought you'd be pleased. They're in good nick and warm too. Hardly used. What's there to fret about? I don't understand you sometimes, Lilly, I'm sure I don't.'

'It's just that they're not from some unidentified, anonymous child who we might never meet. It's...well, it's your child, Sarah. That's different. I mean –'

'Oh I see. A dead child's clothes. You think it's gonna bring you bad luck or sommat. Is that it?'

That was it, yes. Lilly knew it was irrational and totally unreasonable. She certainly didn't have the luxury of turning down good clothes, no matter how old-fashioned they might be and especially where clothes for her daughter were concerned. She softened.

'It's not that I want my little girl to be the best dressed in the school or anything like that. God knows that's not what I'm saying, really it isn't. And please don't think that I don't appreciate your kind gesture, Sarah. Oh, this is all rather awkward. I suppose I'm a bit uneasy about how you'd feel – you and Joe – watching Marilyn playing and running about in your late daughter's clothes. That's all.'

'Well, our daughter hardly got to wear them, poor lass. That's the point. I just wanted you to have first refusal and, here's the thing...'

Sarah was suddenly crying. Quiet, soft tears that bounced off the edge of the sink. The shock of it made Lilly nearly drop a plate from her tea towel.

'Oh Sarah, please don't get upset. I'm being ever so ungrateful. Please forgive me.'

'No, you're alright, luv. I were only trying to say that your little Marilyn is growing up so fast and we feel as though she's become part of our family, like. Both of you have. I've come to see her as one of me own, do you understand me?' She sniffed and wiped her cheek with the shoulder of her cardigan. 'Anyroad, look at me. I'm getting soft in me old age! Soft as they come.'

'Oh Sarah, you're really very kind to both of us.' This was a different Sarah Cockington standing in front of her. A woman worn down by years of war into generous sentimentality, even humility.

'Pay no mind to me, Lilly luv,' Sarah muttered as she

plunged her arms back into the lukewarm water to finish her task. 'What with all that's been going on and poor June and all that. I dunno...'

Lilly put her hand on Sarah's arm, but there was no more to be said on the subject. Marilyn wore the clothes and felt the eyes of the original wearer bearing down on her. That was just the way it had to be.

BLA Unit Spokes Club
5th August 1944.

Lilly darling

I hope this finds you both hale and hearty. (How often I have written those words to you since this war began and heaven only knows what I should do if the answer came back in the negative!)

What excitement there is all about me since the glorious Allied invasion in June! It's pretty electric here I can tell you. We wait for daily updates on the wireless and in our morning briefings. We are fairly bursting to get a move on!

I enclose a picture of me with my two pals Robert - in the middle and Alec - on the right in the shorts with the knobbly knees. He's proudly sporting a new wristwatch sent to him by his mother and father for his birthday last month. Smashing fellows they are too. We were given those pipes by the CO last Christmas, you remember? Don't I look a dashing rake? Out here tobacco is easier to come by than cigarettes you see. Anyway, we have been lounging around most of this week in the club drinking far too much beer. I think the beer is equally as awful here (served up cold can you believe?) as that potato beer stuff they're experimenting with on Joe's allotment that you described in your last letter.

Quite a picture you painted of Sarah all bloated up like a balloon after guzzling most of the clay flagon Joe brought home. What a girl! I wonder what else they will find to make from all the surplus potatoes. No doubt the Ministry will come up trumps with another pamphlet on the matter!

And how goes my little Marilyn? I have become quite a dab hand at making miniature furniture out of pipe cleaners and matchboxes. They are just prototypes and I'm practicing. I think when I get home, I shall set about making Marilyn a big doll's house. I have been thinking about designs for it and it will have electric lights throughout and everything. She will be thrilled with it. There's a promise I shall not forget to keep.

Now that the danger of a German invasion of Blighty has thankfully passed, we must look forward with growing confidence to the end of this war. I wonder how God will help us to rebuild our community afterwards. I often think of that Lilly dear, don't you too?

With everlasting love, your loving Harry.

CHAPTER 24.

In the north transept of Holy Trinity Church, South Shore there was a memorial to James Parrott who had laid the foundation stone. Originally from London, his health was not good and so he frequently visited Blackpool for the fresh sea air. The Preston and Wyre Railway opened in 1840 with a line to Blackpool and due to his failing health, James Parrott was given a free rail ticket for life. He lived, however to the ripe old age of ninety-four and enjoyed the epithet of the Great Old Man of Blackpool. Throughout his long and active public life, James Parrott served on the building committee for the Holy Trinity Church, presenting it with a clock for the tower and setting up a trust fund to keep it in good repair.

Lilly stood reading his memorial stone which read "In memory of James Parrott who died February 21st, 1897, aged 94." The date caught her eye because February 21st was Harry's birthday. Looking at the date etched there in stone gave her a stab of melancholy.

She usually arrived early to choir rehearsals, taking the opportunity to prepare herself physically and mentally for the onslaught of noisy, excited female chatter that would soon engulf her like a battery of hens. Yet, in spite of herself, Lilly had begun to enjoy the Friday evening meetings, their regularity and her short walk to the church, especially in the light summer evenings when the warm weather allowed her to stroll along Lytham Road, over the bridge and then into Dean Street. She was now feeling a tangible sense of belonging and her confidence and singing capability had noticeably grown with each week.

This evening however, Lilly did not much care for singing with thoughts of poor June still uppermost in her mind, but the choir was preparing the Vivaldi Gloria and Requiem mass ready for next Saturday's charity concert for the Blackpool War Widows Fund and her contribution to this auspicious event gave her the impetus to carry on.

She had asked the whole household at Sunny View to come along to the concert and initially she had felt optimistic of their support, not least as it was her first performance of any kind. However, the flood of inane excuses from around the breakfast table made it clear that Vivaldi and cold churches were not especially appealing to her fellow boarders. All except dear Joe who promised he would be there to keep little Marilyn company. Lilly was uncertain as to whether this was from a genuine enthusiasm for the event or simply that he could not bear to see her poorly disguised crestfallen face. She had grown to trust Joe's boundless humanity and realised just how much she depended upon it now. It was his innate generosity of spirit and unfailing bigheartedness that defined him in Lilly's mind and she would always remember this with fondness in the years that followed. Sarah meanwhile felt no such compunction and politely but categorically declined the invitation citing her long-troublesome weak bladder as the main obstacle.

'I'm a slave to it, I'm afraid. Mind you, I wouldn't hold out much hope for me eardrums neither with that lot warbling away! No offence meant, Lilly luv.'

Lilly did not pursue the matter but left the neat little flyer advertising the details of the concert on the table all the same, in the unlikely event that Sarah might change her mind.

Lilly was deep in thought as she sipped her tea inside the little church hall kitchen. She preferred to let the hubbub chink and clatter around her. She hadn't noticed that a tall man with dark hair and glasses had approached her with cup and saucer in hand.

'I say Mrs Stevens, the tea doesn't improve half as much as the singing does, eh?'

Lilly looked up at him. Though a little startled, she noticed immediately how handsome this man was, broad shouldered, urbane and well-dressed. A gentleman from the bass section of the choir.

'Oh well, it whets the whistle anyway.'

'I'm Mr Nuttall, but please do call me David. Everyone

else does here. We haven't been introduced. Miss Chadwick often seems to pass me by for some reason. But you know, I have seen you many times at the school gates when you pick up your little daughter. Although we've not yet spoken, I have wanted the chance to make myself known to you. I'm Marilyn's teacher.'

'Ah *that* Mr Nuttall! Yes, Marilyn has mentioned you to me many times! You have made quite an impression on my little girl. In a good way, I mean, of course!' Lilly let her blushing cheeks build up to a peak as she hid her burning face behind her teacup.

'Are you from –'

'I do like –'

'Oh, I'm sorry, after you – '

'No, no…'

Lilly and Nuttall were speaking over each other but were rescued from any further awkwardness by the loud tapping of the Reverend's baton which summoned them all back to their seats. They smiled and a bond was struck between them. It was the first of several enjoyable and gratifying conversations that they were to share over a cup of tea across the town in the coming weeks and months. This evening, something very pleasant had begun to warm Lilly's bones. As they sauntered reluctantly away from the little church hall kitchen, he gently placed his hand on her arm.

'I have rather an awful confession to make to you Mrs Stevens –'

'Oh please, it's Lilly –'

'Well, yes, I know your Christian name. And I'm afraid it was I who persuaded Miss Chadwick to recruit you here to the choir. Please don't think too badly of me, will you.'

Lilly laughed.

'Oh well, that solves the mystery! I did wonder how she found me.'

Mr Nuttall was evidently relieved and Lilly noticed the broad grin which enhanced his features as they moved across to their respective seats.

As the scant audience took their creaking seats and fussed about with their hats and coats, the air began to fill with cigarette smoke and anticipation. This was the first charity concert that the church had hosted since before the start of the war. Even the Blackpool Gazette and Herald had turned out to cover the event, much to the excitement of the ladies of the choir, while the gentlemen regarded the reporter with a degree of scepticism.

They were now assembled in the cramped vestry ready to process onto the stage with their sheet music arranged neatly inside formal black folders. As regards their attire, they seemed to Lilly to be something of a motley crew. She had stuck her neck out a couple of weeks ago when the controversial subject of white blouses and black floor-length skirts was discussed, by suggesting that blouses should be one uniform shade of brilliant white if the ladies were able to obtain them or make them and that she would be happy to take responsibility for any running repairs on the night as and when required, picturing herself diligently moving among them with thimble and thread attentively heading off any mending emergency. Instead of the polite gratitude which she had expected, she faced resistance, objections and unyielding expressions.

'Well, I don't possess a white blouse, Mrs Stevens and I certainly don't have the coupons for one...'

'If you think I'm going to make my own, Mrs Stevens you'd better think again. I have too much else to do...'

So there they stood, in various shades of white, yellow, beige and grey with their skirts at different lengths.

Lilly was mortified at the motley sight and wondered how the audience would respond to this ramshackle bunch of singers having paid their hard earned one and sixpence to enter the building. The Reverend Christopher sauntered over to Lilly and remarked on her outfit.

'How sophisticated you look this evening, Mrs Stevens, if I may be so bold. Warther delightful, indeed.'

However well-meaning his remarks may have been, the

good vicar was blissfully unaware of the stoney faces and narrowing of eyes which these comments had prompted among the other less sartorially elegant sopranos gathered behind him.

Then, just as the choristers were about to step out onto the modest stage, they became aware of a minor disturbance emanating from the front row of seats. The ladies craned their necks to observe what was disrupting the calm within the audience.

Lilly joined them, also curious as to what was going on out there. Then she spotted a large tabby cat fleeing down the aisle. In hot pursuit was Joe Cockington with his arms outstretched. He was soon able to capture the uninvited guest and Lilly watched with enormous affection and amusement as Joe tenderly but decisively ushered the cat outside the church.

Then, as the self-conscious Joe sheepishly took his seat again next to an extremely embarrassed Marilyn, the concert was allowed to commence.

It was the first time that Lilly had ever reached the school gates early. She had brushed her dark voluminous hair into compliant waves and made sure that her coat was clean and tidy. What was she doing! Like a silly schoolgirl, she was as eager at the prospect of seeing David Nuttall as were the little children around her about leaving the school yard at the end of the afternoon as they ran headlong into the waiting arms of their mothers. Other adults, older ladies, grandmothers, aunts and neighbours had congregated along the low brick wall. They were friendly and chatty but in all that time since Marilyn had joined the school as one of many new girls, Lilly had never progressed beyond casual polite small talk: the weather, the state of the shops and how difficult it all was to keep the kids clean and properly fed these days.

And there he was. As he counted the children by tapping each head as they passed him through the gates and with a kindly nod to acknowledge their "Goodnight sir", he glanced up and caught Lilly's eye.

'Ah hello there, Mrs Stevens, how nice to see you.'

'Oh hello, how are you? Another busy day?' *How inane*, she thought. *Take a deep breath*. As she brushed the hair from her windswept face, she smiled at him and searched for her daughter among the jumble of little bodies.

'Actually, I'm glad I've caught you today.' David moved towards her. Suddenly it was only the two of them on the pavement. The throng of children and adults faded away.

'Oh yes?'

'Well, as we don't have Choir practice again until next month, I was wondering whether you would have some time this week for a cup of tea. With me, that is. If you have the time. Only, I know a lovely little tearoom in the high street. Miss Tilly's. It doesn't get too crowded in there.'

'Oh, yes. I know it well. It's close to where I work. The dress shop. I can meet you on Saturday if you like. Marilyn is looked after by our landlady on Saturdays. And I can get away from the shop by lunchtime. Would that be alright?'

'Splendid. Shall we say one o'clock?'

And that was how it began. Just a simple cup of tea. Usually, Lilly was home by lunchtime on Saturdays. Marilyn depended on it to break up the monotonous boredom of her day. It would be disappointing for her not to see Lilly at that time. *But, blow it all*, Lilly thought to herself, *I do need some excitement in my life. I deserve it*. She had little else. And besides, David Nuttall seemed to want her company.

And she wanted his. It was the first time anything remotely delicious like this had ever happened to her since she had first met Harry back in 1934 at the factory over a hurried lunchtime sandwich and a brew in the canteen.

After all, an innocent cuppa in the high street with David Nuttall wasn't going to be anything clandestine, or underhanded. She was happy and satisfied that there would be nothing reproachable in meeting him for a cuppa in the high street on Saturday afternoon. She would even mention it in her next letter to Harry. And to her Mother. And Laura. Why not let them all know? Even Sarah Cockington could not find anything amiss in a cup of tea with a gentleman schoolteacher.

Anyway, David Nuttall was probably just a bit lonely. As lonely as Lilly was. This war could make anyone feel alone, frighteningly so and in a way in which they had never felt it before. A cold iron-grey loneliness without end.

83 Lansdowne Drive, Hackney, E8.
18th Sept 1944

Dearest Lilly and Marilyn

Mother would scold me for tempting Fate, but you will want to know that, yes we're still standing and the house is in one piece. These new V2s are bringing us the worst Blitz so far as you've no doubt heard in the News. It's terror in the dark, night after night. And the days are sometimes as black as night with dust and smoke from near-by explosions.

But in the face of all this frightful horror, I have some uplifting and happier news to tell you! I want to introduce to you by letter to my new gentleman friend. (Mother so hates the word boyfriend!) His name is Jim Sparks and he is a police officer. He is a lovely man, almost ten years older than me and I am very excited about getting to know him better. Sadly, he is very badly affected by the horrors of his job, Lilly. Some days he tells me that he comes home feeling quite nauseous after he has found the remains of someone's child and or has had to deal with multiple people who had refused to leave their houses, crushed from bombs in their homes, often trapped in their bedrooms. Children, babies, parents all dead. Can you imagine it? Jim told me of one night last year at the start of the V2 raids when he saw a child's hand sticking out from under some rubble and he went to pull the child out - but the arm simply came away in his grip. It must be unspeakably awful for him to experience that!

The Blitz has exposed him to horrors which he has never seen before, but all the same, he does try to shrug it off and take a philosophical view of it all, telling me about the less horrific occasions such as the boy whom he dragged into the brick surface shelter because he was hanging around outside watching dog fights in the sky.

And the firebomb which landed in the kitchen garden at the back of an old lady's house and burned up all her cabbages.

He says how they all give each other nicknames like Dodger and Shorty, that sort of thing. They call him Sparky which he likes and he says it makes them feel that they're all just as worthy as each other. I suppose it does away with any kind of formality and brings them all closer together in their determined fight for the common cause.

It saddened me when you told me how Marilyn was described in her last school report as a "timid little soul, terrified of anything that might go wrong or be a potential problem". I wonder how much the schools really understand. Children across the country have to deal with so much. Here in London, the sight of numerous empty chairs at school after a bad raid must hurt them deeply.

I told you about my friend Jane who got engaged last April. Well, she has had a nervous breakdown and will be spending six months in a mental hospital. She couldn't take much more of these difficult conditions in the munitions factory and now half her road has been destroyed by the V2 attacks just over a month ago. I went to see her mum and took round some of my home-made peppermint lumps which I know Jane loves. By all accounts, she is ashamed she ended up in hospital, poor dear thing. And she's only 19!

I'm afraid all this is rather too gloomy – it is really! I give into frequent moments of nervous anxiety which (don't be cross) have turned me to smoking. Cigarettes calm my fears, you know. After all, how much more can we take?

I will stop here for I'm sure I have left you feeling rather demoralised. Keep your spirits up, dear girl and do please let me know how you are getting on. Mother misses you both and feels the pain of separation from you beyond words, as do I.

Sending you both our love.

Yours affectionately,

Laura

They met in the small chintzy tearoom at the end of the high street just three doors down from Mrs Bennett's shop.

It was crowded, noisy and humid in there, but David Nuttall was already seated at a table in the corner and Lilly was glad that he had taken the initiative as she made her way directly across the room towards him. He stood up as she approached and although his now familiar smile sought to reassure her, she was more than a little hot and flustered.

'Oh, hello. So sorry to keep you waiting. I'm always obliged to wait on the most awkward customers just when I want to get away! Have you been here long?'

'No no, not at all,' said David with that welcoming smile. 'Only long enough to eye up the iced buns whipping past the table. I never thought so many people would turn out today. How the other half lives, eh!'

Lilly had fretted all morning about what they might find to talk about, but the conversation was relaxed and natural. Over their tea and buns they spoke mostly about Marilyn but also about how education might advance after the war. David was eager to describe his career to her and its many ups and downs, setbacks and successes. Lilly told him about how awful it had been when June was killed and how difficult it was proving to understand and get over it. She also talked about Harry and his many business ambitions and how much she was looking forward to them all getting back to normal again.

'He's one very lucky fella, your Harry. But I'm sure he realises that.' David was hard to read. Was he being serious or simply teasing her?

'Oh, I don't know much about that.' She looked wistfully through the steamed-up window at the passers-by scurrying along the moist pavement.

'Sometimes I wonder how things will be when he comes home. I mean, I know he will come home. I know he's very careful. Doesn't take silly risks with his safety like some of his mates do by all accounts. But you know, I wonder if we'll be the same. Well, we can't be, can we? Not really. I mean we've both been through so much while we've been apart.' David sought to rescue her from plunging into a depressive abyss before it was too late.

'Well, then there'll be a whole lot to catch up on and never a shortage of things to talk about between you!' That seemed to him a most witty remark. But at that moment, he sensed that he had lost her, before she was even his to lose.

'You know, he would often say to me, "Lilly, that dress looks lovely on you." When really, I would prefer him to say "Lilly, you look lovely in that dress." There's a subtle difference, you know. It infuriates me, it does really!' She looked up at him and then pulled herself up sharp with a short self-conscious laugh.

'Oh, I am sorry David. Listen to me. I sound so self-absorbed. Please take no notice. I indulge myself something shocking, I do really!' She gasped at her wristwatch.

'I really ought to be getting on home or else my landlady will have my hide!'

'Your landlady? Is she such an ogress?'

'Shh! She may have friends at the next table.'

They laughed as they put on their hats and coats. He tried to help her on with her coat but she was already fastening it up. She had missed his cue.

'Thank you for the tea, David. Please let me reciprocate next time. It'll be my turn to pay.' Lilly felt no self-consciousness at the idea that there would be a next time. David's smile was enigmatic. It might have been anything from chivalry to embarrassment, or just relief that she was keen to meet him again. She hardly cared to think too deeply about it and she glided out of the tea shop and back home with his charming smile fixed in her mind's eye all afternoon.

It was the best birthday that Marilyn could remember. The biggest box among all the others waiting for her on the settee was too tempting to leave until last as Lilly had suggested. Marilyn swooped down on it much to the amusement of the rest of the household who had all gathered on this fine November morning to be with her.

'Oh, but please! Can I open this one?'

She opened it in disbelief. She had only ever known birthdays to bring a paucity of presents and food, tinged with adult undertones of disappointment and impatience that she never fully understood. But today she forgot all of that as she ripped open the brown paper and ribbons and saw the blue box, its bold yellow label and red writing: Bayko building set.

Harry's own fascination with the new building sites springing up across London between the wars and their bold modernity, had given him a keen desire to see Marilyn develop her skills in creating and constructing model houses. It would be instructive and diverting at the same time, he had said to Lilly that day in Regent Street when he first saw the Bayko building set in the toy shop window. Lilly was not so keen. Apart from its inflated price tag, it wasn't the sort of feminine plaything she had in mind for her little girl. She took her mother's determinedly traditional view of what little girls should amuse themselves with, much to the exasperation of the far more enlightened Harry. He felt passionately that a child's creativity should be encouraged at every opportunity and that Lilly was in danger of stifling Marilyn's. It had become something of a standing joke between them when Lilly had tried to keep justifying her reasons for putting off purchasing the Bayko set. Money and time were both in short supply in Blackpool.

Now she was obliged to relent when Harry sent her a postal order for three pounds and suggested she go and purchase this specific model. As she watched Marilyn's face glow as the child stared in awe, tracing with her eager little fingers the outlines of the illustrated rosy- cheeked children on the box who were busy building their model house out of the Bakelite bricks, it evoked in Lilly a sharp painful spasm of regret that Marilyn's little twin siblings were not sitting there with her to help or hinder her progress. She turned her face aside to flick away the tears. How swiftly they still came these days.

'I sent off to Liverpool to get it,' she said in a voice that betrayed her.

'Oo, this looks far too complicated for me!' Ethel sighed as she knelt down beside Marilyn to take a closer look at the box. She knew that her own birthday offering of home-knitted socks would be overlooked for the moment as Marilyn was engrossed in pulling out a multitude of Bakelite pieces onto the rug. Sarah decided for once to indulge the child's noise and messiness.

'No, but it's perfect, is this!' Joe's eyes were alight with excitement. As Marilyn was still exploring inside the box, he picked up the instruction booklet and took it to the window to get a better light.

'The rectangular Bakelite bases have a square grid of holes into which thin metal rods of various lengths can be placed vertically. In order to make larger models, two or more bases can be joined together by means of metal links secured by screws through holes in the bases… Clever in't it!'

Marilyn was swept along by Joe's infectious enthusiasm and she giggled with delight as she watched him leaf through the booklet. She was happy and excited that they might build the little model houses together.

'Read me some more!' she begged him as she gulped down the last drop of Tizer in her glass.

'She'll not see that booklet again!' Sarah interjected as she rose to make a fresh pot of tea, tutting at Joe who continued as though he were reciting from the Holy Book.

'Bakelite bricks, windows and other parts can then be slotted between pairs of rods in order to create the walls of the building. Other commonly used parts include floors and roofs of various types. Oh, look at them roofs Marilyn, they're maroon! And the windows here are dark green, just like them houses up by Stanley Park! It's all very modern and swish, I mean to say!'

'*Swish*? When did you start using words like that, Joe Cockington, eh?' Sarah came back to pick up the teacups and saucers turning to Ethel, 'Has he gone and swallowed that booklet, has he?'

'Well it's probably a lot tastier than her dinners!' Ethel murmured to Lilly and her giggles infected Marilyn too.

The little church hall was packed. It had only just turned eight o'clock and yet several laughing couples and unaccompanied young ladies were twirling and laughing around the floor to the sound of a tinny geriatric band. As Lilly walked in, she immediately wanted to turn tail and run away home. Too many people, too many unfamiliar faces and no Harry by her side to give her courage as he had always done at their beloved Palais on a Friday night after work. She felt so out of place but as this dance was a fund raiser for the choir and she had promised to come along to do her bit, she was obliged to stick it out or at least stay for an hour and then leave.

She lingered a moment too long in the doorway and then involuntarily caught the eye of the only person she had hoped might be there.

His back was turned as she entered the hall but, as if he could sense her standing there at the other side of the hall, he had immediately turned around and was now facing her smiling his broad sunshine smile which held her transfixed in its beam.

'I took the liberty of pouring you out a glass of punch. It has quite a kick to it, I must warn you! But far better than the tea they usually serve up at Choir of course...' David Nuttall often managed to take Lilly's breath away and she gratefully accepted the punch. With a sheepish smile, she sipped as steadily and elegantly as she could manage to mask her trepidation.

'I'm so glad you came. I wasn't sure if you would.' David was aware of her reticence. 'Would you care to find a little table and sit down for a moment?' They found a quiet corner away from the band and smoky chatter where they could be more relaxed. Immediately, they were comfortable in each other's company, impervious to the censure of any prying eyes nearby. A potential issue occurred to Lilly.

'I don't know about you David, but I realise that although I do love a good dance, I have not been to one in all the time that Marilyn and I have been here in Blackpool.'

'No, I know what you mean. I haven't been to a dance since before the war, I used to go often with my wife. I suppose she would just...' He stopped. The words wouldn't come to him at that moment and he didn't feel like trying to find them. Lilly wondered what he had meant to say and where his thoughts were leading.

'Would this be her sort of thing?' She asked tentatively.

David thought carefully before he answered.

'Oh, I dare say she's at a dance right now in fact, as we speak, twirling about some dance floor in Devon with some handsome GI. I wouldn't stop her - anymore than she'd let me stop her, of course. You know how these things go. Or perhaps you don't.'

'I'm sorry, I didn't mean to...' Lilly immediately regretted her prying question. She didn't want him to be gloomy. 'Well, as long as you have a good time this evening. I mean that would be alright by her I suppose?'

David didn't reply. He knocked back his drink, then unceremoniously stood up and nodded towards the bar.

'Would you excuse me Lilly, while I get us some refills? My guess is this stuff will soon run out.'

'Certainly'. Lilly watched him jerk and twist his way across the crowded floor to the bar. She tidied her hair as she waited for him to return. She felt sorry for him and wanted to lighten his evening so that he could say that he had spent it in splendid company. But what right had she to monopolise him? A popular, handsome chap like David Nuttall, he would have lots of people far brighter than she to chat to this evening. However, to her surprise he was heading straight back to her.

'I was right. They have completely run out of punch. And it's not even half past eight! Lemonade alright for you? You don't look like a brown ale sort of girl and that's the only alternative unfortunately.'

They laughed an easy laugh and Lilly realised that there was nowhere else on earth she would rather be at that moment.

'By the way, I'm not particularly strong at the foxtrot, you know. But I can do a very passable quickstep.' The punch had given Lilly a warm glow of confidence.

'Ah well, with me you see, it's the other way around,' David replied. 'I suppose that doesn't bode too well, does it? Anyway, I'm always willing to keep an open mind – if you are.'

If he had intended more than one meaning in that remark, David hid it well. Lilly turned from the dancers to look straight at him.

'David, you know, my little Marilyn adores you. She talks about you all the time and thinks you're a brilliant teacher. I think you might be her first crush. I'm sorry. But I wanted to let you know that. It's just that you always seem to run yourself down about your job and I think that's a rotten shame because obviously you are doing something right.' His deep brown eyes held her gaze and she didn't mind at all.

'It's a good thing I mean something to her. I would so like to make a difference, you see. And it's a cursed nuisance being in a reserved occupation like this. I never once expected that as a simple schoolteacher I would be forbidden from even enlisting under my own initiative.'

'But I understand teaching to be an essential service. *You* must think of it like that, surely. I would say it's vital to the country. Vital to our children at any rate.'

Nuttall was looking squarely at Lilly.

'They wrote to me and told me that I was "required to remain in my post". It was an odd feeling seeing that, I can tell you.'

'But your wife was mightily relieved, I shouldn't wonder?'

'Oh well, I expect so. She's staying down in Devon with her elderly parents for the time being. They called her back in '41 and she seems happier there, safer perhaps. Although I really don't know.' He seemed to need to qualify that last remark in response to Lilly's averted gaze. 'I live for my work now. And for the choral singing too, I must say -'

'How about the Home Guard?' Lilly blurted out. 'They'd welcome you with open arms, I'm sure they would. And my dear landlord is a very keen-'

'Would you dance with me Lilly? Show me how you light-footed Londoners do the quickstep?'

'Yes of course.'

By the time they had reached the dance floor and had worked out how best to ready themselves to pick up the rhythm, the song had come to an abrupt end. They were left high and dry. They were closer now than they had ever been and still Lilly sensed no danger. Why should she? David Nuttall was the most natural, easy-going man she had ever met. Harry would even approve of David if he had been sitting there at their table. Why, the two men would be the greatest of pals, she reasoned. With so much in common, they would probably revel in each other's company, united in ridiculing Lilly and pulling her leg about some nonsense or other. Maybe she would mention David in her next letter. Maybe.

'Are you alright to carry on? It's a slow foxtrot.'

'Of course. Now we've made it this far!' Lilly gripped his hand more tightly and they moved closer to each other.

Well honestly! Eleanor Chadwick tutted to herself as she sipped her tea and watched the dancers over the rim of her pince-nez. *What do they think they're about, carrying on like that? You're heading for tears before bedtime, my dear Mrs Stevens. Silly, silly young lady.*

83 Lansdowne Drive, Hackney, E8.
20th October 1944.

My dear darling Girl

I hope all is well for you and little Marilyn. Laura and I send our love to you both on this rather cold dreary morning as I write this.

I haven't heard from you for a while. I hope all is well? Perhaps you have found much to occupy yourself these past few months and have forgotten your poor old mum?

I enclose a little photograph of the three of you in our little back garden which I thought might cheer you up. Laura's bike that you can see in the background has long been sent in for scrap and she walks everywhere nowadays. (She certainly won't ride in the 'bus either as she thinks it's too risky) The picture has been on my mantle shelf since it was taken just before the war began, but Laura said she thought it might be a good thing if you had it with you there in Blackpool. You can always bring it back when you come home. They say that Hitler and his mob are on the back foot these days. I don't much care to believe what they say in the papers as it's so often nothing but blarney. But if there is any truth in it, then I reckon as you'll be packing your bags soon enough and fetching yourselves back home again. What a pleasant thought that is!

Anyway, look after yourselves and keep safe till we meet again.

Your loving Mother.

It was such a fine, still evening that neither Lilly nor David could bear to go their separate ways home. They strolled towards the bench around the side of the church where only the gravestones could observe them.

'Marilyn got herself in trouble again today, I'm sure you heard,' Lilly began on neutral ground. Marilyn was an easy topic to help ease them into the regular pattern of their conversation.

'Yes Lilly, I wasn't going to mention it, but I take it Marilyn's told you how it was? Miss Eversley's been on the war path again about her precious hedges. It's a particular obsession with her, I think.'

'I had to laugh actually. I mean, what goes on it that seven-year-old head of hers, I cannot begin to guess. What was she doing?'

'Oh apparently, one little boy got caught for picking the leaves off the hedge in the upper yard and as he was being admonished, a little group of kids gathered around him, including your Marilyn. She evidently was absent-mindedly picking at the leaves herself until the teacher noticed what she was doing and turned on her.'

'She's always so absent-minded. Head in the clouds.'

'Well, the teacher sent her off to the headmistress to stand on the black step for half an hour. Then when Miss Eversley found her there, she called her into her office. Marilyn told me she was terrified that she was going to get the cane. But instead, all the old girl asked her was what did she want to do when she left school. As if a seven-year old would know the answer to that!'

'Marilyn told me she said she wanted to be an actress when she grows up. I had to laugh. All little girls say that!'

'Well who knows? After what Marilyn's been through, she certainly has an emotional depth that I've not seen in many kids...' But gently Lilly shook her head at this and he could see this was not a conversation that Lilly wished to pursue. They fell silent for a moment.

The late evening breeze was cool and refreshing on their faces as they both searched for something to say which was impartial and detached. Lilly began looking not at David but straight ahead towards the gates.

'Bad luck about that amusement arcade on the corner of Temple Street and Church Street catching fire like that. They say it's completely demolished. Marilyn and I used to love to go in there...' David responded with only the slightest acknowledgement, so she took a different tack.

'Well, we've certainly waited long enough for this dry weather, haven't we?' David was too distracted, as if this perfect evening was too much for him to endure. He turned abruptly to her.

'Well, I suppose it will have to come to an end sometime. Won't it, Lilly?'

'This weather, you mean?' Lilly knew what he meant, of course. She did not want to be the one to initiate what had come to be the inevitable conversation.

'I'm falling in love with you, Lilly my dear. But then I suppose you'll have already guessed that much.'

Lilly was uncertain how to respond. Was he being serious?

'I never meant for that to happen—'

'No of course you didn't. I'm not going to blame you for any of it. It's me. I'm such an oaf. I warned myself as soon as I met you over that stupid cup of tea in the church hall here. I said to myself. *Watch out Nuttall, old chap. She's just the sort of girl you'd lose your head over.* And of course, you are - and I did.' He laughed but Lilly saw only melancholy in his eyes.

'But what about your wife? She must be far more attractive than I am. More intelligent and witty at any rate.'

'Why must you always denigrate yourself, Lilly? Don't you possess a mirror for heaven's sake? Doesn't Harry ever tell you how smashing you are?'

'Yes, alright David, I suppose so.'

'Well then... It's getting late. Please would you let me walk you home one last time?' He was so desperate to put his arms around her elegant shoulders or to take her hand in his own so that she might never walk away from him. But there was a line that he must not cross. He knew that she was stronger than him and that for Lilly at least, this had been a much-valued friendship at a time when they both needed to fill a void in their lives.

'But what about the Choir, David? You will continue to come? I shouldn't want you to stay away just because of me. I should be miserable.'

'Oh well, we'll cross that bridge when we come to it, shan't we. Besides, I wouldn't want to let my fellow basses down. There's only three of us left in any case now that old Mortimer Arundel has gone AWOL.'

'Never to be seen again?'

They shared a brief laugh.

'Where do you think he's disappeared to, David?'

'Who knows? He just stopped coming. Didn't send word to old Miss Chadwick or the Rev. It's damned rude if you ask me.'

'Oh, but something awful might have happened. You never know these days. I hope it's nothing bad anyway, I do really.'

They had reached the bottom of Keswick Road. They never went any further than that point and David had not once been to the house. It was that line.

'Well then, Mrs Stevens, this is where we say our goodbyes.'

'No, no, not goodbye, not yet, please David. I don't want to lose you from my life just yet. I'm being awful and selfish, I know. But let's just say goodnight for now. Is that alright by you?'

'Take care of yourself, Lilly,' was all David Nuttall could say and he turned from her and lurched off back towards the pier.

Lilly sauntered slowly the last few hundred yards to her gate. She was lost in her thoughts and her heart was beating so fast that it gave her palpitations. She felt that this was a moment for tears of regret and sadness, of longing or disappointment. And yet, she felt none of these and no tears came at that moment. She felt sorry for David and just wished that they could have met under different circumstances, perhaps the four of them, with his wife alongside him (what was her name, had he ever told her? Had she ever asked?) and Harry standing them all a round at the bar. What an excellent time they might all have had as a foursome in peacetime. Well, who knows? That might yet happen, one day. She was always looking forward to the possibilities which lay ahead. And of course, Marilyn would always be pleased to see him, wouldn't she?

CHAPTER 25.

'Hello Mrs Stevens. Can Marilyn come out to play?' Lilly was touched by their earnest plea.

'Yes of course she can,' she smiled down at the two little girls standing on the sun-kissed doorstep. 'Come on in while I fetch Marilyn from the garden. She'll be ever so pleased to see you both.'

But she wasn't. Marilyn preferred to stay where she was. She was not usually anxious about being among her peers. She was turning into a sociable young lady, especially with these sweet little girls, Grace and Sybil Baxter, although Marilyn had breezily informed Lilly one morning without looking up from her bread and margarine that Sybil favoured pulling her hair when she wanted her attention.

'Doesn't that bother you, Marilyn?' asked Lilly, alarmed at this unruly school-girl behaviour.

'No not really. She does it all the time. And to the boys as well. The boys who are smaller than her, that is. Teacher reckons it's only a phrase she's going through.'

'It's phase not phrase, dear. I see. Oh well then, you just mind she doesn't hurt you.'

Lilly wanted Marilyn to have more company of her own age and she was keen to encourage Marilyn's friendships, especially to take the young girl's mind off June's demise. The Baxter sisters lived at the end of the street. The two of them with Marilyn were a tight little unit. They stuck together in the school yard and got themselves into trouble several times for chatting and giggling together in the school assembly blissfully unaware of how loud their whispers were.

Why Marilyn did not feel like playing with them today was a mystery to Lilly. She hoped against hope that this was not the onset of another dreaded bout of sickness, but she persevered until Marilyn reluctantly came into the little hallway and the three of them then skipped off into the sunshine once they felt its enlivening warmth in their bones.

'Mind how you go and don't talk to strangers!' But they waved without turning round and Lilly could only hope that they had heeded her instruction.

They skipped breathlessly all the way down to the park. There was an old hut in the middle of the grounds that had long been abandoned and fallen into disrepair. Often, they would go and play in there, make a camp or pretend it was their own little tea shop. Some days they would arrive there in high anticipation only to find a group of boys had got there first and had set up their own camp, sitting defiantly swinging their muddy legs over the side of the empty window frames and smoking cigarettes, each of them scraping the skin off huge carrots with a tuppence, all no doubt ill-gotten gain. Then the girls would run away resentfully. But today there was no-one there.

'Terrific!' they cried. They clambered onto the wooden decking and began to laugh and dance around. Marilyn did not see the large hole in the middle of the floor and she screamed as she fell backwards hitting her thigh and back against the sharp edge of the broken planks. She was stunned for a moment and after the split-second panic, she realised that she had bruised her legs and lower back. Worse still, she had torn the left side of her dress and the rip was covered in mud. How could she hide this from her mother? How could she escape her scrutiny? Oh well, mum could mend anything, she really could. It would be alright. Her friends helped her up out of the hole and once they were all satisfied that Marilyn had not seriously damaged herself and that they wouldn't have to go home at that very instant, they set about re-creating their tearoom. Still shaken, Marilyn wanted to sob quietly to herself but little Grace was a step ahead of her.

'Now then, Marilyn, seein' as how you've had that nasty fall, you get to be in charge of the tea shop today. In't that so, our Sybil?'

'Aye, you're right about that Gracie.' Then she added, as if it were the most natural comment in the world, 'Our Brian says he saw some old tramp in a cloth cap and breeches stood staring at him from yon woods there. Last Sunday afternoon it were.'

'Oh you're making it up,' said Marilyn, too shocked to believe her.

'Well that's what Brian said and he never tells fibs. Our Philip tells fibs a plenty, but not our Brian.'

'Well, my mum told us not to speak to any strange men, didn't she? So if we see him, we mustn't.'

'But then, what if he comes into our tearoom here and wants a cuppa? What do we do then?'

The three girls looked at each other searching for the answer and looked about the gnarled wooden hut.

'Well then stupid, we mustn't let him come in. Simple,' said Grace with an air of authority.

After a while they got tired of serving their imaginary tea and buns and began to pack up shop and wend their way back to their homes. They looped arms as they dragged their heels and then decided to play a quick game of hopscotch on the wide pavement as they rounded into Keswick Road. Gracie was the tallest and most sporty and agile. Marilyn looked up to her and envied her easy athletic vigour.

'I'm going in for my tea now. See you both tomorrow.' Marilyn waved as she unlatched her gate.

'Never did see him, anyroad, did we? The tramp I mean.'

'Perhaps our Brian did make it up after all.'

But Marilyn's imagination was running riot and she couldn't help wondering whether the old man in the cloth cap might have been there after all and had been watching them all afternoon.

That Saturday evening, after they had cleared the table and washed up the dinner plates, Marilyn was in a silent pensive mood.

'You're very quiet this evening missy,' said Sarah. Marilyn hated it when she called her that. She looked at her mother.

'Something on your mind?' Lilly asked Marilyn as she put down the damp soiled tea towel hoping that Sarah might finally notice it was long overdue for the laundry. Marilyn was doodling on the back of an old shopping list. Lilly noticed that she was writing *Daddy* over and over in little swirls and scribbles. Finally, Marilyn lifted her head and looked directly into her mother's eyes.

'Mummy, what will happen to us when the war is over and Daddy comes home? I mean, where are we going to go? Will we stay here, or...or what will happen?' It was a question which she had long been forming in her mind and one with which everyone else in the house had been grappling for some months. Sarah patted Lilly's arm and without a word left the kitchen. Perhaps she didn't want to hear Lilly's inevitable answer. She already knew it but wanted them to discuss their future in private.

'Well, my love, we'll go back home to London of course. To Edmonton. That's what daddy will want us to do. You won't remember our place of course, you were just a baby, but it's a dear little house and it's got a lovely garden front and back for you to play in. And then we'll see Nana and Auntie Laura again.'

Marilyn fell silent. And then she said what Lilly had been dreading.

'But you see mummy, I really want to stay here in Blackpool. This is my home. I love the sea and the seagulls, and everything! I don't want to go anywhere else. Can't we stay here? Please?'

It had never occurred to Lilly to go anywhere else but back to London.

'Well, I know you love it here, sweetheart and you have made some good friends, but you will make lots of new friends once we go back to London and Daddy will start a new job and we will have our family all around us again. Just as it was before the war.'

'Yes, but like you said, I don't remember any of that, do I? And I really do want to stay here.' Lilly ran her hands through her hair with growing exasperation, her patience trickling away.

'But you know that we were always going to go back to London. That's where we shall carry on our lives. Just as before. And that's where daddy will expect to find us when he comes home.' Marilyn scraped her chair back and stood up.

'No mummy! You can go back. I'm staying here with Ethel and Sarah and Joe and my friends.'

'Alright then, please yourself. I'll send you a postcard from Buckingham Palace.'

'But I won't know anyone in London. Please don't make me go back there. It's so very dark there and full of loud noises and bombs and things! And besides, I must stay here, I *must*!'

'But why, Marilyn? Why must you stay here?'

Marilyn was silent and she sat back down as if pushed there under a heavy weight.

'Come on Marilyn, please tell me. Why must you stay here?'

The little girl gasped through her tears.

'I must wait here. I must wait in case the baby twins come home.'

Lilly wanted to scold her, to grab her and say: *Don't be so silly, Marilyn! You know better than that. I told you how it was. You know the twins are dead. They won't be coming home!* But she could only stare at her daughter, astonished at her sensitivity and defeated by her sentimentality. She grasped her daughter and rocked her gently, just long enough for the shock of what Marilyn had said to subside and for Lilly to restore her own composure.

'Well now, how about we both sleep on it and talk it over again in the morning.'

She had been expecting this of course and had hoped that Marilyn wouldn't have minded or better still had her own strong inclination to return to London once the war was over. She thought she should enlist Harry's help in convincing the child of the merits of picking up the threads of their pre-war days. It was within his gift to make their lives complete again. He would not think twice about returning to London to set up the business of which he had been dreaming and planning for during all these long war years. The family, their friends and all that was once so familiar would gather around them again and bring them joy. All would surely be well once Harry was home. With a jolt of contrition, Lilly found herself wishing she could talk it over with David Nuttall. He would take her hand and guide her thoughts until she was clear on what to do. And Marilyn would listen to him and hang on his every word.

Lilly waited as she watched David take off his coat and hat, carefully brushing out the creases in his sleeves, an odd thing to do, she thought. She had not seen him do that before and it prolonged the silence between them before he sat down in their usual quiet corner of the café. Lilly could sense that something was wrong. She felt the change in him immediately, as one feels the unmistakable change of direction in the wind. A gulf seemed to have opened up between them.

'Everything alright?'

'Yes, hello Lilly, how are you?'

Lilly decided to be patient. He would confide in her surely.

'Well, actually,' she began with a jaunty air which she hoped might brighten his spirits, 'I was hoping for your advice, David. I bought this little pamphlet here a while back, "Improvised Toys for Nurseries and Refugee Camps" so that I can make something fine for Marilyn's Christmas present. I know it's early to be thinking about it yet, but oh, I'm so hopeless when it comes to choosing what to make. It always takes me ages. Here, you have a look, Any ideas? You know her well enough, I'd say.'

David scanned the little booklet with little interest. Lilly noticed that it seemed to take all his effort to focus on the pages.

'Oh, it all looks simple enough. She might like this little toy dog, or whatever it's supposed to be, right here on the cover. You could rise to that couldn't you? Just looks like a match box and some oddments of cloth are all you really need.'

'Oh yes, that's a grand idea! I can do that alright. I just need to-'

'Lilly, dear, something has come up. I would like to discuss it with you.'

Lilly put down the pamphlet. It seemed that improvised toys were not his topic of choice. She waited. A dozen scenarios danced around in her mind. But she looked at him intently and said nothing.

'I had a letter from Louise last month.'

'Your wife Louise?'

'Yes. It seems that she has found a teaching position for me to apply for down in Devon. In Exeter actually. It's a good position. It would suit me down to the ground. I feel I may have just the experience and qualifications they're looking for. Louise very much wants me to join her there. She misses me, she says. And I miss her, of course. I've taken ever such a long time to make a decision. I haven't found it at all straightforward, you know.'

'Well, why not for heaven's sake? You must go ahead and give it a good try, David. If it's what you want. It is what you want, isn't it?'

'Oh yes. it's a good position. Head of the English department in an all-girls school down there. I should say it would be quite a step up for me, if I were successful in getting it. But it's all so unexpected, you see. The point is, Louise wants me and we really do need to try and work things out between us. Make a proper go of it. After all she's my wife....'

'Yes, I know. And you're right of course.' Lilly had picked up a teaspoon and was making spirals in the tablecloth.

'An all-girls school, eh? Mind how many hearts you might break.'

'Oh, I shouldn't care to break anyone's heart, Lilly. That wouldn't do. And anyway, there's no certainty that I would get the position. None at all...'

They looked up from their cups and into each other's eyes for the first time since they had sat down.

'Oh, you'll get it alright. They'd be lucky to have you... Marilyn will be upset of course. I'll break it to her gently this evening when I get home. And mind you keep away from the coast, in case the Germans come that way. And you oughtn't to go near Plymouth. You know how heavy the bombs have been there.' She felt a sting of tears but was not prepared to let him see that. 'Oh David, we have had a lovely time together, haven't we?'

'Oh, certainly we have!' He put his hand tentatively on hers. 'And we would keep in touch of course. I'd write to you to let you know how I'm doing and-'

Lilly screwed up her face and shook her head.

'No, David. I don't think that should happen. No, we shouldn't make any promises like that. There's so much else to think about and now you have a chance to make fresh start...'

So many unspoken sentiments lay between them.

'I shall cherish this time we've had together. I think that you and I are kindred spirits. And I feel a much richer man for having met you, Lilly Stevens.'

'Oh, away with you and your fine speeches. Save them for your interview!' She smiled a broad smile to reassure him that all was well. 'I shan't forget you either, David. Thank you for such a lovely few months. It's been a real tonic for me, in more ways than perhaps you'll ever know!'

'Then you're not cross with me? For going away?'

'Why should I be cross with you? Whatever for? This is your marriage and your career we're talking about here. You must go. Of course you must. It's the best decision for you. There's really nothing more to say, is there?'

They fell silent for what seemed to Lilly to be an excruciating length of time. David's hand was still on hers. Before she could stop herself, she uttered the words that had been poised on her lips for so many weeks.

'You do love her, don't you?'

'We have to try at least,' David replied. 'I believe in the sanctity of marriage. That much I do know. I haven't stopped thinking about her all the time she's been away in Devon. My life hasn't really been complete since she left. I have to be honest with myself. I do want to be there with her.'

'Right, well then enjoy it! For heaven's sake.' Lilly forced a wide grin. 'I'm really very excited for you David. I mean that. Now go on home, pack your suitcases and go to Devon!'

'And you have Harry, that luckiest of lucky fellows! What a homecoming that will be for you when this stupid war is finally over.'

'Let's get out of here, David. Do you mind?' The air in the café had become cloying and oppressive. Lilly was relieved to be out in the street once again where the bright afternoon sunshine could clear her head. Then it was the moment for them to part. The middle of the wide pavement was hardly appropriate for a long last embrace. They shook hands as if they were two casual acquaintances leaving a business conference.

'Take good care of yourself, David. I wish you Godspeed, I really do.'

'You're a very beautiful lady. If I never meet you again, I would always want you to know that.'

Too choked to reply, she smiled once more and nodded. Then she walked off back to the tram stop and picked up her step so that she could get out of sight of him as soon as possible.

She resolved not to turn around and wave back at him, though she dearly wanted to. David stood there watching her until she was out of sight. His heart was aching and he was trembling even in the warm sunshine.

Lilly's walk home that afternoon was a heady mix of relief and sadness. This had indeed been a lovely interlude for her. She smiled as she recollected all the times spent with David over the past months and how these had helped to calm her and bring her joy. She had thrilled at the anticipation of his company and at the sight of him on the other side of the choir room. How they had chatted at the school gates, in the tea breaks at choir and after rehearsals in the little lane that ran to the side of the church. Their afternoon teas and hurried lunchtime meetings. They had even stolen a kiss once when they thought it proper. A light peck on the cheek and a warm embrace.

Lilly knew he had admired her, though he would never have acted in any way improperly. Kindred spirits they may have been, but there was that line which neither of them was able nor willing to cross. She finally had to admit to herself that it had been something more than platonic between them and so she had kept their friendship a secret from everyone, even Marilyn and she had certainly never mentioned anything in her letters to Harry or her family, in spite of her earlier guiltless intentions.

She had grown fond of David but, as secure as she was

in her love for Harry and in his love for her, she could have looked both men in the eye without any self-reproach or sense of shame. And yet, David Nuttall was leaving Blackpool and now Lilly's world would lose much of its complication and intrigue, but also its colour and delight.

CHAPTER 26.

Harry awoke to the deafening sounds of shouting and cheering. German radio had just announced that Adolf Hitler was dead. The circumstances of his death would not become clear until many weeks later and in the meantime, there was much initial reluctance from the Allies to accept this news as true. They were anxious that it might be the beginnings of an elaborate escape plot.

An energetic throng of solders filled the room.

'Stevens, wake up lazy head! Wake up! It's celebration time, old man!'

The radio was blaring out:

In the wake of Herr Hitler's death, leadership of Germany has passed to other high-ranking Nazi officials. Their role will be little more than to prepare for official surrender, which is planned to take place in a week's time when German Chief of Staff, General Alfred Jodl will sign the instrument of unconditional surrender. As Europe now lays shattered, the Nazi horror is finally over. The German nation will be delivered into the hands of its victors "for better or for worse", to quote Herr Jodl...

Harry had seen Berlin. To think of it now as a city lying in abandoned ruins, completely dead and destroyed beyond all recognition, he wondered whether it could ever be rebuilt. He read news reports later describing in meticulous detail this historic outcome which took place at a small schoolhouse in Reims, in North-eastern France, being used at that time as General Eisenhower's headquarters.

Then the official announcement of surrender was made the following day, Tuesday 8 May 1945, 'Victory in Europe' Day. Harry knew that no-one across Britain would need telling twice to get out the bunting, light bonfires and start celebrating the two-day public holiday to celebrate peace in Europe. He sat quietly contemplating how for whole populations across the continent, those years of fear and darkness had become a grim test of endurance and resilience. Surely it had been their war; their homes had been the battlegrounds for Hitler's maniacal delusional venture. Many thousands of unnamed, ordinary people had become reluctant warriors fighting for their very existence and for that of their loved ones, often against the most terrible odds. Now this was their peace, whoever and wherever they were.

They were the young girls who had been called into in the munitions factories in the East End like Lilly's sister, they were the elderly veterans who had lived through the Great War, like Joe and Sarah Cockington - and they were the children who had grown up with the war and knew no way of life other than blackouts, rationing, gas masks, the threat of invasion, the spectre of death hanging around them, stiff upper lips and the unspoken terror of the dreaded telegram. Children like Marilyn who were too young to remember life before the war. Theirs was the future, however uncertain or overwhelming the prospect, surely it must be a peaceful future, a prosperous future. It brought Harry to tears of pride and relief.

Some days later, he received from Lilly the happiest letter she had ever written to him.

'Sunny View', Keswick Road, Blackpool, Lancs.
9th May 1945.

My own dearest Harry.

We were standing in the queue at the dry cleaners yesterday, Marilyn chattering away, when someone suddenly screamed out "Peace! It's peace! The war's over! The fighting in Europe has stopped".

We all started cheering and clapping and crying and shaking hands. It was terrific. Poor Marilyn was rather confused by it all. But I think she soon cottoned on. What a tremendous relief. It's over and we got through it!

My thoughts turn to you, my darling and to our future. How soon will they let you be de-mobbed and come home to us? It's so hard to be patient now that it's all over – well almost. Will they send you to the Pacific to face the Japs? Surely Harry, you have done your bit by now?

I wanted to let you know that I plan to take Marilyn back to London just as soon as I can arrange it. We can stay with Mother and Laura in their flat in Hackney. Marilyn will probably hate Hackney. All the concrete and the bomb sites won't suit her after living so close to the sea these past few years, but I think we ought to go. We need to go home.

I will write to you from there. We shall keep looking forward, shan't we? No sense in looking back.

Your loving wife, Lilly...

Marilyn read the letter again. *"Your loving wife, Lilly."* Yes, she thought as she carefully returned it to its fragile yellowed little envelope. You were indeed a loving wife, Lilly. She wiped the solitary tear that had started to trickle down her cheek and she admonished herself. She was wasting precious time and all this paperwork would need to be boxed up and packed into the car together with Lilly's other personal possessions. Lilly had always been a hoarder since she had come back from Blackpool, a reaction perhaps to her having had so very little in the way of belongings during those dark days of the war. But Marilyn was stunned now to find all those letters sent between Lilly and Harry and between Lilly and her sister and mother throughout the Blackpool years. How evocative these letters were of that time! Lilly had sometimes referred to them in a vague, abstract way.

'Please don't throw the letters and photos away after I'm gone, Marilyn darling,' she would tell her solemnly.

Now Lilly had passed away, a quietly dignified ninety-one years of age and she was reunited at last with her beloved Harry. These flimsy dogeared objects with their corners worn away by time, were too precious to dispose of. Reminders of those difficult years so long ago when Marilyn was just a small child living in someone's else's house in a faraway town. They encapsulated her history and her memories.

Marilyn had been transporting herself back in time to Blackpool, to the little terraced boarding house in Keswick Road all those years ago. It was hard now for her to return to the present, to the task at hand. Lilly's little flat had taken longer than expected to clear.

Marilyn allowed her thoughts to wander just for a little moment longer, back to that thrilling crisp sunshining day in January 1946 when they were a family once again. When her beloved dad eventually came home to them with a whole bunch of medals of his own after almost five years of exemplary military service. "A most capable and reliable man in every way." so said Harry's Release Leave Certificate. She could still recollect the smell of his great coat and the warmth of his smile.

Harry Stevens, artistic, shrewd, determined had set himself up in business after the war as a dress designer, just as he had promised Lilly in those wartime letters packed full of his dreams. He had done very well at it and had called his company Marilyn's Fashions. He had a shop and a factory back in the East End, about a half hour's drive from his home.

When Harry retired, they eventually moved out to Westcliffe on-sea. That was always their cherished plan. Then one dreadful day in August 1973, six months after they moved, when Harry was just sixty-one years old, he died of a sudden heart attack. Marilyn was still in her early thirties.

Although Marilyn had stayed in London for the rest of her life, she had never forgotten her time in Blackpool, young and vulnerable though she was. Lilly had received letters from Sarah Cockington every Christmas and Easter. They no longer ran the boarding house after the war and they had both lived comfortably into their eighties. Marilyn often recalled Mrs Cockington – "Cockie" – to mind and those poor, wretched kittens that she had flung on the fire that day! Marilyn could often still call to mind the sound of their desperate cries, even after all these years.

Marilyn often wondered what had become of poor little Billy Hackett. The last she had seen of him was that rainy afternoon when Billy had taken his modest little bundle of clothes and personal belongings and clutching these close to his chest, was ushered out of the door and led away by the Billeting Officer, a Mrs Eliza Pucklechurch, who huffed and puffed her way down the path and along the street. This was a terrible inconvenience for her, the woman had fumed. Once settled, an evacuated child was not supposed to be called back by his mother. The evacuation scheme would never be a success if this sort of thing was allowed to keep happening.

Billy had gone back to the East End. His mother's dream of taking them both away to the idyllic farm in the rural safety of Essex was not to become a reality. Sarah Cockington never knew how Billy had tried desperately to bring his mother round after she had been knocked unconscious in an air raid in February 1944. The Authorities deemed it unnecessary to inform Sarah, of course. And so, neither would she ever have known that Billy had been found almost starved to death and shivering with cold in that wrecked tenement and that, as they were trying to revive him on the way to the hospital, another bomb had exploded in front of the ambulance sending it crashing into a near-by taxi cab. It would have been Billy's ninth birthday. If she had known about all this, Sarah would perhaps have put up a fight rather than so readily let the little boy be taken away back to London. And of course, the irony would have been too much for her to bear that, had Billy stayed put there with her in Blackpool, he would most likely have survived the war safe and secure in her house until it was his proper time to go home.

And those girls. The tragedy of June's untimely death still played on Marilyn's mind all these years later. Ethel, who had become a Land Girl to escape the horror of it all, had kept in touch with her for years afterwards. She had made Marilyn laugh with all her exploits: a town girl getting to grips with life on the land. On her first day, Ethel had been given a bucket and a three-legged stool and was expected to milk a cow. Although she was always keen and eager to learn, Ethel had never even seen a cow before. Apart from that inauspicious start, working on the land had been a happy experience for her, even though the work was hard and the days long. It was a healthy way of life and she stuck it out and stayed with the Women's Land Army until it was disbanded at the end of November 1950. Marilyn had still kept the note which Ethel had written to Lilly proudly detailing how she had taken part in the final parade at Buckingham Palace in front of the King and Queen in October that year.

Victor Norman, her beloved comedian had had a mixture of successes and failures. A rollercoaster of a career in fact. Lilly and Marilyn tried to keep track of him after the war. Victor's big break had come one night in July 1947 when he was taking odd jobs both on and off stage at the Empire Theatre in Sunderland.

It was the opening night of a new light comedy. One of the principal actors was suddenly taken ill with an asthma attack and Victor was told to call for an ambulance to take him off to hospital. A gaunt young man called Anthony Keith who was playing the lead, suggested that Victor take over the role as he was the only other person who knew the lines.

A top London agent happened to be in the audience that night and was so impressed by the obvious chemistry between these young actors that he visited Victor and Anthony after the show. He was extremely surprised to learn that this had been the first and only time the two men had ever performed together and he immediately decided to sign them up as a new comedy double act.

So, there they were. Norman and Keith – but soon to become known by their burgeoning legions of fans as Mr Sunshine and Mr Smile.

They had themselves one heck of a ball, spending the next five years touring the world: Australia, New Zealand, South Africa, amongst other places, playing at all the big-ticket venues and packing them out night after night. Then they came back to Britain and found themselves working every day and making an impressive £100 a week.

Eventually, it all got a bit too much for Victor and the two men fell out. Then Anthony Keith secured the chance to try his luck with a solo career in America and that was that. Victor was on his own again. But he knew that comedy was in his bones and that was all he had ever really wanted to do. So he soldiered on, taking work whenever and wherever it was offered to him. It was paid work, albeit barely enough to keep the meter topped up. Soon he found that the crowds were less interested in him as a solo act and there he was once again slipping further and further down the bill.

The truth was that after the Norman and Keith partnership was over, Victor simply ran out of steam. Didn't that happen to them all sooner or later? He had certainly had his breaks, his moment in the sun. But the pace, the endless round of lonely digs, the cheerless seaside Sunday afternoons with only a bottle of whiskey to warm his bones as he tested out his new gags in front of a mirror, had all taken their toll and he was tired. His new material became old hat soon enough and seemed irrelevant to the modern crowds.

Television had been the real killer of Victor's career. Audiences were getting used to a different, pacier kind of variety act and they wanted original, bright new talent. Victor had to refine and refresh his material week after week and he could no longer keep it up. Perhaps he was just unwilling to keep it up, but he knew deep down that he simply didn't belong to this new brand of showbusiness with all its stresses and strains.

Victor Norman died alone in his hotel room in Malaga in March 1964 at the age of seventy-three. His failing eyesight had been torturing him for several years and, as the darkness began to envelop him, he knew he wouldn't be able to stand it. It was very swift. The best bottle of Brandy de Jerez and a fist full of Librium. His last engagement had been entertaining a group of wealthy British holiday makers and the heat and late nights had proved too great a strain. By the time the hotel staff found him, it was all over.

His obituary in the papers was brief. It covered his early life and career and mentioned that his one Blackpool summer season during the war was among the happiest moments of his troubled life. Marilyn never threw that little newspaper clipping away.

Such a hotch-potch of different characters, all of them brought together in that Blackpool boarding house. They never would have met, much less lived together in such harmony, but for the war.

Those memories Marilyn had often shared with her own children so that they might know something of that time – and of the darkness of war that perhaps everyone had dreaded so much in different ways, but from which she and her loved ones had all thankfully escaped, together. And when it was finally time to leave behind that Blackpool boarding house and return with Lilly to London, well, perhaps that was when she had realised just how much all the people in it had come to mean to her.

She remembered parting from them that day with a throb of sadness and, as a lump caught in her throat, there she was, once again standing in that little cramped hallway in Keswick Road…

Marilyn watched as Lilly struggled down the stairs with their cases, preparing to say their goodbyes. Lilly was anxious and emotions were running high.

'Here now, let me help you down with those cases. Don't you struggle down on your own.' Joe was only too eager to help, to have something to do rather than just stand there stoically suffering this tortuous agony of parting. But that was the last thing Lilly wanted, any fuss.

'Thank you, Joe. That's kind of you, but we can manage.' She said without looking at him. 'I don't know, they seem ten times as heavy as when we first came. I can't think what we've been accumulating.'

'Are you sure you'll be alright getting on and off them trains?'

'Oh yes, we'll be fine. Don't worry, please Joe.'

'He's such a Mother Hen,' snapped Sarah. 'Here you are, Lilly luv, I've cut you both some sandwiches for your journey. Don't eat them all at once.'

Lilly was suddenly choked with emotion. She stared down at the meagre sandwiches in her hands.

'I don't know what we'd have done without you both. You've been ever so kind to us throughout. It's just such a dreadful wrench now that we must go back to London.'

'Well, we've all had quite a time of it, haven't we, one way or another,' Sarah declared.

'But we're ever so glad you've been here with us. Both of you.' Joe indulged himself in one last tussle of Marilyn's hair. 'And we've seen this young lady thrive and grow into a fine young lass. No doubt about it. Remember that frightened little mouse you brought along with you back in 1940?'

Lilly smiled down at her daughter and thought of all the times of health and sickness, the sorrows, the pains and the laughs that they had all shared together. Too many to count inside a single recollection.

'Yes, of course I do remember.' Then she paused and gave the little girl a gentle nudge.

'Marilyn has something she wants to give to you Joe. Go on Marilyn, there's a good girl.'

'Well, what's all this then?' exclaimed Joe as Marilyn mutely handed him a parcel.

'You shouldn't go buying me gifts, young lady. I've had me birthday. I mean to say...' Joe unwrapped the parcel and took out a small picture frame. But there was no picture inside it. He shot them both a quizzical look.

'It's for your medal, Joe.' Lilly nervously began to explain. 'We know you got a medal in the last war for bravery. And we know what you did in the gas attack to save your pals. We think you should be very proud of that and show off your medal. Don't we Marilyn?'

The little girl was smiling broadly. It had been her idea. She had been much affected by Joe's story when Lilly carefully recounted it to her as they took a walk in the deserted park that bleak Winter's morning before school.

'Then why doesn't Mr Cockington wear his medal? Why doesn't he show it off?' she had asked. In the simplicity of Marilyn's world, it was the obvious thing to do. Bravery deserved a medal and a medal deserved to be seen. She would make sure her Daddy understood that too of course, when he came home. 'So why don't we help Mr Cockington to show it off?'

And then she would not let the matter drop until Lilly had come up with the solution. They had scoured the hardware shops across town. Lilly had even set David Nuttall the task of finding something suitable for the purpose. And finally, she had spotted just the right sized frame and had wrapped it up and stored it away for the most appropriate moment. This now was the right moment and Marilyn was over the moon with excitement.

For weeks she had anticipated Joe's glowing face as he held up the frame with delight. But Joe was too taken aback to say very much, though his heart was bursting.

'Oh, I don't know about that. I only did what any human being would have done in that situation. Besides, who knows, behind any door up and down this very street alone there could be dozens of others who did sommat similar during those times. There's nowt special about me.' He cleared the tightness in his throat.

'Now then, the taxi engine's running and the driver will be keen to get a move on, so shall we…?' Joe had spent what to him was a small fortune on hiring a taxicab to take Lilly and Marilyn and all their paraphernalia to the station on this significant day. It was a special occasion after all. A one-off event and he wanted to treat them like royalty to round off their whole experience in Blackpool with a special delight. It was a shock extravagance for poor old Sarah, but the decision had been quickly and simply justified and it was one which Joe would privately treasure for ever.

Lilly, taking the hint, turned to Ethel. It seemed to Lilly almost the same scene as that first time they met when she and Marilyn had first arrived on that miserable rainy November day long ago. But it was also different in so many ways.

'Well goodbye Ethel, thank you for all the times you've looked after Marilyn for me. You've been such a good friend to us both. I'm so glad you got accepted into the Land Army over in the Dales. I hope it all works out for you. Take good care of yourself, won't you.'

Ethel threw back her head and laughed.

'Oh aye, that I will. Got meself a proper job, eh! A more honourable occupation, as you might say. A new beginning for me anyway. I just needed a change of scene, I suppose.

Well, you know it's not the same carrying on here without our June, so...'

'Well she'd be very proud of you,' said Lilly. 'Rolling up your sleeves and getting stuck in. Gosh, all that mud!'

Ethel let her guard drop just for an instant.

'What a laugh me and June would have had together messing about in all them hay-stacks. Still, I reckon as this country's gonna need us land army girls to carry on feeding all them empty stomachs up and down the country – war or no war...!' Then she brightened as she remembered something that she had been meaning to mention before Lilly left.

'Hey, you won't forget to go and see Victor Norman if he ever fetches up on the London stage, will you? Oh, how I'd love to be there someday and see him for meself!'

'Yes, we will,' Lilly assured her. 'Maybe one day he might even end up at the Palladium, you never know. He might hit the big time indeed! Marilyn would be ever so excited to see her funny Mr Norman again, I'm sure of that.'

Then it was time to be leaving at last. No more delay.

'Right well, this is it. We really must be going.' Lilly clapped her hands with an affected brightness, though she would have preferred in that instant to have found any number of things to distract her from stepping out through the front door.

'Bye now, cheerio, don't forget us!'

'Of course we won't forget you!' Sarah had her hankie out ready. 'Bye bye, you two. Keep in touch with us, won't you. Have a safe journey. Now I know your mam's not on t'telephone, so you will write to let us know when you get home and tell us how you're going on, won't you? Please, luv. Bye-bye, Marilyn.'

Then, as they were tottering out into the street, Marilyn turned round and looked back at her as she raised her hand.

'Goodbye. Thank you for having me,' she said softly and waved. That just about did it for Sarah.

'Oh! Oh, Joe, I'm all choked up. Where's me smelling salts, quick!"

DREADING THE DARK

EPILOGUE

The shock hit me like a wrecking-ball in the face, full on. My brain bailed out as if it needed to detach itself from the reality of what had just happened. As if it could not process the fact that the world, my world, would never be the same place again, even though the physical space around me remained unchanged. It was the 27th of December 2014. The saddest day of my life. There were two messages. We had ignored the phone earlier, so engrossed in an old Bette Davis film that we let it go to voicemail. I never did discover what those messages consisted of. I guess Paul, my husband deemed them too sad, too upsetting for me to hear. But the gist of them was something like: First message – 'Hello, this is Matthew. Mum has had a heart attack. It's looking very bad. We can't bring her round.' Second message: 'This is Matthew. Mum has passed away.' I could hear Paul gasping in that unique way that people do when they first hear a certain kind of terrible news. I immediately assumed that it was one of Paul's own elderly relatives, which would not have been so very unexpected unfortunately. Something was wrong, obviously, but I didn't get much time to work it out as Paul came bursting into the room where I had just settled into tackling a particularly uninspiring jigsaw puzzle.

'Your Mum has died!' he said. Just like that. No cushion, no safety net, no softener. No 'Darling, I'm afraid I have some bad news, you'd better sit down...', like they always do in the movies. That was it. Oh god. My Mum? Mum?

Just a couple of days before, having finished our oversized Christmas day lunch, I remember sitting down on the settee feeling an overwhelming sadness that, for the first time in my life, I wasn't seeing my Mum or Dad at Christmas. My parents were divorced and so Christmas had always been a juggling act between them, but we had always managed it somehow, although not without a degree of guilty feelings on my part that I was letting one or either of them down by whatever decision I had made.

This year, I had the inspired idea of suggesting to my mum that she spend Christmas with my brother Matthew in Spain.

'It will be drier and a whole lot warmer there for sure,' I assured her. Mum had agreed wholeheartedly and set about planning and looking forward to a fortnight's stay with my brother in his new apartment in the town of Zaragoza where he taught English as a second language to young adults.

So, I got up from my lethargy on the settee and resolved to call them both. Dad was abroad on a river cruise and I couldn't reach him, but I dialled mum's mobile and got straight through. She was upbeat, although she sounded a little tired. They were at a party hosted by one of my brother's colleagues. Everyone who met her from Matthew's school referred to her as 'Matthew's Mum', which seemed to amuse her no end. We had a lovely chat until it was getting a little too noisy at her end for us to hear each other, so we finished the call. And, as if on some obscure level, I could sense that it would be the last time I would ever hear her voice, I blurted out 'I love you mum.' It was not the sort of thing we used to say to each other; for us that deep-rooted, fallible love and affection unique between mother and daughter was implicit, tacit, understood. That being the case, my Mum said nothing in response. But I hope she felt what I was feeling.

The last time I had seen her was in late November. We had travelled back to London together from my home in Swansea. I had an interview the following day. When we arrived at Southgate tube station it was a fine Autumn day so we decided to walk to Mum's house, less than a mile away. We were chatting together as we walked down the road from the station when suddenly Mum stopped to catch her breath.

'I just need a moment to rest, sorry,' she gasped. 'Need to recover my mojo…'

She was trying to remain upbeat in a 'this happens all the time when you reach 76 years old!' kind of way.

I was so preoccupied with that stupid interview that I only briefly recognised that Mum's face had turned ashen grey.

She was leaning her whole weight against someone's front garden wall.

In that moment, I could have saved her life. I'm sure I could have. I know it. I could have gently suggested that we seek some help, call a paramedic to gauge whether she needed to go to hospital. Some assistance anyway. But I didn't do it. I didn't do anything.

We just waited there together for a few minutes longer while she recovered her energy and then we continued on home. But how I wish I had acted differently! Had I known that just a few precious weeks remained to her, I would never have ignored her grey complexion in that moment. I would never have left her at all.

Like everyone else, Mum was a flawed human being, but she was gentle and she was kind. She was also very beautiful although I wonder whether anyone had ever told her so. For someone as loyal as she was, it saddens me to think about how little love and contentment she had known throughout her life. An only child, for Lilly had had no more children after she had lost those twins, my mum was the apple of her father's eye and he doted on her. She carried his photo in her purse for the rest of her life. When Harry died relatively young and unexpectedly, the relationship between Lilly and mum became more fractious and strained. At times it deteriorated into periods of irrational bitterness. They seemed to teeter on the brink of the unfathomable distance between them and they never resolved their difficulties.

My dad knew better than to intervene or play mediator. Neither could he find it within himself to make up for that lost love that my Mum craved.

They married young, barely twenty and by the time my brother and I were born ten years later, whatever love there may have been between my parents had all but died. The marriage limped on, punctuating my childhood with stormy rows and stony silences until one day in September 1989, after thirty-one years of marriage and in the midst of a stupid petty row about something inane and unnecessary, my dad suddenly snapped. He stormed upstairs to their bedroom, flung open the top cupboard and dragged out the set of suitcases which my brother and I had bought them as an inspired 30th wedding anniversary present and he began to cram them with the contents of his wardrobe. I tried to stop him, but he threw me aside yelling that this had nothing to do with me.

My mum stood bewildered at the bottom of the stairs looking up and wondering what was going on. The look of incomprehension on her face broke my heart and has burned into my memory ever since...

Even by Zaragoza standards, it was an unusually warm week running up to Christmas that year, 2014. Matthew's school was a trendy sort of place, rather grungy in fact and the reception area looked more like a small-town flea pit cinema than a school. Matthew had to leave Mum to her own devices for much of the time as it was a busy week for him preparing his students for their crucial exams looming large in the New Year. Mum was happy just to mooch around the bustling city streets by herself. She was taken with the town of Zaragoza and always enjoyed the many shops and parks it had to offer the casual tourist with time on their hands. There was much about the place that interested her: its folklore, the local cuisine and landmarks such as the Basílica del Pilar, La Seo Cathedral and the Aljafería Palace.

One morning, Mum was wandering through the twisting cobbled paths of the old town when she suddenly realised that she was lost.

She was never one for studying maps, preferring her own intuition, or if that failed her, she would rely on other peoples'. She had good enough command of Spanish to be able to ask for directions, but at this particular moment, her courage failed her and she began to panic. It took her an hour to recover her bearings and find her way back to more familiar territory.

She was shaken and resolved to sticking to the narrow streets closer to home and to the school where my brother was working, unaware as he was of the stresses she had suffered in those uncertain moments, nor the toll it had taken on her heart.

On the morning of the 27th of December, Matthew left Mum to sleep in while he went early to the school to take his Saturday morning revision class. They had planned to meet at the school after the class and have lunch together. Mum set off for a stroll across the by now familiar town, (though I don't really remember her ever actually strolling). I'm guessing that she was more likely walking hurriedly as she rarely allowed herself a moment to relax. She stepped up the high kerb and entered the school foyer.

'Hello Matthew's Mum!' they greeted her at the reception desk. 'So nice to see you again.' Mum was early and she perched briefly on one of the bare metal pull-down cinema seats as she waited for Matthew to finish his class. Matthew later told me how, as he was coming down the stairs to meet her, he could hear Mum's voice as she chatted to the receptionist.

'Matthew works far too hard. He's very –'

Suddenly Matthew heard what sounded like someone having dropped their bags of shopping. Then he saw her. Mum had simply dropped like a stone onto the cold, unforgiving concrete floor. Somewhere in the confused recounting of this terrible event, Matthew remembered sitting on the stairs as the ambulance drivers tried to resuscitate Mum where she lay. First with a small defibrillator and then with a much larger one. But no response. They discussed taking Mum to hospital, but it was sadly apparent that she had already passed away. Her heart had just given out, exhausted. The most massive heart attack, from which she would never have stood a chance of recovering. And that was it. I only hope that she had known nothing about it. For her, no more pain, no more anxiety. She was gone from us.

Matthew later described to me how Mum had been complaining that she felt as though her chest was on fire. I never have been able to fathom why it didn't occur to either of them that this might be a heart attack and that urgent attention was needed. Or perhaps it had and Mum had simply chosen to ignore it. I will never know, of course.

I think the hardest part of losing my Mum in that way, was that I wasn't there with her at the end. I never had the chance to say goodbye or tell her all the thousands of things that I now know I would have wanted her to hear from me before she left us. Hardly a day goes by when I don't think of Mum. Often, it's the slightest hint of an aroma, or the briefest snippet of a tune or a phrase that she might have used, or even a film that she liked to watch.

When Paul and I went back to Mum's house to begin the grim process of sorting out her effects ready for Probate and for the eventual sale of the house, I came across a slim note pad sitting by itself on the kitchen table. It wasn't in a particularly prominent position, but it seemed to want my attention all the same. We leafed through it and then we saw at the back of the note pad, Mum had scribbled a few lines about where and when she was born, how she had been evacuated to Blackpool with her mother during the war, her marriage and her children. It was nothing more than a sketchy outline of her life and she had never mentioned to me or my brother that she had any intention of writing a memoir or of writing anything for that matter. Then, as I took these notes home with me as part of my cache of treasured mementoes, a seed of an idea suddenly took root and the thought grew more and more distinctly in my mind that this was a story which my mum had wanted me to take up. Recollections of her life in Blackpool, possibly among the happiest and most influential years of her life, never dimmed in Mum's memory. Being no more than a toddler when her mother Lilly took them both up to Blackpool to live out the war in relative safety away from the Blitz, she could not have remembered the main events of that period with any degree of accuracy, but she did have a variety of vivid memories, just snapshots really. Since I had been the one to suggest that mum should write down her Blackpool memories someday as part of our family history, not to be lost to the ravages of time, it was now my responsibility to reconstruct her story, recounting it as faithfully and as accurately as Mum herself had remembered it. I wanted to explore how a young woman's wartime experiences shaped the character traits of her daughter and the relationship between them. This book has evolved from a simple depiction of the camaraderie among a disparate group of individuals sharing the same roof into something far more personal: a chronicle of a wartime childhood punctuated by love and loss - and how it might have determined the life courses of Lilly, Harry and Marilyn Stevens. It was something I just knew I had to do. A clear purpose. A labour of love.

Lilly and Harry, 'Walking Picture' 1937

Harry, Marilyn and Lilly, London circa 1940

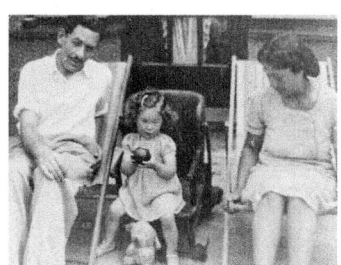

Marilyn aged eighteen months

Harry in uniform, 1940

SOURCES

Harry's poem is taken from Wilfred Owen's poem, On My Songs.

Description of the Blitz of 1940: https://www.bbc.co.uk/teach/the-blitz-eight-months-of-terror/z7dyxyc

News bulletin describing the bombing of a convoy: https://www.bbc.co.uk/teach/school-radio/history-ks2-world-war-2-clips-the-bombinghttps://www.bbc.co.uk/teach/school-radio/history-ks2-world-war-2-clips-the-bombing-of-a-convoy/z7yd47hof-a-convoy/z7yd47h

Churchill's "Never Give In" speech of October 1941: https://youtu.be/jU5uhBpCm1Q

Bulletin announcing D Day: https://www.bbc.co.uk/teach/school-radio/history-ks2-world-war-2-clips-d-day-has-come/z73jkmn

Gardiner, J. War on the Homefront, Carlton books (2007) and the expertise and contribution within her book made by the Imperial War Museum, London

(Author Unknown) Yesterday's Britain, Readers Digest Association (1998)
On This Day, A History of the Modern World in 366 Days, Octopus Publishing Group (2004)

BBC - WW2 People's War - WW2 at the Seaside: Childhood

Memories of Blackpool

Blitz Spirit with Lucy Worsley BBC 2021

Hodgson, G. People's Century, BBC Books (1995)

R.F.Delderfield, The Avenue Goes to War Hodder & Stroughton (1958) - for his depiction of Blackpool in the early years of World War ll.

Faviell, F. A Chelsea Concerto, Dean Street Press (1959) one of the most harrowing and insightful accounts of ordinary lives shattered by the Blitz over London. A most incredible read and very much recommended.

Thanks to Holy Trinity South Shore, Anglican church in Blackpool for its references to James Parrott : Holy Trinity Church, South Shore, Blackpool - Articles (htss.org.uk)
https://www.blackpoolgrand.co.uk/blackpool-world-war

Cook, W. Morecambe and Wise Untold, HarperCollins (2007) for his description of life in Blackpool in the mid-20th Century.

The descriptions of June's murder:

https://blackpoolcrimetour.wordpress.com/2015/06/27/princess-parade-promenade

https://beyondtheblackpool.wordpress.com/2021/01/12/military-murder-at-princess-parade

Ginn, P, Goodman, R. & Langlands, A. Wartime Farm Mitchell Beazley Octopus Publishing Group (2012)

Wartime Farm Christmas, Lion Television for BBC (2012)

Catford, N. Improvised Toys for Nurseries and Refugee Camps London University Press (1942)

Ellis, J. Blackpool At War. History Press (2013)

McCartan, S. Revoe For Ever (1995)

Fred Ackroyd's poems written by Paul Saunders.

All photographs are the property of the author.

ACKNOWLEDGEMENTS

This book has been inspired by real life events as witnessed and recalled through the eyes of my late mum, Marion. She and her mother Lilly (my Nana) spent almost six years in Blackpool staying in a number of different boarding houses during the war and so, Sunny View guest house is an amalgam of these. They escaped the Blitz only to find themselves homeless on their return to the East End as their street had been demolished by Nazi bombs in 1940.

I dedicate this book to my late mum whom I miss every day. I hope she might have found it a faithful evocation of those years which she spent amongst all the different characters with whom she shared the same house.

This account of life in Blackpool and London during the second world war is as authentic and researched-based as I could make it. However, it is in no way meant as an historical account. My aim has been to reconstruct my mother's memories as faithfully as possible although I am bound by the vagaries of her memories and of my own subjective interpretations of her descriptions. For example, Harry's insistence that they leave the East End and flee to Blackpool, the subsequent bombing of their house, the horrific kitten drowning episode, Billy's mortification over the Ex Lax, the chip shop debacle, Lilly's job sewing button-holes to earn her living, her loss of the twins and their being in a dry-cleaners when peace was declared – and the decline into prostitution of the two girls - are all fact. The rest is pure imagination, including all correspondence between the characters, with the exception of the murder of June and the case that ensued. I acknowledge the documentation of this sad event and the memory of Joan Long (1922 - 1944).

There are so many gaps in my knowledge about Lilly and

Marilyn's Blackpool lives. So many questions that I would liked to have asked them had I the foresight to begin this project in their lifetimes. Why did Lilly leave the relative safety of their home in Edmonton, North London and go and live in the East End? Was it to be near to her own mother and sister? Why then did Lilly not take her mother with them to Blackpool (her sister was called up to work in the munitions factory) Perhaps she tried. What really happened when Harry visited them in Keswick Road Blackpool during his leave in early 1942? I have only conjecture to fall back on as well as a good deal of background research to fill in these gaps.

I have checked key dates, events, public information and all other historical details in this book to the very best of my ability. If I have inadvertently overlooked any inaccuracies or omissions anywhere in this book, I beg the indulgence of my reader and I remain receptive to any corrections.

I am extremely grateful to the Home Front Museum in Llandudno https://www.homefrontmuseum.co.uk for the wealth of information and memorabilia which inspired and informed so much in this book with the background details of civilian life during the second world war. I thoroughly recommend this museum to anyone with a keen interest in all things 1940s!

I am also indebted to a number of people who have helped me along the way to bring this project to fruition:

Members of the Lampeter Writers Workshop, my heartfelt thanks for your keen critical eyes, your feedback and your enthusiasm for my fledgling work.

Members of Swansea Little Theatre for their invaluable feedback when I tried out this story before them as a two-hour stage play. Thank you for suggesting that the plot lines needed more space to run and that perhaps I should try writing this story in novel form.

To my dear friends, Cal and Lance, Elizabeth and Jonathan, Ann and Gary, Elaine and Carl, Helena and Dean: I cherish your friendship, support and constant encouragement, more than you will ever know!

Special thanks to my lovely patient proofreader, Elizabeth

Hughes Diolch o galon, fyng ffrind annwyl!

To my dear husband Paul who has consistently and patiently encouraged and supported me in writing this story, you have offered so many insights, humour and feedback throughout this journey. Any success this book might enjoy will be due in no small part to you!

Alison50saunders@gmail.com

ABOUT THE AUTHOR

Alison Saunders

Alison Saunders was brought up in a house full of books and grew up with a passion for reading and creative writing. Originally from London she now lives in rural Wales with her husband Paul. She has had careers in broadcasting, account management and strategic marketing, but in 2024, Alison gave up her day job to concentrate fully on writing and on completing her debut novel, 'Dreading The Dark'. Alison has previously written mostly plays for stage and radio which have been performed across Wales by both professional and amateur companies. An active member of two local writing groups and which have helped her critically analyse and hone her writing skills, Alison is currently developing two further fiction projects and a one woman play which she hopes to perform within the next twelve months.

Printed in Dunstable, United Kingdom